STAR OF BABYLON

STAR OF BABYLON

Barbara Wood

This first world edition published in Great Britain 2005 by
SEVERN HOUSE PUBLISHERS LTD of
9–15 High Street, Sutton, Surrey SM1 1DF.
This first world edition published in the USA 2005 by
SEVERN HOUSE PUBLISHERS INC of
595 Madison Avenue, New York, N.Y. 10022.

To my husband, George,
With love.

British Library Cataloguing in Publication Data

Wood, Barbara, 1947-
   Star of Babylon
   1.   Romantic suspense novels
   I.   Title
   813.5'4 [F]

ISBN 0-7278-6210-3

Typeset by Palimpsest Book Production Ltd.,
Polmont, Stirlingshire, Scotland.
Printed and bound in Great Britain by
MPG Books Ltd., Bodmin, Cornwall.

Prologue

In the darkness of the secret passage, the priestess dared not pause to rest though her legs screamed with pain. Behind her, death was coming – not just for her but for them all. She had to warn the others.

The Library was burning.

She stumbled, scraped her naked shoulder on the rough wall, and nearly fell. But she stayed on her feet, kept running, her lungs starved for oxygen. Even here, at this safe distance, she felt the heat, inhaled the smoke of the conflagration. Would she reach the others in time?

As Philos stripped the warm oils from his bare skin, he wondered by what good fortune he had caught the eye of the most beautiful creature in the world. Artemisia would disagree, of course, complaining that her face was too round, her nose too blunt. But to High Priest Philos she was the moon; a man had but to set eyes upon her luminosity and he was under her spell.

They had just made love, and now she bathed in the scented waters of her private bath. Afterward, they would return separately to the Library, to resume their sacred duties, with no one the wiser to their forbidden love.

Artemisia looked up at him from the steaming water. Philos always removed his wig when he came to her bed. Like all priests, he shaved his scalp. It gave him the look of an eagle, especially with his impressive nose, which she adored. Philos was the handsomest man in the world. And he was hers.

If only they could marry.

But they had been dedicated to the service of the Library, and its secret mission, since before they were born. As children they had taken vows of chastity, easily spoken, since what

1

did a child know of physical love? Should their illicit romance be discovered they would be banished from the priesthood, cut off from the family, and driven into the desert to perish.

Philos turned suddenly. A sound at the door. Someone coming!

She heard it too. 'Hide!' she said.

Too late. The door was flung open and a priestess from the Library stood there, her white gown torn at the shoulders. Stark fright stood on her face. She didn't note the presence of High Priest Philos in Artemisia's chambers. 'The Library is on fire!'

Now they smelled the smoke and, parting the drapes to look out at the night, saw the golden glow amid the Library's precincts. They dressed in haste and ran.

The sight that met their eyes stunned them. Beautiful columns and arches and domes, all aflame. The streets jammed with people, running in and out of the burning buildings, carrying out chairs, tables, books, heaping them onto massive piles and torching them. The frenzied mob lay hand to anything they could, looting the Library complex for jugs of wine, sacred oils, gold lamps.

'We must stop them!' Artemisia cried, but Philos held her back, for now they saw priests and priestesses being dragged out, their robes stripped from their bodies before they were flung onto the bonfires.

'We must save what we can,' Philos said, and, taking her hand, ran with her toward the harbor, where massive walls had protected the Library from the sea for six centuries. Here they found a secret way in, and, plunging into the smoky tunnel, encountered other priests and priestesses, carrying whatever they could rescue from the rioters.

'To the docks,' Philos ordered them. 'Take what you can but save yourselves.'

Philos and Artemisia made their way to the most inner precincts of the Library complex, the Sanctum Sanctorum, where the holiest of books were kept. Using their robes, they hurriedly collected the scrolls, feeling the heat beyond the walls, inhaling the thickening smoke.

They joined their brothers and sisters, all running with whatever precious relics they could save, and made for the

2

harbor. But a mob intercepted, their faces glowing with lust for blood and death. 'Pagans!' they shouted. 'Devil's spawn!'

The priests broke through, but some were caught. The rioters set upon them with clubs, bashing their heads in.

Philos saw that there was no chance for both him and Artemisia to escape – but, with a diversion, one could get away. 'Go!' he said to her, pressing his scrolls into her already burdened arms. 'Take these. I will run that way. They will follow me.'

'Not without you!' Tears streamed down her face.

'My beloved, the books are more precious than my poor life. We will be together again in the Light.'

She ran, and turned back only once to see the mob lay hands upon him and lift him over their heads. The screams came not from Philos but from the frenzied pack of Christians who carried their victim to the bonfire, there to throw him onto the flames.

Philos' final words before fire consumed him: 'Do not let them forget the oath, my love! Do not let them forget!'

The Library had stood for six centuries, built back when Alexandria itself was founded by the great Alexander. For six hundred years, a center of learning and wisdom, enlightenment and thought, a repository of books, letters, and words gathered from the four corners of the earth. Burning now, down to the ground, and everything within – papyrus, parchment, scrolls, men and women – charring to ash that would be carried away on the wind.

From their boats, the survivors huddled together as they clutched what precious treasures they had run with. They took one last look at the hot glow against the night sky, then they turned their backs on their home and loved ones, set sail and rode away on the tide.

Part One

One

Candice Armstrong was about to make the second biggest mistake of her life when a late-night knock at the door interrupted her.

She didn't hear it at first. A Pacific storm pounded the Malibu mountains, threatening to cut the power before she could finish the email she was furiously banging out on her computer – a desperate plea that had to be sent before the electricity went out.

And before her courage left her.

The lights flickered, she whispered a curse, and then she heard the knock, louder this time, insistent.

She checked her watch. Midnight. Who could it be at this hour? She looked at Huffy, who shared the cabin with her, a big overfed Persian cat that didn't like its naps disturbed. The cat slept on.

Candice listened. Maybe she had imagined it, what with the thunder and wind and all.

Knock knock!

She peered through the privacy peephole. A man on the threshold, rain pouring down on him. She couldn't see his face, cast in the shadow of his wide-brimmed hat. Like an old fashioned fedora from the forties. And a trench coat.

'Yes?' she said.

'Dr. Armstrong? Dr. Candice Armstrong?' An authoritative voice.

'Yes.'

He held up a badge. *Los Angeles Police Department.* He

said something – his name probably – but it was drowned out by thunder. 'May I come in?' he said, nearly shouting. 'It's about Professor Masters.'

She blinked. 'Professor Masters?' She inched the door open to get a better look. The stranger was tall and drenched. But that was all she could tell.

'Did you know your phone is out of order?'

She drew the door all the way open. 'It happens every time it rains up here. Come in, Officer. What about the Professor?'

'Detective,' he corrected and stepped inside, his broad shoulders soaked with rain. Candice shut the door against the storm. 'You're hard to find,' he added. As if he had driven all this way in the rain just to tell her that.

It reminded her of something Paul, the last man she had dated, had said when they had broken up because she wouldn't move to Phoenix with him and keep house while he built his law practice. 'This isn't a home, Candice. It's a hideaway.' Was he right? But what was she hiding from? Her best friend had chided her for letting Paul 'get away.' He was a good catch, she had said, as if he were a trout. But Candice wasn't looking to catch a man. Certainly not one who had said, 'Your career is on the skids so you might as well marry me.' Companionship, a loving relationship, these she desired. But they eluded her. Once a man discovered he would not be the center of her life, that Candice's work came first, he didn't stick around. So she had sworn off men altogether.

Which was why she tried not to stare at this tall stranger with the shadowed eyes. He might be handsome, but the hat was pulled low. 'What about the Professor? Is he all right? Is he hurt?'

His eyes swept over the interior of the rustic cabin, as if taking inventory of the Egyptian statuary, oriental carpet, leather ottomans, potted palms, paintings and posters of the Nile and Pyramids. 'He's had an accident, Dr. Armstrong. He's in critical condition and asking for you.'

'Why is he asking for me?' She hadn't had contact with the Professor in over a year.

'I wouldn't know. Your phone doesn't work so I was sent to inform you.' His tone. Did he resent having been sent on this errand?

5

Grabbing car keys and turning out lights, Candice paused at the front door to look back at the computer screen and the email that waited for the 'send' command. A desperate last-ditch effort to salvage her career by explaining her side of what had really happened in the scandalous incident at Pharaoh Tetef's tomb. She would send it later.

But she stopped in the rain and stared at the right front tire of her car. A pancake was not flatter. There was no time to change it.

'I'll drive you,' the detective said. A grudging offer.

He explained nothing further during the drive to the hospital, which was in Santa Monica, ten miles away. He hadn't removed his hat but Candice could see his face more clearly. She guessed he was in his late thirties, with deep creases on either side of his mouth. His nose was big and nicely formed. The profile reminded her of Pharaoh Tuthmoses the Third.

The Pacific Coast Highway was a vision from a demented dream, water washing over the four lanes, mud sliding down the cliffs, lightning streaking across the black sky. Candice couldn't even see the churning waves breaking on the beach, and what little traffic there was crawled.

Her thoughts went to Professor Masters. When was the last time they'd had contact? Lunch, a year ago, after they had finished their collaboration on the Solomon Project. They were friends, and had worked together. Still, why would he be asking for *her*?

She leaned forward, urging the car to go faster.

The detective glanced at his passenger, assessing her. Tense. Wound up. Things on her mind. Not speaking.

He wasn't used to this. A desperate midnight rush to a hospital where a friend lay stricken. A moment that called for nervous chatter. A million questions. Cigarettes. But not Armstrong. Facing straight ahead, eyes fixed on the road but not seeing it, focused on something inside her head.

And then: 'Jericho,' suddenly.

The detective took his eyes off the road. 'What?'

'The first time I worked with Professor Masters. It was at Jericho.'

He blinked. She was carrying on a conversation with herself, in her mind.

6

Her voice was unexpected. It possessed a deep timbre, sounding firm and ripe at the same time, with a flavor that made him think of hot fudge sundaes.

'What happened to the Professor?' she asked. 'Was it a car accident?'

'He fell down some stairs.'

She stared at him. Professor Masters fell down some stairs? 'He could have been killed,' she said, recalling that her former mentor must be nearly seventy.

'He's in critical condition.'

Thunder clapped again and lightening forked across the sky. The midnight hour had taken on a surreal aspect. *Don't die, Professor.*

And then they were swinging off the highway and climbing a road to the top of the bluff. A moment later they were heading down Wilshire Boulevard, where, up ahead through the sweeping windshield wipers, a glowing sign said HOSPITAL EMERGENCY.

The cop slowed the car and pulled into the lot. Candice had expected him to drop her off and drive away, but he parked in a red emergency zone and escorted her through double doors to an elevator, where he pushed Four. Bright-as-day lights now revealed added lines at the corners of his eyes, and a fringe of dark-blond hair beneath the back of the hat, which he still hadn't removed. She noticed also, in mild surprise, that beneath the damp trench coat he wore what looked like a suit jacket, a white shirt with starched collar and a crisply knotted tie of burgundy silk. Had he been called away from a party?

She had expected to see a crowd of worried friends and relatives outside the Intensive Care Unit, but there was no one. Except for a man drinking from the water fountain, the hallway was deserted. And inside no one hovered anxiously at the Professor's bedside. 'Wasn't anyone notified?' she asked when she identified herself at the nursing station.

'Just you,' the nurse said as she directed Candice to one of the cubicles that radiated in a semicircle from a central bank of monitors.

When she saw her old mentor lying on the white sheets, tears sprang to her eyes – the bandage around his fragile head, the IV taped to his hand, the oxygen canula beneath his nose,

7

the heart monitor beeping. His color was awful. He looked ancient.

She glanced at his hands, mottled and bruised where the IV needle had gone in, and an image flashed in her mind, a memory of those finely shaped hands laboring over an ancient papyrus that had crumbled into a thousand tiny fragments. The Professor had spent hours piecing them together, sometimes taking weeks to join two jagged edges. She remembered him with tweezers, laying one yellowed piece against another, each with black squiggles on it. 'Look, Candice,' he had pointed out. 'Remember your alephbet. Watch now.' The Professor referred to the twenty-two letters in ancient Hebrew writing as the 'alephbet,' to distinguish it from today's 'alphabet.' He had made a lifetime's study of the evolution of the earliest written pictographs into a recognizable system of letters, and thus could read ancient Hebrew as if it were the morning paper.

She took one of those hands into her own now, praying that they would reconstruct many more papyri in the years to come. His eyes fluttered open. A moment of confusion, and then recognition. 'Candice. You came . . .'

'Shh, Professor. Save your strength. Yes, I'm here.'

His eyes darted from side to side and his respiration grew shallow. She felt cool dry fingers tighten around her hand. 'Candice . . . Help me . . .' And she bent close to listen.

The detective found a place beside a rolling cart loaded with medical supplies, from where he could keep an eye on the Professor and his visitor. The nurse had tried telephoning Candice Armstrong only to discover that the phone lines in the canyons were out. If she had a cell number, it wasn't listed anywhere. But the old man, confused and excited, had demanded she be sent for, growing agitated, alarming the staff before he lapsed into unconsciousness again, the doctor saying, 'Head trauma, possible subdural bleeding. Have to stabilize first . . .' and thinking that maybe this Candice Armstrong could settle the old man down.

They had found her address in the Professor's wallet; she lived in the Malibu mountains. Since it was an emergency the detective had volunteered to go out into the storm to fetch her. He watched her gentle manner as she bent over the old man. Mid-thirties, dressed in tan wool slacks and cream silk blouse, with a pink cameo brooch at her throat, delicate gold wristwatch – feminine, the cop thought, not a woman who toiled in dirt and ruins. Her longish brown hair was drawn back in a Celtic-knot clip, but hanks of it had escaped and fell forward to hide her face. He thought she might be sort of pretty, but he was no judge.

Her voice, *that* was unique. Like her vocal chords dripped with honey.

Unaware of the policeman's scrutiny, Candice leaned closer to the Professor, who was having difficulty speaking. 'My house . . .' he whispered. 'Go, Candice. Urgent. Before . . . before—'

'It's all right, Professor. You'll be okay. Don't worry.'

But he grew more agitated. 'Pandora. My house.'

'Pandora? Is that your cat? Your dog? Do you want me to feed her? Professor, let me call someone. A family member. Someone from the university.'

His head rolled from side to side. 'No. Only you. Go.' He closed his eyes. 'The Star of Babylon . . .' he whispered.

'The what?'

His eyes remained closed.

'Professor Masters?'

He managed three more words: 'Pandora. The key . . .' And then he lapsed into unconsciousness.

As she and the police detective left the Intensive Care Unit, Candice felt heartsick. The Professor had looked so small and vulnerable. Seven years ago, when they had been in Israel together, he had been a giant.

At the elevators, Candice reached into her purse for her cell phone. 'Hope I can get a cab at this hour,' she murmured as she dialed directory information.

'I'll take you home.'

'I'm not going home. I have to go to the Professor's house. I think he wants me to take care of a pet.'

'I'll take you.' Another reluctant offer. But she accepted.

They ran across the parking lot, where the rain was still coming down hard.

'Bluebell Lane in Westwood,' she said when they climbed into the car. 'I don't know the number but I will recognize the house.'

It was in an upscale neighborhood of West Los Angeles

and as they pulled up to the large Tudor-style home set back from the street, surrounded by neatly clipped hedges, rose bushes and carefully tended lawns, they saw no lights on. Candice jumped out of the car and into the rain.

When the cop caught up with her on the front porch she was hunting through planters and under the door mat. 'He said something about a key. But I can't find it.'

There was no key, but the front door was unlocked.

As they entered the dark foyer, Candice called out, 'Here kitty, kitty. Pandora? Pandy? Hello?'

She listened for a welcoming meow, but all she heard was silence broken by occasional grumbles of thunder.

She ventured farther inside, looking into dark rooms, peering through shadowed doorways as she called, 'Pandora! Pandy! Here kitty kitty.' Memories surfaced: days spent on the Solomon project, the aroma of the Professor's pipe tobacco, his deep mellow voice as he spoke knowingly of things ancient. She prayed he was going to be all right. According to the nurse, the housekeeper had been here when he took the fall. Thank God, otherwise . . .

As she stood in the circular entry wondering how far she should venture into the house, she was startled by a murmured voice. When she realized the detective was no longer standing behind her, she went to the foot of the big staircase and looked up. At the top, in the shadows, she saw him. To her surprise, he was talking on his cell phone.

She couldn't make out what he was saying, but she thought it odd that he should have gone up there. What was he looking for?

She saw a faint light coming from the living room.

Approaching the open doorway, she was instantly drawn to the painting over the fireplace. Executed in the classical style of David or Ingres, it depicted Pandora, the first woman on earth according to Greek mythology, tall and willowy in a flowing gown, looking sad and wistful as she pointed with a slender arm to the box Zeus had just given her.

Rising on her toes, Candice shifted the painting aside. But there was no key secured behind it, no hidden wall safe that might contain a key.

Setting the painting straight, she stood back and considered

10

it. This *had* to be the Pandora the Professor was talking about.

Then Candice noticed Pandora's outstretched arm. Although she was pointing to the gift Zeus had just given her, a box containing all the world's ills, the pale finger could also be seen as pointing right off the canvas and beyond the right side of the frame to an ornately carved wooden box standing on a marble pedestal. Candice recognized it as a cigar humidor and recalled that the Professor had kept it in his study. It looked out of place there against the wall.

She lifted the lid. Her eyes widened. The box contained no cigars but an old book.

Hearing the policeman's footsteps behind her, Candice retrieved the book and held it up to him. 'I think this is what the Professor was asking for.' She gestured to the painting. 'Pandora pointed the way.'

When he didn't say anything, just stood there in shadow while lightening flashed and briefly illuminated a living room filled with antiques and ancient treasures, she said, 'Is it all right if I take this? I'll bring it to the Professor in the morning. I can sign a receipt.'

'I trust you,' he said.

Out on the porch, as they locked the front door and peered into the black rain, Candice said, 'Why were you at the top of the stairs? Did you find something?'

He kept his eyes forward, into the storm. 'I was checking the carpeting, to see where he tripped.'

'I thought I heard you talking to someone on the phone.'

'The housekeeper's husband. She called the ambulance. I wanted to talk to her but she's been sedated.'

Candice gave him a long look. There was a tightness about his jaw, a peculiar tension in his voice. And then an alarming thought occurred to her. 'The Professor's injury wasn't accidental, was it? Is that why a police detective was assigned to the case?'

'I wasn't assigned to it. And his injury *was* accidental.'

'Then why was a policeman sent to fetch me?'

He finally turned deep-set eyes on her. 'I thought you'd realized. John Masters is my father.'

Two

The phone woke her.

By the watery light filtering through the pine boughs beyond her window, Candice saw the time. Too early for the call she was desperately waiting for from San Francisco, informing her she had the job, that her career was saved.

Pushing hair out of her face, she said sleepily into the phone, 'Hello?'

Silence.

'Hello? Who's there?'

Click.

She stared at the phone, then sat all the way up in bed, waking up now and remembering things. She dialed information for the hospital number, was connected to ICU and enquired about the Professor's condition. *Please be all right. Be better. Be sitting up and flirting with the nurses.*

There was no change. 'If he regains consciousness,' she said to the nurse, 'please tell him that Candice Armstrong will be in to see him this morning.'

'Again?'

'What do you mean "again"?'

'You were here just a few minutes ago, Miss Armstrong.'

'No I wasn't.'

'We have you on the sign-in sheet. I'm looking at your signature right here.'

Candice rubbed her eyes. Probably the sheet from last night hadn't been changed. She thanked the nurse and hung up.

Beneath the hot shower, she thought of the detective last night in the rain. 'John Masters is my father.'

He had reached into his coat and brought out the badge again, and this time Candice saw what she had missed before: *Detective Lieutenant Glenn Masters.*

Handing the badge back to him, she had thought how Glenn Masters, still in hat and wet overcoat, looked more like an official surveying a crime scene than a man returning to the home he grew up in. At least, Candice assumed he had grown up there. She knew that it had been the Professor's residence for fifty years; he often boasted how he had bought the place from a silent movie star whom he claimed still haunted it.

'I am so sorry,' she had said. 'This must be difficult for you. I had no right to take you away from your father's bedside. I could have called a cab.'

When he didn't say anything, just slipped his ID back into his breast pocket, Candice murmured, 'I didn't know the Professor had a son.'

They had driven back to her cabin in silence, but before she got out of the car, Candice said, 'Detective Masters, your father said something about a Star of Babylon. Do you know what that is?'

'No.'

She thought of the antique book tucked into her shoulder bag. She had lifted it out, yellow and musty, its title in French. 'Would *you* like to take this to him? It seemed very important to him. He might wake up during the night, and if this book is there—'

'You take it to him. You're the one he asked.'

She stared at him, and when he saw the look on her face, he said, 'My father and I have been estranged for years. When he was taken to the hospital, it wasn't the nurses who informed me of the accident, it was his housekeeper. My father didn't know she had. He didn't know I was there. When he regained consciousness, he asked for only one person: you.' No bitterness or rancor. A simple statement of fact.

Still, she felt guilty, as if she were somehow to blame for the fact that his father had asked for her and not his own son. Especially as she remembered the Professor was a widower. His wife, the detective's mother, had died long ago, Candice recalled, and violently.

Dressing in jeans and a pink silk blouse, Candice took her thoughts into the kitchen where she put Kitty Vittles down for Huffy, who gobbled and purred at the same time. Fixing herself a cup of instant coffee, Candice picked up the book she had found at the Professor's the night before.

Découvertes mésopotamiennes, by Pierre Duchesne,

published in Paris in 1840. Of vital importance to Professor Masters, since it was his only thought as he lay critically injured in a hospital bed.

To someone who didn't know John Masters, it might seem queer that the book had been hidden in a cigar humidor and that the only clue to its whereabouts was a figure in a painting pointing to it. But to those who knew him these were indicators that the book was part of a very important and secret project. Whenever the Professor was working on a new theory he always feared that academic and professional competitors were trying to steal it; he was known to keep his notes and research hidden in various places around the house. When they had worked together on the Solomon Project, Candice had found some of the Professor's most vital notes hidden in the kitchen toaster.

The question was: what was so important about this old book? What did it have to do with the Professor's latest project? For that matter, what *was* the Professor latest project? *'Find the Star of Babylon . . .'*

The phone rang and Candice nearly jumped out of her skin. Reed O'Brien! Telling her she had the job.

'Hello?'

But she heard only silence.

'Hello? What number are you trying to reach?'

Click.

A prankster. Probably one of her former students. She wished she could take the thing off the hook, but she was waiting for a phone call that was going to save her life.

Candice returned to the book. The odor of dust and antiquity rose from its yellowed pages. The text was in French. Besides undergrad courses in Latin and classical Greek, Candice had also studied French and German, since nearly half of all scholarly publications on Egyptology were written in those languages. She was able to translate the title, *Discoveries in Mesopotamia,* and get the gist of what it was about: Pierre Duchesne, French consul in Egypt between 1825 and 1833, making several trips northeastward to the Tigris--Euphrates valley where he indulged his gentlemanly interests in archaeology, wrote a memoir of his travels and filled it with engravings of the objects he had collected and brought back to his country home outside Paris. The pictures (statuettes, fragments of bas reliefs, cuneiform tablets) were unremarkable, and few were accompanied by an explanation or description, most likely because Duchesne himself didn't know what they were. Certainly there were no pictures of anything that could be remotely taken for a star, and there were no chapters or sub-sections titled *Etoile de Babylone.*

'This can't be the key he was asking for,' Candice murmured, wondering if she should go back to the Professor's house and examine the humidor a little more closely.

She was distracted by a shrill sound from her redwood deck where the French doors stood open to damp forest smells and birdsong. Perched on the railing was a mockingbird, greeting the day. His warble sounded like the ringing of a phone, reminding her of the call she awaited from San Francisco – the museum board were making their decision this week.

Candice's career was in crisis. It had never really had a chance to fly, after the disastrous tomb scandal. At thirty-four, she was starting to panic. The museum job meant a rescue, a second chance, and half the Egyptologists in America were hoping to get it. But she had decided that bombarding Reed O'Brien with impulsive emails wasn't going to help her case, so she had not sent last night's email after all.

Inspecting the cover of Duchesne's book, she noted a faded imprint on the inside front cover. *Stokey's Antiquarian Books. Figueroa Street.*

The tire change was no challenge – Candice had learned to take care of herself at an early age. Shutting her computer down, she grabbed her car keys and turned to Huffy, who was giving herself a tongue bath on the sofa, and said, 'If Reed O'Brien calls tell him I accept.'

As she slipped Duchesne's book into her shoulder tote bag and headed out into the gray day, Candice remembered that the Star of Babylon was another name for the Star of Bethlehem. The possibility excited her. Did the Professor's secret project have something to do with the birth of Christ?

15

Three

Candice did not see the suspicious car right away.
Her thoughts were divided, on the Professor – she would visit the hospital after the bookstore – and on Reed O'Brien, thinking maybe she should have sent the email after all.

Reed knew the details of the tomb incident – the whole world did – but perhaps if she told it from *her* point of view, making him see it through her eyes, experiencing it as she had: waking up in camp because she couldn't sleep, noticing a strange light coming from the tomb, going inside, hearing sounds in the burial chamber, creeping forward and looking through to see Professor Barney Faircloth, the director of the dig, standing in front of the open sarcophagus, lifting an object from his pocket and tucking it into the mummy wrappings, closing the coffin, sprinkling dust on the spot where he had placed his gloved hands to make the coffin look untouched, and then backing away, sweeping a broom to cover his footsteps in the dust.

Candice clearing her throat. The director spinning around. The awkward moment. He, a man of years and stature and sterling reputation, she, barely out of school with her brand new PhD in Egyptology.

'Tomorrow's the big day,' he said too loudly. 'Tomorrow we open the sarcophagus and see if my theories are correct.' Faircloth believed that the Aztecs had descended from Egyptians who had crossed the Atlantic on rafts. He had devoted his life to searching for the pharaoh who had launched that ocean-going expedition. He believed he had found him.

Candice had not known what to say. They'd stood in the stony chamber that stunk of rot and decay, with the controversial dead king standing up in his gilded coffin, presumably still sealed.

'I was just—' the director began, gesturing behind himself. 'Making sure.' And then: 'How much did you see?'

'You put something on the mummy.'

She got as far as Vermont and Pico when she finally realized that since leaving Malibu she had seen nothing but a white Taurus with rental plates in her rear mirror. So she made a turn without signaling, and the Taurus followed. She pulled into the parking lot of a strip mall. So did the Taurus. She pulled out, made another turn, and then sped through an orange light until a black SUV filled her mirror. Los Angeles was full of weirdoes.

Faircloth so nervous even his voice sounded sweaty. 'Candice, we all *know* Tetef is the king who sent the expedition. But no one will believe us without proof. All I did was help things along a little.' It was a small amulet engraved with a plumed serpent. It came from the Museo Nacional de Antropología in Mexico City and was about to be discovered on a mummy in the Nile Valley.

Candice had not, as many thought, 'blown the whistle.' She had in fact not known what to do. Dr. Faircloth was her hero. To work on a dig with him was a dream come true. But he had committed one of the worst breeches of ethics in their profession and had asked her not to say anything. So she placed a long-distance call to the man who had mentored her through her dissertation, another Egyptologist of renown and also president of the California Society of Egyptology. She had called in confidence, and had asked only for advice. But he had said, 'I'll take care of it.' And the nightmare had begun.

The white Taurus was back.

She kept her eyes on it as they moved with the heavy traffic. She couldn't see whether the driver was a man or a woman. 'If you are being followed while in your car, drive to the nearest police station,' the instructor of the YMCA self-defense class had said. Fine, except where was the nearest police station?

When Candice saw an opening in the right lane, she pulled over, causing a BMW driver to extend a finger in her direction. Traffic closed and the Taurus was left behind. Candice chose the first side street, a residential neighborhood, and zigzagged her way to Wilshire Boulevard where she joined even heavier traffic.

Candice had not known that her mentor and Faircloth were

17

arch-rivals from way back. Faircloth was publicly disclaimed by the president of the California Society of Egyptology, who added further humiliation by insisting that all of the director's prior works, publications, theses, lectures, even letters to editors be scrutinized for errors, fiction, plagiarism, falsifications. News wires picked it up and an aggressive news team ambushed Candice into a reluctant interview for a popular Sunday night TV magazine. They selected clips out of context and creatively moved statements around, so that Candice wound up looking as if she were accusing Egyptologists of being grave robbers and charlatans.

The backlash was swift and brutal. Candice's colleagues believed the incident should have been handled 'internally.' Although there was no question of Faircloth's guilt, they accused Candice of jealousy, seeking the limelight and being a troublemaker. She was suddenly unwelcome at digs, symposiums, lectures, any place where archaeologists gathered. Her articles went unsold, her theories ignored, and funding for digs did not materialize. Her career was on the skids before it even got started. And then rescue came in the person of Professor John Masters, asking her to join him on his Solomon project.

When she saw the bookstore, she grabbed a space at the curb, parking and locking quickly, and walked with rapid get-out-of-my-way steps to the entrance. Inside, she stayed away from the window, hiding between book stacks, but with a view of the street where she saw the white Taurus crawl by.

She rang the bell at the cash register and the proprietor materialized from the back room, a stooped gentleman named Goff who carried a half-eaten pastrami sandwich in one hand, a napkin in the other. He tucked the fatty ends of the meat into the mustard-smeared bread, and wrapped it in the napkin. As he took a juicy bite and chewed thoughtfully, he said he recognized the Duchesne book, recalling the afternoon Professor Masters had come in to purchase it, six months earlier.

'Paid a lot of money for it,' Mr. Goff said with a thick throat, mustard clotted at the corner of his mouth. 'Duchesne's antiquities collection was destroyed about a hundred years ago in a fire when his house outside of Paris burned down.

Made the book all the more priceless since it was the only record of what Duchesne had collected. Don't think the book had a large printing in the first place. At most, a few hundred copies. Professor Masters told me he had had a copy once, but it was ruined during a storm when a section of his library suffered damage from a leak.'

Candice remembered the incident, and how upset Professor Masters had been over losing a portion of his valuable antique book collection. 'Do you know what was so special about this book, aside from what you have just told me? If the Professor lost his copy five years ago, why did he wait until recently to replace it?'

'It wasn't the book itself he was interested in, just one particular plate. I can show you.' Goff set the sandwich down, wiped his hands on his pants, and carefully lifted the cover to turn the pages with the precision of a surgeon delving layers of muscle.

The memoir had been published in the days before mass photography and so the illustrations were engravings, but executed in such fine and skilled detail that one would swear they were photographs. 'Here it is. Oh!' A piece of paper had been tucked between two pages, small and folded, something written on it. 'Better be careful with this,' Mr. Goff said, handing it to her. 'Might be important.'

Candice slipped the note into her wallet and then studied the picture he had turned to. It was of a clay or stone tablet typical of Mesopotamian culture BCE, the type used for archival records or correspondence. There was writing imprinted on its surface.

'It looks like cuneiform,' she said, 'but I can't identify the language.'

'That was the Professor's interest in it. Said that scholars for decades have tried to identify this language.' Goff addressed his sandwich again, taking another mouthful, savoring the juice and spices. 'Said this tablet was one of a kind. No other sample of this writing ever been found. The way the Professor was acting, well, he didn't tell me anything, of course, but I had the feeling that he had come across *another* stone with this same writing. Wanted to make a comparison between the two.'

19

Candice gave the man a startled look. Had Professor Masters stumbled upon a rare archaeological find?

Before leaving, she noticed a photocopier at the rear of the store and asked Mr. Goff if he would please photocopy the engraving of the mysterious Duchesne tablet. The book was too valuable for constant handling. She would put it away in a safe place and later she would fax the photo of the tablet to a friend who might be able to identify the writing.

While she waited, she surveyed the street. She had not seen the Taurus since coming inside.

As he handed the picture to her, his phone rang, an old black instrument with rotary dial. 'Yello,' he said into it. 'Hold on.' To Candice he said, 'Your name Armstrong?'

She gave him a surprised look. 'Yes.'

He held it out. 'For you.'

How was that possible? No one knew she was here. She took the black receiver cautiously, as if it might sting, and placed it to her ear. 'Candice Armstrong,' she said.

Click.

'Well—' she began, puzzled. And then suddenly, 'Oh my God,' remembering the morning hang-ups, realizing what they meant. *'Oh my God!'*

'You okay?' Mr. Goff called as the door swung shut behind her.

She slipped through two near-misses – one with a city bus – and collected fists and finger gestures as she wove in and out of the noon traffic as fast as she could. If she was pulled over, she would tell the cop she was being robbed and ask for a siren escort.

The rain-slick road to her cabin caused fishtails and one almost-spinout, and when she neared her house her fears were confirmed.

Huffy was yowling in the middle of the road. Candice remembered locking the cat inside.

Someone had broken into her house.

Every morning Glenn Masters woke up with one question on his mind: will today be the day?

The day – that inevitably must come – in which he turned into the creature he feared most: a man of violence.

20

He would ask himself this in the shower, over coffee and bagel, working the daily crossword, and then he would pick up his badge from the dresser and go to Hollywood Division police station, where he would spend another day in the world of violence, keeping himself in check, watching his emotions, guarding against becoming part of that violent world.

The department shrink had warned him that bottling his emotions could have the opposite effect. 'The day will come when you reach your limit, and you'll be out of control,' she had said, and suggested he let off a little steam now and then.

Easy for her to say.

She had then asked him about his love life, which he thought was none of her business, but to which he had replied, 'No complaints.' Sherri was no longer in his life. They had drifted apart after the accident, and there had been no one steady since then. Glenn could not risk falling in love because he knew how connected emotions were and that if he let one out the rest would follow.

Looking around at the police-chaos of Hollywood station, he wondered what the hell he was doing here. After his mother's funeral, he had vomited every night for two weeks, thinking of the violence of her death, how he detested it. Then he had taken tranquilizers to calm his stomach, pills to sleep, and powders to stop him from dreaming. And when he had emerged from the twilight, shaken but steel-cold, he had discovered a new creed had taken root during his mental absence: no violence, ever.

But he had gone into police work. Homicide, no less. Friends asked why he hadn't found a nice quiet monastery in the high peaks of Tibet and lived out his life among the clouds. All Glenn could say was that there were criminals in need of being caught, and that couldn't be done on a mountaintop.

So here he was, a non-violent man in a violent world.

As he surveyed his desk, which groaned beneath his work-load – unsolved cases, witnesses to question, evidence to analyze, and leads to follow up – all he could think about was the old man, lying helpless in a hospital bed.

It was not how he had expected to see his father again. Whenever Glenn had imagined their reunion, it always took

21

place in the family house, in his father's study, the old man sitting dignified in his big leather chair, saying, 'Son, I asked you to come here today because I decided it was time for me to admit I was wrong. I hope you can forgive me.' Glenn, of course, would be forgiving, they would embrace, and then find a way after such a long separation to be father and son again. Instead the long-dreamed-of reunion had taken place in a hospital room with the old man lying unconscious, not even aware his son was there.

'Glenn?'

He turned. Maggie Delaney, a member of his homicide team, was observing him with large eyes. 'Yes?' he said.

'We finally have a lead on that janitor who says he saw something.' She held out a piece of paper.

He stared at it. He couldn't make sense of the words. It was as if seeing his father so helpless had rendered him help-less as well. 'I'm sorry, Mr. Masters,' the surgeon had said on the phone. 'I can't give you a prognosis. We've done all we can. Such a blow to the head wouldn't be so traumatic in a younger man, but your father is seventy . . .'

A horrible image formed now behind Glenn's eyes – his father lying crumpled at the foot of the stairs. What an indig-nity, to trip on a carpet and tumble like a discarded rag doll, to lie on the floor at the mercy of others. What if Mrs. Quiroz hadn't been there? How long might his father have lain there in pain, drooling, wetting his pants, before a mailman, the gardener, a worried neighbor found him? Thank God for Mrs. Quiroz's quick action. Glenn had tried calling her again but she was still under sedation, her husband had said. The shock had been that great.

Stepping into the house after all those years! Memories had rushed at him like ghosts starved for company. Birthday parties, Christmas mornings, breakfasts and dinners dished up by Mrs. Quiroz. And Glenn standing in the doorway of his father's study, the Professor two decades younger, a full head of dark hair, with no resemblance to the frail old creature lying at that moment in a hospital bed, bent over important work on his desk. The son, eighteen years old, standing in that doorway, yearning for his father's comfort, wanting the strong man to take him into his arms and tell him the world wasn't the

22

terrible place it had suddenly become. Glenn clearing his throat. His father looking up. And across the short space and deep silence, reading his father's mind: *Dropping out of school won't bring your mother back, son.*

That was the day Glenn had moved out of the house and gone to the LAPD recruiting office. Dreams of following in his father's scholarly footsteps had been replaced by the reality of becoming a policeman.

'Great. This is good,' he said to Maggie Delaney. Glenn had to rein in his uncooperative thoughts and focus on the note. *Janitor at the Highland Avenue building thinks he saw . . .*

The words faded and the image of Glenn's mother swam before his eyes.

Lenore's face had been radiant as she spoke, and although he had no idea what she was talking about at the time, he had loved every word. But then his father coming into the room, rebuking her. 'Don't fill the boy's head with talk of Doomsday and Armageddon. You promised, Lenore.' She had clammed up, chastened. And that was when Glenn had had his first inkling that his parents shared some horrible, unspeakable secret.

How could he have forgotten?

And what were the words she had spoken . . .?

He pressed his hand to his forehead as if to squeeze the syllables from his brain.

'The Last Things, my darling, *Ta Eschata* in Greek, *De Novissimis* in Latin. The End Days.'

But it made no sense. His mother never spoke of religious things. She was a scientist. Why would she have been speaking to him of such an esoteric concept as the end of the world?

He felt a chill. And a sense of dread.

'Glenn?' Maggie Delaney, waiting for a response.

He frowned at her. *The secret his parents guarded . . .* 'What?' he said.

'Are we going to follow this lead?'

Maggie wasn't the only one who had noticed Glenn's uncharacteristic distraction. Standing in the doorway, Captain Boyle watched his best detective with a critical eye.

Glenn was a mixed bag: unpopular with his brother cops, yet admired and respected by them. He wasn't a player, the word 'team' wasn't in his vocabulary. Yet he made the collars.

23

Once on the scent of a criminal, Glenn Masters never let up. He defined cool. Not your typical action cop. Masters would never burst into a room with both guns blasting. In fact he refused to carry a gun.

But what would he do in a really tough situation? Boyle sometimes wondered. One that he couldn't silver-tongue his way out of, when he was backed into a corner and action was called for? You could never really tell what Masters was thinking. Loner, no close friends. Never hung out at the Cock 'n' Robin, the local cops' watering hole. No current lady friends, as far as the captain knew – although there had been that one, a few years back, mountain climber of all things. What had made him lose interest? Look at him with Delaney. Temporarily assigned to homicide, Maggie Delaney was a plainclothes policewoman who headed the Domestic Violence Unit. Her fantastic body was proof of a daily vigorous workout and she had the eye of every male in the division. But *she* seemed to have eyes only for Glenn Masters. Except he didn't seem to notice. And now he was tuning her out completely.

'Glenn, can I have a word with you? In private?'

Maggie left.

'I just got a call from a hospital,' Boyle said with a puzzled expression. 'They wanted me to let you know that they performed a procedure to release pressure on your father's brain and that he is resting comfortably.' The sentence ended upward, like a question.

The captain waited. When Glenn didn't say anything, Boyle said, 'What's this all about? Your dad is in critical care and you never told us?'

'Captain, with your permission I'd like to take a drive out to South Central and question—'

The older man shook his head and laid a fatherly hand on Glenn's arm. 'Whatever it is, if you don't want to talk about it, well okay. But you haven't taken a vacation day or sick day since I don't know when. Get out of here. Go visit your father.'

'Hey, Glenn!' Another officer across the squad room. 'Phone call. Line two.'

Glenn picked up. He recognized the deep, honeyed voice of Candice Armstrong. 'My cabin was broken into. It was ransacked. I've been robbed.'

24

Four

Trashed. That was the only word for it.

Someone had broken into her home and trashed it. Books swept from shelves and strewn everywhere; statuary smashed; file drawers emptied and papers scattered; even the sofa cushions had been wrenched up and tossed aside.

Candice was blind with fury.

Five minutes after the Malibu sheriffs arrived, Glenn showed up in long black overcoat and fedora. After conferring with the officers at the scene, he moved through the living room, taking in the shambles. He looked into the bedroom. Bed covered with a floral comforter and matching pillow shams, hardwood floor clean and polished, top of the dresser littered with a few pieces of good jewelry and a statuette that, if genuine, might be worth something. None of it touched by the burglar. But a bookcase tipped over, and a drawer filled with papers spilled onto the floor.

A strange kind of break-in.

He glanced into the bathroom, where matching hand towels, embroidered with tiny roses, hung neatly on a rod. Pink soap shaped like shells in a floral dish. A feminine room, he observed, like its owner. On the wall pictures in small frames, arranged decoratively: Candice Armstrong in various settings – high-school graduation day, at a birthday party, with a woman who could be her mother. When he saw one of Candice Armstrong with his father, he stopped.

The Professor, seven years younger, his arm around Candice's shoulders, a sign behind them – JERICHO – in English, Arabic and Hebrew, both grinning into the camera beneath a fierce sun as if they were having the time of their lives. Her hair, longer then, blowing in the wind. Glenn recalled how it had looked the night before, cascading down her cheeks as she bent over the hospital bed—

He caught himself.

25

Never mind her looks. He was investigating a crime scene.

He left the bathroom and looked into a small, windowless room that might have been intended as a storeroom or a sewing room. Scattered on the floor were printouts, charts, notes, colored marker pens, and spiral notebooks. And Candice Armstrong, in a pale-blue blouse and long flower-print skirt, on her knees, tears streaming down her face as she tried to gather it all up.

'Hey,' he said, 'hey.' Taking her by the shoulders and bringing her to her feet. 'Are you all right?'

No! 'Yes.'

'You're sure?'

When she saw how he was looking at her, she read his mind. Pointing to her eyes, she said, 'These are tears of anger. I don't cry at the drop of a hat.'

He looked around the violated room. 'I'd hardly call this a dropped hat.' He reached inside a breast pocket and brought out a folded white handkerchief. 'Here.'

She dried her cheeks, recognizing the scent on the monogrammed linen: Hugo Boss. Classy. Expensive.

He looked at the pink cameo at her throat. It drew the eye down to the source of that incredible voice. 'I'll help you,' Glenn said and bent to pick up books.

The first was a plain-bound volume titled *Land Ownership and Matrilineal Inheritance in New Kingdom Women*, by Candice Armstrong. 'A Dissertation Submitted in Partial Satisfaction of the Requirements for the Degree Doctor of Philosophy in Near Eastern Languages and Cultures. Los Angeles: University of California, Los Angeles; 1994. 1 volume (xi + 301 pages [including 43 figures, 12 tables]). University Microfilms Order No. 7632839. Supervised by Mark Davison.'

He placed it on a shelf and picked up a slender volume titled *Egyptian Love Poems*. It had fallen open to a page that he couldn't help reading:

My boat sails upstream
In time to the stroke of the oarsmen.
I am traveling to Thebes, 'City of the Two Lands.'
And I shall beseech of the god Ptah, Lord of Truth:
'Bring me my fair one tonight.'
The goddess Meshkent is my beloved's tuft of reeds,

The goddess Mayet is her posy of blossoms,
The goddess Neith is her budding lotus,
The goddess Anuket is her blooming flower.

Glenn looked at the title page. *Translated from the original hieroglyphics by Dr. Candice Armstrong.* He shelved the book. Armstrong was smart. He gave her that.

The walls of this curious little room were covered with pictures and maps, notes, newspaper clippings, charts, and what looked like a timeline. Dominating was a blackboard with notes scribbled in white chalk.

Why was Tutankhamon murdered?
KV55: Why male mummy in female coffin?
Why does Nefertiti vanish from the historical record?
Or does she??

The photographs were of Egyptian kings and queens, mostly Akhnaton and Nefertiti. Glenn surmised that this was the nexus of Candice Armstrong's universe, the axis around which her entire life revolved.

'Was anything stolen from this room?'

'I don't know!' she said furiously. She clutched papers to her chest. Her body shook. 'Huffy could have been killed. My last cat was eaten by coyotes. Huffy is never allowed outside!'

As if on cue, the silver Persian jumped up on the desk, tail swishing in agitation. She wasn't used to strangers invading her house. When Glenn scratched the cat behind the ears, Candice stared. 'She never lets anyone touch her.'

'I like cats. Pure honesty. No false pretenses. Dr. Armstrong, you should have called me from the bookstore.' She had told him on the phone about the hang-ups and the call at the bookstore. 'I could have had the sheriffs here in minutes. They might have caught the perpetrator red-handed.' He didn't add the rest: that she should also have waited outside her cabin for the police to arrive, that coming inside was dangerous, the burglar could have still been in there.

'It's a bad habit I'm trying to kick,' she said, returning the damp handkerchief to him. 'Impulsiveness. I always act without thinking.' *Could* she have handled Dr. Faircloth's

27

unethical actions differently? Perhaps if she had waited, given it thought, discussed it with him and other members of the dig. And why worry about it now, ten years later?

'It's all right,' the detective said. He saw the whiteness around her mouth, the tension in her neck, the fear in her eyes. 'You were scared.'

'I still am.'

He looked around the small room again, at the pictures and maps, the notes strewn on the floor, books scattered. Wondering at the burglar's motive. What could he have been looking for in here?

'No one would want this,' Candice said, reading his mind. 'My theory is unpopular. No one would steal it.'

He looked at her. 'Your theory?'

'That Nefertiti was a pharaoh.'

He blinked.

'The historical record proves it, but Egyptologists prefer to relegate her to queenhood.' Candice didn't voice the rest: that her passion to restore Nefertiti to her rightful status was due to her mother. Sybilla Armstrong had been taken advantage of, her ideas stolen, and she had never received credit.

'If the burglar wasn't after your work, then what *was* he interested in?'

'Your father's work. The Star of Babylon. That's the only explanation.'

Eyebrows arched to the brim of his hat. 'All right, take a look around in here. Make a list of things missing. I'm going to have a word with the officers outside.'

The sheriffs were doing a thorough job, dusting for prints, taking pictures of footprints and tire tracks outside. The front door had been jimmied open, Glenn noted, probably with a crowbar. He tried to remain focused, the policeman doing his job, but he kept thinking of Dr. Armstrong, on the floor with her precious papers, looking small and vulnerable.

When she came into the living room, Candice saw that Glenn had removed his hat. She tried not to stare. She always thought that men who wore hats all the time had something to hide, like baldness or thinning, but Glenn Masters' hair was very thick, raked straight back, and that strange hue of blond that turns light in the summer and darkens to brown in the winter.

He had also removed his damp overcoat to reveal a smartly tailored dark sport jacket over gray slacks, and a red silk tie carefully knotted at the collar of an immaculate white shirt. Now she had more of a sense of his build. Not a desk man. Glenn Masters *used* his body.

She wondered if he was married. The Professor had never mentioned a daughter-in-law. But then he had never mentioned a son either.

He came over. 'Dr. Armstrong, why do you think this burglary is connected to my father?'

'The way my house was searched. My valuables weren't touched.' She led him to a table by the French doors. Small brushes and soft cloths, cleaning solutions, mineral oil, cotton balls and swabs. 'My hobby,' she said, gesturing to a glass display case. 'I buy old cameos and clean them. Sometimes I find gems underneath the tarnish and grime.' She pointed to a lavender stone set in a gold oval. 'I bought that for fifty cents at a garage sale and recently had it appraised at a thousand dollars. Why didn't the thief take these?'

'Maybe he doesn't know cameos.'

'Detective, do these look valuable to you?'

He took in the gold and silver, the precious stones, the incredible artistry and skill of the carvings. 'Yes,' he said.

'Easy to carry, easy to sell. Yet he left them. There's something else. I was followed today. A white Ford Taurus, everywhere I went.'

He cleared his throat. He wished she had told him sooner. She was right about being impulsive. 'Did you get the license plate?'

'I didn't see the rear plate, but the front one had a cardboard sign in the frame, the name of the rental agency.'

'I'll phone it in, see if we can track it down.' Wished he had known *that* sooner, too.

'I'm sure it was the same person who kept calling me and hanging up. And I think,' she picked up her tote bag and brought out Duchesne's book, 'this is what he was looking for.'

She showed Glenn the picture of the unidentifiable tablet. 'The proprietor of the bookstore said this was a unique stone, and that there were supposedly no others like it in the world. Yet he had a feeling your father might have actually found another one. Do you know anything about that?'

29

Glenn shook his head.

'Does this look familiar or mean anything to you?'

He gave the picture a long scrutiny. 'My father was an expert in cuneiform. He was always bent over pieces of clay like this, imprinted with little wedge-shaped marks.'

'But does this mean anything to you?'

He shook his head again. 'It's no language I'm familiar with. The stone itself is unusual, too. Most cuneiform was written on baked clay tablets. But this appears to be a hard stone with writing etched into it, as if made to endure. And notice how smoothly worn it is, as if passed down through generations. This tablet did not sit in a library or archive somewhere. It was handled and used. But the language I don't recognize.'

'Neither do I. I made a photocopy of the picture. I have a friend I can fax it to. If anyone on this planet will be able to identify this language, it's him. Now the note.' She retrieved her wallet. 'This was tucked next to the picture of the tablet.' She handed it to him. 'That's your father's handwriting.'

He frowned over the words. '"Is the answer in the tomb of Nakht?" What does that mean?'

'I don't know. Nakht was a nobleman who lived in the Eighteenth Dynasty in Egypt, my area of expertise. That might be why your father asked for me. Maybe he thought I could answer this question.'

'But what exactly is the question?'

'That is something I am going to have to figure out.' Candice pushed a strand of hair from her forehead.

'But what was my father working on that—' he began. He blinked. Their eyes met. And suddenly both were thinking the same thing.

'We'll take my car,' Glenn said.

When they arrived at the house on Bluebell Lane, they saw before the car rolled to a stop, in the gray light of the drizzly afternoon, the shattered front window.

Candice wanted to rush in, but Glenn held her back. The intruder might still be inside.

They proceeded with caution, Glenn calling the Santa Monica police on his cell phone as they made their way up the path. They paused in the foyer as they had the night before, but this time Candice's skin crawled with fear as she imagined masked gunmen in every shadow. Glenn did a cursory search, turning on lights, looking and listening. When he was satisfied that the intruder was gone, he and Candice assessed the damage.

Although the house was in less disarray than Candice's, it had been searched, and the method was identical: valuables such as TVs and VCRs, a bottle filled with coins, the kitchen sugar jar stuffed with dollar bills, had gone untouched, while books had been dislodged from shelves, and drawers emptied out. They found the Pandora painting askew, the humidor lying broken on the floor.

As Candice bent to pick up the shattered box, she detected the strong scent of the small cigars the Professor liked to smoke – Las Cabrillas, petit coronas imported from Honduras that gave off delicate oak and peppery aromas.

In the Professor's office they found lying on the carpet a brass plaque that had been given to him by his students: *It is the glory of God to conceal a matter, but the glory of kings to search out a matter – Proverbs 25:2.*

Next to the plaque lay a copy of *International Antiquities Marketplace Quarterly*. Candice picked it up. She noted the date of the issue – six months ago. Professor Masters hadn't been interested in replacing the Duchesne book until six months ago when, according to Mr. Goff, he had come in with an urgent request to have the book located. Now she knew why. A page had been torn out of the magazine, from the classified section, sellers' ads.

Replacing the magazine where she found it, Candice brought her hands to her nose. Had the lingering scent of the coronas been transferred from the broken humidor to her skin? She smelled nothing. And yet when she took her hands away she still detected the oak-peppery aroma.

Odd.

'Here's something,' Glenn said as he inspected a deep drawer that had been forced open. 'My father's correspondence file. He was meticulous about keeping records and copies of everything.' Some of the files were very thick and went back forty years. The entire B file was gone.

Candice looked over her shoulder into the shadows that crouched in the corners. The back of her neck crawled as the feeling of being watched sharpened. And that curious aroma . . .

'Detective—' she began.

He held up a hand. She saw by the way he surveyed the room that he had felt something, too. Did he also smell the cigar?

'Stay here,' he whispered, and she watched him move cautiously to the other doorway, the one that led to the kitchen and back rooms of the house.

Candice didn't want to stay behind. She still felt eyes watching her, and that corona . . .

Someone had been smoking it before she and Glenn arrived!

She whirled around. But there was nothing there, just dark shadows making grotesque shapes out of mundane items. She listened for the detective's footsteps, but the house was eerily silent. She wanted to call out to him, but knew she should remain silent.

And then: *creak!*

Her head snapped up. Someone was on the floor above. Had Detective Masters climbed a back stairway?

Her heart raced, her mouth ran dry. Stealing away from the desk, she tiptoed to the door that led to the main entry. The cigar smell grew stronger.

He was in the house!

Candice ran back to the desk and fumbled for the brass letter-opener she had seen there. As she curled her fingers around the handle, she was startled by the sudden crash from above.

'Detective Masters?' she called.

And then: thudding overhead, heavy footfall, the sounds of a struggle. Dashing to the foot of the stairs, she looked up into the darkness at the top. 'Detective?'

Another crash, a brief silence, and then the sound of thunder – coming down the stairs.

'Is that—' she began. A silhouette flew out of the shadows – large and man-shaped. It knocked her to the floor as it rushed past. She shouted, 'Hey!' and in the next instant another shape shot down the stairs, Detective Masters in hot pursuit, flying past her and out the front door.

Candice jumped to her feet and followed, reaching the door in time to see Masters tackle the intruder and bring him down to the soggy grass. The other man was smaller but more agile, and quickly squirmed away, scrambling to his feet to deliver a hard kick to Glenn's shoulder. Glenn was on his feet and throwing a roundhouse punch that knocked the other man onto his back.

Candice ran out into the rain, the letter-opener in her hand. She watched for an opening. When the intruder's back was to her, an easy target, Glenn slammed the man in the jaw, sending him reeling backwards to crash into Candice, causing her to drop the weapon. As Glenn came after him, the stranger took flight, the detective close on his heels, down the sloping lawn to the slick sidewalk where they disappeared behind a hedge.

Retrieving the letter-opener, Candice went after them, and, when she rounded the hedge, saw them in another clinch, delivering jabs and trying to topple each other. The smaller man pulled free and bolted into the street. As Glenn pursued, a car appeared from nowhere, bearing down on them, coming to a fishtailing halt. The driver flung the passenger door open and the intruder jumped in. Glenn grabbed the door handle and pounded on the window. But as the car zoomed off, he had to let go, flying off to land against the concrete post of a street lamp.

'Damn!' he shouted, slamming his fist into the post.

Candice was out of breath when she reached him. 'Are you all right?' His knuckles were bleeding.

'Did you get the license plate?'

'I couldn't even get the make of the car.'

Glenn peered through the rain toward the end of the street, his chest heaving, jaw clenched with fury. Then he turned to Candice, his face filled with rage. 'The bastard smoked one of my father's cigars! While burglarizing his house!'

A beeping sound joined the whisper of rain. Glenn's pager. The hospital. His father had regained consciousness and was lucid, but his condition was critical. The doctor advised Glenn to come at once.

Five

Glenn jammed on the brakes, causing the car to fishtail on the wet asphalt and Candice to jolt forward against her shoulder restraint.

'What!' she said, looking around for what it was they almost hit.

'That man,' Glenn said, sounding puzzled. 'I know him.'

She followed his line of sight to a long black limousine that took up a five-minute parking zone in front of the hospital. Three men, coming out of the building, walked toward it. A curious trio, Candice thought, observing their body language. The man in the middle seemed to be the boss, the two flanking him, and wearing sunglasses on an overcast day, subordinates. One was African-American, tall and skinny, the other a white man around fifty, with a most remarkable strawberry mark on his left cheek, roughly the size and shape of a human hand, as if he had been slapped hard and it had stayed. Both were dressed casually in tan slacks and white shirts open at the collar.

The man in the middle was shorter, in his late-sixties, Candice guessed, with white hair and a white beard, neatly trimmed. His attire was odd, even for Southern California, because of the rain: pleated white shorts, white Adidas and white knee-high socks, white polo shirt with a cable V-neck sweater over his shoulders, the sleeves tied casually on his chest, as if he had been called away from a tennis court or yacht.

She looked at Glenn. He had a strange look on his face. 'Who is he?' she asked.

'Someone from my past,' he said, his tone incredulous. 'From a long time ago . . .'

Glenn took the nearest space, and when he got out of the car the older man spotted him at once.

He came over, the two companions following a pace or two behind. Bodyguards? Candice wondered. But they didn't appear to have been hired for their physique. 'Hello, son,' the man said in a soft voice as he extended a sinewy, sunburned arm.

'Philo,' Glenn said. It had been twenty years.

They shook hands. 'I came as soon as I heard. It's a cryin' shame.' Philo Thibodeau was gently spoken, his accent Southern. 'My own dear wife passed on three years ago. Do you remember Sandrine? And now your father.' He drew in a deep breath and squinted toward the hospital, as if his

34

hooded gray eyes could see through the steel and masonry right into the intensive care unit, and what he saw there saddened him. 'When I heard about your father's accident, it got me thinkin' about the times when we all—' Overcome, he clasped his hands, which were clad in expensive leather gloves. 'They wouldn't let me in. Family only, they said.'

While he spoke, Candice glanced at the other two men and was shocked to find them both staring at her from behind dark glasses. She looked away, then back. Unseen eyes seemed to bore into her. It gave her a chill and she suddenly had a queer feeling about this trio.

'Call me if you need anything, son. I'll be in town for as long as necessary. The Beverly Hills Hotel.'

As they watched the limousine drive away, Candice said, 'Who was that?'

Glenn's tone was one of bafflement. 'Philo Thibodeau. Texas billionaire. His family owns half of Houston, and his companies own the other half. He was a close friend of my parents a long time ago. His wife and my mother were sorority sisters. The last time I saw him was twenty years ago, at my mother's funeral. I had forgotten about him. Strange . . .'

Candice was familiar with the name. Philo Thibodeau, she recalled, owned corporations, whole towns, an NFL team, a cable network that showed blockbuster movies, a chain of hotels, and most of the cattle in Texas – one of those men who always seemed to be in the background when important people were photographed, the ubiquitous philanthropist/supporter seen at charity balls, political rallies, and state occasions. Wasn't he a close friend of the President of the United States?

Glenn said nothing further and lightly touched her elbow as they joined the busy foot traffic going into the hospital. But they didn't get far.

'Dr. Armstrong,' he said, stopping, removing his hat and putting a hand to his forehead. 'You go on up. I'll be there in a minute. I just have to wash my hands.' In the stark lighting of the hospital lobby, she saw that he had gone pale.

Glenn watched her head toward the elevators, then he found the men's room, where he soaked a paper towel under the faucet and ran it over his face and the back of his neck. His hands shook and his heart was pounding, and he didn't know why.

He hadn't thought of Philo Thibodeau in twenty years. After his mother's death, Glenn had worked hard at putting his past and all bad memories, all emotions behind him. He'd climbed mountains to fight his anger; he'd scaled impossible rocks to forget what a terrible world this was. From Wyoming to Switzerland, Tasmania to Montana, he had clipped his way up rock faces and crushed the past beneath the soles of his La Sportivas, pushing his body and his heart to the limit of endurance, to leave anger, hate, love, and passions at the base of the mountains far below. And he had succeeded.

Until today, just now, minutes ago, when the face of a man he had forgotten had cracked through the barrier around his heart, as if Thibodeau were scaling Glenn, rock-climbing a human the way humans climbed rocks.

Why had the encounter unnerved him? Glenn saw in the mirror how white he had gone. He couldn't name his emotions. Couldn't recall anything about Philo that should suddenly upset him. But he knew one thing: seeing Thibodeau again was not good. Not good at all.

When Candice was admitted into the ICU, she approached the bed with disbelieving eyes. John Masters looked smaller, more fragile. His eyes were open but unfocused, his features twisted in confusion. 'Professor? Can you hear me?'

A memory: the day John Masters had presented his paper on the Solomon project before an illustrious audience of eight hundred. He had concluded his speech with, 'I could not have done it without the assistance of the very bright and capable Dr. Candice Armstrong.' He had then asked her to stand so she could receive applause. She hadn't been expecting it.

She took Duchesne's book out of her tote bag and brought it into the light. 'I did as you asked,' she said, holding it where he could see it. 'I've brought the book.'

The old man's eyes fixed on it. 'Yes, yes. Key . . .' A breathy, papery voice. 'The Star of Babylon,' he gasped. 'Must find it. *Urgent*—'

'Where is it? Where shall I look?'

Candice thought of the day she met him, at a lecture he was giving in Royce Hall. An imposing figure, sixty-two years old at the time, robust and silver haired like a patriarch of old, his skin bronzed by the sun of Moses and Solomon. She had known of his controversial reputation. The Professor was dedicated to proving the historical validity of Old Testament stories, finding proof outside of the Bible that Solomon and Abraham really lived.

On that fateful afternoon eight years ago, he had been fielding questions when Candice had stood up and said, 'Professor Masters, how do you reconcile the fact that the cartouche of Pharaoh Akhnaton's god – and "heavenly father" – Aton bears the name Amram with the fact that the same name is attributed to Moses' father in the Bible?'

The audience did not like the question, a few people actually booed her, but John Masters was delighted. Here was a person with chutzpah, he thought, a young woman not afraid to reference an unpopular theory, and with the courage to voice it. He had recognized her, of course. And he did not believe she was responsible for Barney Faircloth's downfall. She had been right to expose the rogue's unethical practices and she deserved a second chance.

That had been the beginning of their friendship. Because of her expertise in hieroglyphics, he invited her to work with him on the King Solomon project and it had been a perfect marriage of their two disciplines, Bible analysis and Egyptology.

'*Professor,*' she whispered now. '*What is the Star of Babylon?*'

His lids fluttered open again. Labored breathing, words barely spilling from his mouth. 'Bring it home. The Star of Babylon will be safe here.'

'Yes,' she said, for lack of anything else to say, since she didn't know what they were talking about. 'I will find the Star of Babylon and bring it back. Rest now.'

He closed his eyes and lapsed into a deep sleep. Candice remained at the bedside, remembering when she had walked with John Masters beneath a hot sun, listening to him speak Hebrew and Arabic, loving the sound of it, wishing he were her father, because her own father had died in Viet Nam at the age of nineteen, before she was born.

Remembering this man's son, the detective, and wondering if he was all right, Candice left the ICU and ran into a man pacing in the hall. 'Ian!' she said in surprise.

Sir Ian Hawthorne. One of Britain's foremost archaeologists.

37

Forty-three, tall, ruddy complexion, bleached blond hair in need of a trim, as usual. He always made Candice think of an ageing lifeguard. His attire didn't suit a knight of the realm: rumpled khaki trousers, faded denim shirt, gold-rimmed glasses filmy with dust.

'What a surprise,' she said. 'I didn't know you were in town.'

Hawthorne kissed her on the cheek. 'I'm attending the symposium on New Testament archaeology over at UCLA.'

'Are you presenting a paper?'

'Alas, no. My God, Candice, you look smashing. How long has it been?'

'Four years. The seminar in Hawaii.' She looked around. 'Is Melanie with you?'

'I'm afraid Melanie and I are history.'

'I'm sorry.'

'I was visiting Conroy over at UCLA when he told me the news about John Masters. Shocking. The nurses won't let me in. They say I have to be a relative or the Queen of England. Alas, I am neither.'

The elevator opened and Glenn stepped out. The hat was back on his head, Candice noticed, but he was still pale. She made introductions.

As they shook hands, Glenn saw Hawthorne's bloodshot eyes and suspected the capillaries had less to do with archaeological toil beneath the sun than with what came in a bottle. From two arm-lengths, Glenn could smell the alcohol.

'I'll get back to the symposium then. It was good to see you again, Candice. Perhaps we can get together. Detective, I hope your father has a speedy recovery.'

When Hawthorne was gone, Glenn stood silently staring down the corridor, rolling things around in his mind. 'You should stay at a friend's house,' he said to Candice.

'You think the burglar might come back?'

Something was bothering him. Philo Thibodeau suddenly appearing, in tennis whites, and now this Sir Somebody in archaeology. Both coming to the hospital, concerned about his father. And his father's house broken into, Candice's as well.

Glenn Masters did not believe in coincidences.

* * *

'Darling!' Sybilla Armstrong said as she greeted her daughter, saucer eyes sizing up the handsome stranger accompanying Candice. After leaving the hospital, they had returned to the cabin, where Candice packed a suitcase and wrangled Huffy into a carrier. Then they had driven to Sybilla Armstrong's house and stepped back in time fifty years.

'How awful,' Sybilla said, drawing them into her amazing hilltop home. 'Burglary! And I thought Malibu Canyon was safe. Thank God you weren't home at the time.'

Her voice had the same resonance and richness of tone as her daughter's, Glenn noticed. Full-bodied. Luscious and ripe, making him suddenly crave a peach. She had pyramid-shaped hair, parted in the middle and so frizzed out on the sides that it was flat on top. She wore a colorful Pucci tunic over black tights, and big dangly hoop earrings that caught the light. A woman who marched to the beat of her own drum. And rich, if Glenn was any judge of real estate.

Sybilla Armstrong lived on top of a hill in a fabulous glass and stucco house built back in the fifties. Not a big house, but the view of the city was 360, and now that it was evening the city glimmered with lights and a kidney-shaped pool shimmered pale green beyond glass doors. The retro decor was an eyeful, Calder mobiles suspended from the ceiling.

'Detective, may I fix you a drink?'

'No thank you. I have to get back to the station.' And do some checking on Philo Thibodeau and Ian Hawthorne.

He wanted to say something more to Candice, a warning, to lock doors and windows and not let strangers in. But he didn't want to alarm these two women alone in a house on a hill. Outside, he called for a black-and-white and twenty-four-hour surveillance.

Sir Ian was not surprised that Jessica Randolph was staying in the most expensive suite at the most expensive hotel in Los Angeles. It was her style. Only the best, costliest, rarest and most perfect was good enough for Ms. Randolph, dealer in antiques, art, and artifacts.

Although Ian knew her well, and their history went way back, and they occasionally kept in touch since both maintained residences in London, they were not what one would call close. So what perplexed him now, as he knocked on her hotel room door at this late hour, was why she had called him out of the blue. What could she possibly want from a down-on-his-luck, near-penniless archaeologist whose glory, Ian was sad to say, lay behind him?

The door opened to reveal stunning red hair framing aristocratic features. Jessica was not only rich, she was beautiful.

'Ian, darling!' she enthused in an aura of Chanel and sophistication. She wore a lounging set of dazzling turquoise silk.

'I was quite surprised when I got your message,' he said as he stepped inside, Jessica closing the door behind him. 'I didn't know you were in LA. The last I heard you were in Istanbul, conducting the auction of a seventeenth-century crown.'

'I was, darling. The sale concluded two days ago.' She sent him a smug smile. 'My commission was five hundred thousand.'

He tried not to let his envy show. 'How did you know where to find me?'

She swept ahead of him in a walk Ian imagined had taken her years to perfect. 'I had heard you were attending the New Testament symposium, so I telephoned and they were kind enough to tell me which hotel you are staying at. Help yourself to some champagne, darling. I'll just be a moment.'

Ian ignored the champagne and went to the well-stocked bar. As he poured himself a glass of Glenlivet he tried not to make eye contact with the sunburned, ruddy-faced, jaded-looking gent in the mirror. Ian knew he was handsome – enough society columns had said so – but he didn't feel particularly so. 'Dashing, eligible, debonair,' they all twittered, as if he were a regular feature at Wimbledon and Churchill Downs. Those days, alas, were gone. Now, at forty-three, Sir Ian was in debt, out of new ideas, and drinking far too much.

Jessica was on the phone speaking French, fluently and with a flawless accent. Ian understood enough to grasp that she was on a conference call conducting an auction between buyers in Singapore and Quebec. The item was a Rembrandt for sale in Paris.

As he watched her, Ian marveled again at what an amazing creature she was. Blood didn't run in Jessica Randolph's veins, liquid money did. She even spoke a peculiar language – the nouns and verbs of dollars, cents, pounds, marks, rubles. Her favorite music was the sound of cash registers. She judged a man's looks not by his face but by his wallet. To Jessica, there were no ugly millionaires.

Ian eyed the room service cart. Typical of Jessica, she had ordered caviar, most likely the rarest and most expensive, and he noticed that the small spoon had been used, a few crackers gone. But most of the caviar was still there, neglected, to be cleaned away with the crumbs and orange rinds. That was her way. She never ate the whole of anything, just a bite, and then discarded the rest, as if to show she could. Jessica's true appetite was not for food, anyway, but for cash. Her bank account fattened, never her body.

He suspected she was a completely invented woman. No one really knew her background, her roots. He would wager that Jessica Randolph wasn't even her real name. She and Ian had been romantically entangled briefly, years ago, when Jessica was still climbing her platinum ladder. Looking back, he could see that it wasn't really 'romantic.' They certainly had never made love. Having sex. That was all.

'What do you know about the Star of Babylon?' she said, snapping her phone shut.

His blond eyebrows arched. 'The Star of Babylon?'

'You always have an ear to the grapevine, darling. I wondered if you had heard any scuttlebutt about such an object?'

'No idea. What is it?'

'If I knew,' she said dryly, 'I wouldn't be asking about it, I would be *selling* it.' She lit a cigarette and blew smoke through her nostrils. 'I thought perhaps Candice Armstrong might have said something.'

'Candice! Why should she? And how do you know Candice?'

'I know her from her reputation,' Jessica said vaguely.

'Is that why you asked me here? You could just as well have asked me that on the phone.'

'I want to ask you a favor.' She swept away from him again – Jessica never just walked. 'I have to leave for London tonight,' she said. 'Something unexpected has come up. But

41

one of my clients is interested in an item called the Star of Babylon. I was wondering if you could keep an ear open. The symposium you're attending has drawn hundreds of scholars and archaeologists from around the world. There's bound to be *some* talk.'

'For God's sake, Jessica,' he said impatiently. 'I haven't the faintest idea what the Star of Babylon is. Is it a necklace? A mosaic? What?'

She matched him impatience for impatience. 'I don't know, Ian. I am simply asking you to keep your antenna up. It's very important.' She puffed, blew smoke, then: 'It could mean a lot of money. And I would be willing to share, pay you a finder's fee.'

That surprised him. 'Well I'm only here for two more days myself and then it's back to Jordan.'

'Yes, I heard. A floor, isn't it?' Making it sound insignificant. 'Just think, darling, what a nice juicy commission from me could mean.'

Jessica winked and it grated on Ian. He wanted to shout, 'You win! You're richer and more successful than I am! You're sleek and mysterious and the world is your personal oyster.' Instead he smiled and toasted her with his glass.

He resented her smug superiority, and he didn't like being at her mercy. But the sad truth was, he needed money. He had spent the past week dodging a bookmaker whom he owed nearly a thousand pounds in unlucky bets.

'Very well, love,' he said, setting down his emptied glass. 'I suppose it can't hurt to put some feelers out tomorrow, see what people know about this mysterious Star of Babylon.'

After Ian left, Jessica smiled in anticipation. She knew he thought her a cold, heartless fish. Never mind. It was none of his business that she had had her eye on only one man for most of her life and that she had recently come to a decision: to make that man hers.

And Jessica was willing to risk everything to that end. Even if it meant stealing the Star of Babylon.

Even if it meant *killing* for the Star of Babylon.

Six

S ybilla had already left for her business trip. Candice had
found a note in the kitchen:

> You'll get the San Francisco job, darling. No one knows
> ancient Egypt like you. You are unsurpassed. What
> happened to Dr. Faircloth is in the past and Mr. O'Brien
> knows this. He won't cut off the museum's nose to spite
> its face.

Candice wished she had her mother's optimism. But as she was
getting dressed earlier she had received only one call, and it
wasn't from San Francisco. Detective Masters, calling to see if
Candice and her mother were okay, no surprise visitors during
the night? 'I ran a check on your friend,' he had then said.

'My friend?'

'Hawthorne's registered for the seminar, just like he said,
and attended yesterday's lectures.'

'You checked up on Ian? Ian isn't a thief.'

'Ideas get stolen everyday.'

'Every profession has its unethical element,' she had said
defensively. 'Sir Ian is a respected and honored man in his field.
He would never stoop to anything so low as taking advantage
of a colleague in dire straits.' Although, Candice had heard that
Ian had fallen on hard times. Gambling debts, they said.

Was his sudden appearance on the scene just a coincidence?
Or was there another reason? The detective was too suspicious of people, she told herself. And then decided she didn't
blame him.

Last night, Glenn Masters standing at his father's bedside,
solemnly and silently, with his hand on the rail, gazing down
at the old man, as if in prayer. He had not removed his hat,
and Candice could not tell by his posture what he was thinking.
Masters was an enigma. She sensed an air of melancholy below

43

the controlled surface, as if two personalities inhabited the body, the stiff detective, and the hidden man who had yet to reveal himself. Why did he seem to be constantly holding himself in check, as if he feared the slightest slip would make him let go and—

What? Let fly some unimaginable temper? Outrageous laughing fits? Waterfalls of tears? She couldn't imagine the *other* Glenn Masters and wondered if perhaps he had been held so long in check that even if he were given the opportunity to let loose, he could not.

At the door to the Intensive Care Unit, she pressed the buzzer marked RING FOR ENTRY. The nurse at the desk said with a frown, 'Miss Armstrong? But you're already signed in.'

'Again?' One would think the staff of an Intensive Care Unit would be more careful with sign-in sheets. 'I was here last night,' she began, about to point out that it must be an old sign-in sheet, that they had made the same mistake yesterday morning, when she glanced in the direction of the Professor's bed and saw a woman, slim and red haired, leaning over him. 'Who's that?' she said.

The nurse's puzzled expression deepened. 'That's Candice Armstrong.'

'I'm Candice Armstrong!'

The sound of her voice caught the attention of the redhead, who looked up, stared, and then, picking up her purse, darted away from the bedside.

'Wait a minute—' Candice said as the woman swept past.

Candice ran after her, but the woman ducked into an elevator before Candice could reach her, the doors closing on a thirty-something face with stunning features.

Candice had never seen her before in her life.

She took the stairs and reached the lobby in time to see the impostor hurry through the double doors and out to the busy patient-loading area. Dodging wheelchairs and stretchers, Candice pursued, calling out, 'Wait! Who are you?'

The woman ran across the parking lot slick with light rain, and into the multi-level parking structure adjacent to the hospital.

Candice sprinted across the pavement after her, weaving between cars, trying to keep the redhead in sight. But she lost her, the red hair vanishing into the darkness of the concrete building.

44

Slipping inside, surrounded by massive walls where the slightest sound echoed, Candice paused and listened.

Which way?

She heard the staccato step of high heels on the next level up. Candice pursued. Up the ramp and around the corner. There she was, the redhead, getting into a red Mustang convertible, top down, with red leather upholstery.

'Hey!' Candice shouted.

The woman didn't look her way, just turned the ignition and backed the car out of the space. In the pause to shift gears, Candice reached the car and pounded the trunk. 'Don't you dare drive off! Who are you? Why are you impersonating me?'

A quick glance in the rear mirror and the redhead shifted gears. The Mustang flew out from under Candice's hands, squealed up and around the corner to the next level and was gone.

Candice stared after it. She had failed to get the license plate number.

As she turned back toward the exit, she heard a sound that made her stop. An engine gunning. Driver sitting either in indecision or anticipation. Gunning and then a roar and a squeal of tires and in the next instant the red Mustang was flying back around the corner and coming straight toward her.

Candice bolted.

The red Mustang pursued, tires screeching around each turn to the next level up. Candice ran, jumping over the low walls, going higher up in the structure as the red Mustang kept coming. She fell when the heel of her shoe broke, and scrambled back to her feet seconds before the bumper of the Mustang brushed her. She had no way to go but up, and to the top, where the final level was open to the sky and there would be nowhere else to go.

Why was this woman trying to run her down?

She climbed the last low wall, ran with all her strength and breath up the incline, the engine roaring behind her, tires screaming on the concrete, until she reached the top of the parking structure. She stopped for only a second – many empty spaces, a row of parked cars, and the overcast sky above.

She turned. The Mustang was racing straight for her. 'Are you crazy?' she shouted.

She saw red hair flying, pale hands gripping the steering wheel, eyes hidden behind dark glasses.

Candice ran to the edge, to the waist-high wall, where she was trapped. Nowhere to go from here but down. Five stories. 'Help!' But the wind carried her voice away. The people on the sidewalk below did not look up.

There was a fire escape on the outside of the building, just feet away. Candice ran toward it and froze. She was terrified of heights. She looked down, the street and people spun crazily, and Candice fell back.

Frantically looking around, seeing the Mustang approaching – the crazy woman bent on squashing her like a bug – Candice saw the row of parked cars: BMWs, Mercedes, Porsches, even a Rolls Royce. The doctors' parking area. Which meant car alarms. She clambered up onto the nearest, a pale-blue Lexus, and jumped from one hood to the next, setting off alarms as the Mustang roared alongside. A cacophony of sirens and claxons echoed down through the parking structure, sure to bring security guards.

But when Candice reached the last car and jumped down, with no place to go, nowhere to run, she saw the Mustang, heedless of the alarms, racing straight toward her.

'She just kept coming at me! It was crazy! In a public parking structure in broad daylight!'

The ER doctor wanted to give Candice a sedative, but she turned it down. She wanted to keep the edge. She wanted to remember. In the last second, as the Mustang was hurtling toward Candice to crush her against an SUV, the redhead had spun her car in a tight U and raced back down the ramp. From hearing all the sirens, knowing people would be coming, Candice supposed.

Glenn remained standing in the curtained cubicle while Candice sat on the gurney, legs dangling. She wore a skirt with a ruffled hem. He tried not to look at how it brushed her calves. 'You shouldn't have gone after her,' he said.

It sounded like an accusation. 'She was impersonating me! I wasn't going to hang around and wait for a policeman. I want to know what she wants with the Professor.'

'There was a witness,' he said calmly. 'Who got the license

46

plate number. We'll track her down. Are you okay to visit the ICU?'

'I am so mad!' Candice hissed as she grabbed her things. Her house burglarized, Huffy left to wander outside, someone impersonating her and then trying to kill her with a car.

Glenn didn't blame her, but he thought she could do with some self-control.

In the elevator, where they joined visitors holding flowers and balloons, Candice could not read Glenn's expression. The ubiquitous fedora – this one navy blue – sat low on his forehead to shadow his eyes. But she could sense agitation. Because of what had happened to her? Or something else?

They stepped out of the elevator and saw a crowd of people in the corridor. They rushed forward when they saw Glenn, surrounded him, shaking his hand and expressing concern and worry.

The billionaire Philo Thibodeau was there in white slacks, white tailored shirt with a crest embroidered on the pocket and top button undone, the collar open to reveal a bronzed throat that contrasted with the white beard above it. Accompanying him were the two mismatched men Candice thought might be bodyguards, although they were slight of build and didn't carry weapons. She sensed an air of arrogance and superiority about them, the way they carried themselves, seemed to look down at the others, like a pair of peacocks. When she heard the African-American say something to Philo, she revised her prior assessment: not African-American, just African. The man spoke with a distinctive accent. Kenyan? The one with the hand-shaped strawberry mark on his cheek had his eyes on her again, watching Candice the way he had the day before, from behind dark glasses.

It gave her the creeps.

The crowd around Glenn was mixed: young people and old, a racial rainbow, a woman in an Indian sari, an Asian gentleman in a gray silk suit and a wispy beard down to his belt. Solemn, worried people. And Glenn in the center, looking puzzled. *He does not know them.*

'Hello,' came a silken voice at her side. 'You are Dr. Armstrong, are you not?'

Candice turned a startled look to a woman who was small

and plump and, with her feathered hat, resembled a quail. In her late-sixties and looking vaguely familiar.

'I recognize you from the picture on your book of Egyptian love poetry,' the woman said in a sweet voice. 'Your interpretation of the *wadjet* symbol. Very insightful. You have captured the spirit of the ancient Egyptians where other translators have failed.' The lady smiled. 'I'm in the field myself.' She held out a gloved hand. 'Mildred Stillwater.'

Candice stared at her. She was one of the foremost experts in ancient Near Eastern languages. 'Dr. Stillwater! This is such an honor. I use your book all the time to cross-check my hieroglyphics.'

The woman smiled. 'We are here to pay respects to John. If he is awake, will you please tell him that I am here and that he is in my thoughts?'

'I'm sure he will appreciate your prayers.'

An odd light came into Stillwater's eyes as she said, 'We don't pray, my dear. But John knows that. He will understand.'

Thibodeau was instantly at Mildred's side, smiling graciously and saying, 'I don't think we need bother Dr. Armstrong right now . . .' He guided her away.

Ian Hawthorne was among the group, an oatmeal cableknit sweater setting off his ruddy complexion. 'I leave the day after tomorrow, Candice. Back to Jordan.' He shrugged. 'It's not much of a dig, but at least it's mine.'

Glenn interrupted. 'Dr. Armstrong, we can go in now.'

Ian took her arm. 'Listen, Candice, I leave in a couple of days, if there's anything you need, anything I can do . . .' He shifted his eyes toward the ICU. 'I rather like the old man.' And he slipped her a card with his various phone numbers on it.

Thanking him, she followed Glenn into the unit, where he flashed his badge and began questioning the staff. The red-haired woman had visited his father several times, they said, each time signing in as Candice Armstrong. Did they know if the woman had had any dialogue with his father? They did not know. While Glenn was occupied, asking to see the sign-in sheets, Candice went to the bedside and looked down at her old mentor.

The Professor's condition had worsened, his face the color of ashes. She took his hand. It felt like cool bones wrapped in old paper. His profile reminded her of the mummy of Seti the First, a grand and noble monarch. His sudden shrinkage alarmed her. He had been so robust and vigorous just a few years earlier. How could age accelerate like this?

She wished she could pray. But Candice was not religious; her mother hadn't raised her in any specific beliefs, they had never gone to church. Candice thought of all the sacred texts the Professor had deciphered and analyzed in his life, illuminating holy words for others. He had never discussed religion with her on a personal level, only as an aspect of the ancient peoples he studied. What prayer would he like her to recite now? she wondered.

It took her a moment to realize his eyes were open.

'Professor?' she said softly.

The eyes stared at the ceiling, unblinking.

Candice leaned over, positioning herself in his line of sight. The eyes were unfocused and glassy.

'Professor?' she said again a little louder.

The eyes shifted slightly in their aged sockets. Filmy pupils found Candice's face and fixed there. She felt movement in the hand she clasped. His chest rose with effort as he drew in a breath and said in a whisper, '*Jebel Mara . . .*'

His mouth was lopsided, as if he had suffered a stroke. She leaned closer. 'What did you say?'

His tongue and lips were dry; his jaw seemed to creak with movement. 'Jebel . . .' he said, 'mara . . .'

'What is Jebel Mara?'

For an instant his eyes cleared and he recognized her. 'Candice,' he said. 'Star of Babylon . . .'

'Yes, Professor. I'm looking for it. Don't tire yourself. I'll find it. I will bring it back to you.'

His face crinkled with worry and effort. She sensed his agitation coming back and it alarmed her. Should she call the nurse?

'Promise, Candice. Jebel Mara . . .'

'I promise,' she said, seeing the spark begin to fade behind his eyes, feeling the hand relax its grip on hers. 'I will find the Star of Babylon. You just rest now.'

When she joined Glenn at the nursing station, he was telling the staff that he did not like the idea of strangers having easy access to his father. He was going to post a police guard outside the unit and they were to check the ID of anyone asking to see Professor Masters. 'The list is short,' he said with a furious expression. 'Myself and Dr. Armstrong here. If anyone else tries to see my father, you are to contact me immediately, is that clear?' And the redhead, should she show up again, was to be detained.

When the automatic door swung away, they saw that the crowd outside had grown, hospital security ordering them to disperse. One woman protested. An elderly Hispanic lady with long silver-black braids and skin like aged ivory, insisting she be allowed to see Señor Glenn. 'There!' She rushed forward. '*Lo siento*,' she said. 'I am so sorry.'

Glenn put a hand on her arm. 'It's all right, Mrs. Quiroz, it wasn't your fault. Accidents happen.'

'I was upset when I call you that night. I don't think, you know? I should have told you. And then my husband, he came and took me home.'

Glenn's manner was soft, patient. 'Tell me what, Mrs. Quiroz?' he asked gently.

'Señor Glenn, I want to tell you but I forget. Your father, he was writing a letter before he fell. I see it and I put it away. I see your name on it. It say "Dear Glenn," so I know it special. I think, maybe cops come and take it. So I put it away. But, *Dios mio*, I cannot remember where I put it!'

'It's all right, Mrs. Quiroz. I'll find it.'

'I wanted it to be safe.'

'Why did you think the letter wouldn't be safe?' Glenn asked. And then: 'Mrs. Quiroz, why did you think cops would take it?'

'Because your father,' she crossed herself, the rosary in her hand clicking, 'Señor Glenn, there was someone with him up those stairs.'

Glenn stiffened. 'What do you mean?'

'I work late, you know? The Professor, he told me to go home, but I promised I would clean up, there was mud on the kitchen floor because of the rain. The Professor, he was writing a letter. And then I hear the doorbell. They go upstairs, I don't know who. And then I hear arguing, you know? The Professor is upset. And then I hear the noise like thunder. I run, and I find him lying on the floor, and I hear footsteps running outside.'

'Mrs. Quiroz,' Glenn said in controlled, measured words, 'what are you saying?'

'Your father, he did not trip. The Professor, he took those stairs a hundred times a day. He was careful. He would not fall. Señor Glenn, your father was *pushed*.'

Seven

R unning.
    As fast as he could. Legs pumping to the point of pain. Heart and lungs straining. Increasing the speed on the treadmill; raising the incline; pushing himself to the limit.

Someone tried to murder his father.

Sweat poured off Glenn's face and neck and body, hands clenched into fists, arms going like pistons, feet pounding the rubber belt. Even the machine, now, starting to sound strained, as if nearing its limit.

The anger – when Mrs. Quiroz said, 'Your father was pushed.' Right there, in the hospital corridor, Glenn had wanted to explode, let all his emotions out and the consequences be damned. Instead he had said, 'Are you sure?' Asked questions. Jotted words in his notepad. Outwardly calm, inside boiling with rage.

And then he had noticed that Philo Thibodeau was no longer among those clustered outside the ICU. Glenn immediately called the Beverly Hills Hotel. No Philo Thibodeau registered. He called his station and assigned a man to contact all the hotels in Beverly Hills and Los Angeles. 'Find Philo Thibodeau.'

He had then taken Candice Armstrong home, the pink cameo throbbing in the hollow of her throat, as if the engraved goddess were herself filled with rage and indignation. Glenn had made sure Candice was okay alone in her mother's house, that the black-and-white was stationed outside, that her doors and windows were locked before he left. The paleness of her face, the whiteness around her mouth, the husky voice going huskier as she said, 'Find who did it, Detective.'

Nudging the treadmill's speed higher, raising the incline as far as it would go, he reached deep inside himself for the last reserves of energy, forced his lungs to gulp air, his heart to pump blood. He could not stop running. If he did he would go out of control.

Final report: no Philo Thibodeau registered at any Beverly Hills or Los Angeles hotels. 'Check the airports,' Glenn had said.

And there it was: Los Angeles International Airport, private jet owned by Philo Thibodeau getting clearance to take off one hour after Mrs. Quiroz had uttered her explosive statement. Destination: Singapore.

Glenn kicked himself. He should have thought of that first, should have nailed Thibodeau yesterday in the parking lot when his instincts had told him that this man's sudden appearance was not a good thing. He had no evidence, nothing to connect the billionaire to the attack on his father, to the two burglaries, to the redhead who had tried to run Candice Armstrong down with her car. Yet he knew all the same. Thibodeau was behind it all.

He had had enough.

Slowing the treadmill, Glenn eased his run, reined in his fury, allowed his legs to throttle down to a leisurely jog until it was safe to turn off the machine and come to a standstill.

But the only thing standing still was his body. Glenn's mind raced. He was not going to be lulled into a false sense of security just because Thibodeau was thousands of miles away. A net would be cast, as far and wide as the planet itself. Philo was not going to escape.

In the meantime, Glenn had ordered copies of his father's phone records and bank statements to look for frequently called numbers, or any unusual amounts paid out. Tomorrow detectives were going to canvas the staff and students at the university; Mr. Goff at the bookstore; the residents on Bluebell Lane; grocery delivery boys; gardeners; the postman – everyone who had had contact with his father.

Glenn vowed to get answers, before Philo struck again.

Candice unbuttoned her blouse with shaking hands.

She was still reeling from shock. The Professor, *pushed* down the stairs. The image haunted her. How he must have felt when he lost his balance, the helplessness, bruising and breaking his fragile body as he hit the risers, knowing that someone had done this to him, that he might not make it to the bottom alive.

Someone was trying to steal the Star of Babylon.

Candice wanted to scream and shout and break every dish and cup and glass in her mother's house. Instead she had made phone calls to see if anyone had back issues of *International Antiquities Marketplace Quarterly* – what was it the Professor had bought, and from whom? She had then considered contacting her few friends in the field, to see what the word was on the Star of Babylon, but decided against it. The Professor kept his work secret, so would she.

She had spent the evening searching for the Star of Babylon in general historical sources, had run Internet searches on Roman legends, medieval manuscripts, a rumor attributed to Marco Polo, to learn that the Star of Babylon could be a seven-pointed star symbol or an actual star in the sky – Capella, the sixth largest star in the heavens – or it could refer to the goddess Ishtar. Finally, she faxed the photocopy of the Duchesne stone to the editor of *Ancient Near East Texts*. If anybody could identify the alphabet, it would be him.

And what was Jebel Mara? Was it one word or two? Was it a place? She was tempted to ask Ian Hawthorne. It sounded Arabic or Hebrew and Ian's area of expertise was Jerusalem from the Babylonian occupation to the Roman conquest. His knowledge was unsurpassed in those centuries, and his keen eye was remarkable. Ian could just look at a piece of pottery and tell you which Maccabee was in power at the time of its firing. But she couldn't ask him.

As she went into her mother's kitschy bedroom, she stopped to part the drapes and look out. The black-and-white police cruiser was still parked in the driveway. The cop behind the wheel waved to her. She waved back.

Glenn Masters had insisted upon protection. She was glad. She felt safer with the policeman out there, now that night had fallen and she was alone in her mother's house on a hilltop.

Glenn Masters. Candice was startled at her reaction when he came into the ER cubicle. A small thrill at the sight of him, a sudden sense of feeling safe. It had been a long time since a man had had that effect on her. She could not even remember who or when. There was something about the detective's tallness and his coolness that made her feel like a damsel in distress. She was surprised to find she liked it.

She wondered again if he was married. He wore a plain gold band, but it was on his right hand—

Candice stopped herself. *Don't go there.*

Sybilla's bedroom was, like the rest of the house, a step back into the fifties. Her only concession to the modern age was a digital clock on the Danish teak night table, and the framed picture next to it, from 1969. A young soldier looking like a little boy in dress-up clothes. Candice's nineteen-year-old father, killed in Viet Nam.

A sound. From somewhere in the house.

'Huffy?' she called out. Candice tried to relax, knowing it was the near miss in the parking structure that had her on edge. The cat was obviously exploring.

She opened the bedroom closet for a bathrobe.

Sybilla dressed in style, if flamboyantly. Scarlet rayons, midnight-blue silks, daffodil cottons and creamy linens, all with matching accessories. Candice found a silk kimono printed with apple and cherry blossoms.

After receiving the condolence telegram from the military, Sybilla had dropped out of college and gotten a job as a secretary at an advertising agency. She was smart and creative and full of fresh ideas – all of which her boss used, taking credit for himself. While Mr. Wyatt got raises and promotions, Sybilla remained an unrewarded secretary. The cosmetic account, when Candice was twelve, was the final straw.

A phone jangled suddenly, followed by a hum. The fax machine! Candice ran to it, praying her editor friend had identified the alphabet on the Duchesne stone. Her face fell when she read the report: 'Unidentifiable.'

Returning to the bathroom, she peeled off her clothes, and turned on the shower. The tub was inviting, but she couldn't afford to take the time for a luxurious soak. A quick shower and back to work. But as she was about to step in, she heard a sound. Listened. It wasn't the fax.

Peering through the doorway into the bedroom, where soft light cast subtle shadows, she saw the living room and, beyond, the glittery view of Los Angeles at night. The shimmering pool cast shadows upon the garden walls, and pale-green lights danced over the living-room walls, looking almost like human shapes. 'Huffy?' she called. What was that cat getting into out there?

Candice slipped into the shower.

It had been Sybilla's dream to be an advertising executive herself one day, with her own office and secretary, her own accounts, even though it was a male-dominated field. She continued to attend night school and take more classes to improve her skills and education. Success was just around the corner. And then came the cosmetic manufacturer. They needed new names for a fragrance line they had been putting out for years, perfumes with the names of flowers, now outdated. Sybilla came up with new names like Passion, Desire, and Love. Colognes and lotions with names like Sweet Dreams, Spring Rain, Autumn Smoke. It had done the trick. Sales skyrocketed. Mr. Wyatt was made a partner in the firm, and Sybilla didn't even get a handshake.

Sybilla had then done the unthinkable. She had confronted Mr. Wyatt and demanded credit for her work. He fired her. She went to the other partners, she spoke out in letters to editors, on local radio stations. She would not let up, not even after Mr. Wyatt, under pressure, offered to take her back with a raise. Credit, she said, repeatedly. Tell them these were my ideas.

Going directly to one of the clients did it, a lingerie manufacturer on the verge of bringing out a new line of intimate fashions. Sybilla revealed that prior ad campaigns for their products had been her work, and she offered to work on this latest line for free.

The outcome was nothing less than spectacular. When Sybilla opened her own small agency, two of Mr. Wyatt's clients went with her, willing to take a risk. They were not disappointed. More clients followed, the new agency grew, so that today Sybilla Armstrong Creations handled only top-flight clients and raked in the money. Because she had had the courage to fight for what was right.

And now, like Mr. Wyatt, someone was trying to steal the Professor's ideas. Candice would not stand for it.

Turning off the shower and opening the steam-covered door, she saw the lights glimmer and ripple on the bedroom walls, as if someone were swimming in the pool. Had a wind come up? Trees created haunting shapes on the garden walls, making it look as if shadowy figures had climbed over.

She chastised herself for feeling edgy. There was a policeman outside, after all. And then another policeman, Glenn Masters, materialized in her mind.

That little leap of her heart again. Traitorous organ, defying her brain. Candice did not want to think about the detective, or any man, but her heart had a mind of its own. She pushed the image away – his sudden appearance at the ICU, tall man in handsome fedora, tilted just right on his head.

Stop!

She had more important things to think about. The project in San Francisco, a television series on Egyptian women – wives, mothers, bakers, singers, dancers, seamstresses and queens – Candice would do almost anything to land the job. The Professor and the mysterious Star of Babylon – where to look next?

As she reached for the bath towel, she thought of the last time she had seen the Professor, a year ago, lunch on campus at UCLA, where the Professor still taught. She recalled now something he had said when she had spoken passionately about ancient Egypt. 'You are searching for something, Candice.'

'Answers!' she had replied with enthusiasm. 'The solutions to mysteries. What became of Nefertiti after the collapse of her husband's reign? Who was the Pharaoh of the Exodus?'

'No,' he had countered thoughtfully. 'You are searching for your soul.'

Crash!

She jumped. Listened, watched the shadows climbing the walls, her heart racing. Huffy, with her long impossible tail, must have knocked something off a shelf.

Still, better investigate.

As Glenn stepped out of the shower, toweling off his sinewy torso, he caught a glimpse of his back in the mirror, the ugly jagged scar on his right shoulder blade. He remembered the day he had gotten it, when he had thought he was about to die. Sherri had been with him that day. He recalled her pale face looking down at him. He wondered what she was doing now. Still climbing, most likely. It was funny how you could be so close

56

to a person, even thinking of marriage, and then the mutual interest is removed and the two of you drift apart. It turned out that all that had held their relationship together was mountains.

His thoughts shifted to Candice Armstrong.

Gutsy, but too impulsive. A risk-taker. Glenn knew about the Barney Faircloth scandal and Tetef's tomb. She had courage, he gave her that, but Glenn would have gone about it differently, quietly, methodically, and by the book. The end result would have been the same – Faircloth's ruined reputation – but there would not have been a backlash on him as there had been on Candice. Now her career was in shambles. An impatient woman. Not one you would want for a climbing partner.

Pulling on black drawstring pants and a black T-shirt, he went to the phone to get a report from the station. Nothing new on the case.

Why wasn't she married? Or was she married to her career? The fury and passion that had burned in her eyes, glowed on her skin, when she was picking things off the floor of the small room that was the center of her universe – a mother defending her children.

Candice Armstrong was too dominant in his mind. It troubled him. Forcing her back, he focused upon Philo Thibodeau. A man he had not thought about in years yet whose sudden appearance set off alarms at the back of his mind.

And triggered memories: of his mother, Lenore, the Professor, and their close friends, Sandrine Thibodeau and her husband, Philo.

The four had been thick. Sandrine and Lenore had gone on occasional junkets from which the husbands were barred. Whenever Glenn asked where they had gone, his mother would pat his cheek and say, 'Just girl stuff, darling.' He had always figured it was an exclusive spa in Switzerland where they soaked in mud and drank ghastly teas. He recalled now disliking Philo back then, yet could not pinpoint why. Maybe it was the way Philo had made Glenn's mother laugh, or the way he always helped her on with her coat, touching her in ways that Glenn, at eight or twelve or fifteen, thought inappropriate. And her husband, the Professor, oblivious.

Morven.

He froze. Where did *that* come from?

And then another memory, long buried, suddenly in his mind: after his mother's funeral, Glenn suffering from insomnia, finally forcing himself to take sleeping pills. Waking foggily in the night to hear voices downstairs, shouting, angry, two men, one man threatening to kill the other. Glenn so out of it he was unable to identify the two, couldn't make out what they were arguing about. And then drifting back to sleep, the incident forgotten.

Remembering it now, twenty years later. Why? And what or who was Morven?

The past was coming back, riding on the tails of hobgoblins he had slain long ago. Or thought he had. Grabbing overcoat and car keys, Glenn decided to take a closer look around his father's house.

Still dripping from the shower, Candice slipped into the kimono and tied the sash, and went to investigate Huffy's shenanigans. 'Where are you, you silly cat?' she called. 'What are you doing out here?'

The living room had the feel of an aquarium, cast in the shimmering lime-green light from the pool, and with the languor from the hot shower Candice felt as if she swam between the furniture. She found a shattered vase in the front entryway. It had stood on a pedestal that Huffy had clearly wanted to investigate. Candice hoped it wasn't expensive.

When the phone rang, she jumped.

And then she ran. She had given Reed O'Brien in San Francisco her mother's number. 'Hello?' Breathlessly.

Silence.

'Hello?'

Click.

She stared at the silent instrument.

And terror washed over her.

Glenn was driving down Wilshire when his cell phone rang. Hollywood station. 'Ran down that Mustang, Detective. Rented by a woman named Jane Smith. Turned in this afternoon. No leads from there.'

'Credit card?'

'ID and credit card look bogus, Detective.'

'Anything yet from Singapore?'

'Thibodeau's still in the air.'

Glenn swore under his breath. There was no guarantee that Philo would land in Singapore. He could change his route and wind up anywhere in the world.

'Get in touch with Interpol, tell them we need . . .'

Candice got Detective Masters' voicemail.

She disconnected and hit the redial button.

Voicemail again!

Should she tell the policeman outside? But maybe that was what the caller wanted her to do, so he could nab her as she came out.

She looked out the window and saw the cop parked there. He hadn't moved since the last time she looked. He sat in shadow. She could not see his face. Had he fallen asleep? Should she go out and wake him?

She heard another sound. She whirled. 'Huffy?' she called, sharply this time.

No response.

The back of Candice's neck prickled. *She was not alone in the house.*

Glenn placed five more calls from his car. It was nearly midnight in Los Angeles but dawn on the other side of the world. People up and working, people who would find Philo Thibodeau.

He ignored the call-waiting signal. Whoever it was would call back.

Creeping through the living room, Candice seized the fireplace poker and gripped it with both hands. She wanted to turn on the lights. The shadows on the walls distorted things, made it look like thirty people were advancing on her. But lights might give the intruder an advantage. The pool filter had switched on, filling the night air with a hum that blanketed other sounds.

'I've called the police,' she said. 'And there's a cop outside.'

She walked slowly over the gold shag carpet, tightrope-like, poker held over her shoulder as if she were a batter at home plate. 'You might as well leave. You won't get anything here.'

Was it the redhead? Had she rolled her flashy Mustang to a silent stop outside, tiptoed through the bushes, unseen by the officer? But how had she gotten in?

And then Candice saw the service door that led to the patio. It stood open.

She began to shake. She gauged the distance between herself and the front door and the policeman in the driveway. Could she make it?

He got her from behind. She had not heard or sensed him coming. Strong arms around her waist, lifting her, feet off the floor. The poker flying out of her hands. She tried to scream. A sweaty hand clamped over her mouth.

'Shut up!' he hissed. 'If you scream I'll kill you.'

Instead of struggling forward to get away, Candice threw her weight backwards. It caught him off guard, unbalanced him. He fell against the wall and she shot out of his grip. Made it a few feet before he caught the hem of her bathrobe.

She fell. Scrambled on all fours. She had dropped her cell phone. All she had to do was hit the redial and get Glenn Masters. But where was it?

She kicked at her attacker. But he was on her again, yanking her up by one arm, covering her mouth.

She saw his reflection in the entryway mirror. The light was dim but she made out the head, bald on top with hair growing all around, long and tied in a pony tail that fell between his shoulder blades. He was stocky and powerfully built, in jeans and Hawaiian shirt.

'Where is it?' he growled.

He took his hand away long enough for her to say, 'Where is what?'

'The Star of Babylon.'

'I don't—'

Felt something sharp at her throat. Caught a glint in the mirror. A knife. '*Where is it?*' Words riding on garlic breath. 'Tell me or you will wind up like the Professor.'

She tried to stall for time. But the blade was biting into her skin. He was going to kill her right there in her mother's house on the hill.

60

'Please—' she began.

The knife pierced skin. Blood trickled down her neck. She cried out.

Remembering the self-defense class at the Y, Candice snapped her head back and caught him on the face. She heard a crack as her skull connected with his nose. His hold loosened for an instant. She jabbed her elbow into his ribs and ran like hell.

He came after her.

She flew out the door, shouting, down the driveway, pounding on the door of the black-and-white. She pulled it open and the officer slumped out onto the driveway. Jumping over him, Candice got behind the wheel, pulled the door shut and slammed the locks down.

The man with the knife came staggering down the driveway. He scrambled up onto the hood. His face ran with blood.

Candice saw the console between the seats – techno-gizmos that she had no idea how to use. Pounding buttons and flipping switches, she grabbed the radio microphone and shouted into it. 'Help! I'm in a police car and there's a man on my windshield.' Banged on the console, hitting everything she could until the red and blue lights flashed on, strobing Technicolor bursts on trees and walls.

A static-noisy response: 'Stay calm, ma'am. We can't understand you if you shout. What is your location?'

The key was in the ignition. She turned it. 'Hedgewood!' she screamed, shifting the car out of 'Park.' As soon as the Crown Victoria began to roll backwards, the siren blared to life, ear-splitting and startling.

Making sure she was clear of the officer slumped in the driveway, she stepped on the gas, raced the cruiser in reverse, then slammed on the brake. Her assailant flew against the windshield, smearing it red. But he held.

She gassed it again, whipping the wheel to the left and right, making him swing to and fro on the hood. 'I'm at the top of Hedgewood Drive. Bel Air! Someone is trying to kill me!'

The squad car flew backwards down the driveway, siren screaming, lights strobing, and when it crashed into a massive oak that had withstood centuries of earthquakes, mudslides, wildfires, hawks, bark beetle, Indians, and Boy Scouts, the man flew off the hood, slammed to the ground and lay still.

61

Candice kept shouting into the microphone while another siren could be heard in the distance, and the person on the radio told her help was on the way and to stay calm, and she saw her attacker stagger to his feet, glance her way, then bolt into the shrubs and vanish.

'Is he dead?' she asked the paramedic who was dressing her neck wound. They were loading the stricken officer into the ambulance.

'Just knocked unconscious, ma'am.'

They heard an engine gunning up the narrow road, tires screeching to a halt. Glenn flew out of his car and ran up to Candice, saying, 'Are you all right?' before he even reached her.

'Damn it,' she said.

He looked at her – the flimsy kimono drawn tight across her breasts, the silk damp in places and clinging to her body – then he went to talk to the officers at the scene.

On his way back to her, he stopped to look at the damaged police cruiser. 'You got him good. Blood all over the cruiser, and a trail of blood leading from the house into the bushes.' A note of admiration in his voice, imagining her at the wheel of the Crown Vic, trying to shake off her attacker. 'We've alerted the local emergency rooms to watch for a broken nose and facial injuries. Although I doubt he would be stupid enough to go to a hospital.' He consulted his notepad. 'Aloha shirt?'

'It's the best I can do. It had blue palm trees.'

The voice again, like warm whiskey poured over hot stones. It still took him by surprise. He squinted at the house on the hilltop with no neighbors. 'You can't stay here.'

'I won't put friends in jeopardy, and I have no other family. A hotel, I guess.'

He looked at the cameo on her bandaged throat – a delicate goddess stained with blood – and spoke words he didn't want to speak: 'I know where you will be safe.'

'Where?'

The last place on earth he wanted her to be. 'My house,' he said.

Eight

'It's easy,' Rossi said as he absently scratched the straw-berry mark on his cheek. It didn't itch, but he always thought it should. 'The man I've hired is good and keeps his mouth shut. The plan is, he gains entrance to the ICU disguised as a flower-delivery guy, lost, looking for the patient he's supposed to be delivering the bouquet to. In the two minutes it takes the nurses to throw him out, he scopes out the place. I go in a few minutes later pretending to be a relative.'

Philo Thibodeau gently stroked the blue-point Siamese cat in his lap. Outside, glorious breakers crashed on a Southern California beach. 'There is a police guard outside the unit.'

Rossi finished filling the hypodermic syringe. 'No problem.'

'They are checking ID.'

'Also not a problem.'

'How long will it take?'

'Death by potassium injection can be immediate, so I'll inject distally to the heart. The leg, probably. This will give me time to get out of the ICU.' He capped the needle and slipped the whole assembly up his sleeve, fastening his cuff. 'By the time he arrests, I'll be long gone. They won't connect me with it.'

'Is there a chance they can resuscitate him quickly?' Philo was thinking of time.

Rossi shook his head. 'They won't know the cause of the arrest. They'll be administering the wrong drugs. To counteract the K he'd need insulin by IV push, glucose, calcium gluconate. They wouldn't think of any of these.' Rossi had been a doctor, once. 'They'll keep at it, maybe fifteen minutes, half an hour, depending, before they give up and pronounce him.'

Philo tickled the purring cat under its diamond collar.

*　　*　　*

63

Glenn did not want her here. But the man who had attacked her was most likely the man who had pushed his father down the stairs. Glenn felt responsible for her safety.

Or so he told himself. The deeper reason, which he would not admit to, had more to do with the way she had sat shivering on the tailgate of the ambulance, bandage around her neck, bare thigh exposed where the silk kimono had fallen away, sitting there delicate and vulnerable, yet she had fought off her attacker and done him enough damage to leave a bloody trail. He couldn't stop thinking about it, which meant Candice Armstrong was starting to get under his skin in a way that threatened the safekeeping of his emotions. During the drive from her mother's house she had mentioned the possibility of a job in San Francisco. He hoped she got it.

They rode the eight floors up to Glenn's condo in silence, with not even elevator music to break the tension. Glenn's mind a tilt-a-whirl of questions: Who had pushed his father? Where was the letter that Mrs. Quiroz had hidden away? Did it contain the identity of the attacker? And what was the significance of *Morven,* a sudden, inexplicable memory from the past?

Candice, at his side, trying to keep her cool. At the paramedic's urging, she had helped herself to a bottle of tranquilizers in her mother's medicine cabinet, but she had yet to take one. It was after midnight, she wanted to stay alert. She had not called her mother in New York, didn't want Sybilla to know yet what was going on. When they had dropped Huffy off at a friend's house, Candice had not told her friend of the attack, saying the bandage on her neck covered a bee sting.

As Glenn unlocked the front door, Candice said, 'Why don't you go to the hospital and sit with your father? I'll be all right here.'

'I won't leave you alone. And my father wouldn't be aware of my presence anyway. They'll call if they need me.'

If *they* need me. Not if *he* needs me. Why the rift? she wanted to ask. What had stood between father and son all these years that stood between them even now, in this hour of tragedy?

Glenn had arrived at her mother's house in a trench coat, which he now shed, and his appearance surprised her. No suit, no slacks or shirt, but black drawstring pants and a T-shirt that fit snugly over tight muscles and a lean waist. The black gave him a look of power and control.

Candice looked away. Until her career was back on track, she would do without relationships. Therefore she convinced herself that Glenn Masters was just another good-looking guy who wore a T-shirt well.

The condo was a showcase of suede furniture in burgundy and gray, chrome lamps, Indian rugs, live palm trees in huge pots.

Candice saw that one wall was devoted to pictures of mountains, bluffs, rocks, cliffs, boulders, in black and white and color, five inches by five inches to poster size. As Glenn went into the kitchen, Candice looked more closely at the pictures and discovered that there was a person on nearly every rock face. They were all Glenn, scaling impossibly flat and steep walls like a fly. There was also a woman in some of the pictures, lean and tough and sharing Glenn's rope. Candice read the labels: Eagle Crag, Hong Kong; Gola Island, Donegal, Ireland; Grampians, Australia.

He emerged from the kitchen with two tall glasses filled with ice cubes and orange juice. Noting her interest in the pictures, he said, 'When my mother was killed I turned into one very angry kid. I was eighteen and needed anger management. There was no such thing twenty years ago, so a friend got me interested in climbing.'

The woman in the pictures?

'It looks dangerous.'

'It can be. It can also be exhilarating. You should try it.'

'I get dizzy on a step ladder,' she said. 'Part of my graduate studies, I worked on an excavation near the Great Pyramid. My professor challenged me to climb up with him, a race to see who got to the top of Cheops first. I could have made the climb *up*, it was the getting down that I knew I couldn't do. We saw tourists up there, on top of the pyramid, stranded because they were too terrified to climb down, and an Egyptian military helicopter had to lift them off. That would be me, airlifted off the top of the Great Pyramid. Does it work? For your anger, I mean?' She touched her neck.

'I stopped climbing. What's wrong?'

65

'This bandage is too tight.'

He led her to the burgundy suede sofa where he set the glasses on woven Navajo coasters. 'I'll redo the dressing.'

When he returned with a first-aid kit, she said, 'Why did you stop climbing?' Wondering if it had to do with the woman on the ropes.

'Accident, blew out my knee,' he said, sitting next to her, snapping open the white metal case with the red cross on it. He gently peeled back the dressing on her neck and frowned.

'What?' she said, imagining her carotid artery spurting. Glenn reached behind her neck with both hands to lift up her hair and untie the pink ribbon. Candice caught her breath at the unexpected touch of his fingertips on her bare skin.

'Your cameo is bloody.'

He dropped the necklace into her cupped hands and returned to the neck wound that had stopped oozing but needed to be cleaned better. As he soaked a cotton ball in antiseptic, they heard the rain outside start again.

He dabbed her neck as lightly as possible. Glenn had dealt with stab wounds, bullet wounds, bludgeoned skulls, legs bones protruding through flesh, and even avulsed limbs. But this small cut terrified him. And enraged him as well. Her neck so white and delicate – she could be a cameo herself – violated. He wanted to find the bastard and slit *his* neck.

Candice saw the vein throbbing at Glenn's temple. She wondered what he was thinking. About his father, no doubt. Estranged, yet he still cared.

'Why cameos?' Glenn asked, the silence, her nearness making him uncomfortable. She had changed before leaving her mother's house – a blouse of barely-there sheer fabric and flowing skirt with a fluttery hemline. Her hair drawn carelessly up in its clip. Her skin giving off the residue of bath scent – freesia or peony?

'I enjoy hunting for them,' she said, his touch like a butterfly on her neck. She didn't meet his eyes. He sat too close for that. She would have looked into them and rethought her decision about avoiding relationships. 'Cleaning them up, bringing beautiful ladies back to life.'

'Like Nefertiti,' he said with a quick smile. He patted the wound dry and squeezed ointment onto his finger, applied it

66

gently as he said, 'Why do you think she was a king?' because he needed to take the focus off what he was doing, their physical closeness, and shift it somewhere else, for both their sakes, because he sensed Candice's ill-ease as well.

She looked past his shoulder, at a portrait over the fireplace. 'My theory is unpopular.' In San Francisco, Reed O'Brien, saying across his impressive desk, 'If we give you the documentary, Candice, you can't have anything in it about Nefertiti being a pharaoh. Too radical. The series is about women in traditional roles in ancient Egypt. Not as female kings.'

'Archaeologists allow Hatshepsut to be a pharaoh because there is no getting around the evidence,' she said as Glenn turned to the first-aid box and lifted out gauze, tape and scissors. He was not finished with her neck. More touching, more closeness. 'But one woman king is enough for the conservative male-dominated world of Egyptology.'

Glenn placed a sterile pad over the cut, then took Candice's hand and placed it there, to hold the gauze in place, his fingers lifting her wrist as if it were made of porcelain. 'But why do *you* think Nefertiti was a king?'

She moved her gaze from the portrait to the closed drapes, beyond which rain caressed the windows. The way Glenn had lifted her hand to her own neck. He was only dressing a wound, she told herself. Yet it had felt intimate. 'It's in the written record. Temple blocks have been uncovered showing new and unexpected depictions of Nefertiti. On some she is standing next to Akhnaton, *the same size as he* – wives were *always* depicted smaller than the kings – and in others she is portrayed in kingly regalia smiting enemies of Egypt on her boat.'

Strip. Snip. And one piece of tape went tenderly over the pad. 'She could just have been a strong queen,' he said.

He had to bend his head to see what he was doing. Candice noticed how perfectly he had combed his hair straight back over his head. She detected the Hugo Boss again. 'There's more. The instant Nefertiti disappears from history, a person named Smenkhare appears.'

Strip. Snip. The second piece went into place and the job was done. 'Akhnaton's homosexual lover.

67

'That's the prevailing theory, based on bas reliefs showing Smenkhare sitting on Akhnaton's lap, kissing him. But was Smenkhare really a young man, or was it Nefertiti in her newly elevated role as co-regent? One of Smenkhare's titles was Nefer-neferu-Aton, which was also Nefertiti's title.'

He sat back, inspecting his handiwork. 'It's a better dressing,' he said, sounding a little proud of himself, but relieved also now that he could put distance between them and had no more reason to touch her. 'Proof is going to be hard to find. The Amarna tombs have all been explored by now.'

Candice was impressed he knew this. 'We look beyond the Amarna tombs. Akhnaton's temples and buildings were torn down after the collapse of the Eighteenth Dynasty and the blocks were used to build new structures. We have only found a few. We'll find more.'

He snapped the first-aid kit shut. 'And you are going to find them and restore Nefertiti to her rightful glory.'

'Yes,' she said. Candice wanted to ask about the woman who had climbed mountains with him: had she been part of his accident, was he still seeing her? But it was none of her business. All the same, she wanted to know.

She watched his hands, finely shaped, as he picked up remnants of gauze and bandage, and noticed a curious scar on his right hand, next to the pinkie finger. A wound received in the line of duty? A bullet grazing—

'I was born with polydactyly,' he said, seeing what had caught her eye.

'I didn't mean to stare.'

'It's all right. I had an extra finger. It was removed when I was nine.'

'Nine! Why so late?'

'My mother didn't want it removed. She was adamant about it.'

'Why?'

'It ran in her family; her father had six fingers on his right hand. Maybe she was proud of it. But my father won out in the end and off came the extra digit.'

'Kids in school must have teased you about it.'

'Actually, they thought it was cool. Afterwards, I was just ordinary.'

She wanted to say, 'You are far from ordinary.' Instead she asked, 'Do you like being a cop?'

It wasn't a matter of liking. Going after criminals was in Glenn's blood, in every breath he drew. He planned never to retire but to die with his badge on. 'I guess I must,' he said, 'after twenty years.'

'Is it dangerous?'

'It has its light moments,' he said, seeing the remnants of fear in her eyes, seeing that she needed a light moment herself. 'When I was a patrolman, my partner and I chased a drunk driver down Pacific Coast Highway. We pulled him over and charged him with DUI. The guy was clearly drunk, but he argued that he wasn't and demanded that I prove it. I pointed to the upper half of a traffic-light pole that was lying across the hood of his car.'

As she reached for the frosty glass of orange juice, her eyes were drawn again to the family portrait hung above the fire-place. 'That was painted thirty Christmases ago,' Glenn said. 'My mother and father – well, you recognize the old man. And me, eight years old.'

It fascinated her. The Professor, with a full head of black hair and black piercing eyes, a strikingly handsome man. And the smiling boy wearing a suit and proper little gentleman's tie. Candice saw the right hand resting on the left, the sixth finger visible. But it was the woman who arrested her. Glenn's mother, who had died violently. 'She's stunning,' Candice said.

'She was a professor of mathematics. That was what my parents had in common, their passion for finding small parti-cles and putting them together to make larger truths: my father handled clay and papyrus fragments, my mother, numbers and digits.'

He looked at Candice, as if debating a decision, then did something that surprised her. He removed the gold band from the ring finger of his right hand. 'This was my mother's,' he said, showing it to her.

Now she saw that it wasn't a plain band at all, but that Glenn wore the ring turned around, so that the bezel was hidden: a beautiful square ruby with gold filaments woven above it, like tongues of fire. 'There's an inscription on the inside, circling the band.'

69

She read: *Fiat Lux.* '"Let there be light."'

'My mother always told me it would be mine someday. Little did she know,' he added, taking the ring back and replacing it on his finger, 'that the "someday" lay closer in her future than she thought.'

He got up and went to the window. When he drew open the drapes, Candice saw a small balcony with potted plants. Beyond, the city lights dancing and swimming in the rain.

'She was murdered,' he said with his back to her. 'I was seventeen and she was coming out of a convenience store when a guy hit her over the head with a hammer, grabbed her purse and ran. A witness said the attacker was a white male, tall and skinny, maybe blond, maybe bald, it had all happened so fast. The police went about it very methodically. It took months of dogged work but they found the guy and he confessed.'

He turned to face her. 'My mother was killed in a random act of violence. I needed to know why. Does that make sense?'

It did to Candice, whose father had died in a meaningless war. 'How did they find him?'

'The hammer. That was how they traced him. They searched the area in widening circles and found a shed with tools. The hammer had blood and hair on it. My mother's. The witness who had seen the crime picked the murderer out of a line-up. He died in prison, serving life. I was a freshman at UCLA, planning to follow in my father's profession, but I developed this thing about justice and catching criminals. The day I turned eighteen, I quit in the middle of the semester and went to the LAPD recruiting office.'

And you've been catching bad guys ever since. Now she understood the source of the estrangement, the son going his own way, dashing the father's dreams.

His eyes flickered and she knew she had come too close to seeing the hidden man. 'It's late,' he said. 'I'll take you to the guest room.'

He carried her overnight bag, even though it was light and her only wound was a scratch on her neck. Treating her like a princess.

Up the stairs and down a hall. A door stood ajar and the interior so caught her by surprise that she jolted to a stop.

The room was full of paintings, stacked on the floor, on

70

easels – an artist's studio. Sliding glass doors and a balcony that overlooked the tops of trees, bare now in the early spring rain, but which would come into full leaf and flower in a few weeks. It would be a sunny room, made all the sunnier by the subjects of the paintings.

The canvases appeared to be abstracts of galaxies, star clusters and nebulae, but all white – ivory on white, splashes of opalescent snow and silver-pearl, surrounded by golden haloes and nacreous clouds tinted saffron and topaz, shot through with the barest traces of blue, sapphire, aquamarine, lapis and turquoise. Though the paintings were similar, they were all different, some explosive, others softly incandescent.

And then she realized: he painted light.

'It's something I saw during my accident. I was making a free solo on Blacktail Butte in Wyoming—'

'Free solo?'

'Rock climbing without gear, just a chalk bag and shoes. I took a fall. It was a screamer. That means it was a long one. While I was falling I saw this light.' He pointed to the canvases propped up around the room, nailed to the walls, splashes of brightness and radiance. 'I've been trying to recapture it since. I think it's something called the Luminance, but I'm not sure.'

'The Luminance?'

'The word came into my mind as I was falling. I've never heard it before. At least, I don't think I have.'

Whatever the Luminance was, it was breathtakingly beautiful. 'Do you sell them?'

'They're not for sale.'

Watching his manner, the way he cleared his throat, shifted his weight, she realized no one saw these paintings, that she hadn't been meant to see them either. But now that she had, what did it mean?

As they started to leave the studio, Glenn frowned and looked around. 'That's strange,' he said.

'What?'

'One of the paintings is missing.'

'Are you sure?'

'It was right here.' He pointed to a spot by the walk-in closet. 'One of the older ones.'

'Could someone have taken it?'

71

His frown deepened. Why would someone break into his condo and take one painting? And then he said, 'Mrs. Charles, the lady who comes in once a week to clean. I tell her to skip this room but she insists that if I don't let her vacuum we will be buried in dust. That would be it. She moved the painting, put it somewhere else.'

Glenn paused once more by the door, as if not convinced Mrs. Charles was the culprit, and as he did Candice got another look at the art work and was startled to see what, from this distance, could not be seen close up.

There was a face in nearly every painting.

The doctor in the crisp white lab coat, stethoscope draped around his neck, sauntered down the hospital corridor. It was late, few people were about. He nodded congenially to the uniformed policeman stationed outside the ICU. The policeman nodded back, glancing at the doc's ID badge.

'So who do they have in there? Some celebrity?'

'Attempted murder. High security risk.' The cop looked bored.

'Good luck,' said the doctor and he sauntered away.

He continued down the hall, paused at the water fountain, took a drink, looked back, then walked on. Turning the corner, he stopped and looked at his watch, marking the time since Rossi had administered the potassium. Cardiac arrest should be imminent.

As Glenn opened the door to the guest bedroom, his cell phone chimed. It was the hospital. 'What? Yes, thank you. I'll be there in about thirty minutes.' He listened, then said, 'I appreciate that, nurse, but this is a police investigation and I need to ask my father a few questions.'

As he disconnected the call and punched in another number, he said to Candice, 'That was the ICU. My father has rallied. The pressure is off his brain, he is alert, talking and coherent.'

'Thank God,' Candice said.

'Maybe he can tell us who pushed him.' The second conversation was even briefer, a report to police headquarters, telling them to put additional security outside the Intensive Care Unit. Now that the Professor was awake, he was in greater danger.

*   *   *

72

'*Code Blue, ICU. Code Blue, ICU.*'

The team came running – people in white lab coats, green scrubs, technician uniforms. The doctor at the end of the corridor joined them, slipping inside the unit when the doors opened.

The plan had gone like clockwork, just as Mr. Rossi had promised. The phony flower-delivery guy had managed to get into the ICU, act confused, argue with the nurses and, before he was escorted out, had memorized the patient list on the chalkboard: bed #1, John Masters; bed #8, Richard Chatzky. He had reported this to Rossi, who had then presented himself at the ICU as Richard Chatzky's cousin.

It got him in. After that it was a no-brainer. When the nurses weren't looking, Rossi injected the potassium into the comatose Chatzky's leg. All Philo Thibodeau, in a doctor's white coat, stethoscope and fake ID badge on his lapel, had to do was wait for the code blue.

As the rest of the crash team rushed to the arresting Chatzky, Philo slipped away and went to bed number one, seven cubicles away from the action, where John Masters lay, starting his recovery from his fall down the stairs. Listening to the chaos at the other end of the unit – calls for Lidocaine, the paddles, all the things Rossi had assured him would prolong the resuscitative efforts and therefore give him time with Masters – Philo bent over the bed and said, 'Hi, John. Remember me?'

Glenn pulled his car to a squealing stop in the hospital parking lot, and they both jumped out, in a hurry now, anxious to see the Professor before anything else happened. Candice had never fully thanked him for everything he had done for her. Now she could. And Glenn had decided it was time to mend the twenty-year rift.

The Professor's eyes fluttered open. He frowned. Then his face cleared. 'You!' he whispered.

Philo smiled. 'In the flesh. Again.'

The cool institutional air was filled with voices as everyone talked at once at the other end of the unit – '*Straight line. Still no pressure.*' '*We need blood gases, damn it.*'

73

'I won't tell you,' John Masters gasped.

Philo leaned close. 'I am not here about the Star of Babylon. I'm going to let your son and the Armstrong woman find it for me. I'm here to tell you Lenore will never be yours.'

'What—'

Philo laid his hand over the Professor's throat, placing thumb and middle finger over each carotid artery. 'She was mine,' he said quietly, but loud enough to be heard over the shouts at the end of the unit, where Mr. Chatzky was not responding to resuscitative attempts. 'Lenore was never yours. And now she will be mine forever.'

'He isn't responding!'

Philo applied gentle pressure on the arteries as John Masters struggled feebly. 'It is your fault she was killed,' Philo said quietly, pressing harder. 'Had she been married to me, she would have been watched, protected. But you allowed her to be murdered.'

John Masters tried to pry the hand from his throat, but Philo was stronger.

'Get a priest!'

The Professor's eyes bulged, his lips turned cyanotic. Philo continued to smile as he watched the life ebb from the man he had hated for forty-five years.

Nine

*T*he commotion at the ICU, breaking into a run, relief at *discovering the team wasn't working on his father, bending over the bed: 'Dad? It's me.' Waiting for a response. 'Dad?' Candice saying, 'The monitor! It's flat!' Glenn shouting for help. The nurses confused – another arrest? A second team called, the crash cart rushed in, paddles. 'Clear!' Long needles into John Masters' chest, confusion, his father growing white and then yellow. More drugs ordered. Up the defib voltage. Glenn and Candice standing anxious and fearful, ignored by the frantic team, both thinking this could not be happening, because they* *had things to say to the man in the bed, until, finally, someone said, 'Call it. I'm sorry, Detective. It looks like it was a stroke.'*

Glenn had relentlessly interrogated the staff, the team, the cop outside, the janitors in the hall. A cardiac arrest at the time of his father's unexpected demise was no coincidence. Had anyone seen anything? The uniformed cop mentioned a doctor – white hair, white beard, some kind of Southern accent.

Glenn had sent Candice home in a taxi, to his condo, with orders to get some sleep. He said he would be there soon. But by the time he got there, it was past dawn and Candice was gone. She had left a note: she had gone back to her cabin to check on things. A Mr. French had called, saying it was urgent, that the two of them were to be at his office at noon. He was John Masters' lawyer and it was regarding the will.

So Glenn now paced outside the attorney's office, furious with himself – he should have placed better security around his father. He went to the window and looked out at the morning rain, the parking lot below. They couldn't start the meeting without Candice.

He struggled to rein in his emotions – fury and grief and something he could not identify. He needed a cool head. There was work to be done. The letter Mrs. Quiroz had spoken of, he had to find it. He had called her again that morning but she still couldn't remember where she had put it. And the mysterious Morven – the word haunted him. It was strangely familiar . . .

There was her car. He could see her through the windshield, slender arms in pink sleeves, reminding him again of how she had looked last night, the airy-floaty fabric of her blouse, like gossamer, and her scent, an elusive flower he could not identify.

A dangerous woman, Glenn thought. Last night, as the sheet was being drawn over his father's face, Candice had put her arms around Glenn. He had tentatively put his arms around her, lightly, awkwardly, and then he had drawn away. He wanted to grieve, but in his own way, in his own time, when he could do it in a controlled, disciplined manner. Not breaking down because of how Candice Armstrong had felt in his embrace.

As Candice pulled into the parking lot, she looked up and saw Glenn Masters standing in the window, looking down.

After waking up in his condo, to discover he had not yet

come home from the hospital, Candice had gone to her Malibu cabin to find it undisturbed, checked messages – nothing from San Francisco – called to see how Huffy was doing, showered and changed, and now she was here at the law offices of Whalen, Adams & French, wondering why she had been mentioned in the Professor's will.

Stepping out of the elevator, she found Glenn in the foyer, pacing, the shoulders of his long black overcoat and the brim of his fedora sparkling with rain drops. He had arrived just minutes ahead of her.

'Are you all right?' she said. 'You didn't come home.'

'I went to the station to get my team together. Philo murdered my father and we're going to catch him.'

'Detective,' she said, hesitantly, 'I am so sorry about last night. Because of me you weren't at your father's side when he passed away.'

He stopped her. 'It isn't your fault, Dr. Armstrong. The responsibility was mine, the decision was mine. I should have swallowed my pride and reconciled with him long before this. It's just something I am going to have to live with.'

But she could see by the look in his eyes that it was not going to be an easy thing to live with.

'Now listen,' he said. 'You are in danger. The killer is going to assume my father passed his secrets to you.'

'And to you.'

'I can take care of myself.'

'So can I.'

'No you can't.' He looked at the dressing on her neck, the pink cameo clean again and resting in the hollow of her throat. Then remembered the trail of blood. 'Well,' he said, 'maybe you can.'

Finally Mr. French – tall, polished and professional – called them into the private conference room and invited them to take seats at the large table. He sat at its head and produced the voluminous document that was John Masters' last will and testament.

First, condolences, such a shock. Then: 'It was your father's wish,' Mr. French said, 'that the contents of his will be made known immediately upon his death. It was imperative, he said, that no time be lost.'

76

Before he began, Glenn asked Mr. French, who had been his father's attorney for years, if he knew what Morven was. But the lawyer said, 'Morven? Is it a person?'

'Do you know Philo Thibodeau?'

'I know *of* him, but I have never met him. His wife and your mother were friends, I recall. Sorority sisters, was it?'

When Mr. French started with the general dividing up of John Masters' estate, Glenn was surprised at how wealthy his father had been. He and Candice listened with strained patience as Mr. French listed the various dispersals. And then: 'To Candice Armstrong I leave all rights to the Solomon project.'

Candice was moved. Even though she had helped him with his research, the project was totally the fruit of John Masters' genius. The book continued to sell on college campuses and in museums and would provide a welcome addition to her income. But more important was the thought that he had left a little of himself to her.

'To my son, Glenn, I leave the remainder of my estate, that is, once the above items have been distributed. He is to have the house and grounds upon which it stands, and all furnishings within.' Listening, Glenn twisted the gold ring on his right hand. Twisted it with a nervous vengeance. 'And also to my son,' Mr. French cleared his throat, 'I leave the Star of Babylon.'

Glenn snapped his head up. 'Does he say what the Star of Babylon is?'

'I'm sorry. There is nothing more. But I was instructed to give you this.' He handed across a small envelope. 'It contains the key to your father's safety deposit box. Perhaps what you are looking for is there.'

The bank manager, a small gray man with the unlikely name of Vermillion, escorted them to the vault and then to a private room with table and chairs, inviting them to take their time, to push that button should they require assistance, and could he get them anything, coffee, in the meantime?

Both declined and waited for him to close the door.

Then Glenn, removing his hat and setting it aside, opened the box.

It held one item: a battered cardboard container the size and shape of a shoebox. Partially wrapped in brown paper and string, it bore two addresses – sender and recipient – in almost undecipherable writing, and an assortment of foreign stamps. Inside was the original packing material, which turned out to be crumpled pages from a Moscow newspaper.

In the box were two objects. The first was a map, very old, the paper yellow and brittle and nearly falling apart from having been folded and unfolded many times. It was crudely drawn, as if by a shaky hand, and the place names and notations were in Russian. There was an X at the far edge, with an arrow pointing to it.

Attached to the map with a paper clip was the torn-out page from *International Antiquities Marketplace Quarterly*. Candice scanned it and found just one classified advertisement for an address in Moscow: a Mr. Sergei Baskov. The ad was for the sale of a clay tablet, Mesopotamian, language and date unknown.

'The seller's name begins with B,' she pointed out. 'The missing B folder from your father's correspondence files? And Baskov ... As I recall, there was an early twentieth-century theologian, I believe, Russian, named Ivan Baskov, specializing in Semitic languages. There have been rumors for years that he found something in the desert and that he died before he could publish it. If the story is true, whatever Baskov found must still be out there, waiting to be rediscovered.'

Glenn twisted the gold ring around and around. 'So my father was planning a dig. Maybe in a place called Jebel Mara.'

They parted the crumpled paper to expose the object within. 'My God,' Glenn said.

Candice stared in shock. 'It's the other tablet. The one with the alphabet that matches Duchesne's.'

Beneath the bright lights the inscribed cuneiform was clear. The same unidentifiable symbols. 'There's something written here,' Candice said, noticing a scribble in the margin of the magazine page. In the Professor's distinctive hand: *The tablets were buried with the Star of Babylon.*

She looked at Glenn. 'Ivan Baskov was exploring the region of the Tigris and Euphrates rivers. He must have stumbled upon a cache of tablets. Like Duchesne did. Maybe Duchesne's tablet is from the same cache.'

Glenn fixed his eyes on the fragment, which looked fragile, as if the slightest whisper of air would reduce it to dust. He sat motionless, twisting the gold ring, a man in deep thought. Candice imagined this was how he studied crime-scene evidence. Or painted his canvases of light. Finally, he said, 'Dr. Armstrong, did you notice anything unusual about the writing on the Duchesne stone?'

'You mean aside from it being unidentifiable? No. I haven't had time to study it.'

'None of the symbols is repeated.'

Her eyes widened. 'You noticed that?'

'Twenty-two symbols, each different, none repeated.'

'It's an alphabet,' she said.

'Yes. Or a secret code of some kind. Maybe a cipher.'

'The key!' she said suddenly. 'That would explain why the Duchesne stone isn't made of clay but of a durable substance. It's the key to the encryption, the key your father was talking about! With the Duchesne stone we can decipher what's written on this fragment. All we have to do is figure out which language it replaces.'

Glenn delicately poked a finger through the newspaper shreddings and came out with a scrap of white paper. 'It looks like my father already broke the code. That must be what is written on this fragment.'

Candice read the phrase: *the astronomer's wife.* 'Detective, the note I found in the Duchesne book – "Is the answer in the tomb of Nakht?" Since your father tucked it into the page with the picture of the tablet, I assume it means he thought the tablet was Eighteenth Dynasty, or maybe that there was a reference to Nakht in that perplexing cuneiform. Nakht was a scribe holding the title Astronomer of Amon at the temple of Karnak, somewhere between the years 1500 and 1315 BCE His wife, Tawy, was a musician of Amon. Beyond this, nothing else is known about the two; it's even unclear which king they served under. Nakht's tomb, near the Valley of the Kings, is famous for its murals. I examined them, and although the occupant was an astronomer there are no stars in them.'

She pictured Lady Tawy in the Nakht murals, holding a musical instrument, Chantress of Amon. Was the Star of Babylon connected to *her*, not to her husband? And what did an Eighteenth Dynasty Egyptian nobleman have to do with Babylon, which didn't reach its peak until a thousand years later? 'Why a secret code, Detective? Why isn't this just written in the alphabet of whatever language it is?'

'Maybe this was a secret society. Guardians of forbidden knowledge.'

His cell phone rang.

It was Mrs. Quiroz. She remembered where she had hidden his father's letter.

Ten

Jessica Randolph hadn't intended to chase Candice Armstrong with her Mustang. But indignation had gotten the best of her. Candice pounding on her car, insisting she stop. Once she had gone after her, Jessica had found she enjoyed it. She would like to have gone all the way, finish the job. Maybe she still would.

Slipping out of bed and into a satin dressing gown, she moved quietly so not to disturb the man who still slept among the rumpled sheets. She glanced at him in disdain. Member of Parliament, rich and influential, married with four children, and quite possibly the worst sex partner she had ever had. But, then, that wasn't the point of their affair. Physical gratification had never been high on Jessica Randolph's list. Her passion was acquisition, and this man had social connections to the owners of some of the most impressive personal collections in Britain. At the moment, Jessica was on the trail of a fifth-century manuscript, and this man knew where it was and how to persuade the current owner to sell.

Jessica trod barefoot on apricot carpet so thick that her toes disappeared into the rich pile. The bedroom was beyond luxurious, filled with precious antiques, costly furniture, the finest drapes and crystal chandeliers. It was Jessica's home, personally decorated by her. She always brought her lovers here, making it a firm rule never to go to their places, or to meet at hotels or hideaways. Everything in Jessica's life had to be on her own grounds, whether it was bargaining for the rights to a Ming vase or spending an hour of intimacy with a man. Her eight-room apartment was in the toniest section of London. It was not her only residence.

Tonight, everything was going to change. Come the dawn, no more lovers. Just one man. The man she had waited for nearly all her life.

A snore erupted from beneath the satin counterpane. He had asked too many questions. But, as always, Jessica had artfully sidestepped them. Her past was none of anyone's business; where she had come from and what she had had to do to achieve her high place in the art world was her own personal secret and not fodder for gossip.

If the scandal sheets ever found out . . .

When she heard the phone ring in the outer room, she hurriedly slipped out of the bedroom, closed the door, and reached the instrument before her maid could. Jessica kept permanent house staffs at all her residences. They were hand picked for their discretion and ability to keep their mouths shut.

It was her ultra-private line, the number known to only a few. 'Jessica here.'

The caller's voice was somber: 'Professor Masters is dead.'

'I see. What about the Star of Babylon?' All business, not missing a beat.

'We'll be keeping a close watch on his son, Glenn. This could either suddenly get very simple for us, or very complicated.'

'And Candice Armstrong?'

'She'll be put out of the picture tonight. Wait for my call.'

The letter was in the study, Mrs. Quiroz had said. The letter John Masters had been writing to his son when he was interrupted by murder.

Glenn pulled at the yellow police tape with ferocity, as if he could tear the house down. When they stepped inside, he hit a light switch and the overhead crystal chandelier blazed into brilliance. The house had a dampish smell, as if it hadn't been occupied in years. How quickly the living depart, Candice thought.

They found the letter rolled up and nestled in a vase that held silk irises. Thirty years of working for the Professor and some of his secretive ways had rubbed off on Mrs. Quiroz.

81

Glenn stood in the center of the Oriental carpet, holding the 'scroll,' as if weighing it.

'I think,' Candice said, needing to fill the silence, but also wanting to help him take this painful step, 'that your father assumed someone at the hospital would contact you. It's what they do, call the family. That's why he asked for me. It wasn't instead of you, it was *as well as* you.'

He raised his eyes and they held a look of such naked gratitude that she had to turn away.

The phone rang and they jumped. It was a computerized telemarketing message that Glenn clicked into silence. Then he saw the message light blinking on the answering machine. There were several calls. Hitting the 'Play' button, he and Candice listened to messages of condolence, offers for free trial cable service, one wrong number, and then: 'Professor Masters, this is Elias Konstantine again.' Heavily accented English. 'I am sorry it took me so long, but you understand, with the paper work, the fees – well, I can take you to Jebel Mara. But it is imperative that you come to Damascus at once. And I must warn you it is very dangerous here. You come at your own peril, Professor Masters. A man came to me today and asked me to take him to Jebel Mara. I told him I did not know this place. I fear you have rivals.'

'Damascus!' Candice blurted. 'So your father *was* planning a dig. And Jebel Mara is a place! But how can someone else know about it? The Professor told only me.'

Glenn, still holding his father's rolled-up letter, as if he had no idea how to unfurl it, said, 'In the correspondence file that was stolen from this desk. Sergei Baskov must have written to my father about Jebel Mara.'

'So we each have part of the puzzle,' Candice said, imagining a global treasure hunt.

Glenn picked up the phone and called the station. When he disconnected, he said to Candice, 'No leads on the burglaries. And we still can't locate Philo Thibodeau.' He pondered Konstantine's last word: *rivals*.

His father's killer had gone after the Star of Babylon. Which meant that he, too, would have to go.

He removed his hat, the elegant black fedora with the satin band, placed it gently on the desk. Almost ritualistically,

Candice thought, watching him unfurl the letter, take a deep breath, hold the paper to the light, bracing himself for what was about to be revealed.

When he said, out loud, '"Dear Son,"' Candice said, 'You don't have to read it to me'

'You're involved in this, Dr. Armstrong. You have a right to know what is in this letter.' But that wasn't the reason. Glenn felt safer reading the letter out loud, making the private words public, putting distance between himself and grief over his father's death.

'"Dear son,"' Glenn began, '"Since you are reading this letter, I am dead, either by misadventure or natural causes or an accident while on my dig in Syria. Possibly I died before embarking on my quest, which I ask you to carry on for me. If I am buried in Syria, then I beg you to continue whatever it was I started there.

'"Forgive me, my son, I write in urgency for I am in grave danger. And now, because of me, so are you. There are things of vital importance I must tell you about. But first it is time to make peace with you."'

Glenn's eyes pricked with tears as he read his father's words in the dying afternoon light. Candice switched the desk lamp on.

'"By now you will have gone through my things, and the items in my safe deposit box, and you know from Sergei Baskov's correspondence that the Star of Babylon is at Jebel Mara. Because I believe the Star will lead you to the Eighteenth Dynasty of ancient Egypt and an astonishing revelation there, I advise you to seek the help of Dr. Candice Armstrong. Perhaps you recall she assisted me on the Solomon project. She is a good person, and a top flight Egyptologist. Further, she can be trusted."'

Shadows crept into the room, drawing close, as if to listen. 'We think that age brings wisdom,' John Masters had written. 'At least, I had always thought so. But it isn't so. What age does is make us wise to the fact that we *lack* wisdom.'

Glenn paused. Cleared his throat. Stepped closer to the lamp.

'"I can only imagine what it must have been like for you after your mother's death. I was too devastated to console you. How many times have I wished I had the nerve, or more humility to bring this up and mend our fences? But so often, when we got together, things fell apart. I've spent my life piecing broken things together, and so now do you, son, as a detective. Yet between us we can't patch up our own shattered relationship.

"'I know you think I am embarrassed by the fact that you are a policeman,' Glenn continued, his voice tight. 'This is not so. I am proud of you. But I am too stubborn to speak these words. If you are reading this letter, it means I did not take the first step to bridge the silence between us. It means I am dead. If that is so, then please know, son, that I love you with all my being, that I have always loved you and am so proud of you that there are no words to express the depth of my feelings.'"

Glenn pressed fingertips to his eyes. Candice waited.

Rain began to fall again beyond the windows. Glenn moved closer still to the lamp, the letter trembling in his hand. "'And now to business. Son, I have handed you a soup of mysteries, made up of questions without answers. And there is another thing you do not know: for years I protected you from something. I should have told you about Morven and the Luminance long ago.'"

Candice's eyes widened. *The Luminance!*

"'It is time you knew the truth. I have kept it from you all these years for your own safety's sake. You never knew about your mother's real work.'" Glenn stopped, his forehead knotted in a frown. Her *real work*?

"'You must read it for yourself,'" he continued, "'in her journal. I never showed this to you. After her death, I put it away. It is in her nightstand, where she always kept it. Read it, son. You need to know what you are up against, the forces you are facing.'"

Glenn looked up at the ceiling, as if to peer through the plaster and beams and carpeting above to see the journal in its drawer.

He finished reading. "'Philo Thibodeau is a madman. He has embraced Nostradamus and taken to heart the prophecy of century seven, quatrain eighty-three. Do not let Philo get the Star of Babylon. He will use it for evil. I speak of nothing less than Armageddon, for I believe he plans a great devastation—'"

Glenn stopped.

'Go on,' Candice said.

'That's it. There is no more. This was when he was interrupted.' He stared at the last word and the space following it in which a doorbell rang and a man's life came to an end.

Candice shivered. The late-afternoon shadows had brought a chill with them. Dampness settled over the house like a creeping fog. 'What did he mean, "a great devastation"?' Picturing the Star of Babylon as a nuclear weapon left in the desert by some Middle Eastern dictator. She looked at Glenn, his face cast in shadow. 'What is written on the tablets that your father so desperately wanted to get hold of them?' She touched the bandage on her neck: someone had almost killed her for the tablets. 'Something Biblical? A prophecy maybe?' *The end of the world.*

Dropping the letter on the desk, Glenn wordlessly left the study. Candice heard him run up the stairs, move around in a room above, then return to the study with a book in his hand. His mother's journal.

A beautiful, dainty book. Nine inches by six, covered in shimmering emerald silk, the pages ivory and gold-edged with a red ribbon place marker. It closed with a magnetic flap. Glenn opened it to a random page and saw his mother's handwriting: *There is no death.*

He snapped it shut and pressed the magnetic closure. Not now, not yet. This was more than a book, it was his heart. And his heart was his Achilles heel, which he guarded with his life.

'The Nostradamus prophecy,' Candice said. 'Perhaps that will tell us something.'

Glenn looked around the study, recalling an antique volume his father had had for years. It was in the library. He found it and came back to the desk to flip through the pages. The chapters, called centuries, were arranged in one hundred four-lined poems each. Finding century seven, he quickly flipped to the later quatrains but they ended at forty-two.

He put the book down. It was time to act. Picking up the phone, he said to Candice, 'My father's murderer is no longer in the United States because there is nothing more for him here. He will try to persuade or force Elias Konstantine to take him to Jebel Mara. That is where I will find him.'

'Where *we* will find him,' she corrected.

He stared at her. 'What?'

'I'm going with you,' she said. 'I promised your father.'

When he realized what she was saying, Glenn flew into a

85

panic. Candice looked at him with eyes wide and expressive, damp with tears. He had no defenses against her. He could *not* allow her to go to Syria with him.

He searched for words that sounded convincing. 'I can't allow it. Too much risk. If Philo Thibodeau is the man I am after, he is rich and powerful with every resource at his fingertips.'

'It will be two against one.' When she saw that he was resolute, she added, 'I'll be a help, not a hindrance, Detective. I'm an archaeologist. How are you going to find the Star of Babylon?'

Keep it professional, stay in control. 'The same way I find a murderer. I follow leads.'

'How will you get into Syria? It takes weeks to get a visa.'

'An emergency visa. International police courtesy. We do it all the time.' Into the phone he said, 'Masters here. I need to speak with Captain Boyle. It's urgent.' While he waited, he said, 'Leave this to me, Dr. Armstrong. By the time you obtain a visa I will have already caught the perpetrator.'

She brought out her own cell phone. As if they were dueling.

'What are you doing?' he said.

'I'm calling Ian Hawthorne. He said he was going back to Jordan. He's directing a dig there. He can get me into the country as one of his staff. From Amman it's an easy hop to Damascus.'

'Dr. Armstrong—'

When Hawthorne answered, she said, 'Ian, it's Candice. You said to call you if I needed a favor. Well, I need one badly.'

Glenn scowled.

Ending her brief conversation, she slipped the phone into her purse and misread Glenn's look. 'Don't worry, I'm not going to tell him why I need to go. I won't tell him anything about the Star of Babylon unless I absolutely have to. And he won't ask. Ian is a gentleman.'

Glenn tried another tack. 'Dr. Armstrong, your presence will jeopardize my investigation.'

Her beeper chirped. She looked at the digital read-out. Area code 409. San Francisco.

'I have to take this call,' she said.

Heart pounding, she dialed the cell phone and reached O'Brien. 'We heard about John Masters. What a terrible loss to the scholarly world.' A pause. 'We have decided on you, Candice. You have the job.'

She stared at the cold fireplace, black and tidy and clean of ashes. Felt Glenn's eyes on her. Heard the rain outside.

She had the job.

'Oh,' she said.

Glenn staring at her. 'What?'

'I have the job, Detective. The one I told you about.'

Relief washed over him. She was going to San Francisco.

Candice, still gripping the phone, Reed saying four hundred miles away, 'Are you still there?' She was suddenly giddy. They believed in her! They had set the Faircloth incident aside and judged her on her merits. Validated by her peers, at last.

And then she looked at Glenn, his brooding features, the emerald-green book in his hand, and she remembered something. Putting her hand over the phone, relegating Reed O'Brien and his good news to a limbo of silence, she said, 'Detective, if you find the Star of Babylon and the tablets, what will you do with them?'

He blinked at the unexpected the question. 'Turn them over to the authorities, why?'

'Your father wanted them brought here, to be safe, he said.'

'It is illegal to remove antiquities or any cultural treasures from a country. Whatever the Star turns out to be, and the tablets if I find them, it is my duty to turn it all over to the Syrian government.'

'But your father—'

'My duty is to the law, Dr. Armstrong.'

Seeing the set look of his features, the clenched jaw, Candice realized that there were no more questions, no more decisions to be made. Her way lay clear and distinct before her. 'Bring the Star of Babylon home,' John Masters had said.

She returned to Reed who was on hold in San Francisco. 'I can't accept. I'm sorry.'

'What!' Glenn grabbed her wrist. 'Take the job. Go to San Francisco.'

She shook off his hand and disconnected the call.

'I can't believe you did that.'

Neither can I. 'I know what I am doing.'

'Damn it, Dr. Armstrong, don't you know how dangerous this is? If I'm not following my father's killer, then *he* will be following *you*!'

She thrust out her chin to press down her disappointment. The San Francisco project would have saved her life. 'Even better. I'll be the bait.' Brave words, spoken with little courage. Could he see how scared she really was? Then she remembered Reed's news. Despite her unpopularity and a career swathed in scandal, O'Brien and the museum board had recognized her true merits and skills. If they had confidence in her, so should she.

I can do this.

Glenn scowled. 'I thought you were working on your impulsiveness.'

'I am not being impulsive.'

He wanted to say she should add stubbornness to the list. 'You can't go.'

'You can't stop me.' She met his eyes in challenge, feeling confident. But when his eyes met hers, she felt her heart do an alarming leap. And she realized it was one thing to say goodnight to a sexy man on her doorstep and retreat into her cabin and put him out of her mind, another to travel halfway around the world with him, in close and constant company. But she had made a promise to find the tablets and bring them home. A little will power was all it would take to resist the tall detective's charms.

As Candice stood there challenging him, Glenn heard the deepening of her already deep voice, and it made him feel itchy in his skin and think of steamy nights and rumpled sheets. It was for this reason he could not allow her to go – she distracted him in the worst way. He had an appointment with violence somewhere on the other side of the globe and he needed to be strong. But if she was determined to go, then he was equally determined to find a way, once they were in Damascus, to convince her to go back to the United States – using force, if necessary.

Eleven

They met in secret.

On the fortieth floor of a high-rise building that overlooked the glittering lights of Houston, twenty-two people. Under the cloak of night, a somber gathering, whispering into the high-rise after hours, passing quietly through the lobby, where the regular security guard had been replaced by someone known to them. They wasted no time with frivolous banter or personal conversation, but took their seats around a large conference table illuminated by overhead lights. Each carried a dossier, each prepared to deliver a report. The leather chairs around the table were placed in half shadow; occasionally, the flash of gold, platinum, or gemstone on wrists and fingers bespoke the wealth of these people and, by extension, their power. They were not all Americans. The majority had flown in from other nations. And they did not always meet in this building, or in the United States, but because they were here tonight it fell to Philo Thibodeau, whose petrochemical corporation owned this high-rise, to chair the meeting.

He stood at the head of the table, his white hair illuminated by a soft spotlight. He was dressed in a white sweater pulled over a white shirt, and white slacks. The clothes were spotless. Philo changed several times a day. Although the others had poured water or coffee for themselves, no cup or glass stood near Philo's place. He never ate or drank in the company of others. No one, not even his wife, had ever seen Philo Thibodeau take a sip or a bite of anything.

He said to the man on his right, 'Mr. Greene, we begin with you.'

The man opened his folder, cleared his throat and read from the report inside. 'Roger Fieldstone, arrested for possessing items stolen from the Getty Museum in Malibu. His trial starts next week in Los Angeles Superior Court.'

Thibodeau made a tsk-ing sound. 'We need quick damage control on this one. Who's the presiding judge? Is he one of ours?'

The man consulted his notes. 'Judge Norma Brown.'

'Ah yes. Good woman. I'll give her a call. Reassign Fieldstone. That was sloppy work. Something low profile. The spectrometry lab.'

The next to report was a man whose hands, holding a cream-colored folder, were as black as dominoes. 'We are on the trail of a book rumored to be the diary of one of the earliest anthropologists to visit East Africa. It purports to contain descriptions of religious rituals he secretly observed. I meet with the seller next week.'

'Excellent, Mr. Kimbata,' Thibodeau said. 'Next.'

Around the table they went, each giving a report, speaking in low tones in words accented by their native tongues. A stoop-backed man with thick heavy glasses said, 'In the latest *Antiquities Quarterly* there is a Cretan stele engraved in Linear B being offered.'

Thibodeau held up a hand. 'A forgery. Next?'

Mr. Yamamoto from Tokyo said, 'For the silk scroll containing previously unknown text from the Tao, the seller is asking five million.'

The group spent a moment consulting, nodding their heads or shaking them, until they agreed the price was fair.

The last member to report, a financial wizard and Wall Street watcher, announced the election of a mutual acquaintance to the office of CEO in a vast and powerful corporation. There were nods of approval, and Thibodeau let out a long low whistle. Having that corporation in their pocket was a dream come true.

And then it was his turn. 'I have received news, ladies and gentlemen, that Dr. Candice Armstrong is going after the Star of Babylon.'

A member spoke up, Mr. Barney Voorhees, Minister of Culture for a small European nation: 'It takes weeks to get a visa for Syria. We can still stop her.'

'She has asked Ian Hawthorne for help,' Philo said. 'He has connections in Jordan, and he knows which palms to grease to gain her swift admittance. Once in Damascus, Armstrong will be linking up with a man named Elias Konstantine.'

'What about Glenn Masters?'

'He is going as well.'

'Is there no way we can stop them?' came a voice from the half shadows, a man speaking with an Australian accent.

'There are ways,' Thibodeau said. But at this point he no longer wanted them stopped. Let them find the Star of Babylon, and then Armstrong and Masters would be expendable. Philo did not voice this thought to his companions.

After everyone left, to return to their lives as bankers and politicians, scientists and poets, to friends and families who knew nothing of their involvement with an ancient, secret society, after he was alone at the top of the high-rise, Thibodeau slipped into the adjoining office where a man waited.

'Buschhorn won't sell,' the man reported. He had a lantern jaw and a gap between his front teeth. Built like a bulldozer he was used to getting his way. In this instance, however, he had not succeeded.

Philo shook his head regretfully. He preferred making acquisitions peacefully and in a civilized manner. But when he encountered resistance, further measures were necessary.

This, too, was something the other members did not know.

Sammy was her savior.

If it hadn't been for his precious company these past few years, Britta Buschhorn would not have survived. Which was why she fed him the best food, gave him the best toys, and allowed him complete freedom of the house for two hours everyday.

The luckiest cockatiel in the world.

Britta lived alone in an apartment overlooking Hederichstrasse in Frankfurt, Germany. Only forty-two years old, yet her hair was as white as the feathers of the bird that perched on her shoulder. Britta's eyes were large and haunted because they had seen too much. She had been tortured by rebels who had taken over the medical clinic where she and her husband had worked in a Southeast Asian jungle. Held for months in darkness and near-starvation, out of twenty-nine clinic workers, Britta was the only one to survive.

Sammy had pulled her through. A sweet-tempered cockatiel that wolf-whistled when Britta disrobed to shower, shared her lunches of pumpernickel and sausage, demanded head scratches, and filled the apartment with comical sounds. He was the companionship and love in her world of fighting for human rights. A member of Amnesty International, Britta wrote letters, gave speeches, arranged protest parades, and kept an eye on a world of injustice. Sammy was the antidote to that dark world.

The wheelchair was motorized. A luxury, but necessary – her arms had been broken by the rebels and had never regained their full strength. As she rode to the bird cage, Sammy on her shoulder, she told him that he would have a treat later if he would be a good boy and take his afternoon nap. Sammy gave a little squawk, playfully nipped her earlobe, and rode on her hand into the cage. Restored to his perch, he cocked his head, lifted his beautiful white crest, and seemed to weigh which snack to enjoy first, the cuttlebone or the hard-boiled egg. Britta thought she heard her front door open. But that couldn't be. It was locked.

When she looked over her shoulder, two men stood there in raincoats; one was a black man, the other a white man with a red blotch on his cheek.

A third man, older, white haired, white bearded, entered from behind, the two men stepping aside, like a sea parting for a prophet. He wore white slacks and a white open-necked shirt beneath a long cream-colored cashmere coat, as if to defy the dreary overcast day outside. Filling her small apartment with an impressive stance, he said, 'Do not be afraid, Frau Buschhorn.' Philo spoke flawless German with a trace of an American accent. 'We have not come to harm you.'

'Who are you? What do you want?' Britta demanded. She swung her chair around to face the intruders squarely, to show them she was not easily intimidated.

Philo paused to take her measure. Tough woman. Hair whitened prematurely, like his own. He knew her story; it had made international headlines when she had escaped from her captors and was found by tourists. Now Britta Buschhorn was an icon for human rights around the world. Philo knew what she was thinking: that there was nothing he could do to her that the rebels had not already done.

She was mistaken.

He reached into his pocket and brought out a small book. During their captivity, Britta's husband Jacob had experienced a series of mystical visions. In his darkness he had seen light; in his pain he had felt God; in the screams of his tortured colleagues he had heard the whispered voice of God; and when he had fallen unconscious from the pain, he had been lifted out of himself and into a gentle cradle of love.

Jacob had revealed these visions to his fellow captives, to give them hope and comfort, and had recorded them on scraps of paper in the clinic, using chalk, charcoal, pencils when the rebels were not watching. After recuperating in hospital and returning home, Britta had turned to the writings for solace. Thinking that the messages of hope should be shared with the world, she had published them in a small book. The words of hope, wisdom and comfort were instantly popular and had become a best seller. Jacob Buschhorn's visions had been translated into languages around the world, including English, the edition Philo now held in his hand.

'We have come for the original papers this was translated from.'

Now she understood. 'You're the man who has been trying to buy them.' There had been several offers, the last amounting to one million American dollars.

'I am,' Philo said softly. 'And now I have come to take them.'

She reached for the phone. Philo was at her side in two strides, touching the back of his hand with gentle fingertips. 'Do not be afraid,' he said, his deep gray eyes catching her, holding her, unblinking, the power of his soul shining through. 'We will not harm you. I promise.'

She held onto the phone. 'You cannot have the papers.'

'My associates are going to search your flat. But they will do it neatly and respectfully. I have ordered them to leave everything as they found it. If they leave anything the way it should not be, tell me and I will correct it.'

'Search all you want,' she said defiantly.

'We shall.' And he went into the kitchen.

Britta picked up the phone and started to dial. Then she heard the silence and realized the instrument was dead. She replaced it on the cradle and watched the man in the long cream-colored cashmere overcoat make himself at home in her kitchen. She refused to be afraid of him. He could search all he wanted, he would not find the papers. And Britta already knew that no powers of persuasion were going to force her to disclose their whereabouts.

'My associates and I are not thugs or criminals,' Philo said as he retrieved the tea kettle from the stove. 'We are knights on a sacred quest, members of the most ancient and most holy society on earth, and our mission cannot be impeded by personal vanities.'

She glared at him in defiance. They could take anything they wanted, they could strip her apartment bare. Britta had been in this place before, survived it, was beyond it.

He filled the kettle in the small sink. 'Listen to what I have to say now, Frau Buschhorn.' He turned to look at her with his dark-gray eyes. 'It is important that you know.'

The kettle went onto the burner and Philo turned on the flame. 'Our roots lie in a priesthood of antiquity, a fraternity of men and women who were the guardians of knowledge. This was three hundred years before the birth of Christ, when Alexander the Great experienced a vision in which he was told to collect all the knowledge in the world.' While Thibodeau busied himself with cups, saucers, spoons, finding milk in the small refrigerator and a sugar bowl on the table, in Britta's tiny bedroom the two men went neatly and systematically about searching her things.

'To achieve his goal,' Thibodeau continued, locating a ceramic creamer and pouring the milk into it, 'Alexander's successor, King Ptolemy, sent letters to all kings, queens, emperors and governors on earth requesting the works of their poets and writers, thinkers and prophets, books sacred and secular, songs and hymns, and then he dispatched agents to all the cities of Asia, Africa, and Europe to collect them. Foreign ships calling in at Alexandria were searched for scrolls and manuscripts, and if any were found they were taken to the Great Library – a massive complex of buildings – where they were scrupulously copied.'

He found a small brown teapot. In the bedroom, Britta's closet was examined with the scrutiny of police detectives examining a crime scene. Britta held her ground, a frail woman in a wheelchair, refusing to be cowed by three strangers violating her privacy. In his cage by the window, Sammy the cockatiel preened his feathers without concern.

'Two centuries later,' Thibodeau went on, 'Ptolemy's descendent, Cleopatra, expanded and enriched the Library by continuing to send emissaries out into the world to bring back books and knowledge. It is said that by the time of Jesus the Alexandrian library contained copies and translations of all the known books of the world. Think of it, Frau Buschhorn. *All the known books of the world.*'

94

Thibodeau lifted a tray from behind the toaster, protected it with a placemat he found in a drawer, and set napkins, spoons, cups, sugar and milk on it. Carrying these into the living room, he said, 'All those books were made available to scholars who were invited from the far corners of the world to study manuscripts in Chinese, Arabic, Hebrew; the works of Plato, Caesar, and Ptah-Hotep; a population of brilliant minds moving through the great lecture halls, gardens and museums of the library complex. It was a university, Frau Buschhorn, the first in the world. A beacon of light, just like the famous Alexandria lighthouse.'

The kettle whistled. Philo returned to the kitchen and when he crossed in front of the window he blotted out the pale light. There was a moment of utter darkness and then light again, and Britta felt a chill run up her spine.

He came back with the teapot, steam pluming from its spout. While Philo poured, Sammy in his cage entertained himself with shiny large beads and little bells that made ringing sounds.

The two men had finished in the bedroom and now searched the living room, quietly, tidily. Late-afternoon shadows fell across the carpet and the intruders. The man who spoke – she recognized Philo Thibodeau from news photos of the American billionaire shaking hands with the Chancellor of Germany – kept his voice soft and mellifluous, even while uttering her complex language, a look of compassion in his eyes, as if he genuinely regretted this intrusion.

'In the year 391 CE, the Patriarch of Alexandria eyed the Great Library, where all the wisdom of the ancients was preserved, and suspected that as long as this knowledge existed people would be less inclined to believe the Gospels of Jesus Christ. So he asked permission from Emperor Theodosius, who was already bent on seeing that paganism was annihilated, to destroy the Library. A Christian mob, worked up by fiery rhetoric and talk of Satan, attacked the Library with torches. In an orgy of sanctimonious hatred, they brought books and scrolls from the library and burned them upon huge bonfires in the streets of Alexandria while the priests and priestesses tried to escape. Can you picture it, Frau Buschhorn?'

Despite herself, Britta pictured it: *against a backdrop of brilliant yellow flames licking the night sky, men and women furtively gathering together, the priests with their shaven heads, the priestesses in long black wigs, their white robes fluttering as they frantically fill their arms and baskets with as many books as they can carry. Outside, a frenzied mob laying hands on library workers and throwing them onto the bonfires, to make flesh and papyrus blacken together.*

'It is estimated that nearly half a million books were burned that day.' He handed her a cup, poured one for himself and set it aside, to leave it untouched. Britta's likewise remained untouched.

'That is historical fact,' Thibodeau said, pulling up a chair to face her, 'the burning of the Library. But what history does *not* know is that many of the priests and priestesses who were the guardians of the Library and keepers of the world's knowledge managed to flee with their lives – and with something more.'

The two men, finished with their search of the living room and finding nothing, went to stand by the front door.

'The priests fled Alexandria,' Thibodeau continued, 'with whatever precious books and scrolls they could carry – legend says that one priestess even slipped a basket beneath her gown to make herself look pregnant, a basket filled with the prophecies of the Delphic Oracles. They regrouped on Cyprus. From there they moved north into Spain and then to France, always moving ahead of anti-pagan prejudice. Eventually some of them were Christianized, but that did not affect their sworn oath to protect the writings, pagan though they be. Down through the centuries, while other works were being destroyed by intolerant minds, the Alexandrian priests preserved what they had rescued from the fire, and continued to search for other writings, for that was their sacred injunction.'

When Philo paused to give her a chance to absorb this, Britta said, 'I am not afraid of you.'

His eyebrows arched. 'I did not expect you would be, Frau Buschhorn. I thought it only fair to let you know why we are going to take your husband's papers.'

He added cream to her tea, two lumps of sugar. Britta saw a curious gold ring flash on his right hand: the bezel was a square ruby with gold filaments woven above it, like tongues of fire.

In his cage by the window, Sammy slept.

'The secret society grew. Members accompanied the conquistadors and padres to the Americas, where they rescued sacred Aztec and Maya manuscripts. They sailed to Australia with the first convicts and listened to the Aborigines and wrote down their wisdom. There is no corner of the world whose sacredness the Society has not explored. As anthropologists, explorers and missionaries they moved among the Indians of Tierra del Fuego at the tip of South America. They observed hidden tribes in New Guinea and Africa. Everything they learned from them about the divine, the spiritual, and prophecy was brought back to reside with the Torah, the teachings of Christ, the words of Buddha and Mohammed, the enlightenment of Lao Tzu and Confucius.'

He was beginning to frighten her. Political rebels were one thing, a madman another. 'But you have the book,' Britta said, trying to keep her voice strong.

He looked at the slender volume he had placed on the table. 'It is not enough. For our purpose, sacred writings must be as pure and as close to the source as they can be.'

He removed his ring and showed her the inscription on the inside of the band. *Fiat Lux.* 'Let there be light,' he said. 'Light cannot be flawed. But this,' he pointed to the book of Jacob Buschhorn's spiritual epiphanies, 'is flawed because it was edited and therefore sheds no light.'

Replacing the ring on his finger, he flashed her a smile and her heart jumped. She had no idea what this stranger was talking about, but he scared her.

When she said nothing, just sat in her motorized chair with her hands clasped tightly in her lap, he said, 'You haven't touched your tea.'

The light outside, already dreary because of the overcast day, was beginning to fade, drawing the apartment into somber shadow.

'Those papers are all I have of the man I loved,' she said, her voice tremulous now. 'Without them, I have nothing.' And realized in a sharp panic that this was true: without the original words of Jacob's visions, words spoken in the middle of darkness and pain and despair, without the original paper, scavenged from drawers and boxes and waste baskets, scraps that connected her to those days of despair and hope, she could not go on.

97

Philo took her hands in his and said with passion, 'I must have those papers,' his voice low and solemn, yet possessing force.

'For your selfish collection,' Britta said bitterly, wanting to spit in the face of this man in the expensive cashmere coat who kneeled before her lifeless legs.

'Oh, not for my collection,' Philo said, and a new light came into his eyes. His voice dropped to nearly a whisper, yet still contained power. 'You could not possibly understand my work, or the path that I walk. What I am about is above mortal men, above your comprehension.' She felt his fingers tighten, his hands go damp, and energy pass from him to her. She could not look away. 'A glorious moment is coming, and you will be part of it, Frau Buschhorn. But those papers are vital to that moment of glory. *I will have them.*'

Philo rose and looked at Sammy's cage, where the white and yellow cockatiel slumbered. 'Beautiful bird,' he said, peering through the bars. 'Does he suffer from night frights? Cockatiels are prone to that. No one knows why. They wake up suddenly scared and thrash about in their cages in panic. Nightmares, do you suppose?'

She kept her eye on him, and when Thibodeau reached into his coat and brought out white gloves, she caught her breath.

'Humans are the same as cockatiels,' Philo said as he reached up to open the cage. 'The bird is unable to see well enough in the dark to realize it is safe, and so it is thrown into a panic. So it is with us. We do not see well enough in the dark to know we are safe. And we *are* safe, Frau Buschhorn. Take my word on this, for *I* see well enough in the dark. I see what is around us and what lies ahead for us. There is no darkness, only brilliance.' His hand paused on the latch. 'How old is he?'

'Ten.' She swallowed. Her mouth had gone dry.

'Did you know that cockatiels can live up to twenty-five years? I know one that is in its thirties. You can look forward to two more decades of loving companionship with this fine creature.'

'What are you going to do?'

'I am going to walk out of this apartment with those papers.'

She lifted her chin. 'You cannot have them.'

'Frau Buschhorn . . .' A gentle, teasing tone.

She held her silence.

98

Philo opened the cage.

'Please—'

He looked at her. The question stood in his eyes.

Her voice broke. When she had thought that, after her ordeal at the hands of the rebels, nothing could touch her again, she had not imagined a man like Philo Thibodeau. 'I can't let you have them. Jacob's blood and sweat and tears are in those papers. To give them up would be to give *him* up.'

'And that is why I need them, for the blood, sweat and tears.' He reached in and gently captured the bird with both hands. Sensing no danger, Sammy bent his head for a friendly scratch while Britta looked on in fresh terror.

Philo kneeled by the wheelchair, Sammy between his gloved hands, the crest going up and down. 'Where are the papers?'

Tears filled her eyes. 'Please don't do this.'

Philo brought Sammy to eye level and whistled. Sammy stared, cocking his head in curiosity, crest rising. Philo whistled again and Sammy whistled back.

And then Philo, reciting from the English translation of Britta Buschhorn's book, said solemnly, '"God said: 'Be calm for all is as it should be. This is the way of things. It is My way. There is a light at the end and you will shine in the brilliant vault of heaven.'"'

Tears filled Britta's eyes at the sound of her husband's words.

'"God said: 'You are My glory, Jacob Buschhorn, you and your fellow martyrs. Heaven and its angels await you.'"'

Britta began to sob, and Sammy, finally sensing danger, screeched.

'"God said: 'Nothing happens without a purpose. Nothing happens without My making it so.'"'

'"God said: 'You are not alone. I am with you.'"'

Sammy's cry grew piercing and filled with panic. Britta, thrown back to the nightmare days in the jungle clinic when the captives had thought each day was their last, and her husband, under torture, had spoken words of solace for his fellow victims, said, 'Please—' tears streaming down her cheeks.

Philo's voice, soft and reverent. '"God said: 'I, the light, have come into the world.'"'

Sammy's screeching filled the air. Wild fear stood in the bird's eyes as it struggled against Philo's hold.

99

'You're hurting him!' Britta cried.

'Where are the papers?'

'Don't hurt my little Sammy. Please, I beg.'

'Where are the papers?'

She gulped for air.

'Where are the papers?'

Britta wore the papers under her blouse, next to her heart. It was how she had smuggled them out when she escaped, how she had worn them when she brought her husband's body back to Germany, and at his funeral, and now always, keeping him close to her.

But she looked at Sammy, terrified in the stranger's grasp, and she brought it out – a yellow silk bag on a black cord, still warm from her breast. One of the strangers took it from her, opened it and showed the contents to Philo – pieces of unmatched paper, stained and smeared, the writing cramped and shaky. Jacob Buschhorn's original descriptions of his God visions.

Philo rose and gently replaced the bird in the cage. It hopped on its perch, feathers ruffled but otherwise unharmed.

They said goodbye to the sobbing woman and, as they emerged downstairs in the dying day, the man with the strawberry mark said, 'Congratulations, Philo.'

But Philo had never doubted he would be successful in obtaining the papers. As a Knight of the Flame, the blood of heroes ran in his veins . . .

Twelve

Southern France, 1096

Sir Alaric, the Comte de Valliers, galloped a league ahead of his men, pressing his war horse to a faster pace.

Rewards awaited him. Margot, with her arms the whiteness of milk, her lips the sweetness of wine. Never was his ardor so great as when he did battle. And this last one had been a great fight, his enemy vanquished, prizes won. Now it was time for bed – but not to sleep.

It had been a good campaign: only twelve of his men dead (compared to thirty-two of the Baron's) and worthy spoils – kegs of wine, textiles from the East, a few fat sheep, and the Baron's own spirited war horse. Alaric's men were looking forward to getting back to the farms from which they had been seized to fight their liege lord's battle, back to wives and children who had not seen husbands and fathers for months, to resume their old lives until the call to serve their lord again.

Alaric himself was looking forward to a reunion with his beloved. He also looked forward to an evening with his brother, Baudoin, who, due to a leg wound from a prior battle, had been left out of this campaign and would be eager to hear every detail.

He spurred his war horse, an Andalusian stallion named Tonnerre – 'thunder' – to go faster, faster. Alaric carried a surprise for Margot. A piece of Christ's True Cross! Not that Alaric himself believed in it. He suspected that if all the splinters of the True Cross were laid end to end they would traverse the land of the Franks and back.

Alaric rode through the spring rain, a man no longer in the springtime of his youth but, at thirty-five, entering the autumn of his life. A man of merry disposition, handsome and robust, with long yellow hair and closely cropped yellow beard, green eyed, virile, passionate, and in love. He decided he had had enough of warring and wenching for a while. Now was time to spend with Margot, his lady, the center of his universe. Time to stay home, do his duty by her and get her with child. Blessed, patient Margot who suffered her knight's absences like a true high-born lady. Did a luckier man live?

Unbeknownst to Alaric, farther up the road, coming from the opposite direction, another man galloped in haste. But his mission had nothing to do with bedding fine ladies or boasting of the spoils of battle. His was a holy mission.

Brother Christofle had ridden day and night since leaving Paris, and now it was raining, ribbons of mud in the road, the steed's hooves slipping as it galloped the last mile. He carried important news: the call to God's work in Jerusalem.

He reached the manor house at the same time as the count,

both galloping into the rain-sodden yard where stable boys ran out to take charge of the horses. 'My lord,' the monk began as he slipped from his saddle.

'Wine!' bellowed Alaric good naturedly. 'And meat!' Servants dipped hasty bows and ran back into the house. Removing his helmet, Alaric said, 'God's teeth, who in blazes are *you*?'

'Brother Christofle, of the Order of Alexandrians.'

Alaric grunted.

'I have come with urgent news, my lord,' the monk said with such gravity, the rain pouring down his face, that Alaric wanted to laugh. He clapped his big hand on the man's shoulder and boomed, 'Come, good brother, and warm your backside at my hearth!'

They entered the great hall where rushes were strewn on the floor and tapestries covered the walls. Alaric strode directly to the enormous fireplace where inviting flames leaped and danced.

'My lord,' Brother Christofle said, 'a word, please. I come on an urgent matter.'

Alaric laughed as he tossed off his wet cloak to reveal muddy and bloodstained mail beneath. Two young squires helped their lord remove his battle costume and began drying his naked body with thick warm towels. As Alaric stood there, with no modesty or shame, the fire's glow illuminating a robust body bearing the many scars of a fighting man, he said, 'Nothing is more urgent than paying my respects to the lady of this house.' He dipped his fingers in a bowl of perfumed water and patted his cheeks. 'But I would not go to her with the stink of battle still upon me.'

A servant appeared with wine. Alaric selected a flagon and quaffed deeply as he sized up his curious visitor.

The monk was a bowlegged, shaven-headed little man with a breast and belly that sagged beneath his robe. His hood and cowl were soiled like the rest of him, and he smelled of sweat, beer and compost. Alaric scratched his ribs and belched with gusto. 'What's your news then?'

Hiking up his sodden robe and presenting his bare buttocks to the fire, Brother Christofle said, 'All over Christendom princes and dukes are calling men to arms. A mighty force is

102

building, my lord, readying for a glorious march to the Holy Land to rescue Jerusalem from the hands of the infidel.'

Alaric had already heard of the expedition to the East. When Pope Urban had made his impassioned speech the previous spring, thousands had shouted, 'God wills it!' And now Christian-fever was sweeping the land.

He listened with no interest to what his visitor had to say. Alaric had bedroom matters on his mind.

'The Turks have wrought terrible injury upon our people,' the little man continued. 'They round up Christians and force circumcision upon them. They set upon Christian pilgrims, tie them to horses and drag them through the streets of Jerusalem.'

Alaric turned this way and that as the young squires rubbed and massaged his chilled body back to life. Another flagon of wine. Alaric observed his curious guest over the rim as he drank.

Christofle was a strange sort of monk. He wore no crucifix upon his person, hung no rosary from his belt, nor peppered his speech, as holy men were wont, with 'God' and 'Jesus' and 'Mary.' And his rhetoric grew more vivid and eloquent as his passion grew, painting pictures of torture, slavery, and disembowelment, and, although the monk could have been making it up as he went along, Alaric knew it must all be true, the Turks being what they were.

As for Brother Christofle's private opinions: atrocities and religion aside, he suspected the truth behind Urban's call. Europe was a hotbed of wars, battles, skirmishes, lords laying siege to neighbors' lands and houses on whims, bored with humdrum castle life, no sooner returning home from a small victory than having the vanquished neighbor regroup and attack and start it all over again. As if the map of Europe were a giant chessboard, the game constantly in motion with no regard for human life or the possibility of peace. Squabbling, the monk thought, like pigs fighting over scraps. Urban, that wisest of pontiffs, saw a way to unify his people – by giving them a common enemy.

'My lord, your fellow knights are sewing crosses to their garments, painting them on their helmets and shields, and calling themselves cross-bearers. They will march under the banner of Jesus Christ. It is to be a holy war.'

Alaric was unmoved. As his two young squires helped him

into a long soft robe of fox fur, Alaric perused the platter of roast pigeon that was presented to him. All of his appetites were clamoring for attention, so that he hardly knew which to satisfy first. And there was Margot, upstairs . . .

'Godfrey of Bouillon sold the city of Verdun and mort-gaged his estates to come up with the money to pay his soldiers. Should Alaric of Valliers do less?'

'I am not a religious man, good brother,' Alaric said, impa-tient to join Margot.

'You go not for religion but to rescue ancient books. It is your duty, Alaric, to bring those books back to France.'

The count blinked. Rescuing books? What a worthless occupation! Alaric was not literate; he could barely write his name. Margot, on the other hand, could read – she even owned books. It excited him now, to picture her, and was anxious to unlace her imprisoning bodice.

Seeing his host's attention wander, Christofle hastily added, 'Among the books are letters, precious and carefully preserved, written by St. Mary Magdalene herself in her own hand. These must be saved! It is a lofty quest, my lord.'

But Alaric's stomach growled in an unlofty way, and another part of him stirred as well, as he thought of Margot beneath bedclothes.

As Alaric sucked on a pigeon bone, Christofle said, 'The letters are kept in a house in Jerusalem, the home of a wealthy merchant who is one of our Order, on a small street off the Via Dolorosa, near Herod's Gate. The letters were brought to the Great Library in Alexandria by a rabbi named Joseph, in the year of Our Lord eighty-two. The blessed saint had passed them to him upon her death, asking him to take them to the safest place in the world. He knew the guardians of the Library would protect the letters from those who opposed the power of the Magdalene. She had many followers but there were those who wanted to destroy her writings. The rabbi said he would come back for them, but he never did. When the Library was set on fire, a priestess rescued the letters and carried them to Cyprus, and from there to Jerusalem where they have reposed since.'

Alaric tossed the bone into the fire and wiped his greasy fingers on his fur robe. He frowned. What was this prattle of a library? And then he thought: letters written by the Magdalene! What a prize for his beloved Margot.

'You are charged with this holy duty, my lord—' And then Brother Christofle was momentarily taken aback by his sudden notice of the young knight's deformity.

Alaric saw what had caught the man's eye. Alaric had six fingers on his right hand. Considered a lucky sign, as his grandfather had also had this trait and had been a great warrior, the extra digit made him a formidable swordsman. His brother Baudoin did not have the sixth finger, which was perhaps why the two had been competitive since an early age, when they had gone together to an uncle's house to train for knighthood.

'Why should I bother myself over books?'

Brother Christofle struggled to conceal his bitterness and disillusionment. In the last Alexandrian house he had visited, in Rouen, the lord had called him 'Swagbelly' and driven him off with a stick. But Christofle forgave the man, ignorant blowhard that he was. Mentally grousing about his miserable lot, Christofle envied Alaric his robustness and health. He even appeared to have all of his teeth, which he showed off every time he threw back his head and laughed. But Christofle, like most men who reached the age of fifty, daily counted his dwindling teeth and dreaded the day when he would no longer be able to chew bread and meat but must do with gruel. And what good was life then? Why live? *The mission*, he reminded himself. While an Alexandrian remained who drew breath, there was still hope.

Or so he tried to believe.

Sniffing with self-righteousness, Christofle said, 'You are an Alexandrian!' He drew back the voluminous sleeve of his robe. 'This is the ring which identifies us. You have one.'

Alaric wrinkled his nose. The ring looked familiar. Then he remembered: his father had given him one upon his thirteenth birthday, accompanied by a tale of heroic priests who had fled a fire carrying books. There was even such a book in this house, he seemed to recall, albeit in scroll form, brittle and stored away, not seen by human eyes in centuries.

'Three hundred years before the birth of Christ, a general named Alexander conquered Egypt, and while he was there he visited the Oracle of Amon in the desert. There Alexander experienced a blinding vision of glorious light in which God told him to build a city that was to surpass all others past and future, a city that would be the Light of the World, a center of learning, enlightenment, and tolerance. It was called Alexandria. The young general was to have ruled his empire from there, but he died in Persia, at the age of thirty-three. His son later returned to Alexandria to begin building the Great Library and university. But three hundred years after Christ the Library was set afire.

'The Alexandrians were scattered over the continents,' the monk said. 'And now our brothers in Jerusalem are in peril, as are the sacred documents they protect.'

Alaric gave him a blank look.

'You took an oath, did you not?'

Alaric searched his memory. His father had told the tale by rote, having learned it from his mother. As far as Alaric knew, no one in his family had ever met another Alexandrian. In fact, they never gave the Society a thought. But yes, he had taken an oath, the content of which escaped him now. 'Am I bound to it?' he asked.

God's blood! Christofle had played out this drama in too many houses. The Society might as well not exist. It was like a tree whose leaves and limbs are dead and the trunk rotting. Only he and a thriving few – the roots as it were – kept the mission alive. Without him and his stalwart brethren, the Alexandrians might die away altogether.

His robe steaming and stinking up the air, Christofle eyed the platter of roast pigeons, the flagons of wine, thought of the scented woman upstairs – and was bitter. He had forsaken such pleasures for a brotherhood that was doomed to die out because men thought more of their appetites than of God. He thought of the houses he visited throughout Europe, where he saw ancient treasures – so many allowed to deteriorate because their purpose was forgotten. When the Alexandrians first fled to Cyprus it was agreed that for the safety of the treasures they should scatter. But now he saw the folly in that, for by separating they had weakened the Order. The monastery on Cyprus was the largest concentration of Alexandrians, and they numbered exactly twelve – twelve aging men, each older than the last, concerned more with their bowels than with scrolls.

Christofle did not mention this to Alaric, whom he saw as

106

the Order's last chance. This expedition to the Holy Land could imbue the Alexandrians with fresh vigor. If he could just get it through this numbskull knight's head.

'Forgive me, good brother, but I must see my lady. Enjoy the comforts of my house, we have wine and meat in plenty. Perhaps tomorrow we can talk, or the day after . . .' Alaric added vaguely.

'But, my lord—'

The count was gone.

Alaric listened at the heavy door and, hearing silence, pictured his beautiful Margot in slumber, thick lashes resting on white cheekbones. He opened the door upon the dimly lit chamber. The windows, fitted with oiled parchment, were shuttered against the spring rain. Large wall hangings, depicting Bible scenes, reduced the chill, while flames on fat candles danced in drafts. Margot's clothes were draped over the cedar chest by the bed, and on top of them the jewel-handled dagger she always kept nearby.

The bed drapes were closed. Alaric thrust them aside, declaring, 'I have a surprise for you, my love!' But it was Margot who had a surprise for *him*. She lay naked in bed, long hair tousled upon the pillow, and next to her, equally naked, Baudoin, his brother.

No one would later be able to put together what happened that night, least of all Alaric himself, for a blackness came over him at the sight of the two, and his fighting arm came to life on its own, snatching the jewel-handled dagger and lifting it high. To strike what? He did not know. But if his intention had been to rend a pillow, he did just that, for Baudoin and Margot, waking suddenly, rolled away from the blow in time to save themselves.

But not for long. Alaric charged after them like an enraged bull, mindless and bellowing, the red flag of jealousy blinding his eyes. His target was Baudoin, who had the audacity to search for his own sword among his clothes, with not a word of explanation or apology, while Margot, covering her nakedness with her arms, shivered by the fireplace and watched with terrified eyes.

Baudoin had one advantage – he was well rested. But Alaric

had the advantage of rage. Spewing epithets, calling his brother every name under the sun, he lunged again and again, his aim off, his eyes blinded by tears. Forsaking the dagger, he ran to the wall, from where he snatched an ancestral sword on display. This, too, had been made for a six-fingered man, which gave Alaric a further advantage in that he had greater force, a wider swing.

Tossing off his fur robe so that he stood as naked as his brother, he lunged again at Baudoin.

They dueled, firelight casting their tall shadows on the walls as metal clanged. Margot threw herself between them, screaming at them to stop. But they pushed her aside, as first one brother lunged, the other parrying, and then the other on the offense, and the first defending.

Alaric's sword flew out of his grip. Dodging a thrust, he leaped to the floor where he snatched up the jewel-handled dagger again. As Baudoin rushed at him, Alaric swung his leg out and kicked Baudoin's feet from under him. Baudoin scrambled away as Alaric jabbed at the air.

Finally Baudoin was backed against a wall, his sword lying on the floor. Alaric raised his arm, both hands on the hilt of the dagger for the lethal downward thrust, and, in the last moment, Baudoin seized Margot, yanking her to him as a human shield, too late for Alaric, who completed the thrust, plunging the blade into her breast and tearing with such force that his knuckles scraped exposed ribs.

A startled look on her beautiful face, and she slipped gracefully from Baudoin's hold.

The brothers froze.

And then a cry thundered from Alaric's throat. *'I will kill you!'*

Baudoin bolted from the room, disappearing so quickly behind a drapery that Alaric had to blink. He blundered after him, encountering men in the hall who had come running at the sound of commotion, startled at the sight of the naked Baudoin pushing past them, and Alaric, likewise naked, bloodied and frenzied, raging past, screaming like a madman with froth on his lips.

As Alaric's men seized him and held him back, Baudoin made his escape with the aid of his own loyal men, who got him out of the castle before Alaric could renew his pursuit.

In the terrible days to come, Alaric would not look back and wonder at his sudden attack, would not wonder that he did not demand an explanation or apology, or offer his brother an honorable duel. Alaric would already know why: the secret glances at the dinner table, Margot and Baudoin walking in the garden, Margot's petulance when Alaric came home from an absence – signs so obvious, yet Alaric had turned a blind eye.

'It is not your fault, sire,' his men told him. Like most knights of means, Alaric maintained a handful of professional soldiers, fiercely loyal to him, who between battles spent their days sporting and keeping their gear ready for the next fight. They had never seen their lord so out of his wits.

'It was my hand that killed her!' he bellowed.

'A blow meant for your brother, sire.'

His grief turned to rage and thirst for revenge. 'Find my brother! He made me kill my beloved Margot! For that he shall die! I shall hunt him down to the ends of the earth.'

Brother Christofle interceded, to implore Alaric to forget this tragedy and ride to Jerusalem under God's banner. There was honor in it.

But Alaric would not go to Jerusalem. He had to find Baudoin and duel to the death. *That* was where his true honor lay.

'There are higher purposes than revenge, my lord, there is a higher love than that of man for woman, or brother for brother – it is man's love for God. You must set aside this madness of the flesh and take up the cross.'

But the knight was insane with grief and listened not to reason.

Christofle panicked. He had been desperately counting on Alaric to go to the Holy Land. So he did something he had never done in his life. He told a lie. I do it for the Order, he told himself, to save the Alexandrians. He tried to believe this, for he could not bear the real reason why he had come to the house of Alaric of Valliers, the dark secret that ate away at his soul.

The lie he told was this: 'If it is after your brother you must go, then go east, for where else would Baudoin run but to the cause that would grant him redemption?' Christofle did not for a minute believe this. Baudoin, knowing his brother's thirst for revenge, would get as far away from people who would

109

know him as he could. Perhaps he was already at the coast, plotting his crossing to England.

But it made sense to Alaric. Baudoin had slept with his brother's wife and had murdered her in a most heinous way. The wretch would seek absolution in Jerusalem, for Pope Urban had promised the forgiveness of all sins for those who rode on God's mission.

Thus did Alaric join Brother Christofle's quest to save holy books, but he went with blood-thirst in his heart and but one thought in his mind: to find his brother and exact revenge.

Brother Christofle made the announcement in the town over which Alaric was lord, declaring that all who followed their liege to Jerusalem would be granted absolution from all sins and guaranteed entrance to Heaven. Their rush to join did not surprise him. For these people, life was brutal and short, a brief spell between the mysteries of birth and death. And they were very much concerned about their souls. Total absolution to these sinners meant more than all the gold in Christendom. The peasants were the first to volunteer – serfs without rights, owned by their lord, forbidden to leave their farms, who worked so hard that their expected lifespan was twenty-five years. They seized the opportunity to leave that hardship, to travel with their lord, and gain absolution from their sins. Then came the tradesmen and townsfolk, who consisted of adulterers, pickpockets, thieves, malcontents, idealistic youths, men thirsting for adventure, women escaping abusive husbands and fathers, a mendicant priest, a murderer, and a wretched one-eyed beggar. Alaric didn't bother to learn their names, nor did he outfit them as other lords were doing, being so embroiled in his grief and hatred and thirst for revenge on Baudoin. Alaric's poor 'army' painted crosses on their helmets, their shirts, however they could mark themselves, but when they arrived in Lyon to join other bands of cross-bearers, they were ashamed at how miserable they appeared. Some defected to other knights to get a sword and a cloak with a cross on it (although these had been sewn so hastily they were crooked, off-center, and rendered in large stitches, but they were better than nothing and proclaimed the wearer to be a pilgrim on a holy mission).

Alaric rode at the head of his ragtag mob. He wore a coat

of mail, a mail hood, and an iron helmet. He carried a kite-shaped shield, a sword, and a lance with a pennant that showed him to be a man of rank. His sword was double-edged with an iron crossguard and firm grip, customized to accommodate his sixth finger. He had found the Alexandrian ring his father had left to him, a plain, blocky thing of gold, with a motto inscribed on it which Alaric could not read. He remembered nothing of what his father had told him of the Alexandrians, and he recalled nothing of the oath he had been made to recite as a boy. But it mattered not. He was not riding to Jerusalem for *them.*

As they set off on their holy cause, Brother Christofle was filled with a sense of foreboding. Alaric's attitude toward the quest was one of indifference, his soul was conflicted, his eyes burning with vengeance. A combination that could only spell disaster.

The unruly bunch grew more so, as it occurred to them that men who faced absolution from sins at the end of this journey should seize the opportunity to enjoy themselves on the way. Whoring, gambling, thieving, lying, cheating, and a modicum of killing became the norm. Along the way, they were joined by peasants and the poor, riding in ox carts or on foot, shouldering their few possessions. When the growing force camped outside Cologne, rumors flew that the ghost of Charlemagne had appeared to bless these people in their march to Jerusalem.

Alaric was oblivious. Whenever they made camp, his man-at-arms saw that the horses were safely picketed with a sentry standing guard. This was a knight's duty, but the Comte de Valliers had forgotten his duties. He did not seek out other Alexandrians in the mob, as Brother Christofle urged, neither did those other men desire the company of their kind. Each was caught up in his own personal vision of valor, bravery, and riches at the end of this march. Of books they cared not a wit, but they would bring them back, since that was their mandate.

Alaric searched for his brother in every hamlet, village, and town, going among the people and asking, 'Does anyone know Baudoin of Valliers? Has anyone seen or heard of him?' When new armies joined his group, he rode among the men searching their faces for his brother.

111

Christofle, alarmed that Alaric's passion for revenge had not subsided, but seemed in fact to grow, cautioned him. 'Have you thought that it is you who could end up dead in a duel with Baudoin?'

'I care not whether I live or die, for the only thing I ever loved is gone forever. The life is gone from me. Wine tastes like water, meat is sawdust in my mouth. All joy and happiness have been stamped out of me. All that remains is one desire: to sink my dagger into my brother's breast.'

Days blended into nights, and nights into weeks, and the expedition grew. Knights who once raided one another's lands now rode side by side, bent on rescuing the Holy Land from the infidel. More groups followed, including the Pope's own army. News spread across Europe and more men answered the sacred call, lords and vassals, barons and dukes, princes and knights, marching together with broadsword and axe, crossbow and crucifix.

Brother Christofle's despair grew as he repeatedly abjured Alaric to awaken to this holy quest, to act like a knight and a man of honor. But poison flowed in Alaric's veins. He let his beard go untrimmed, his hair grow ragged, his clothes filthy. He was becoming indistinguishable from the wretched one-eyed beggar who walked with the mendicant priest and begged crusts from soldiers. After a while, Christofle became fixated on the beggar: the man seemed to personify the hopelessness of this expedition, for surely this ragtag mob could not be called a proper army, and surely they could never take so great a prize as Jerusalem. We are like that wretch, Christofle thought, haunted by the sight of the man, diseased, poor, overlooked by Heaven. We might paint crosses on our shields and cry, 'To Jerusalem!' but in the end, beneath our flesh, we are all one-eyed beggars.

At night he dreamed of Cunegonde.

In his youth Brother Christofle had been very much in love with a girl named Cunegonde, and she with him. Her father had brought her to the monastery to take the Alexandrian oath and receive the ring. They had enjoyed an exquisite secret love affair, and when her father took her away she promised to write. But Christofle never heard from her. As weeks and months and a year went by, his despair and misery deepened. He sent letters to her but received no replies, until finally he heard from her father informing him that Cunegonde was married and he was to leave her alone. That was when Christofle decided to dedicate his life to the Order and forsake all worldly pleasures.

Now, thirty years later, he was wondering what it had all been for. A man's life had to count for more than a stool with his name on it in a monastery no one had ever heard of. While the world had enjoyed its seasons and its wars, its romances and pageants, while people everywhere had frolicked and made babies and cursed one another and died, Christofle had moldered within stone walls like the decaying books he served, a bitter old man.

This then was Christofle's dark secret, the real reason he marched to Jerusalem.

Alaric also dreamed.

Nightmares, in which he killed Margot over and over, trying to stop his hand from plunging, waking in a sweat to the fresh horror and grief of it all. He cried to Christofle, 'I close my eyes but sleep does not take pity on me. Through eyelids gritty from sleeplessness I see her beauty, her lips, her hair. How she smiled at the touch of my hand, the flames that shot through me when I stroked her naked breast. Never have I desired her so as I do now, when I know that I have lost her forever.'

The great multitude arrived at the city of Mainz, where the vast band of pilgrims from the various regions of Lorraine, eastern France, Bavaria, and Alemannia were joined by more than fifteen thousand military men and foot soldiers. From there they continued on to the kingdom of Hungary, an army innumerable as the sands of the sea, joyously making their way to Jerusalem.

Descending into the kingdom of Hungary, the large body of men and women bivouacked on a plain beside a river, there to await a greater army coming to join them.

At the beginning, they were welcomed by the king and granted permission to buy the necessaries of life. Peace was ordered on both sides as the king worried that an outbreak should arise from so large an army. But as they delayed there for several days, awaiting the arrival of Christian forces from the south, they grew restless, drank beyond measure and violated the peace which had been commanded. Other knights and princes disciplined the men under them, but Alaric ignored his soldiers and their needs. Christofle advised, 'Men need to ride under a banner, my lord, to fight for a united cause.' He wanted to add, 'They need a dedicated leader, too,' but held his tongue.

Despair and disappointment grew in the monk, who moved through the massive encampment and observed other Alexandrians, men who should have held themselves to a higher standard but who drank and whored and gambled with the commonest foot soldier. Again and again he tried to remind them of their purpose, but they cared not for the suffering and sacrifices of their distant ancestors, they loathed the written word and were contemptuous of books. A few drove Christofle off with sticks, ordering him to stay away from them.

The restless cross-bearers, realizing that fabled Jerusalem was a lot farther away than they had imagined, decided to steal from the Hungarians – taking wine, grain, sheep and cattle, murdering those who resisted. Again the dukes and nobles meted out punishment and kept their people in line, but Alaric's band grew ever more rude, undisciplined, and haughty.

No one knew how the disaster started, and the record afterward was filled with conflicting accounts because the chroniclers – lettered men who had pictured themselves calmly sitting at a battle's edge and writing down what they saw – were caught unawares and, before they knew it, were in the fray.

But most agreed that the tragedy occurred because raping and pillaging had become the pastime of the bored and restless pilgrims. As a reprisal, Hungarians ambushed those camped on the perimeter and robbed them and beat them. Some of the dukes and princes attempted to mend the peace by saying, 'Are we not all Christians?' A shaky peace of sorts was declared, but when some of Alaric's men sought to buy necessities from the magistrate of the city, the official, thinking it a pretense and regarding them as spies, forbade the sale of anything to them. Angered, Alaric's men began forcibly to seize and lead away the herds of cattle and sheep from nearby farms. The Hungarians fought back.

Passions rose, insults were hurled. 'Why don't you march to Jerusalem?' the pilgrims shouted, implying that the Hungarians were not Christian. Whereby the Hungarians shouted back, 'And why don't *you* march to Jerusalem?' implying that the pilgrims were malingering.

Other cross-bearers rallied to the aid of their brothers, as well as Frankish and Allemani knights, reluctantly impelled to protect their men. Fighting broke out, with soldiers pouring from the city, yelling battle cries as they descended upon the pilgrims. Arrows began to fly, swords to clash. And the dead and wounded began to fall.

The battle escalated and Brother Christofle ran to Alaric. 'My lord, you must call your men back else you will have no one to march to Jerusalem with you.'

But Alaric cared not.

Each side now was determined to avenge wrongs, both real and imagined, pilgrims and Hungarians alike believing themselves to be the injured party, and by noon a full-scale conflict was under way.

The sound of metal against metal, metal against flesh filled the air. Men screamed, blood flowed. Horses shrieked and reared, trampling the living. The sound of arrows was like flies as archers discharged volley after volley into the air. The warriors gave the horses their heads and away they went after them, the bowmen and archers, the spearmen charging. It was a hideous, clashing, thundering, shrieking, howling confusion.

Alaric could no longer ignore the call, for he was by nature and training a fighting man. By the time he was seated atop Tonnerre, the horse whinnying and rolling its eyes at the smell of blood, the Hungarians were fighting resolutely and without fear. Those who were trampled underfoot by the cross-bearers' horses still lunged with their spears at those who charged over them, and many a Frank was slain as he stooped to lop off the hand of his victim in token of triumph. The reek of blood outdid the reek of sweating soldiers, and ravens circled down from the sky in ever growing flocks.

Then the tide of battle changed when the Hungarians saw

that a separate contingent under the leadership of a Frankish duke had entered the city, where women were being attacked, children put to the sword. They ran in rescue and that was their undoing. The cross-bearers' war horses rounded upon them and the archers and spearmen moved in for the kill.

In the delirium of bloodlust, both sides prolonged the massacre, in the city and on the plain, plunging their spears into all they saw, slaying men who had already laid down their arms, braining children with their clubs. Pilgrims and Hungarians lost many that day, in a battle that had no name, that would not be recorded in history, but that would mark with shame the beginning of what would become known as the First Crusade.

A few skirmishes continued here and there. Dismounted by now, Alaric fought hand to hand. As he clashed swords with a fierce-looking Hungarian, he heard a Frank shout, 'Look out, my lord!' He whirled in time to see the one-eyed beggar take a blade in his belly – a mortal thrust that had been meant for Alaric. The slayer, a man in a red tunic and a horned helmet, seeing Alaric's mighty sword, took flight.

The dust began to clear and Alaric saw the carnage. A man used to battle, he had never witnessed anything as obscene as this. Already ravens were picking out the eyes of the corpses, and some of those still living. Women made their way through bodies, weeping, searching for their menfolk. Babies that had lost both parents sat in the dirt shrieking. Where was the nobility in this? Where the holy cause of Pope Urban's call?

Alaric felt a great heaviness drop away from him, as if his armor fell from his body. His heart jumped and strained in his breast, and he felt fresh blood flowing in his veins again, washing away the poison. He felt as if he had woken up from a long sleep. In the midst of so much death, Alaric had never felt so alive.

He went in search of Christofle, who had escaped injury by hiding in a tent. He said to the monk, 'Because of my selfish preoccupation with my troubles I led my people into slaughter. I am sick at heart to realize what I have done. Good monk, I wish to find my brother, but no longer for revenge; I wish to beg his forgiveness, and to forgive him.

116

For life is short and we cannot spend it in hate. But I fear that I cannot go on, nor can I turn back! Tell me what to do, good monk!'

And then he heard his name whispered on the wind: 'Alaric . . .' He followed it and found the one-eyed beggar, barely alive, still clutching the blade in his belly. But now Alaric saw what he had not seen before, for the beggar's hat had fallen off. The flaxen hair like his own. And the good eye was blue. Snatching away the eye patch, Alaric gazed upon the face of his brother.

'I followed you . . .' Baudoin gasped, 'for atonement. I am ashamed for what I did. I wanted to fight at your side . . .'

'Speak not, brother,' Alaric said, choking on tears.

'I want to say she seduced me, but I desired her, brother. We cannot lay blame upon Margot. You were absent so many times . . .'

Alaric lifted Baudoin in his arms and cradled him against his breast. 'Long campaigns make for an unfulfilled wife, my brother. I sought booty and glory when I should have been pursuing Margot. We are all three to blame in this tragedy, and are at the same time all three blameless.'

'Can you forgive me?'

'If you forgive me.'

Baudoin died, and Alaric lifted his face to the sky, an anguished howl pouring from his throat. He shot to his feet and searched for the soldier in the red tunic and horned helmet. A new revenge burned in Alaric's gut, this time to slay his brother's killer. Seeing the man across the field, Alaric gave chase, his pulse thundering in his temples, his heart galloping like a war horse. A bloody cry tore from his throat and he lifted his broad sword high. The Hungarian, unarmed, cowered.

And then . . .

A bright light. It came from nowhere and everywhere, sharp, piercing Alaric's eyes. He fell to his knees, stupefied. The light expanded and brightened, eddied and flowed around him, became the universe. Alaric felt weightless, as if he were soaring like an eagle, but he saw no earth below, no people, no city. Just light – cool and calming, all around him. But he was not alone, for he sensed the presence of beings nearby, luminous entities without form, swirling about him. He had

117

never felt such sweet joy, such exhilaration. No victorious battle, no passion in a woman's arms matched this utter ecstasy.

And then he saw . . . a vision.

It so overwhelmed him that he collapsed to the ground and covered his head with his arms. He heard a voice within the light – or, rather, *felt* it, as if the voice were speaking not to his ears but to his heart. And his heart was moved. 'Yes!' Alaric cried. 'Yes!'

The light receded and Alaric found himself on the ground, his face in the dirt, sobbing like a child.

Staggering to his feet, dashing the tears from his eyes, he sought out Christofle and said to him, 'In my vanity I believed myself to be a good knight. I condemned my brother for dishonorable behavior. Yet I am no better than he! I entered into a holy covenant with no thought for my men or our cause but wrapped in a cloak of selfishness. I have not upheld the standards of knighthood. I have been false to my vows. But now I shall atone!'

He described his vision, at which Christofle marveled, for no Alexandrian since the great Alexander himself had experienced the God-light. 'It was most miraculous, Christofle! The voice that spoke to me belonged to a High Priest named Philos. He told me he was my distant forefather, that I am descended from him, and because of this royal blood flows in my veins.'

'Praise be!' cried Christofle, throwing himself at the knight's feet.

'I will go to Jerusalem, but not for my own sake, because I know now there is redemption in forgiveness. As I forgive my brother, I am redeemed, just as I pray these poor creatures will forgive me.' He looked around at the dead. 'I will go to Jerusalem for a higher cause. All this was meant to be, I see that now,' Alaric said. 'I realize in my new wisdom that what happened between my brother and Margot and me was meant to open my eyes to the life I had been living – living only for myself – and to bring me to this place so that I might hear the call to reunite the Alexandrians and resume our sacred mission.'

In the blinding light Alaric had seen himself arrayed in the glorious costume of a cross-bearer, on a handsome steed, carrying a banner and leading a force of thousands, all dressed as he, and he knew what they would be called: Knights of the Flame. They would ride with honor to Jerusalem, take the holy city from the heathen, and rescue the holy books.

As Alaric spoke, Christofle witnessed a miraculous physical transformation: as if the light of Alaric's vision had lodged within his soul and now burned outwardly, for the Count of Valliers glowed with pride and honor and a sense of purpose. He had become most handsome, had grown in stature and confidence, and he spoke compellingly. A man who was going to be a great leader, a hero for whom men would die.

Christofle broke down and confessed now the secret that had poisoned his soul: that he was no better than any other member of this miserable expedition. That he had spouted noble causes but the truth was that he had come out of pitiful pride. 'I was bitter because I had lost my beloved Cunegonde, and because of this consigned myself to the Order. But the Order is dying out! Others born into the Alexandrians leave, they do not care, they do not want to carry on a mission that is thirteen hundred years old. What has it to do with them? As I visited the homes of Alexandrians, and saw how well they lived while the precious scrolls and books in their care were decomposing, I realized all my years of sacrifice had been in vain. That was why I placed all my hopes in you, my lord, why I kept pushing you. It was for myself, so that I might die having lived a life that counted for something at least. I wanted you to ride for *my* sake, not God's, and for this I am ashamed!'

Alaric laid a hand on the weeping monk's head. 'You will ride with us, good brother, as a Knight of the Flame, and generations to come will remember you for your sacrifice, valor, and heroic deeds, and praise your name.'

Alaric was anxious now to be on his way back to France to raise his great army of Alexandrians. He would find his scattered brothers and reunite them, resurrect the glory of old, the glory of Alexander himself. And the noble Knights of the Flame would ride to Jerusalem to rescue the precious words of blessed Mary Magdalene and bring them safely home.

119

Part Two

Thirteen

M oussa drove like a maniac.

The hour was late. He had collected his father's three visitors at the airport and now raced his 1957 canary-yellow Chevrolet through the sleeping city of Damascus, his passengers gripping their seats and holding on for life.

They rode in silence through this *Arabian Nights* fantasy of fountains, minarets, and mysterious alleyways – Damascus, made famous by Lawrence of Arabia. Candice had visited here once. Her driver had kept up a cheerful running commentary. Not Moussa Konstantine. After the initial friendly greeting and a rounding up of their luggage, he had fallen serious and quiet, rushing them from the terminal to his car, glancing frequently over his shoulder, and now this dash through the city, as though they were being chased.

Candice sensed something was wrong. She looked at the back of Glenn's head. He sat in the passenger seat next to the taciturn Moussa. Did he, too, sense something amiss?

They turned northwest to where picturesque Mount Qassioun, visible in the moonlight, rose above the city. This was the district of Al Mouhajarine, where luxurious homes and villas enjoyed a panoramic view of Damascus. To the west mountains stood, but to the east a desert extended for thousands of miles all the way to the Indian Ocean. And somewhere in that vast wilderness lay the Star of Babylon.

They drove past dark buildings and closed shops, food stalls shuttered for the night, mosques silhouetted against the stars, the streets only occasionally illuminated in the orange glow

120

of street lamps – a deserted city, Damascus, not known for its night life – until Moussa slowed and parked the Chevrolet beside a curb, looked up and down the dark street before hurriedly escorting his passengers to a gate set in a high wall. The man who greeted them in the moonlit courtyard was their host, an effusive Elias Konstantine.

Short, barrel-chested, with arching eyebrows and a completely hairless head, his white cotton shirt setting off his olive complexion to handsome effect. 'Come in, come in! Welcome to my home!'

Another hurried dash through a courtyard where fountains trickled and bougainvillea climbed walls.

As they passed under an oriental archway and entered a foyer where a marble floor gleamed like glass, Mr. Konstantine said, 'Such sad circumstances that occasion our meeting, Mr. Masters. I respected your father, may God grant him peace.'

He led them along a corridor whose walls were lined with magnificent religious icons, some quite old, the gold leaf frames starting to flake. When he saw Candice staring at an arresting portrait of young man on a red horse, spearing a fallen enemy, Konstantine said, 'That is St. Demetrios. We are Greek Catholics and very proud of our most ancient religion.'

The villa's interior was a blend of traditional and modern, with rich oriental furnishings among Turkish columns, one corner filled with computer, stereo, and wide-screen television. Mr. Konstantine explained that he was in the import–export business, and it was obvious to his guests that business was good.

'In a moment my daughter will serve refreshment. Now then,' he turned a solemn face to them, 'I am sorry but I cannot take you to Jebel Mara after all.'

'What!'

Glenn laid a hand on Candice's arm. 'Mr. Konstantine, if it's a matter of money—'

'It is a matter of danger,' the Syrian said. 'When your father contacted me times were safer. There is the trouble in Iraq, but also people have been asking me questions. I fear my house is being watched. I cannot risk my family's safety. I am sorry, you are on your own.'

Glenn, Candice, and Ian Hawthorne exchanged looks. They

were thinking the same thing: two Americans and one Brit on their own in the Syrian desert. They had been counting on Konstantine's protection. Now they had none.

A young woman entered with a platter bearing a silver teapot and glasses, followed by two more women carrying serving trays laden with cheese and bread, hard-boiled eggs and olives, butter and honey, and fruit. But Konstantine's guests were not hungry.

'Is there anyone else who can take us?' Candice said, sitting on a divan piled with cushions.

'I am sorry.'

'Can you at least tell us where Jebel Mara is?' Glenn asked, remaining on his feet.

'It is a small mountain range just north of Palmyra.'

'Palmyra!' Candice said. 'But that's a tourist spot!'

Ian groaned. 'It's been eighty years since Baskov was there. That's a lot of tourists. What if one of *them* found the Star of Babylon? It might at this moment be adorning a fireplace mantle in Cheshire. Worse, being used as an ashtray!'

Glenn twisted the gold band on his right ring finger. Candice guessed what he would do next: flash his badge, talk some police talk, use muscle and maybe even threaten to bring in the local cops. He surprised her by saying, 'I do not know you, Mr. Konstantine, so I am going to assume you are a man of reason and therefore can be reasoned with.'

Konstantine spread his hands. 'I am a wealthy man. I do not want money.'

'I am not offering money. Let me tell you what we are looking for.'

The Syrian folded his arms and sat back, the look on his face telling Glenn he was wasting his breath.

Glenn filled him in on Pierre Duchesne and the stone he had found with mysterious writing on it, and a Russian named Baskov, who, in the 1920s, retraced Duchesne's footsteps in the hope of finding more tablets. 'We believe Baskov found the tablets but he came down with a fever and had to return to Moscow, where he died soon after. We think Baskov could not have carried his find with him – perhaps it was too large or too fragile, or he was being watched – so he drew a map to help him locate it again. The map and the fragment remained in his family, most likely forgotten, stored away in a trunk or attic, until the collapse of the Soviet Union. Baskov's great-grandson placed an advertisement for these two items in a magazine, where my father saw it.'

Despite himself, Konstantine's small black eyes twinkled with interest. 'And what do you think you are going to find? An ancient library?'

'Or an archive of some kind, yes.'

'And what is the Star of Babylon?'

Glenn took the measure of this man who moments earlier had been a godsend and was now an obstacle, and drew in a breath. Glenn had no idea what the Star of Babylon was, whether a place, an object, the remains of a temple, a celestial event, or an astronomical measure. And he could not tell Elias Konstantine that they were in a race against a man who was planning some sort of Armageddon using the tablets as his license. So he said to the Greek Catholic with a gold cross glinting in black chest hairs, 'It is the Star of Bethlehem.'

Konstantine did not see the looks on the others' faces, Candice and Ian staring at their friend. The Syrian leaned forward in sudden interest and said, 'One of the Three Wise Men came from Babylon. Do the tablets contain an account of our Savior's birth, written by the hand of one of the Magi himself?'

'That is our theory.'

Konstantine pursed his lips. 'Do you have this map with you?'

Glenn turned to Candice, who retrieved the map from her tote bag. 'This is a photocopy,' she said, looking at Glenn in amazement.

Konstantine frowned over it for some seconds. 'I cannot identify these markings.'

'Neither can we. But we assume the large X marks the location of the Star of Bethlehem.'

He rose. 'I will make phone calls.'

When their host left the room, Candice stared at Glenn. 'You lied to him,' she said.

'Not exactly. The Star of Babylon *is* another name for the Star of Bethlehem, and the tablets *might* be an account of the Magi's journey.'

'You lied.'

123

'If you can't motivate a man with money, try religion,' he said, pointing to the icon of St. Demetrios, of which Konstantine had spoken so reverently.

'We shall leave just before dawn,' Konstantine announced when he rejoined them. 'It is too hazardous to drive at night.'

Candice welcomed the chance to grab some sleep. She was taken to the women's side of the house, Ian and Glenn to separate quarters.

The city was still sleeping when, roused from fitful naps, Candice, Glenn, and Ian filled their stomachs with thick coffee and date-stuffed pita bread, then settled into Moussa's canary-yellow Chevrolet. The sky to the east was pinking.

They went in three cars, Konstantine and his visitors in the first, with Moussa driving, the other two cars to carry extra gasoline, spare tires, belts, and motor parts as the road was going to be rough and there was only one gas station on the highway between Damascus and Palmyra. Breakdowns, Konstantine had said somberly, were as common as sand flies.

They traveled down the slope into the valley, along winding narrow residential roads, past walled gardens, elegant mausoleums, silent cafés, and reached the river, followed it, passing administrative buildings, embassies, luxury hotels and the University of Damascus. Little traffic was on the wide avenue, a few peasants with donkeys and carts, slogging toward the marketplace.

When they crossed the river and passed the National Museum, dark, looming, and huge, Konstantine's cell phone rang. A brief dialogue, then: 'We are being followed.' He barked an order into the phone, then told Moussa to turn at the next street.

Moussa pulled the wheel sharply to the left and headed down An Nasr Avenue toward the central post office and taxi station, deserted now, with a few people arriving with crates of chickens. The other two cars continued on, but the one they thought was following, a pink Nissan van, dented, no license plate or identifying marks, headlights dark, turned and closed in on Moussa. 'Go faster,' Konstantine said, turning in his seat to look back.

Moussa pressed the pedal, but the pursuer sped up and closed the gap. Candice and Glenn looked back. The interior of the van was dark, impossible to see how many were inside.

The walls of the old city loomed ahead. 'Go!' Konstantine said, bracing his hand on the dashboard, Glenn, Ian, and Candice grabbing hold of the back of the front seat.

They plunged into a maze of crooked streets and dead-end alleys, a city from the past, with ornate balconies leaning over narrow lanes toward each other, bazaars dark and deserted. Nearby was Straight Street, where two thousand years ago a traveler named Paul experienced an epiphany.

Moussa tried to lose the pursuer, making sharp turns, back-tracking, circling around, guiding the Chevrolet down lanes so narrow that Glenn and Candice thought the yellow paint would get scraped off, tires squealing, hitting potholes, jarring the passengers.

The Nissan stayed with them.

'What do they want?' Ian shouted when the Chevy's right front tire caught the edge of a sunken pit in the middle of the street, and he and Glenn and Candice were thrown so high they banged their heads on the roof of the car. 'Why don't we just stop and talk?'

'These men do not wish to talk,' Konstantine shot back, his brows lowered furiously over his eyes.

They reached the eastern edge of the old city, where shop windows displayed Christian icons, statues, prayer books. And caught in the twin beams: an old man in long jellabah, leading a donkey.

Moussa leaned on the horn. Candice covered her eyes. Ian shouted something and the Chevy swerved sharply, rode up onto the broken sidewalk, crashed into an empty stall, scattering boards and planks, swerved back onto the road, landed with a crash and kept going.

They looked back to see the van make the same maneuver, barely missing the old man, who stood frozen in the street.

Through a Roman gate, past a cemetery, the van in close pursuit, crossing the river again in a dizzying race, going faster, the three in the back seat being thrown to the right and left as Moussa executed quick, sharp turns, past mosques, a church, speeding around a deserted traffic circle, past the Olympic Stadium and finally onto the major highway with signs pointing to Homs, Aleppo, and Baghdad, the pink van still on their tail. There was little traffic; nonetheless, Moussa had to deal with slow-moving trucks, motor scooters, and the occasional minibus, weaving in and out as the Nissan followed.

When the highway straightened, he pressed the gas pedal all the way to the floor and the Chevrolet shot up to its top speed. The van fell behind but quickly caught up.

Konstantine swore in Greek, then in Arabic, and finally, for good measure, in English.

And then Ian, muttering, 'Bugger it,' reached into the duffel bag between his legs and produced a gun.

'Oh my God!' Candice cried.

He rolled the window down and leaned out.

'Are you out of your mind?' Glenn shouted.

'Just going to shoot out a tire or two.'

'You'll kill someone!' Glenn seized Ian's arm. Pulled him back inside. They struggled.

The gun went off, straight up through the roof of the Chevrolet. Behind, the shot startled the pursuing driver. He lost control, tried to regain it, over corrected. The van swerved, hit a pothole, flew into the air and came down in a roll, going over and over as Glenn and Ian, Candice and Mr. Konstantine watched in horror through the rear window.

The Nissan landed upside down and burst into flame. A ball of fire billowed up to the night sky, the men inside screaming, unable to get out.

The ancient document fluttered in Jessica Randolph's hands as she studied the medieval script beneath the bright Mediterranean sun.

She wondered why Philo was so anxious to get his hands on it. This letter had nothing in common with the other acquisitions, mostly religious writings, she had made for him through the years.

'It is what you wanted, isn't it?' asked her companion, Terry Leslie, owner of the yacht, offering Jessica a crystal flute of champagne. One week earlier, Jessica and Terry had met in the yacht's salon, with its dramatic bar and plush sofas, doors standing open to a large aft deck. There, on a table meant for marine charts, Jessica had laid out the plan of a museum in Melbourne, Australia. A wealthy collector had donated a collection to the museum, and among the items catalogued was an eleventh-century letter written by a Raymond of Toulouse. Philo Thibodeau wanted that letter.

Terry Leslie had studied the plan, which identified the museum's lighting system, control panels, doorways, air ducts, electrical wiring, emergency power, sensors, and monitors. The map had also come with a roster of security guards and schedule of inspection rounds. Terry had then scanned a report accompanying the layout, picking up key phrases: *windows are non-opening polycarbonate plastic*; *perimeter canine patrol*; *impact sensors*. The museum had the best in top-notch security.

Piece of cake.

One week later, Terry delivered.

'It's perfect,' Jessica said to the burglar, whose high-end thefts had paid not only for this pleasure craft but for a villa in Spain, a condo in Hollywood, and a fleet of luxury cars.

Terry Leslie boasted, 'I've pulled fifty-six capers and never bungled one. I'll never get caught,' she added with a laugh, because she knew the police were looking for a man.

Jessica studied the letter, mentally translating the Medieval French. In the year 1048, Raymond of Toulouse had written to his local Bishop of suspicions regarding a secret pagan society dedicated to the preservation of heretical writings against the day the Anti-Christ would rise up and take over the world. Raymond mentioned a fortress in the Pyrenees.

Why was Philo so anxious to get his hands on this?

And then she thought: it is not the letter itself that's valuable, it's what's written in it.

A secret society.

While the yacht rose and fell on the gentle sea, and her hostess sampled crab meat dipped in melted butter, Jessica's keen mind worked its myriad cogs and wheels.

A society of what? The Holy Grail? The Blood of Christ? A society that not even Jessica, whose job it was to know such secrets, had ever heard of, so secret, she thought, it made the Knights Templar look like exhibitionists.

Raymond of Toulouse had written: *they are identified by their ring of flames.*

Ring of flames?

The ring on Philo's right hand!

Was *he* a member of this secret society?

Behind the dark glasses that protected her eyes from the glaring sun, and behind her green eyes, her mind raced. This was an unexpected windfall. And she realized how valuable the letter was – not to Philo but to her.

Jessica wanted Thibodeau. To be his partner in wealth and power. When Sandrine died three years ago, Jessica had seen her chance. Philo was a widower now, no wife to stand in the way. But he didn't look at Jessica the way other men did. Nothing she did seduced him even an inch. So she had decided she must resort to other means. Her first plan was to lure him with the Star of Babylon. Failing that – since the plan depended upon the success of Candice Armstrong and Glenn Masters – contingency plans must be set in place.

This letter was perfect.

Jessica smiled to herself. She had learned long ago – before the breast implants, the nose job, the name change; in the days of nickel and dime grifting when she was always one step ahead of the bunko squad – that the smart con always had a back-up plan. If the first trick failed, and if the back-up failed, Plan C had to be implemented.

She would get Philo by any means possible, even if she had to resort to murder.

Fourteen

Philo knew they were searching for him. The Los Angeles police. To question him in connection with John Masters' death. He was unconcerned. They would never find him, and even if they should it would be too late.

Philo sat in a glass living room surrounded by sky. The twenty thousand square foot penthouse thirty stories above the city of Houston was inaccessible from the ground floor. The elevators – Philo's personal one and the ones for servants and supplies – started at this floor and only went up, Philo coming and going from this residence by way of helicopter.

If police were watching the building, hoping to catch him, they had a long wait.

Thibodeau was dressed in white flannel slacks and a white silk shirt, believing white to be the only proper color for a true Southern gentleman. His only concession to color was the pale yellow ascot at his throat and matching silk handkerchief tucked into the shirt pocket.

His residence was likewise all white: sofas, carpet, walls, flowers, even the white marble coffee table that measured ten feet by six. A perfect setting for the newly acquired painting that hung over the white marble fireplace, where flames danced at the hearth.

An abstract of white upon light, gemstone yellows shot with sky-blue, pearl upon snow upon incandescence – it could only be a representation of the Luminance. Lenore must have broken her promise to John and told their son about the secret order. How else could Glenn have known of the Luminance? He had talent. Standing in the studio while the detective was at the hospital, Philo had studied all the paintings and had seen the gradual evolution of Glenn's vision. The later paintings, those with the face in them, came close to the ultimate truth. Philo took it as a sign. Everything was falling into place.

Soon, Lenore, soon . . .

He sipped his expensive scotch. Philo was alone in the white living room – it was the only way he could drink.

Philo never ate or drank in the presence of others. No one saw him sleep. No one joined him in the men's room. These habits were not seemly for a man of his sacred calling. That was Jesus' mistake, eating and drinking with his companions, confusing them, making them wonder how the Son of God could need food and wine. Not even Philo's wife, Sandrine, had seen him eat. His last meal in the company of another person had been the picnic with Lenore.

On the day his life had changed forever.

He looked again at the Polaroid photo that had been delivered earlier. Glenn Masters and Candice Armstrong at an airport, waiting to board a flight, unaware they were being photographed. Looking at each other, a brief glance captured on film. On the surface: anger, irritation, impatience, each not wanting the other along. But Philo saw yearning there also, an attraction so primal that not even the subjects themselves were aware of it. This was how he must have looked before he was aware of his love for Lenore.

Back on the day he had taken the first step on his final path to destiny . . .

Philo had thought she was naked. Standing nude in the stream and bathing her ivory skin. But as he crept closer he saw that she was wearing an ankle-length sheath as pale as her skin. And she wasn't exactly bathing but scooping water from the stream she stood in, raising it high over her head to let the water trickle from her fingers. It looked like diamonds.

As he circled around to get a better look, he saw small breasts and narrow hips, long hair and long legs. He guessed she was his own age, fifteen. When he saw her face he was taken by the beauty of it and he knew she mustn't see him. He might be rich and his parents the cream of Houston society, but girls still had eyes and they either looked right through Philo or laughed because he was short with a roundish face sporting too many freckles. He couldn't bear such a snub from this beautiful creature. But his foot snapped a dry twig and violet eyes searched the forest, found him, and held him.

'Hello,' she said.

He stepped out. 'These woods are haunted.'

'I know. Water doesn't fall right. I think the laws of physics are different here.' She blushed. 'I'm going to be a physicist.'

Philo could only swallow. It was 1948 and girls didn't dream of being physicists. But she could have said she wanted to be a coal miner, he was that spellbound.

He knew who she was. Lenore Rousseau, her father a member of the Alexandrians, with a lineage that went back as far as Philo's.

'We might be a democratic society,' Philo's mother had repeatedly told him, 'with no member placed higher than another, but the fact remains that only a handful of members can trace their ancestry back to the beginnings of the order as *we* can, three hundred years before the priests were forced into exile. You are the direct descendent of High Priest Philos and Princess Artemisia, and you must never forget, Philo, that you are superior to all the others.'

It was Lenore's first time in this place; she had been brought here for her initiation. Philo, who had been initiated the summer before, on his fourteenth birthday, had offered to help her through the process. 'It's easy really,' he said, his adolescent voice breaking as he felt those violet eyes on him, 'some fasting and meditating, a few questions, and then the oaths of loyalty and secrecy.' After which, the novice was admitted into the esoteric wisdom of the ancients, indoctrinated into the mission of the Alexandrians. But Philo did not mention this part. She had to swear her vow of secrecy and allegiance first.

Lenore looked down at the water swirling about her feet and made a small cry of dismay. 'All these stones. I shall never make it back to shore.' Ten inches away.

Philo held out his hand and she paused to delve right into and through his trembling soul with those astonishing eyes, and said, 'You are so gallant. My knight in armor.'

She delivered her hand, cool and slick from the water, into his sweaty adolescent paw, and he bravely assisted her out of the stream, she delicate and otherworldly, pink nipples visible through the sheath, her long hair curly and fairylike, he lumpish and awkward and homely with his Texas hick accent.

She had neither laughed at him nor looked right through him. She had called him gallant. In that moment Philo vowed that he would spend the rest of his life making himself worthy of her.

In the next few years he grew, not by much, a couple more inches, and then stopped. To compensate for lack of stature he polished his style, but who to emulate? His own father was a weak, quiet man, chosen by Philo's aggressive mother for his money and his genes, a man passionately devoted to stamp-collecting and avoiding his wife. Hardly a role model for a boy.

Philo didn't have to look far. Robert E. Lee, the great Confederate General of the Civil War, considered at one time the handsomest man in the South and the truest gentleman. Lee had lost the war but had held no grudges. He had set himself as an example for fellow Southerners, hoping the bitterness of losing the war would be forgotten and the creating of a unified America could begin. He exemplified the highest standards, the most chivalrous conduct, and the finest traits of manliness. These were the qualities, Lee averred, that marked

131

the Southern gentleman: moderation, self-control, duty, sincerity, consideration of others, courage, special regard for ladies, courtesy, honor, and deep religious conviction. They would become Philo's, who would embrace Robert E. Lee's virtues and practice them everyday of his life. Even in the future, when he was forced to kill, it would be with compassion and respect for his victim and an assurance that they would be held in special light with God.

And as Robert E. Lee was referred to as 'the last gentle knight,' and since Philo himself descended from Crusader knights, he adopted the title as his own.

In only one area did he disagree with his idol. Lee had said, 'There are things in the Bible which I may not be able to explain, but I fully accept as the infallible Word of God, and receive its teachings as inspired by the Holy Spirit.'

The error lay in the fact that God did not exist, therefore there could be no *word* of God.

Philo worked on his speech – deleting Southern slang, like 'might could,' 'boy howdy,' and 'running aloose,' – his bearing (he walked tall for a short man), his manners, the very swivel of his head when speaking. He cultivated a lordly outlook and tolerant philosophy. He studied hard and earned top grades. He won awards and graduated with honors. All for Lenore, his violet-eyed wood nymph who had called him gallant.

Except for the occasional social events at the homes of members around the world, they saw little of each other after the encounter in the glade, Lenore living in California, Philo in Texas. But she was never out of his mind, and everything he did, every endeavor he undertook, every breath he drew was for Lenore; and when Philo thought of the future he saw her at his side.

In his modern white penthouse, he recalled words Lenore had written to him long ago, in a letter preciously kept and memorized:

My dear Philo, we humans have been growing up all these eons. We were children when God created us. His laws are proof of this. The first ones dealt with morality – the laws of Hamurabi, Moses, Confucius. These were rules for us to live our lives by. But now we have grown

132

up and God is revealing more astounding laws to us –
those of physics and astronomy, and of the quantum
world. Every day we see it in the news, science making
wondrous discoveries. God preparing us for a paradigm
shift of immense proportions. We stand at the brink of
the miraculous.

It always struck Philo how Lenore would refer to God, even
though she was an Alexandrian and the Alexandrians did not
believe in the existence of God. But that was just part of her
glorious complexity. Lenore was passionate about the
Luminance, and few who drifted into her golden sphere went
away unchanged. And she was to be his.

There was only one obstacle. Bathsheba Thibodeau.

People had been afraid of Philo's mother back then. Not
because she was the wealthiest society hostess in the southern
United States and that one's placement or non-placement on
her invitation list spelled social success or doom. People
feared her because she spoke to the dead. They needed to be
reassured, she said. And Philo was sure the dead listened.
Everybody listened to Bathsheba

A formidable woman with a bloodline that went back over
two thousand years – unlike that of her inconsequential husband,
who could only trace his lineage back to the *Mayflower* –
Bathsheba ruled with the proverbial iron hand. And the center
of this fiercely ruled universe was her only child: Philo.

Her real name was Jimmynell, but she thought it 'too
Texas and too silly' so she had changed it to Bathsheba, wife
of David and mother of Solomon, because even at age eight
she had been devoted to the fundamental Word of the Bible
and already knew that she was someday going to be a woman
to be reckoned with. The Bathsheba of old had connived to
put her son on the throne of Israel. No such lowly ambition
for Bathsheba Thibodeau. She had loftier plans than that for
Philo.

From his earliest days, Philo had understood that he was
to be singled out for specialness. Only one thing confused
him: if his parents didn't believe in God, why did they go to
church every Sunday, and why was he made to commit the
Bible to heart? Bathsheba kept saying that someday he would

understand, and then, on the day of his initiation into the Order, when he was fourteen, he did understand.

On his twenty-first birthday, when he graduated with honors from Texas A&M, his mother kissed him in the sunlight, stroked his hair and whispered into his ear, 'Remember that you are of royal blood, my son. Royal blood.'

Thus was he ready to take his rightful place as leader of the Alexandrians, the first in their twenty-three hundred years of existence. With Lenore Rousseau at his side.

He had thought his mother would be an obstacle to the marriage, but she had surprised him by blessing and even encouraging the union. And so, when Philo was twenty-one, they went on a picnic, where he planned to propose. 'Philo, you have put me on a pedestal,' Lenore said. 'I don't belong there. I am just a woman. I have my flaws and weaknesses. I can't live up to the image you have of me.'

And he thought: her humility and modesty only add to her perfection. On bended knee: 'Lenore, you are my glory, the radiance that lights my way. Lenore, you are my soul.'

'What do you want of me?'

'I beg that you be my lady, that you permit me to serve you, to hold you in my heart, and that I may dedicate my life and purpose to you.'

'Philo, I am getting married.'

'Is he a physicist?' Philo had asked, he recalled later, when it was all over. A fire had been lit, deep within him, just the barest spark, like a stone against flint, but there now, growing, fanned by the winds blowing through his soul. He didn't give a damn if the man were a physicist. He didn't even know why he asked.

'He is in the school of Near Eastern studies.'

Flames leaped within Philo. She had given the man form and purpose. Philo looked at the crusts of bread from the sandwiches, the pits from their olives, orange rinds, empty soda bottles – evidence that they had consumed food together. He knew he could never again eat in the presence of another person.

'Please wish me well,' she had said, violet eyes beseeching him.

'I wish you well,' he had said, because that was what Robert E. Lee would have said, a gentleman never exhibiting the baser emotions, certainly not in front of a lady. He had lost and, like the good loser Lee had been, would accept it graciously.

But a conflagration raged inside him as he drove home in the Alfa Romeo he had received for graduating magna cum laude. The internal fire burned not from anger nor hatred nor disappointment, but from the need to lash back at Lenore. Hurt her. Cause her the pain she had caused him. Yet he could not! Though she was the igniter of the inferno in his soul, it was insupportable that Philo should blame her, his flawless, blameless Lenore.

But the fire needed to be set free, to be released from within him or it would consume him and Philo would perish. *Someone had to pay.*

His father was in his study, as usual, shoulders stooped over his stamp collection, examining a one-inch-square piece of paper with a magnifying glass as if working on a cure for cancer. His father, who had never held a real job in his life, wealthy by inheritance, once handsome but now gray and faded after two decades with the indomitable Bathsheba.

Bathsheba in the seance room, talking to spirits, giving them orders, really, instructing the dead to be patient. He had never understood the root of his mother's need to tell ghosts what to do. He thought it had something to do with her coming from the world's longest lineage, which made her feel immortal, somehow, honing even more sharply within her the smug superiority the living innately felt over the dead.

Philo found himself in the main living room, staring at the painting over the fireplace, a horrific scene depicting the Alexandrian priests running from the mob, the Library burning in the background. He reached up and tore it down. The massive framed canvas crashed to the floor and he kicked it into the fireplace. It felt good, kicking those priests. Again and again with his foot, his eyes red with rage, kicking the priests because he could not kick Lenore.

The canvas caught flame. Philo seized the frame and dragged the burning painting across the carpet and through the house, leaving a trail of flames behind, starting fires here and there, locking the door to his father's study, locking the door to the seance room, seeing red, flames, fire everywhere. He was still making his way through the enormous mansion when the first siren screamed in the night, and neighbors were gathering in concern and awe. He heard screams inside the house, too.

Smoke inhalation and second-degree burns laid him up in a Houston hospital where, in his pain-racked delirium, he walked with Jesus.

When Philo was nine years old Bathsheba had taken him to an old-fashioned fire-and-brimstone tent revival on the outskirts of town, where a Texas shit-kicker preacher had spewed hell and damnation over the perspiring heads of the congregants. Bathsheba loved tent revivals because she said the dead liked to attend them (although, as she later argued with the preacher, God was *not* present in the tent). And while the preacher preached, Philo had wondered if Jesus talked like a Texas good old boy. In his coma, as millions of burned-raw nerve endings danced beneath special bandages and morphine swam through his veins and his brain floated in an amniotic sac of narcotics and hallucinogens, Philo met Jesus by the Sea of Galilee, and discovered he had been right when he was nine years old – Jesus *did* talk like a Texas good old boy. And what he said to Philo was this: 'You did a good job, son, but you ain't done yet. God's waitin' on you, but He won't wait forever. But before you go, let me tell you something about that little gal you was set on marrying.'

Philo lay in a coma for three days. When he came out of it, they told him he had nearly died. They were wrong. He *had* died.

And was resurrected.

Like Jesus, Philo had suffered a martyr's death, had roamed the nether realms of Heaven, Hell, and assorted underworlds and a few foreign countries for three days, and then was brought back to life to begin his great journey. But the difference between himself and his predecessor, Philo understood as fresh power surged through his blood, was that Jesus was merely baptized with water. Philo was baptized with fire. Proof of his redemption and transformation was his hair. When the bandages were removed from the parts of him that had been cleansed by fire, the twenty-one-year-old's hair was discovered to have gone stark white.

He took it as a sign.

A great work lay ahead of him, a road to glory and to God. Philo knew now that Lenore understood this. Blessed prescient woman, she had *known*. And because of this, for the sake of Philo's sacred mission, she had committed the ultimate sacrifice.

He understood so much now because Jesus had explained it all. Lenore was too high and lofty to marry a work-in-progress. She knew this, because she was insightful and brilliant, whereas he himself had not seen it. She understood that Philo was the Chosen One, on an epic journey, and she must not stand in his way.

For this, Lenore was prepared to commit the ultimate sacrifice: marrying a man she did not love. (And she *had* to marry. She needed a protector and respectability.) Philo now heard the real words behind her 'No.' She was saying: I will join you, Philo, but not right now, for I will only stand in your way. I will be with John Masters until you have risen high enough, and then I will be with you.

He no longer hated John Masters but rather felt sorry for him, because the poor man believed that Lenore loved him, and Philo thought that when the time came for John to be put out of the way, Philo would be merciful.

From his hospital bed, the twenty-one-year-old learned from a team of lawyers that he had inherited an astounding fortune, plus assorted lucrative corporations, high-priced properties, blue chip stocks and the hefty life insurance policies on his parents. But these riches mattered not to Philo, who was one day going to own the world.

The fire was investigated and found accidental. 'Sparks from a fireplace,' was the official report, and the arson investigator smiled as he deposited a hundred thousand dollars in a secret account.

As Philo prepared to take over a financial empire, and begin his secret, holy quest, he couldn't understand what everyone was so upset about. It was a glorious moment, a day of rejoicing. Why so glum over what had happened to his parents? They had been martyred in order that their only son should make the journey into the Underworld to spend three days undergoing his glorious transformation, and then to be resurrected into his new life. Everyone should be happy for Bathsheba. Now she could bully the dead in person.

Stirring from his memories, Philo set aside his drink and picked up the Polaroid of Candice and Glenn at the airport. With a pair of scissors, he sheered the picture in half, keeping Glenn Masters between thumb and forefinger and carrying the other half to the fireplace, where he dropped Candice Armstrong in pale-pink blouse, long flouncy skirt, dark hair drawn up in a clip, into the flames and watched her curl, blacken, and turn to ash. A symbolic death for now, soon to be a reality.

The power of flame, Philo thought in ecstasy.

He picked up a phone. Dialed. Listened to the report of a terrible car accident on the outskirts of Damascus.

He hung up and pondered this latest news. The men had perished in fire. A further sign that the End was coming.

He shuddered in a paroxysm of passion. *Soon, Lenore* . . .

Soon the whole world was going to know the rapture of fire.

Fifteen

S tranded. In the middle of nowhere.

'We have no idea where we are, thanks to John Wayne here,' Glenn said as he squinted in the direction of the rising sun. Dawn was breaking over the Syrian plateau, a desolate sight.

'I should think you would be grateful,' Ian grumbled, lighting a cigarette. 'If I hadn't fired, those bastards would have caught us and sold us into slavery. I want my gun back.'

'Go to hell.'

'It's not yours—'

'Will you *stop*!' Candice cried. The two men had been bickering since Konstantine had dropped them off and returned to Damascus. 'We have to figure a way to get to Palmyra.'

They turned, both thinking she was beautiful when she was angry.

'What do you suggest?' Ian said. 'We can't go back to the main highway, not with maniacs searching for us. Probably bent on revenge now, after what happened.'

The van rolling over. Landing upside down. Bursting into flame. Men trapped and screaming inside.

It haunted the threesome.

It had infuriated Konstantine. 'I was insane to let you talk me into this,' he had said when, after driving long enough to make sure no other cars were in pursuit and it was safe to stop, they had driven off the main road onto a dirt track that carried them into an olive grove. 'I knew the risk was too great. We go back to Damascus.'

But the three Westerners had agreed on one thing: to push on to Palmyra.

'I cannot take you,' Konstantine had said.

They had tried bribing his men, offering generous fees for taking them, but the men had seen a car burst into flames, and the screams of the victims still rang in their ears. 'We must think of our families,' Konstantine had said after Moussa had placed their gear on the dirt and gotten back behind the wheel of the Chevrolet. And then they were gone.

'We have to stay off the beaten track,' Glenn said now, reluctantly agreeing with Ian. 'The friends of those men,' *in the burning wreckage*, 'will be looking for us.' And if Philo was behind it, the search party would have trebled and quadrupled by now. They could trust no one who came along. 'We need another strategy.'

'For crying out loud,' Candice muttered, snatching up her nylon carry-all and marching around a thicket of chickpea shrubs. Glenn and Ian heard the zipper open, contents rifled, Candice's sighs of exasperation as she did something mysterious behind the shrub. When she emerged they saw she had changed from the flouncy skirt and gauzy blouse into conservative slacks and a long-sleeved blouse of midnight blue silk, buttoned up to her throat.

'What—' Glenn and Ian began.

Shouldering her carry-all and knapsack, she traipsed out of the orchard, back, to their shock, to the main highway where, in the breaking dawn, she began waving at the light traffic whizzing by.

'Oh God!' Ian said. Glenn was already running after her.

Too late. Candice had only to flag the next vehicle and it came to a screeching, swerving halt.

The driver and passengers turned out not to be men intent on killing them, but a party of brothers heading home after a weekend of selling olives in the Damascus marketplace. Cheerful young men only too happy to accommodate the foreigners in the back seat of their clunky old Mercedes. '*Ahlan wa sahlan!*' they shouted as the car squealed off the dirt and back onto the road. 'Welcome to Syria!'

'That was reckless,' Glenn muttered to Candice in the back seat. They were squashed together, as one of the brothers made up a fourth on the cramped seat.

'It got us a ride, didn't it?' she said from the corner of her mouth. 'Leave it up to you and Ian, and we'd have stayed there until the Second Coming.'

'No need to get snotty,' Glenn said, and he unpinned his arm to lay it along the back of the seat, but there was no room with all the goods piled there, so he put his arm around Candice's shoulders and left it there.

They stopped at a village seventy miles from Palmyra, where the foreigners were invited to lunch and could not refuse – a village famous for brothers, their hosts boasted, for here was the very spot where Cain slew Abel. The five sisters of the four brothers brought out platters of eggs and yogurt, bread and oil, and, because this was a special occasion, a chicken was slaughtered and roasted just for the guests. Because their hosts spoke no English, Ian translated a lively discussion that ranged from films – the brothers were Jackie Chan fans – to America's military presence in the Middle East. There was no rancor, as the brothers understood that what governments do has nothing to do with people.

The feast was held beneath the shade of a massive sycamore, where dogs slept in the dust, children clustered to ogle the strangers, and the three Westerners kept an anxious eye on the road from the highway.

But no one came looking for them, and finally handshakes and embraces, the brothers refusing money offered by the guests, sent the travelers on their way. A farmer and his son took them further, in a rusty old truck, two lively Syrians who treated their American guests to a driving tour around an Omayyad castle perched on a hilltop, followed by a stop for sugared tea and a layered flaky pastry filled with nuts and drenched in honey.

140

The ruins of Palmyra rose abruptly from the desert, brilliant-gold in the dying sun, hinting of the grandeur of the city once ruled by the extraordinary warrior queen Zenobia. The farmer dropped his passengers off in the heart of the 'new' town, refusing to be paid and wishing them luck.

Luck, however, was not with them, as they discovered that the tourist season had begun and there was not a vacancy to be found.

'There's always camping,' Glenn said as they walked into the cool lobby of the last hotel.

But Candice had seen the so-called camping area in the hotel grounds. It was sleeping under the stars and no facilities. She was in desperate need of a shower.

The desk clerk of the Lotus Hotel apologized and said, as all the other hotels had said, that they were full, but, for a fee, they were welcome to find space in the garden, where already young travelers were staking out territory with sleeping bags. Candice saw room keys in the cubbyholes and asked about them. 'Those are guests who have not yet arrived. But they have reservations, madam. Paid in advance,' he added significantly.

She looked around the lobby, crowded with tourists and luggage, a man asleep on a sofa, his head on his backpack. Digging into her tote bag, she brought out a roll of currency – American. 'If one of the rooms opens up, please hold it for me.'

They hired a driver to take them to Jebel Mara. The plan was to visit with the local Bedouins to see if any of the old people remembered Baskov's work there. As it was just eighty years ago, it might still be in the local memory.

As they left the golden ruins behind, the driver pointed out the Bedouin encampments dotting the flat landscape. 'They are a wandering people,' he said in good English, 'because their flocks must move continually in search of fresh pastures. Of course, now many of our Bedouins have settled down to sedentary lives, no longer roaming.'

Even such settled ones as those camped fifteen miles north of the Palmyra oasis still lived in the portable black goat-hair tents of their ancestors, as the visitors now saw in a shallow depression that held a cluster of tents of different sizes, open fronts facing leeward. Men sat in the shade smoking water

141

pipes and playing backgammon while children and dogs ran around and women peeked shyly from behind tent flaps.

A man came out to greet them, tall and dignified, wearing a jellabah under a jacket, a black-checkered kaffiyeh over his head and shoulders. He introduced himself as Sheikh Abdu and welcomed the strangers to his tent.

As Ian engaged him in a dialogue in Arabic, explaining their purpose there – to seek the origins of an old story – Candice looked past the encampment toward the jagged upthrusts rising a thousand feet and called, in this flat land, 'jebel,' mountains. Her heart raced. Was the Star of Babylon near at hand?

Sheikh Abdu invited the three inside, and as they entered the tent they saw a TV set propped up on a camel saddle, wires running from it to an outdoor generator. Men seated on woven rugs rose and bowed politely, most of them in long jellabahs, but two young ones in blue jeans with cell phones hooked to their belts.

Women wearing bright red and yellow dresses, gold glinting on their hands and arms, served sweet tea and barley cakes, and retreated behind the blanket that separated the men's side of the tent from the women's.

Before getting down to the reason for the visit, Glenn asked Ian to inquire if other foreigners had come by also looking for the place where an old story had taken place at Jebel Mara. A red-haired woman, perhaps? An American with white hair and a white beard? But the three were the first strangers to visit the camp since the previous autumn.

Sheikh Abdu listened politely as Ian explained their desire to locate the place a foreigner named Baskov had worked, three or four generations ago. The sheikh conferred with his companions, their dialogue animated. Over the years legends and myths have a way of becoming altered, distorted, as they are told around campfires, embellished upon, and exaggerated until little of the original is recognizable. Nonetheless, the kernel of this particular story remained: a crazy European digging in the desert for old stones.

As Ian translated for his companions, saying, 'We're in luck. They know this story,' he was interrupted by one old man who suddenly spoke up, talking rapidly and with excitement.

142

Candice and Glenn waited for Ian, his expression darkening to consternation. He questioned the elder, others joined in, a rapid exchange with gestures, until finally he turned to his friends and said, 'This is not the Jebel Mara of Ivan Baskov.'

'What!' Candice's hopes plummeted. 'But they know the story!'

'Yes, but they say it didn't happen here. There's *another* Jebel Mara.'

'Another? Do they know where?' Glenn spread out his GEO map of Syria and they all looked at it, crowding around, talking and chattering, shaking their heads, arguing, laughing, frowning, many brown fingers pointing to myriad spots hundreds of miles apart. But gradually, as each man scratched his head and consulted with his comrades, as they tossed out what could not be and focused on what *must* be, as memories were subjected to keen and honest scrutiny, there was a narrowing down of the facts and, therefore, of the possible locales for Baskov's adventure. 'Here!' the sheikh finally said with pride.

Of course, nothing on the map was labeled 'Jebel Mara.' It could not be that simple. 'Bugger,' Ian muttered. 'It looks like we have to follow the southeast track out of Palmyra until we get just past Wadi Awarid, where we turn north for a few miles until we travel east toward the Al Rutaymah salt lakes – but not reaching them. Here,' he said as he tapped a great blank spot on the map, 'is Wadi Raisa. Nearby they say we'll find Jebel Mara.'

Glenn looked doubtful. 'Are these men sure?'

Ian shrugged. 'Who can say?' His troubled look returned. 'They're saying it's a very desolate, very inhospitable region. Any people we run into will most likely be brigands, looters, and soldiers who've gone AWOL.'

The hotel desk clerk was pleased to see Candice. A room had suddenly become available, he said. Leaving Ian at the downstairs bar, and Glenn to head for the nearest police station, she went up to her room.

The room was stuffy. Opening the French doors that led to the balcony, Candice left the front door open to allow breezes through and went into the bathroom. She peeled away the Band-Aid. The cut on her neck was healing. She left it uncovered.

Returning to the room, she unpacked her carry-all. Candice had brought along a book titled *Bible Hebrew Source Book,* because the 'astronomer's wife' fragment was in Hebrew. This, at least, was something she had been able to determine before leaving California: that the alphabet on the Duchesne stone was indeed a substitution cipher for the ancient Hebrew alphabet. In between the pages of the book, Candice had folded the photocopy of the Duchesne stone.

She thought of the unexpected meeting with the woman in the corridor outside the ICU. Dr. Mildred Stillwater had published the reference book forty years ago and it had remained an essential tool for archaeologists and Bible scholars since. Where had she been all these years?

Candice thought of the other peculiar people in the corridor. Were they really there to pay homage to a respected colleague, or were they after the Star of Babylon?

She went out onto the balcony where a deepening dusk was filled with the perfume of the night: jasmine and honey-suckle blooming in the garden; lamb roasting on an open spit; coffee brewing, dark and rich; and the desert itself, dusty, ancient. Palmyra, 'Bride of the Desert.' City of cara-vans and trade routes, where cultures met and mingled and clashed. A thousand palms with shaggy green crowns. People had lived here as far back as seventy-five hundred years ago. The Romans had brought their gods and laws to this city.

Lifting her face to the breeze, Candice closed her eyes and slipped into another world. She pictured this oasis as it must have been centuries ago, the people, the marketplace, a hand-some Roman centurion on his high-stepping horse . . .

A knock on her open door.

She turned to see Glenn framed there. She was still in her fantasy and he had walked into it, the handsome centurion wearing a plumed helmet, scarlet cloak, shining military breast-plate, sword at his side – symbol of power around the world.

'I thought you might be interested to hear what I've found so far,' he said, stepping inside, scowling. 'You shouldn't leave your door open.'

The centurion vanished and it was Glenn Masters again – no longer in helmet and cloak but sexy all the same in black

144

cargo pants and blue chambray shirt – once more telling her what she should and should not do.

'I made discreet inquiries around town. No one has been asking about Jebel Mara. No one hired a guide and a car to take them there. No one asking about Baskov or the Star of Babylon.'

He joined her on the balcony, where date palms stood silhouetted against the darkening sky and the first stars.

Candice moved to the rail and quickly drew back. 'What's wrong?' he asked.

'I don't like heights.'

'We're only one floor up.'

'That's one too many for me. I get dizzy when I have a high opinion of something.'

She caught the quick, amused smile. And then it was replaced by a serious look. He was no doubt wondering what to do next, how to get them to Jebel Mara. 'We'll find someone else to take us,' she said. As if it would be as easy as calling for a taxi.

But that wasn't what Glenn had been thinking about. He was thinking he would like to paint Candice by moonlight.

Glenn fixed his eyes on the ruins – in the deepening gloom Palmyra with its streets and columns and arches looked almost like a modern city. 'I went to the local police and filed a report on the car that followed us out of Damascus. I told them of our situation. They'll keep an eye out for anyone asking about Jebel Mara or the Star of Babylon. And they will be escorting you to the airport in the morning.'

She snapped her head around. 'What?'

He turned to her. 'I told them that I am pursuing a criminal and that you are in danger. They want you out of their town as quickly and quietly as possible.'

'You had no right.'

'I had every right.'

'I'm not leaving.'

That voice. Why did it still catch him by surprise? Candice looked like she should have a higher voice, that soprano tones should rise from the slender throat where a cameo goddess kept a vigilant eye on a knife wound.

'I've hired a car and a driver,' he said. 'I head out into the desert at dawn.'

'I'm going with you.'

'No.'

'Then I'll get my own car and driver.'

'And go alone?'

'I wanted to go alone in the first place.' No help from anybody. Even though it terrified her. 'Listen, we don't have the luxury of time. Your father said Philo is planning a great devastation. Armageddon. What if he's using the Star of Babylon as an excuse to blow up the world?'

'All the more reason for me to travel alone.'

'And all the more reason for me to go with you!'

'Look, it isn't going to happen, Dr. Armstrong. The police have put the word out: no one is to hire themselves out to you. This is a small town and word travels fast, especially when it comes from the police.'

'How can you abandon me like this?'

'I'm not abandoning you. I'm putting you under police protection. I need to travel alone, and I need to travel fast.'

'You talk as if I were an invalid or a millstone—'

He took her by the shoulders, gripped hard. 'Damn it, Candice, I could never forgive myself if anything happened to you! How many deaths in my life do you think I can take?'

That stopped her. His tone angry, but his eyes imploring. She felt the bezel of his ring, always turned to the palm of his hand, dig into her flesh, and she imagined a permanent mark being emblazoned there, the scarlet ruby and gold flames branding fire on her skin.

Neither knew what to say next, when, looking past Glenn's shoulder at white marble columns rising ghostly in the moon-light, Candice saw a man standing among them. The familiar Hawaiian shirt.

'Hey!' she said.

'What?'

'That's him!' she said, and suddenly she was gone.

Glenn sprinted after her, out of the room, down the corridor and the stairs to the lobby in time to see Candice fly through the open doors onto the terrace where patrons were dining. She vanished into shadow.

Swearing softly, he took off after her.

Candice ran over broken pavement, between towering

columns, up stairways leading nowhere, around sunken baths where the rich had once bathed, and past niches where the gods had once stood, until she arrived at the remains of a sacrificial altar. She wasn't alone. There were tourists here, talking, laughing, snapping pictures, saying, 'Cheese!'

She saw the Hawaiian shirt vanish around a corner and she followed.

Losing him again, she stopped to listen. Nearby, his footsteps paused and then moved on. Candice continued to follow, drawing deeper into a maze of columns, windowless chambers, crumbling arches. There were no tourists here, just ghosts.

'Come out where I can see you!' she shouted, her voice echoing. She looked back. The temple sanctuary blocked her view of the hotel. She could no longer hear music or voices. Just the wind. She picked up a rock and, hearing a sound, bolted around an arch to run smack into Glenn.

'Did you see him?' she said breathlessly.

'Hold on! Which way did he go?'

'I don't know. Best if we split up,' she said, starting in one direction.

Glenn put a hand on her arm. 'Safer if we stay together.'

But Candice continued in her intended direction, leaving Glenn to go in the other. Headstrong, he thought. Impulsive, stubborn, and now headstrong. 'Wait a minute,' he said, taking her arm. 'Tell me exactly what you saw from the balcony.'

'It was him – same long hair in a ponytail, head bald on top. And the shirt with blue palm trees.'

'You could see his face?'

'He was looking at me.'

Glenn blinked. 'He was looking right at you?'

'Yes, just standing there— Oh no!'

They ran together, through the ruins, across the dining terrace where the guests were startled a second time, up the stairs and down the corridor to find Candice's room exactly as they had left it – with the door standing open.

'What's missing?' Glenn said, immediately opening cupboards, pulling out drawers, as if it were his room.

She found it right off. The photocopy of the Duchesne stone. Gone from Mildred Stillwater's book. Now she wouldn't be able to translate what she found. 'A ruse,' she said. 'He purposely lured me outside so an accomplice could search my room!'

'Where's the map?' But it was still in her knapsack.

Glenn frowned at his watch, torn between leaving right away for Jebel Mara and staying to make sure Candice was safe until the police took her to the airport in the morning. Candice wanted only one thing: to go out and search for her attacker, turn the town upside down if she had to. But Palmyra was swarming with tourists. She would never find him.

Seeing Glenn's scowl she said, 'Don't say a word. I know what you're thinking.'

'You do not know what I'm thinking.'

'You're thinking that I'm impulsive and because of it we have this setback.'

'Okay, you know what I'm thinking.'

'Well,' hands on hips, 'they know where we are and they're going to follow us to Jebel Mara. Now what?'

'First of all, *I'm* going to Jebel Mara. You're going back to LA. There is no way on earth I am going to let you continue with this.'

'I'll try to curb my impulsiveness.'

'You never can and you know it. Running out there like that.'

'He could have gotten away.'

'He *did* get away!'

'Good Lord, is a referee needed?'

They turned to see Ian in the doorway. 'Air traffic control at Damascus International has asked you to keep it down, they can't hear their pilots.'

He saw how they glared at each other, faces red, practically toe to toe. 'I'm happy to report good news. I've hired two chaps to drive us to Jebel Mara.' He grinned. 'Well, one of you say thank you at least.'

They referred to it simply as the Organization, and François Orléans had been working for the Organization for nearly twenty years. It was a long time as far as this sort of job went, but not long enough for him to remember when it had been called the International Criminal Police Organization – a

148

mouthful, so people began to refer to the Organization by its telegraphic address, 'Interpol', and the name had stuck.

While Interpol was involved in many battles – the world-wide fights against organized crime, drug trafficking, weapons smuggling – François was involved in none of these. A sign on the door to his office read, *Interpol – Oeuvres d'art volées* Stolen works of art.

Because his job was his life, François had never married, and thus, having almost no family except for a distant cousin in Marseilles, was single-mindedly devoted to his work. Tonight he was the burning midnight oil, drinking thick coffee and smoking Gauloises, as he squinted at a nearly impossible to believe report: an entire collection of Louis XV furniture – sofas, chairs, armoires, desks – had been stolen in broad daylight from a house in Paris. He shook his head at the sheer brazenness of the robbery.

And the victim, as chance would have it, was a politician, which was why the case had been given to Orléans, who was more than just a policeman, he was a diplomat. Necessary in his specialty. Cultural works could sometimes spark touchy issues, especially if they involved religion or a national hero.

Orléans possessed additional skills as well. The other agents at Interpol claimed that François' real gift lay in his knowing everything. It wasn't just that he was schooled in art. François' knowledge of the art world was in his blood, bred into him when he was an infant and his mother had been a curator at the Louvre Museum in Paris. Had he wanted to go into any other profession, he couldn't. Not that he had ever wanted to. He loved art and objects of culture. More, he felt protective of them. But his real talent lay in his memory. 'Photographic,' everyone called it. His colleagues even teased him about being better than a computer, because when they asked him about something the search didn't take as long and he was more precise in his reply.

Setting aside the report on the stolen furniture, he leaned back in his creaking chair and massaged his neck. He would assign the case to Reverdy, a bulldog Brit who never gave up. François himself no longer did the 'donkey' work. He was a desk man with the highest seniority one could have without being a member of the General Assembly or the Executive Committee, both of which kept their members high-profile.

François not only wanted a low profile, it was necessary for his *real* work.

Work which Interpol knew nothing about.

His fax suddenly hummed to life, and he went to it with hope. He was expecting a report on Jessica Randolph. The grapevine said she was going after an eleventh-century letter that had recently been donated to a private museum in Melbourne, Australia. Not that Jessica would commit the thievery herself; Randolph was a woman who never dirtied her own pretty little hands. She would contract someone, and François had a good idea who.

But the report wasn't on the sexy art dealer after all.

Britta Buschhorn, reporting the theft of her husband's notes. She had told the authorities in Frankfurt, who had declared the Buschhorn notes a 'national treasure' and turned the case over to the International Police Organization – marking it 'urgent' and 'top priority.'

François set the report down and pulled out a pack of Gauloises. Using a gold lighter, he puffed a new cigarette to life. Then he picked up the report, touched the flame to the corner, watched it blaze, and dropped it into the wastebasket. As Francois Orléans, related to the French royal family that descended through the younger brother of Louis XIV, who had been a member of the Alexandrians, watched the report turn to cinders, the ring on his right hand, with a square ruby and gold filaments, reflected back the flames.

Sixteen

Fire helped him to focus.

Philo concentrated on the heart of the flames, to get to the soul of the heat. Although no one had openly accused him of burning his parents alive, rumors sprang up after the funeral. It wasn't natural the way the young man was so taken with fire, people said. A fraternity brother had jokingly called him 'Philo the Pyro,' in front of others. His charred body was found a week later in the burned wreckage of his car. No one used the nickname again.

Nor did Philo burn anyone again. His was a path of right-eousness, a messianic calling. It wouldn't do to leave a trail of blackened corpses. Philo invented other means of persuasion and removal, and his rise to power was swift.

But fire remained central to his life, as it did to all Alexandrians – the vast membership that was spread around the globe, ordinary people leading secret lives, held together by an oath that was older than Jesus Christ. Philo kept flames burning in his various residences, in fireplaces and pits, on candles and oil, reminders of his holy task and of the day he and Lenore would stand side by side in God's brilliant light.

But here was the most precious flame of all, on the entire planet; among all the candles that burned in churches and temples and synagogues and holy places, this lone flame was the most special, most sacred of all.

And here he came daily to draw sustenance from it, and to speak to the woman he had loved nearly all his life, and whom he would love for all eternity.

'People are afraid of me, my dearest.' His voice gentle, echoing softly off marble and crystal walls. A man standing alone beneath a gemstone sun. 'Why? I am a benevolent man. I am a gentleman. I am the kindest of souls. Yet people fear me.'

He shook his white head, baffled by the machinations of the human psyche. It seemed that the more beneficent he was, the scarier he was.

He was taken back to his last conversation with her, twenty years ago. They were talking about Glenn. He would be eighteen in a few months and Lenore wanted to plan his initiation into the Order.

Before they said goodbye, Philo had expressed his love and devotion to her, as he always did, and she had said, 'Philo, I love you as a brother and a friend. But John has my heart. I will never cheat on him.'

It was what he adored most about her. The sacrifice she was making, living with a man she did not love, putting up such a brave facade. He had taken her face between her hands and said, 'My brave little actress. Even with me, you put up a front.'

Those were their last precious words together. The phone

call – he couldn't remember whose voice at the other end – to say that Lenore was dead, had been killed, had been hit over the head with a goddamn hammer, and Philo had gone out of his mind with grief, a grief so deep and vast and insupportable that he wanted to curse God, but there was no God to curse.

And then it came to him that Lenore wasn't dead after all. John Masters had lied, to keep her for himself, the funeral a sham. Philo searched the world for her. When he saw a woman on the street who looked like her, he would follow, sick and aching and hollow inside, trying to catch up, but trying not to at the same time because deep down he knew it wasn't her and was afraid to face the truth. He had walked his last mile when he came to a standstill in front of the George V Hotel in Paris and realized that the funeral had been real, Lenore was dead.

He continued to search, this time for meaning, for the purpose of life, along the boulevards of the modern big cities and down the narrow alleys of small ancient towns, in high-rise buildings and in mud hovels, in deserts and on mountaintops. He asked wise men and idiots, anyone who could tell him *why.*

And then one day, when he found himself crushed by a crowd on the banks of the Ganges River – how he got there he couldn't say – Philo, in the midst of half-naked people, himself wearing a suit and tie and long black overcoat, as he walked into the sacred healing waters, filling his thousand-dollar Italian loafers with the mud and grime of India's lifeblood, felt a strange power surge through him, a sudden understanding of things. And it came to him: *Lenore died for a reason.*

And Philo, on the crowded banks of the ancient sacred river, knew that reason.

Before returning home to his wife Sandrine, who would ask no questions, he stopped at the Taj Mahal and was thinking that here was a monument worthy of Lenore, when two red-faced Australians with backpacks arrived, acting drunk and silly. 'Look at it, folks,' one said loudly, his voice violating the serenity of the place, 'Taj Mahal, the greatest erection man has ever made for woman.' And his mate brayed like a donkey.

Philo followed them to their seedy hotel, noted the room number, and returned later that night while they slept off an evening of too much beer. When they stirred from their stupor at two o'clock in the morning, they found themselves tied up: one on the bed, spreadeagled and naked from the waist down, the other sitting up in a chair. 'You disrespected a lady's resting place,' Philo said quietly from the shadows. 'You need a lesson that will remind you in the future to be respectful of ladies' tombs. One of you will be punished, one of you will watch; in this way you will always remember. This is Dr. Banarjee. He is a surgeon. Don't try to talk, or you'll swallow that wad of cotton he put in your mouth. Dr. Banarjee cares not who you are, where you come from, nor why you came to his country to blaspheme. I have paid him one hundred thousand dollars to stem the propagation of a bloodline that disrespects women.'

Through the open shutters music drifted from the courtyard below, the twangy tones of a sitar and a man singing sadly in Hindustani. Sandalwood incense filled the air as the operation was performed with precision and local anesthesia. The young man in the chair got sick and fainted when the first of the three small organs was removed, and he came to as Dr. Banarjee was demonstrating to the young man's friend how to pee through a straw for the rest of his life.

Then Philo went home to build his own monument to the respectful memory of a woman.

He heard a soft cough behind him; the man with the strawberry mark, waiting by the entrance to the chapel. Mr. Rossi was the only other person Philo permitted to step on the hallowed ground.

Once Philo had become aware of his messianic calling, he had decided he needed apostles. But unlike Jesus, whom Philo thought egotistical in requiring twelve, he made do with just three.

But they needed to be drawn from the Alexandrian pool, men who believed most devoutly in the holy cause; they must be unmarried and otherwise unencumbered; intelligent and educated; and they must have impeccable bloodlines. The first man he called descended from an astonishing pedigree – the great Brother Christofle himself, who had accompanied Alaric and the Knights of the Flame to Jerusalem. Although Christofle never married the mother of his son – in fact, it was believed Christofle was unaware he had sired a son – the fact that Cunegonde was herself an Alexandrian made the lineage

153

legitimate. (Rossi owned the letters written by Cunegonde as proof, letters to Christofle, telling him she had borne him a child. It was suspected that Christofle never received the letters, as they had remained in Cunegonde's family until they came into Rossi's possession.) In honor of their illustrious ancestor, all firstborn males in Rossi's family had been named Christopher. When Philo called, Christopher Rossi had left his lucrative medical practice and taken up Philo's cause. So strong was his belief in the Alexandrian mission, and in Philo, that he would willingly die for both.

The second man Philo found in Nairobi, Kenya – Peter Mbutu, in whose veins flowed the blood of ancient Ethiopian kings. He resigned from his position as Minister of Wildlife and Natural Resources and joined Philo in his holy cause.

The third, recruited from an old Russian bloodline, turned out to be a disappointment, as he rapidly gained ideas above himself, deciding it was Philo who should serve *him*. Philo demoted the man by arranging for his private business jet to crash into the side of a Hawaiian volcano.

To Mr. Rossi, who had politely interrupted Philo's visit to Lenore, Philo raised a questioning eyebrow.

'Your phone call.' Rossi held out the telephone. The gesture was by no means subservient or obsequious. Rossi was arrogant and vain, because he descended from the great Christofle, who had helped to reunite the Alexandrians. Philo admired Rossi's utter conceit and conviction that he was better than all people on earth – with the exception of the master he served, of course.

The call Philo had been waiting for: the man with the bombs.

A brief discussion. 'How quickly can you have the apparatus in place?'

'They are custom built and the mechanisms are delicate. You said timing on the detonation was crucial. Give us a week.'

A week. Philo would be in possession of the Star of Babylon by then, if Glenn Masters and Candice Armstrong did their jobs.

Handing the cell phone back, he dismissed Rossi and returned to Lenore.

Four centuries ago an emperor lost his beloved empress to childbirth, and so overpowered by grief was he, he decided she must lie in the finest sepulcher ever. The Taj Mahal, its domes and arches and spires of white marble and perfect symmetry mirrored in the reflecting pool with the deep blue sky above. Philo had thought: *this* was a monument worthy of Lenore.

It took twenty-two years and twenty thousand men to build the Taj Mahal. Philo's monument, a crystal chapel of precious metals and stones in a private park outside of Houston, Texas, patrolled by guards behind a high fence, took three years and a hundred men. While the creation of this memorial to his beloved did not bring answers, it had brought solace. Here he would come to nourish his soul. There would be no tourists allowed here. No one profaning Lenore's blessed memory by snapping pictures or making lewd and disrespectful comments. This sanctuary was for Philo alone. Not even John Masters knew of it, nor his son. They could visit the crude grave in the public cemetery and delude themselves that they were paying homage to wife and mother. But only Philo honored Lenore in the way she deserved.

Not even Sandrine had known about the chapel.

The wife had been for appearances, to keep other women away, to allow Philo to focus on his mission. Perhaps as the Magdalene had been for Jesus. After recovering from the tragedy of losing his parents and his family home being burned to the ground, Philo, recognizing his sacred calling in the world, had decided he needed a spouse. He had searched for and found her: Sandrine Smith, a vision in white ermines and pink diamonds, pleasant but cold at heart, attractive, a social climber. After a respectable courtship that involved expensive dinners, theater, the opera, rodeos, Texas barbecues, and occasions at the Governor's mansion and the White House, he prepared himself to outline his plans as clearly as possible to leave no doubt. 'Sandrine Smith,' he planned to say, 'I want you for my wife. I can never love you for my heart belongs to another, but I will respect you and protect you, I will always be there for you. You will have my money, my name, and my social standing. And I will give you children. You will enjoy a rich and happy life with me.'

On the evening of the proposal, before Philo could speak, Sandrine had said, 'Philo, I think you are going to ask me to marry you. I will tell you now that my answer is yes. But I do not love you and never will. I will honor you and give you children. But beyond that I am not interested in bedroom matters and expect separate sleeping arrangements. As to your needs, I ask only that you be discreet and never humiliate or embarrass me.'

It was a match, Houston social wags declared, made in heaven.

The marriage had worked as both intended, and when Sandrine was diagnosed with cancer Philo saw it as a sign that the final days had begun. Therefore, when he took her out of the hospital, saying he would take care of her at home, and the doctors explained about the chemotherapy, its dosage and administration, he withheld it, injecting Sandrine with plain water and administering sugar pills. It was for her own good. Once Lenore was back in his life, Sandrine would have no place in it.

On the day the crystal chapel was completed, seventeen years ago, one year before he found and married Sandrine, on that pivotal day Philo had sent the workers away, sent his assistants and bodyguards away, and had stood humbly and alone beneath the glittering transparent dome. He lit the eternal flame, and as it danced in the golden bowl, swayed and quivered, casting sparkles and shadows on the marble altars and pillars, it had drawn Philo's gaze into its hot yellow heart. He saw the soul of the flame burn and glow. He felt its heat, smelled the fragrant oil that fed its fire. And a voice spoke to him: *'The dead are not dead. How could you have forgotten?'*

Philo had cried out on that day seventeen years ago, his voice echoing up to the glass and gold ceiling. His mother's voice, reminding him that life after death was a cornerstone of the Alexandrian faith.

He had fallen to his knees, oblivious of sharp pains shooting through his legs, the marble floor so cold and hard. He had shivered. Looked up at the blazing sun through the glass ceiling, his eyes stinging with tears. How could he have forgotten that he would be reunited with Lenore one day?

But *when*? cried his anguished heart. Philo was fifty years old. Was he to live another forty years in this lonely torment?

He had thrown himself forward, stretching his arms out on the polished marble, cruciform like a priest taking vows, and wept until the floor swam with his tears.

Lenore, Lenore. Life empty and pointless without her on this earth.

And then the fragment of a tragic poem drifted into his mind, like a ghost whispering with misty breath, taunting and mocking:

'Tell this soul with sorrow laden if, within the distant
   Aidenn,
It shall clasp a sainted maiden whom the angels name
   Lenore –
Clasp a rare and radiant maiden whom the angels
   name Lenore.'
Quoth the raven, 'Nevermore.'

No! cried Philo's tortured soul. She is *not* nevermore!

But how, but how? Pounding the marble with fists that began to bleed. And then: '*Do not cry when loved ones die, for they will be with you again. They walk in the clouds until the day they walk again on earth, when Grandfather Creator joins his children.*' A chorus singing in his brain, the Topaa Indians of Southern California, extinct now but their beliefs saved and protected in Philo's personal archives.

Louder grew the chorus in his head: '*It is written in the book of Daniel that those who sleep in the dust of the earth will awake to eternal life.*'

Sopranos and baritones raised lofty voices in the cranial vault of Philo's brain, a hundred choirs singing: '*And Jesus said, "I am the resurrection and the life. Who believes in me will live, even though he dies."*'

Philo's head pricked and sizzled with fire as the voices collided, clashed, came together in perfect harmony. He cried for them to stop, but louder the voices grew, quoting Confucius: '*Treat the spirits of the dead as if they were present,*' and St. Augustine: '*At the Resurrection, the substance of our bodies will be reunited. Omnipotent God will gather all the particles that have been consumed by fire or by beasts, or dissolved into ashes and dust, and make us bodily again.*'

In his inflamed, tortured head rose the cacophony of voices that he knew were the voices of Alexandrians calling to him down through the ages, shouting to him from the Other Side, as Bathsheba Thibodeau had once shouted at the dead; Alexandrians named Marcus and Julia, Theodoric and Guillem, the Count of Toulouse, the Baron of Rosslyn, Egill the Dane, Mary MacLeod, Andri de Chartres, Charles Brynmorgan, reciting for him the great collected works of the secret society, reminding him what he should believe.

'Stop!' he shouted, covering his ears.

The din had ended. But in the silence, another voice, that of a poet named Yeats, reciting softly: *'How many loved your moments of glad grace,/And loved your beauty with love false or true,/But one man loved the pilgrim soul in you . . .'*

Philo held his breath. He blinked at the marble beneath his face. The words echoing and then fading in his mind: *Her pilgrim soul . . .*

And it came to him. Just like that. As if the sunbeams in the chapel had cut a fine incision into his skull, piercing through bone to the gray matter, and then to the seat of his consciousness. He had known all along why Lenore had had to die – so that he might be free to pursue his holy task on earth. But what he had forgotten was that Lenore was waiting to come back to him.

Philo had sat up then, that day seventeen years ago, brain still on fire but quiet now, and cooling down, and he had looked into sunbeams and seen a question written there: *why did he have to wait?*

Rising to his feet, he had felt new energy tremble along his nerves and sinews and muscles, his skin and hair alive as if reborn into a second resurrection.

He knew why Lenore had died. To set him on this new path. He also knew what he must do. *How* he must do it he learned exactly fourteen hours later between the covers of a three-hundred-year-old book. *The Prophecies of Nostradamus*, century 7, quatrain 83.

And now, seventeen years later, after his single-minded pursuit of a solitary goal, with the Star of Babylon soon to be his, and the bomb broker setting his pyrotechnic magic in place, Philo's glorious destiny, and the prophecy of a Renaissance astrologer, were about to be witnessed by the world.

Seventeen

Glenn debated whether to tell Candice what he had just read in his mother's journal.

Dawn was breaking over the vast Syrian plateau, nothing for miles around. Candice was asleep in the back seat of the tan Pontiac. The lead car, a Toyota Landcruiser, had broken down and the two men hired in Palmyra were attempting to fix it while Ian Hawthorne watched, smoking and chatting with them in Arabic.

They had made a hasty exit from Palmyra under the cover of night, making sure this time that they weren't followed. With the hired men driving the two vehicles, Glenn and Candice and Ian had caught some badly needed shut-eye, to be wakened when they came to a stop at the side of the road. Ian had gotten out to stretch his legs and have a cigarette, while Glenn, moving to the front seat of the Pontiac, had opened his mother's journal. What he read there had shocked him.

Candice's eyes fluttered open. She stared up at the ceiling of the car where torn lining drooped. Then she rolled her head and squinted at Glenn. 'Where are we?'

God. He had wondered, and now he knew. That voice – honey-dipped during the day, but even huskier, more seductive, when she first woke up. 'The Toyota broke down.' He pointed through the windshield.

She sat up and peered out. Daybreak revealed desolation from horizon to horizon. Luckily a nearby formation of twisted boulders provided privacy to answer the call of nature. When Candice returned, Glenn handed her a bottle of water, cheese, and bread.

She saw shadows around his eyes. Had he gotten any sleep? Then she noticed the journal in his lap. He had found something. Something not good.

'There are things in here that are bringing back memories,' he said as she settled in the back seat, legs curled under her as she ate ravenously. 'Things I forgot long ago, or probably made myself forget. I think,' he said, the words difficult to speak, 'my parents belonged to a secret society called the Alexandrians.'

The bread stopped at her lips. 'Secret society? You mean like the Masons or the Rosicrucians?'

'I recall a story my mother told me about the Great Library at Alexandria, and a secret priesthood that escaped the burning in the fourth century. In the eleventh century they were Crusaders who called themselves the Knights of the Flame. I thought it was a fairy tale, but now I think it was real. My parents were members.' He looked at his ring, the ruby and gold. 'That's what this signifies. Membership in the secret society.'

'What is the purpose of this society?'

'I don't know. Mother wrote in her journal that my father had forbidden her to tell me about it. She was to wait until I was eighteen. But she died before my birthday.'

'Does it have something to do with the Luminance?'

He stared at her. The light he had seen when he fell from a rock face and thought he was about to die. Had the vision actually been a *memory*? Had his terrified mind reached back into his childhood and plucked a life-saving recollection? If his mother had described the Luminance to him, that was what he had seen, and what he had been trying to recreate with paints on canvas.

'The Society has a purpose. It isn't just a social group, it is supposed to *do* something. I just don't know what.' He shook his head. The answers would come in time. 'It's this part that worries me.'

He had decided to tell her, let her know how truly dangerous their situation was, hoping it would convince her to go back to Los Angeles.

'"Philo frightens me,"' Glenn read out loud. '"I sense a growing mania. Sandrine seems not to be aware of it, or perhaps she chooses to ignore it. Where will it lead? There are things I suspect he has done. I am afraid to speak of them. I cannot tell the police, for that would mean exposing the Society. And I cannot tell John because Philo is a forbidden subject between us. Can I take my fears to other members? But everyone seems to worship Philo. Mildred Stillwater, so obviously in love with him, giving up her life to live in his shadow. So I must keep these thoughts to myself. I hope that after Glenn is initiated into the Order, together we can do something about Philo, for I am convinced now that Philo plans to subvert the Luminance to his own evil end.'"

Glenn fell silent. If Philo's mania was growing then, two decades ago, what was the extent of it *now*? 'I did some digging into Philo's background. His parents died in a mysterious fire. There were rumors afterward, but nothing proven.'

'They think Philo did it? His own parents?' Candice shivered. 'But if he's going to cause mass destruction, what does he need the Baskov tablets for?' And once again the crazy thought went through her mind that the Star of Babylon was not an ancient thing but a modern thing, a machine of unthinkable, terrible power. 'What about the reference to Nostradamus in your father's letter? Were you able to find that quatrain?'

He shook his head. 'Every reference I found said century seven has only ever had forty-two stanzas.'

'Did your father maybe write the wrong chapter number?'

'I thought of that. But every number eighty-three in the other nine chapters make no sense. Nostradamus is a dead end.'

Glenn thought of the argument he had heard in the middle of the night twenty years ago, one man threatening another. Mrs. Quiroz saying his father was pushed down the stairs. Had Philo come back to carry out that twenty-year-old threat? But why now?

Because his father had found the Star of Babylon.

Glenn squinted toward the west, the direction from which they had come, and wondered if Philo's henchmen were already on their way, right now, speeding down the highway, coming to get them. He looked to the east. Or had Philo already figured out where the Star of Babylon was, and were he and his henchmen already there? I've faced criminals before, Glenn thought, six homeboys in an alley, but what if Philo has brought twenty, a hundred men? What then?

He looked at Candice, recalling how he had thought in Palmyra that he could paint her by moonlight. He wondered how a man could go from never having drawn a line in his life to picking up paint and brushes and painting his soul on canvas. Trying to capture the Luminance. Now wanting to capture another luminance, Candice Armstrong.

161

'So you understand why you have to go back,' he said. 'There's no predicting what Philo will do when I catch up with him.'

'And let you face it alone?' She got out of the car, stretched in the dawn breeze. Go back to Los Angeles. To home and security, to Huffy and the cozy cabin in the mountains. To a plum job in San Francisco – if Reed would forgive her – and out of the path of a man described as a maniac and planning great destruction. Candice wanted more than anything to go back. 'I'm staying,' she said.

He was not surprised. Glenn was infuriated with her, yet also felt grudging admiration. She certainly was no coward. He couldn't help being impressed. No pushover, this woman. A fighter. The LAPD could use her. That was why his father had asked for her. If anyone could find the Star of Babylon, it would be Candice Armstrong.

'Yallah!'

They turned to see Ian waving cheerily. The Toyota had been fixed.

But when their driver returned to the Pontiac, he was scowling. He pointed to the eastern horizon, where, in the distance, a great storm was sweeping majestically across the desert, lightning flickering through the cloud masses, thunder rumbling. 'That is not a good sign.'

As they resumed their race along the deserted highway, the two expert drivers zipping around potholes until they arrived at the end of the asphalt and handled the gravel and dirt track with skill, Candice retreated into her thoughts. Once they had found the tablets, Glenn was going to take them to the Syrian government. She had hoped she would be in possession of them long enough for her to translate them. But now the Duchesne key was gone. Whatever was written on the tablets would remain a mystery.

Hawaiian Shirt, standing among the ruins, looking right at her.

In retrospect, such an obvious lure. She should have quietly told Glenn, they could have snuck out of the room – locking it – and gone in search of the man, grabbing him, getting answers out of him. Instead she had barged out like an angry rhino.

Where did this impulsiveness come from? A friend had once

suggested that she subconsciously sabotaged her own efforts at success. The Faircloth incident, for example. *Could* she have handled his duplicity better, quietly, through channels, so that there was no backlash against her? But why would a person purposely, if subconsciously, sabotage her own efforts?

Because the fear of failure was greater than the hope of success.

Candice saw fields of wild flowers whiz by, the march of majestic clouds across a sky that went on for ever, and she saw herself in this unforgiving desert light clearer than she ever had before: since she could never top her mother's achievement, she was afraid to try.

She closed her eyes. Please, God, let the tablets be out here. Let me find them and bring them back and fulfill my promise to a dying man. Let me be successful in this one endeavor.

Glenn thought she had gone to sleep, her head resting on the back of the seat, eyes closed. He was not pleased with this turn of events. In Palmyra he had had a chance to get Candice to return to California, the police escorting her onto the plane. But then Ian had materialized in the doorway, announcing good news. 'I've hired two chaps to drive us to Jebel Mara. Well, one of you say thank you at least.'

Gratitude was the last thing Glenn had felt. He had had no choice but to take Candice along. She would have gone with Ian, and it was safer for the three of them to travel together. And now here he was, after a hasty escape from Palmyra, furtively and under darkness, trying not to think of the gun he still carried – Ian's, which he refused to give back – and that it had nudged him one step closer to a dreaded, inevitable act of violence.

They had left all semblance of highway now and bounced along a desert track. They encountered no people – no Bedouins, tourists, soldiers, brigands, or wanderers – only gazelles, jackals and hares, and immense flocks of migratory birds that flew up out of the scrubby grass. As they continued eastward, leaving civilization far behind, a sense of isolation and loneliness came over the small group, and they began to realize how vulnerable they really were, how dependent upon telephones and gasoline and modern gadgets. What if both cars broke down, or they ran out of gas? What if the battery in Ian's satellite phone ran down? Each tried to imagine what it had been like for Baskov out there, eighty years ago.

When they entered a flat gravel plain interrupted by upthrusts of tortured rock, queer geological formations, as if some great drama involving rock and lava had taken place here millions of years ago, everyone kept a sharp lookout, for they had entered the area indicated by Sheikh Abdu.

At noon they found the first landmark – an unexpected collection of cliffs and jagged mountains, standing up on the plateau as if placed by a giant's hand. The sight was sudden and awe-inspiring. The vehicles halted and everyone got out.

As they scanned the rocky spine through binoculars, Candice wondering if it was her imagination or did the wind sound lonelier out here, Glenn said, 'That has to be Jebel Mara – it's just as Sheikh Abdu described it. But it doesn't conform to Baskov's map.'

They climbed back into the cars and drove until they came to the base of the great rock massif, which rose a thousand feet and stretched, like the spine of a dinosaur, in each direction as far as the eye could see.

They looked around in silence, thinking they might as well be on the moon, it was all so stark and barren. Here and there a meager rain pool; here and there a struggling tuft of vegetation. But otherwise a harsh and inhospitable wilderness.

They tried positioning themselves according to Baskov's map again but to no avail. None of his drawings or symbols conformed to the topography around them.

Southward, a dramatic watercourse, dry at the moment, was carved into the limestone plateau and ended at the rock massif.

'It doesn't make sense,' Glenn said, using binoculars to follow the wadi to the base of the mountain. 'The water comes from the south, but it has nowhere to go.'

They searched the south face of the towering escarpment and could not fathom the mystery of where flood waters emptied from the wadi.

One of the drivers found the place, shouting, 'Yallah!' to bring the others running.

A narrow defile in the rock, so inconspicuous it had to be

viewed from a precise angle to be seen. The crevasse was too narrow for the vehicles so they decided to go in on foot. But when the two drivers held back, protesting, Ian said, 'They won't go in there. They say it is haunted. Bad magic. They're afraid of this place.'

'Tell them to set up camp then,' Glenn said.

The threesome plunged into the enormous fissure, tramping over cool sand that was covered with the tracks of scorpions and snakes. The darkness closed behind them, cutting off the light so that they followed the twisting and meandering tunnel completely blind. Glenn had taken the lead, feeling his way along the cool walls. 'Watch your head here,' he said, and his voice echoed up to the invisible ceiling. They stopped now and then to listen, and Candice felt the back of her neck prickle. She imagined dens of snakes, hordes of tarantulas.

'I hope this leads somewhere,' Ian said in the darkness, bringing up the rear and banging his head after Glenn's warning. 'Wouldn't want to get buried alive.'

And then: up ahead – light.

'Good God!' Ian blurted when they emerged into full sunshine.

They stood in dumbfounded silence, eyes wide and unblinking. The mountain was hollow and open to the sky, forming a valley that stretched for miles, with crags and tors rising on either side. This was where the ancient wadi had emptied its flood waters, through the narrow defile, cut and carved by millennia of raging waters, rushing through the mountain to sculpt this incredible hidden valley.

But it was no ordinary valley. The sandy floor was cobblestoned in places, with patches of ancient pavement. Littered about were pieces of columns that had toppled long ago. Crumbled arches stood over what had once been a wide avenue. And on either side, carved into the cliffs, gaping openings that could only have been windows and doors. An eerie wind whistled down the valley, carrying fine silt, blowing hot and cold, and moaning like unhappy ghosts. The intruders were unable to speak.

They had found a lost city.

Eighteen

'It's like a smaller version of Petra,' Ian said. 'Definitely Nabataean.'

'I have never heard of this place,' Candice said, awe in her voice.

'Wait a minute,' said Ian, snapping his fingers. 'I know what this is. Of course! Jebel Mara wouldn't be its historic name. Jebel Mara is Arabic for Bitter Mountain, a nickname no doubt given to this place long after the city was abandoned and legends of haunting and bad magic became attached to it. This is Daedana, a crossroads in ancient times! Caravans from Babylon passed through here, then to Palmyra, and from there to the Mediterranean.'

'A city of cliff-dwellers,' Glenn said, reminded of the southwest pueblos of Arizona and New Mexico. The entire settlement had been carved out of living rock, stairways cut into the cliffs leading to ledges that were the thresholds of houses that had been scooped out of the mountain.

The three climbed up and shone flashlights into openings to find empty square chambers devoid of murals or carvings. They read the graffiti of centuries – *C'est moi, Philippe Agoustin. 1702.*

'Think we'll find Baskov's autograph in here?' Ian asked. No one answered as they continued their sweep of the ghost town, exploring structures that had once been stables, eating establishments, shrines to unknown gods, even a multi-tiered amphitheater carved into the mountainside. When they came to the end, Glenn and Candice understood why they had not heard of this place. Daedana had been scavenged and picked clean long ago so that there was nothing of value here, not even to archaeologists. And no one lived here, because of the legends of hauntings and curses.

Where was the Star of Babylon?

Somewhere over the plateau, a desert storm raged. By the

166

time a rumbling sound rolled over the hidden valley, causing the intruders to look up at the blue sky and wonder why they were hearing thunder, Glenn was puzzling over another mystery. 'Where does the water go?' he asked again, picturing the dry wadi that ended at the narrow defile.

Retracing their steps back through the crevasse, realizing that this had been the main route into the city, they emerged to squint southward down the wadi, shading their eyes in the noon glare. This time they spotted what they had not seen before – a high limestone ridge forming a natural basin that caught rainwater. Long ago, humans had extended it to create a dam across the wadi, with artificial channels to funnel off the floodwaters and carry them away from the entrance to the city and around the mountain. Tramping over the sand, they found evidence of man-made sluices, pipes, conduits.

'Look here,' Glenn said, squatting to brush debris from a stone runnel leading to the perimeter of Daedana. 'They created catchment channels that fed storage cisterns cut into the rock over there. They would have had flooding in winter, drought in summer, so they practiced a form of water conservation.'

Candice was walking away back toward the defile. 'Where are you going?' Glenn said.

'To look for the Star of Babylon. There's plenty of daylight yet.'

'First we need to set up a secure camp, and then work out a watch schedule. We'll take turns standing guard.'

She stood her ground, hands on her hips, dark hair flying free from its clip to dance in the desert wind.

'The Star of Babylon isn't going anywhere,' Glenn said in exasperation, admiring her stubbornness, but also annoyed. There was that power again, the ability to manipulate his emotions. He wondered if she was aware of it. 'And unless you want Hawaiian Shirt to visit you in your tent tonight—'

'Yes, you're right,' she said at last.

They selected a hard flat spot of high ground – a necessary precaution in a region prone to violent flash floods – and at the base of a defensible escarpment. Anyone coming to visit had to approach from the west, a 180-degree view for those in the camp, giving them time to prepare.

As the day retreated, the hired men erected tents for the

three Westerners – they themselves would sleep in the vehicles. A campfire roared to life, food was produced, coffee set to brew. There was little talk, and afterward the two Syrians, Ian, and Glenn divided up the night to take turns sitting watch. Although Candice insisted on taking a turn, the four men voted her down. Glenn kept the gun with him at all times.

In the west, the setting sun shot rays of red and gold through storm clouds, while the east flashed with sheet lightning. Distant thunder grumbled and, overhead, tatters of gray cloud raced before the evening wind as night deepened. Soon rain began to fall, lightly, refreshingly. It didn't last long, and the gentle squall moved on. The moon rose in a breathtakingly clear sky, and a cool wind fanned the steppe, drying grasses and flowers while Candice and her companions slept and dreamed.

Dawn broke radiant and flawless over the silent wilderness. Fleecy white clouds dotted the blue sky, a solitary lark flew and sang over the encampment. Nothing out of the ordinary had happened during the night. Each man sitting watch had heard silence and seen darkness. No vehicles coming from the direction of Palmyra.

After coffee and bread, they returned to the deserted city.

Hearing more thunder in the distance, the sound muffled in the hidden valley, Glenn and Candice and Ian walked down the main avenue, scanning the facades of dwellings that had once housed merchants, artists, travelers, soldiers, prostitutes, and politicians. Though they knew the city was deserted, they had the eerie feeling of being watched from the dark doorways and gaping windows.

'Why didn't Duchesne or Baskov mention finding a lost city?' Candice wondered out loud.

'So that no one could come after the tablets,' Ian said. 'They both intended to return.'

They had walked the length of the valley, past the main square, where columns still stood, around a fountain filled with dust, and beyond the amphitheater, when they found it.

The only facade along the entire length of the street that had rubble piled at its entrance. And, crudely etched into the rock face: a five-pointed star.

They climbed the stone stairway to the ledge and frowned at the wall of rocks and debris. Up and down the street doorways gaped like giant black mouths. But this doorway had been filled in. Baskov re-burying his find?

They got to work clearing the rubble, hurriedly, aware of time running out. The two hired men had been instructed to stand guard at the entrance of the defile, and to shout an alarm should anyone come driving up.

Candice's heart raced as she tore at the stones. Now they would have all the answers: what the Star of Babylon was, why Philo Thibodeau would kill to get it, what Professor Masters meant by 'a great devastation.'

The last rock fell away and there was a brief rush of musty air, the sound of gravel falling on the other side, echoing in emptiness.

They had broken through.

The opening to the house looked like the opening to a miniature gold mine. Broken, mismatched columns had been placed long ago to shore up the stone door frame.

'Probably Baskov's work,' Glenn surmised. 'Had his men drag pieces of pillar over to keep the lintel up. It's cracked.'

'It doesn't look too stable,' Ian observed.

'This is odd,' Candice said, running her fingers around the edges of Baskov's opening.

'Bricks,' said Glenn. 'Did we see any in the other doorways?'

'No . . .' The ancient doorway had clearly been bricked up long ago, the brick not contiguous with the stone around the door. Duchesne and Baskov had created a hole wide enough for a person to crawl through.

Ian handed Candice the flashlight and said, 'The honor is yours, my dear. After all, you are the discoverer.'

She took the flashlight, looked at it in her hand, then turned and offered it to Glenn. 'Your father left the Star of Babylon to you.'

Glenn took the flashlight and, positioning himself in front of the small opening, focused the beam inside.

'What do you see?' Ian said with excitement, thinking of Howard Carter, who had made the famous pronouncement: 'I see wonderful things.'

But Glenn said, 'Darkness.'

They worked on the ancient doorway, knocking down bricks that might have stood there for two thousand years. Candice

169

helped, straining with effort, her face getting smeared with dust, perspiration sprouting on her forehead. The sun was overhead by the time they were able to step inside.

The chamber was small and appeared to be the only room in the dwelling.

Ian said, 'This must have been an apartment house of some kind. People living in single-room habitats.'

'Do you see any tablets?' Candice said.

The air smelled musty, fusty – *old*. And the three golden circles created by the flashlight beams exposed only bits and pieces of clay that *might* have come from crumbled tablets. However, fragments bearing what appeared to be practice writing, or cuneiform with errors, were scattered about, indicating that records had at least been written here. But the main stash, from which they believed Duchesne's stone and the Baskov fragment came, was not in evidence.

'Here's one!' Ian shouted in triumph, and dust sifted down from the ceiling. 'Thank God Baskov missed one.'

Candice was instantly at his side, shining her light on the small square lump of hardened clay and she saw at once that it was covered with the wedge-shaped symbols of Duchesne's coded alphabet. Retrieving the soft hand broom from her belt, she kneeled and gently brushed sand from the face of the tablet, her heart racing. 'I need to take a picture. But I need something for scale,' she said, and Ian offered his wristwatch. As Candice laid the watch alongside the tablet, she accidentally touched it, and in an instant, before her startled eyes, the tablet disintegrated.

'Good Lord,' said Ian. 'How on earth did that happen?'

Candice thought she would cry. She hadn't even gotten a snapshot of the writing, and now it was reduced to useless powder.

And then Glenn, suddenly, softly: 'Okay, everyone. Don't move.' A policeman at a crime scene.

'What is it?'

They followed the line of his flashlight beam, and when they saw what it illuminated on the floor their eyes widened in astonishment.

A human skeleton.

'Is this a tomb?' Candice said in bafflement.

170

'Something about this doesn't make sense,' Ian said as he swept his light over the walls. 'Hello, what's that?'

Something etched into the wall.

Candice took a closer look. 'It looks like Hebrew or Aramaic. Ian, can you make this out?'

He translated haltingly: 'Babylon . . . is . . . here.' Tracing it with his fingertip. '*Of* Babylon. Yes, that's it. Something of Babylon . . . is here.'

'What's that first word? Does it say "star"?'

'I can't make out the first word. The symbols don't—' He turned to Candice. 'Do you have that Hebrew source book with you?'

'It's in my knapsack in the trunk of the Pontiac. Be back in a minute!' And she was off before Glenn could caution her to be careful.

When she returned with the backpack slung over her shoulder, she was already thumbing through Mildred Stillwater's book. 'I can't find it,' she said when she stepped inside the chamber. 'That first word isn't listed.'

'But surely it says "star,"' Ian insisted. 'What else could come before "of Babylon"?'

Bringing her flashlight up to the wall again, she studied the markings, and said, 'It isn't Hebrew, Ian. This first word is Persian. And it *is* star.'

'"The Star of Babylon is here"!' Ian said in triumph. He looked around. 'But where? I don't see a star. D'you suppose Baskov took it with him?'

Glenn spoke up. 'There is a notch in front of "star." Does it have any significance?'

Ian said dismissively, 'A flaw in the wall.'

But Candice, with a magnifying glass, said, 'Glenn, you're right. This notch was etched with the words. It's a sign that signifies this is a proper name. I overlooked it! That's why the first word is Persian. Because it isn't a word, it's a name! *Esther*.' She turned wide eyes to her companions. 'Persian for star.'

'"Esther of Babylon is here,"' Ian said. 'Baskov got the translation wrong. The Star of Babylon isn't an object or a symbol or a place – it's a *person*. '

'And this is her tomb,' Ian said.

171

The three stood silent, looking at the skeleton, until Glenn said, 'I don't think this is a tomb.'

'What else could it be?'

'I believe we are standing in a house after all.' He swept his flashlight beam around. 'All this broken pottery. Jugs and pots.'

'For the afterlife,' Ian said. 'They were merely symbolic. Not intended for actual use.'

'Would a tomb have a cooking hearth?'

'Of course! Tombs held all sorts of symbolic objects.'

But Glenn pointed out that the hearth was blackened, as if it had been used, not just placed there symbolically for the deceased. 'And here.' He ran his light over the walls to illuminate the bricked-in window.

'You might be right,' Candice said, thinking of the other facades along this avenue – each with a doorway and a gaping window – and wondering why whoever had buried Esther here had converted her home into a tomb.

'We don't even know how old these bones are,' Glenn said. 'She might have only been here a few hundred years.'

That was when Ian picked up the lamp.

'Astonishing,' he said. 'This is Greek manufacture!' He spoke with excitement. 'As you know, lamps started out as saucers, with a wick swimming in the oil. Gradually, pottery lamps came to be made with enclosed bodies. The Greeks produced an entirely closed lamp which prevented the oil from spilling – like this one. Another of their—'

'Can you give us a date?' Glenn interrupted impatiently.

'The earliest are dated to the fifth century BCE and found predominantly in Greece and Southern Italy. That this lamp traveled so far indicates contact with other nations was being established.'

Candice's eyebrows arched. 'Are you saying that lamp is twenty-five hundred years old?'

'A century either way, yes. Without a doubt.'

Glenn said, 'But that doesn't mean this lamp was buried here then. It could have been used for centuries afterward.'

'Doubtful,' said Ian. 'First of all, like all household pottery, lamps broke easily. The best preserved ones we have came from tombs, where, of course, they were not used. But for a clay lamp to last for centuries? Not likely. Besides, during the Hellenistic period, potters began adding geometrical designs, and also made the lamps more durable. People, like people everywhere, would have tossed out the old for the new, more fashionable model.'

'But we don't know this for a fact,' said Glenn Masters, the homicide detective. 'We can't go jumping to conclusions.'

'The lamp was found with cuneiform tablets,' Candice interjected, 'and we know that cuneiform began to be replaced by the Aramaic script during the Persian period, somewhere around the seventh century. It's safe to assume for now that this house, or whatever it is, was sealed some time in that period. That would coincide with the Babylonian Captivity, one of your father's pet subjects.' She looked at Glenn. 'Am I right?'

'My father devoted his life to three periods of the Bible: the Exodus, the reign of Solomon, and the Captivity. You helped him to solve the Solomon question, Dr. Armstrong, which leaves the other two. And since we are quite a distance from the Red Sea . . .' He left his sentence hanging.

'But what did this woman,' Candice said softly, shining her light on what was left of brittle bone and fragile skull, 'have to do with the Babylonian Captivity?'

'And *is* she the Esther,' Ian added, 'referred to by the inscription on the wall?'

As the sun moved across the sky, shadows shifting and moving within the buried chamber, the three intruders looked at one another in silent question. They had discovered the Star of Babylon, but they now faced a bigger mystery: what *was* this place and why had this woman been buried here?

They had to step outside, the chamber becoming close and musty. They inhaled the clean wind sweeping down the valley, filled their lungs with air and sunshine and the sky and life, to throw off the dust and death they had found.

Ian lit a cigarette. 'So is *she* the astronomer's wife mentioned in the Baskov fragment?'

Candice shook her head in bafflement. 'We seem to have two astronomers a thousand years apart. The Professor wondered if the answer to all of this was in the tomb of Nakht. Nakht was an astronomer, but what connection he has with a woman who lived a thousand years later, I don't know.'

Ian ground out his half-smoked cigarette and they returned to the chamber. Candice began taking pictures, laying down a ruler for scale, labeling each object, trying not to disturb anything.

'What I want to know is,' Ian said as he examined a broken lamp, 'why was she buried inside a house? Why not put her in a grave?'

Candice lay the ruler alongside a fragment of pottery with writing on it and said, 'Maybe she died of something contagious and no one wanted to touch the corpse. So they just bricked the house up.' She looked over at Glenn, who was sitting on his heels deep in thought, his eyebrows forming a deep furrow of concentration. 'What is it?' she asked. 'What have you found?'

He pointed to the skeleton's right hand, in which was clasped an iron nail. 'I think if you match the tip of that implement with the scratch marks in the wall, you will find that it is what carved the letters.'

Candice kneeled next to him and stared at the nail still wedged between the skeletal phalanges. 'She must have etched those words just before she died. Maybe she knew she wouldn't be buried in a normal tomb. Maybe others in the settlement had already died the same way and were bricked up where they lay. She didn't want to be forgotten.'

But Glenn was formulating a different theory. He went to the segment of the wall that had once contained a window and ran his flashlight over it. Then he picked up a broken bowl and turned it over in his hands. Finally he said, 'These bowls and jars are not symbolic, because they did at one time contain grain and wine. There is only residue now, which means someone drank the wine and ate the grain.'

'The men who buried her,' Ian said. 'It often happened. Food meant for the deceased was consumed by the grave diggers.'

'Then why the lamps?'

'Symbolic, as I said.'

'They look like they were burned. And for a very long time.'

'What's unusual about that?' Candice said. 'We have established that this was a domicile prior to be being converted into a tomb. Esther used those items before she died.'

Glenn turned his light to the brick window, illuminating what they had not seen before: soot on the bricks. 'The window was ventilation for the fire, as you can see from the blackened traces from the hearth upward. Do you see these sooty bricks?'

'Are you saying that Esther was still alive when this house was bricked up?' Candice looked at the pots and jugs, and suddenly they took on a new, horrible significance. 'But why bury someone alive, and then give them stuff to eat and drink?'

Glenn scowled. 'A punishment maybe.'

'Or a sacrifice?' Candice murmured. She dropped to one knee and, using a camel-hair brush, gently dusted sand away from objects. Sunlight poured over things buried for centuries: brushes, pens, inkpots. 'Was she sealed up in here to write something?' Candice said.

'That doesn't make sense,' Ian observed. 'If someone was forcing her write something, why seal her up? They would never get the tablets.'

'Maybe she wasn't sealed in to *make* her write something,' Glenn offered, 'but to stop her. Maybe Esther was writing something forbidden and this was her punishment, to be bricked up with her forbidden writing.'

The three said nothing for a moment. If Esther had indeed been buried alive, what was her crime? What was she writing that would warrant such an unthinkable punishment? And why were the tablets written in a secret code?

The Professor's letter: *I speak of nothing less than Armageddon* . . .

Candice broke the silence. 'Since the tablets aren't here, we can assume Baskov carried them out, and then fell ill.'

'He would have hidden them,' Ian added. 'And then he drew a map to the hiding place. It all makes sense now. We were using the map in the wrong place.'

As they stepped out of the chamber and into the bright sunlight, Glenn paused one last time to look back at the doorway into the mysterious house carved into a cliff, and he felt something dance around the edge of his consciousness, an annoyingly elusive thought that seemed important yet which he could not grasp. Something about Esther's imprisonment. Something they had overlooked . . .

It came to him when they reached the defile, where he stopped and looked back down the valley littered with ruins. 'You two go on,' he said. 'I want to check something.'

He climbed back up to the entrance of Esther's house and stood there, thinking it was a mistake to come back, because he felt anger starting to boil within him, and sadness and grief, and other emotions that he had managed to keep in a box and which were now starting to break out. Esther's house was like Candice Armstrong, he realized – it had the power to weaken him.

But as he turned to leave, he saw her climbing the rubble-strewn stairs, dark hair shiny in the sunlight.

When she reached the top, he said, 'Where's Hawthorne?'

'He wants to study Baskov's map. What did you come back for?'

'Tell me how cuneiform tablets were made.'

'Well, you take a lump of clay and shape it somewhat like a rounded deck of cards, imprint your stylus into it and then set the clay out in the sun to bake.'

'What would happen if you didn't? What if tablets were just left inside to air dry?'

'They wouldn't last long. The sun is needed to harden the clay. Otherwise they would be too fragile and end up returning to dust.' Her eyes widened. 'The tablet that disintegrated! The one we thought Baskov had overlooked!'

'It had been written on but it had not been sunbaked. That's why Baskov didn't take it. He probably found others just like it and discovered that they disintegrated at a single touch. It bothered me; I couldn't put my finger on it. And then I realized: Esther alone in her tomb, sealed up, knowing she is going to die, but so dedicated to her personal cause that, even in the face of imminent death, *she continued to write*.'

He turned and delivered himself back into the cool darkness of the chamber. 'She didn't try to dig her way out of this house,' he said, policeman in charge of a crime scene, scanning the walls with his flashlight. 'There's no sign of violence, no claw marks, no indication that she did anything other than return to her tablets and continue to commit her words to clay.'

He went to the window, placed his hand on the bricks and tried not to imagine how Esther must have felt to see the layers of brick go up until the sunlight was gone.

Candice joined him, standing close. 'Knowing this,' she said softly, 'you see now that we have to take the tablets back to the United States. The Syrian government might store them away, they might get caught in the same bureaucratic red tape that kept the Dead Sea Scrolls from public eye for decades.'

But Glenn strengthened his resolve. Esther was not his concern. He had come to find a killer.

And then he heard a sound. 'What was that?'

Candice persisted. 'Your father knew what he was talking about. If we find the tablets, and then let them out of our possession, Philo could get hold of them. He's rich enough to bribe government officials.'

'I thought I heard—' She blocked his way. Something outside the entrance, maybe just an animal scavenging, but he should check.

'Glenn, please say you agree with me.'

The cave-in took them by surprise.

A sudden roaring sound. The lintel cracking, collapsing. A deafening rockslide as the roof gave way and the story above Esther's house came crashing down.

And then daylight was gone, plunging Glenn and Candice into total darkness.

Nineteen

They sat up, coughing, barely able to breathe with so much dust filling the air. Glenn turned his flashlight on. 'Are you all right?'

Candice's face was taut with fright. She nodded.

He looked around. The entrance was completely blocked.

'What happened?' Her voice shook.

'The broken lintel gave way.'

'They'll start digging us out, won't they?'

Glenn covered his mouth; the dust was so thick. 'If they can, if Ian can persuade the two men to come into the valley. They'll say this was the bad magic they were afraid of and that we had been warned.'

He tried to budge the rocks but they were jammed in solid. Candice started shouting for help.

'It's no use,' Glenn said. They can't hear us.'

Terror gripped them. Like Esther, they had been buried alive.

Glenn swept his flashlight over the walls, then picked up a stone and began methodically tapping, starting with the bricked-up window.

'What are you looking for?'

'A way out.'

Candice looked at him as if he were crazy. They were trapped in a stone box. All the habitations in the mountain had only one door, one window. There were no openings between the apartments, no basements or attics.

But he kept at it, *tap tap*, hearing only the dull response of solid rock. 'Help me,' he said.

She picked up a stone. 'If there were a way out, wouldn't Esther have used it?'

'Maybe it wasn't a way out back then.'

'What do you mean?'

'See if you can find a hollow spot.'

She began tapping. Listening. Realizing they had little air and that the flashlight batteries wouldn't last for ever. She tapped every inch of the north wall, from the floor to the top, growing frantic now, feeling the chamber close in on her like a tomb.

And then: *tap* – hollow response.

'Step back,' Glenn said and kicked at the wall until he broke through. They felt a rush of stale air. 'This is why Esther didn't escape through here. It's a water conduit. In her day it would have been filled with water.'

It looked narrow. 'Can we fit?' Candice asked.

'It'll be tight.'

They had to go on hands and knees, holding flashlights, Glenn leading the way to brush centuries of gravel from their path. They came to a turn, and another, creeping mole-like into a black void, Candice feeling the mountain all around them, the air thin and rank smelling.

'Where are we?' she asked, terrified they were going to be trapped in the maze. 'I've lost my bearings.'

'We're heading steadily eastward.'

'We are?' It didn't feel that way to her. 'What's east?'

'These tunnels empty somewhere. My guess is at the edge of the escarpment.'

Her hand slipped. She saw that it was wet. 'Glenn? This tunnel isn't dry. There's been water in here. Recently!'

He didn't say anything.

They came to a juncture of three tunnels branching off at different levels. When Glenn reached for the top-most opening, Candice said, 'Shouldn't we be going *down*?'

'We have to go up,' he said.

And she knew why: the lower tunnels would be filled with water.

He climbed up and into the next level, then reached down for her. She clasped his hand and he pulled her up. She said nothing after that, knowing only that their upward climb meant they would come out somewhere on top of the mountain.

'What's that?' she said suddenly. The mountain was starting to shake. 'Earthquake!' Candice cried.

But it wasn't an earthquake. Something much worse. 'Water,' Glenn said. 'And it's heading this way!'

The flash flood had its origins in the craggy cliffs far to the south, where a storm had been raging over the desert. The run-off into narrow ravines and dry wadis had collected into violent torrents, gathering momentum until it rushed through the watercourse that headed straight for the ancient city. There, the swift current funneled off into the man-made conduits that connected to the tunnels honeycombing the mountain.

'I see light!' Glenn said. 'Up ahead. We must be near the end.'

The shaking grew stronger, and an unnatural roar filled the tunnels, like that of a horrific beast chasing them. The air in the tunnel grew dense, Candice's ears popped, trickles of water now ran beneath her.

The flood was right behind them.

When they reached the end of the tunnel, they saw an opening on the eastern side of the mountain, large enough for them to both stand in. It was a sheer drop to the desert far below.

As the roaring grew closer, Glenn quickly assessed the situation. They couldn't go down so they would have to climb up.

There was a ledge a few feet to the right, jutting out and just big enough. 'Hang on!'

He reached out and swung himself over, grasping the rock face and sending gravel raining down. Then he reached for Candice. 'Give me your hand.'

'I can't!'

'You can do it. Hurry!' The vibration in the tunnel grew stronger. The roar was deafening, her feet now swirling in water.

She was frozen, her eyes shut tight. Feeling the wide open space all around, the sheer drop hundreds of feet down. 'I can't!'

'Don't look down. Just take my hand. *Now!*'

She shot her arm out and made contact with Glenn. In one great effort he pulled her across, and she landed against him just as water spewed violently from the tunnel, a geyser shooting straight out and tumbling down in a waterfall to the desert below.

Candice kept her eyes tightly shut as she clung to Glenn, the mountain vibrating as if to shake them off, with pebbles and sand raining down on them and their small rock ledge threatening to give way.

The water subsided and then dwindled. The mountain grew still, but Candice kept shaking. She didn't want to open her eyes, but when she did she saw Glenn's perspiring neck and, immediately behind it, the sandstone wall. Behind her nothing but open space for hundreds of feet down and thousands of miles around and up to the sky.

'You okay?' he said.

She nodded mutely.

'Now we climb.'

He surveyed the wall. Vertical in places, but inclined in others, with cracks and crevices good for handholds and foot placements.

'We'll go up and over. Now listen . . . try to smear if you can.'

'Smear?' she squeaked.

'Place as much surface area of the bottom of your shoe on the rock to get the most hold. Don't tiptoe. Watch where I put my hands. Use the same handholds.'

In order to begin, he had to remove his arm from around her waist, and Candice felt herself begin to fall.

'Hold on!' he shouted and she grabbed a small outcropping of rock.

They began inching upward, one step at a time, Glenn finding handholds, reaching for Candice, placing her hands where his had been. He would have given anything for pitons and rope.

He watched Candice, her hair flying in the wind. She froze at points and had to be coaxed to move up. Her foot slipped and she screamed and grabbed for him; he caught her arm and held her as her knapsack slipped off her shoulder and plunged to the soggy sand far below.

'Try not to chicken-wing!' he shouted, fighting the wind that snatched his words away. 'Your elbows are pointed out and back at a bad angle. Watch me. Keep your elbows like mine.'

She looked past him, horror dawning on her face. 'Oh God.'

'What?' He turned and saw it. The horizon was moving toward them.

'It's a squall. Headed this way!'

They resumed the climb.

The squall drew closer, black clouds rolling with thunder and flashing with fork lightning. The wind increased, threatening to tear the frail humans from the rock face. Candice frantically grabbed for handholds, sending showers of rubble down the slope.

'Don't fight it!' Glenn shouted. 'Don't fight the mountain. Let it help you up.'

She forced herself to stop, to lean her full weight against the rock and acquiesce, even though fear made her want to keep scrambling upward. She rested her cheek on the stony wall and breathed in the dust and age. The wind tried to pluck her free, carry her away, but Candice leaned into the ancient mountain as she might into a lover's embrace, and let the crag hold her. The warmth of the day exuded from the rock and into her skin, an unexpectedly comforting feel. She closed her eyes. Her breathing slowed. These rough, ancient rocks, scoured by wind and time, felt like an old friend now, strong and steady, like the giant oaks that surrounded her cabin in Malibu, comforting solid presences, nothing to be afraid of.

She felt she could go on.

They reached a spot where Glenn saw only smooth rock face. No cracks, no handholds. He couldn't back down because his last foothold had broken away. They were trapped on the windy face of the mountain with a thunder machine spewing lightning and rain racing toward them.

And then: 'I've got one!' Candice cried as she stretched her arm up, grabbed hold, scaled up past Glenn, found sure footing, then reached down for him. She pulled him up, and after that it was as if they had climbed together all their lives, up and over, reaching, hauling, Glenn sometimes leading, sometimes Candice, now with grace in her climb, certainty in her movements, face skyward, as if she saw a treasure up in the reddening clouds that would be awarded to the first to reach the summit.

Finally, at the last step, pulling themselves up to the crest, standing on top of the mountain the squall passed by behind them, spraying them with wind and mist, heading away from Daedana and out onto the plateau.

In front of them, the scarlet sun was making its fiery exit from the world, washing all of nature in red and gold, while black thunder clouds rolled around the sky, their bellies blazing gold.

Candice froze there on the summit, wide eyed, mouth open, face pale and drawn.

'It's okay,' Glenn said, understanding how she felt – he had seen it in novice climbers: the relief of being alive, reeling with the aftershocks of terror. And the panic of being so high up in open space. Many went down the mountain never to climb again. 'Take my hand.'

She didn't move.

'You'll be all right,' he said, thinking of the professor who had challenged her to a race up the Great Pyramid, Candice declining because she knew she would freeze at the top. But there were no helicopters here to lift her off. 'We have to climb down,' Glenn said, taking her hand. 'You'll be all right. I won't let go.'

They found an easy trail down, created two millennia ago by the water engineers of Daedana.

At the camp, the Toyota was gone, and so were the hired men. No sign of Ian, although his duffel was in the passenger seat of the Pontiac. They ran back through the defile, where they saw Ian madly digging at the rubble in front of Esther's house.

'My God,' he said when he saw them. 'You got out!' Blood was streaming down his forehead.

'What happened?'

'I don't know. I was at the camp. The bastards hit me over the head and that's all I remember. When I came to, the Toyota was gone. They took everything – the water, the food, the satellite phone, both your backpacks, my money, travelers' checks. Even,' he said miserably as he held up his wrist, 'my watch. And they took the keys to the Pontiac! We're stranded here. Without any way to get help.'

Twenty

The hired men did not get Candice's backpack. Ian was wrong about that. She had had it with her in Esther's house, dropped it making the climb, and had retrieved it from the boggy desert floor at the base of the cliffs. Glenn's backpack was gone but he was unconcerned. His money, passport, and identification papers had been secured in one of the zippered pockets of his cargo pants. Nor had the drivers made off with the Pontiac keys, as Ian had thought. They were in Candice's backpack; she had absently placed them there after retrieving Mildred Stillwater's book from the locked trunk of the car. Bottled water, bread and dates and cheese, it turned out, were also in the Pontiac.

'Not a total loss then,' Ian said as they raced across the plain toward Wadi Raisa.

His companions said nothing, Glenn at the wheel, Candice in the back seat, her face to the open window, eyes closed to the desert wind. They felt more vulnerable than ever, now that it was just the three of them, easy prey to the looters, bandits, and army deserters who roamed this wasteland close to the Iraqi border. And the threat from the west as well, the two hired drivers no doubt having reported to someone in Palmyra the Americans' whereabouts, and that they had found the Star of Babylon and were closing in on the tablets.

Before leaving Jebel Mara the three had caught sleep in

naps while taking turns sitting watch, Ian insisting on having his gun back, but Glenn holding onto it. During the night wild dogs had caught and ravaged a gazelle, leaving bloody remains too close to the camp for everyone's comfort. As Glenn had slept, while the wild dogs howled in the desert, he had dreamed again about the night twenty years before, after his mother's funeral, when he had been wakened by two men shouting. 'I will kill you!' one had yelled. This time a new piece had been added to the puzzle: the other man had retorted with the word 'blood.' Was it his father who had said it, or Philo Thibodeau?

He looked in the rearview mirror, Candice reflected there. Something was wrong. She had barely spoken since their ordeal on Jebel Mara. Was it fear? She had frozen on the summit, had been in such a grip of terror that it frightened her even now. He had seen it before. He himself had experienced it, after the fall in which he had seen the Luminance. Glenn had wondered if he would have the nerve to climb again, so he had tried it, challenged Mt. Saint Helena and made it to the top.

The plateau grew lighter as the sun climbed, a dry sea of tawny sand that stretched to the ends of the earth. 'There it is,' Glenn said. 'Wadi Raisa.'

'It goes on forever,' Candice observed as they studied the watercourse stretching away from them in bright morning sunlight.

Ian scowled at the deep gorge cut into the limestone plateau. The desert ravine had its beginnings somewhere to the southeast and continued northward where, eventually, it would empty its occasional rain water into the Euphrates River. 'Baskov could have buried those tablets a hundred miles from here,' he said.

Leaving the Pontiac on high ground, and locking it just in case, the three trudged along the sandy floor, scanning the rocky walls.

'Has it occurred to either of you,' Ian said, 'that the tablets might not even have stayed long in their hiding place? I mean, we've got a feverish Russian trying to bury a precious find. What's to stop his men from digging it right back up and selling the tablets on the black market?'

'We would have heard of some of them over the past eighty

184

years,' Glenn said, watching a lone hawk circle overhead. '*Something* would have shown up in museums or private collections.'

'Then how did Baskov convince his chaps to leave the tablets buried?'

'Maybe he just worked some old-fashioned magic. Put a curse on the tablets. Or promised the men more money when he returned.'

'Or he could have killed them.'

Glenn stopped and looked at him. Ian's eyes were hidden behind dark lenses. 'Why would you say that?'

'What surer way to make certain the find stayed untouched? Another sure way would have been to come to this ravine alone and hide the tablets without help and in such a way that they couldn't be found by anyone, not even a mouse.' He squinted down the length of barren, rocky miles before them. 'I have a feeling it's going to be a long, grueling search.'

'Or not,' Candice said. She was pointing at a strange sight: thirty feet above the ground, six rusting gasoline cans piled neatly against the rock face. Faded writing discernible on one of them: *Anglo-Persian Oil Company.*

'That's what British Petroleum was called when it was first formed,' Ian said. 'Those cans are at least eighty years old!'

The jerrycans had been filled with sand to give them ballast against wind and rain. Ian and Glenn managed to pull them away from the rock face, exposing an opening. Candice shone her light inside and saw a metal box.

Making sure no desert creatures inhabited the small space, she reached in and carefully dislodged the box, bringing it out onto the rocky ledge. It was an old tool box, locked and rusted shut.

Glenn produced a Swiss Army knife, and as he started to pry up the lid Ian said, 'They're probably smashed to bits after all this time. And all the handling by Baskov. Sunbaked clay doesn't hold up well.'

But when Glenn lifted the lid, Ian blurted, 'Good God!'

'Baskov packed them in his clothes!' said Candice. 'And look,' she said, delicately picking off a cluster of fibers. 'Remnants of a basket. This must be what Esther stored the tablets in. These are unbelievably well preserved.'

The three stared in awe at the small lumps of clay imprinted with words over two thousand years old, recorded by a woman who had been buried alive for writing them.

Although they had agreed to take turns sitting watch during the night, Glenn had yet to yield his post to Ian. He still didn't want to leave when he heard footsteps coming up the rocky trail to the promontory where he sat looking out over the starlit desert, so he said, 'I can take another hour.' But it wasn't Hawthorne.

Candice, carrying two cups, holding one out. 'Ian made coffee.' She sat next to him on the boulder, holding her own cup, resting her elbows on her knees.

'Did you find anything in the tablets?' he asked.

The Russian theologian had packed the fragile tablets in layers, using a linen shirt, so that Candice was able carefully to lift out the first layer, to find more clay tablets underneath, and beneath them a white silk scarf. Lifting this out, she had received a shock. The bottom layer was no longer clay tablets but pieces of ceramic in varying sizes and shapes, and all were written on in ink – not in the coded alphabet, but in Hebrew!

Had Esther written *two* stories?

'Unfortunately,' she said now, quietly, afraid to make their presence known even though she saw not a single soul in the vast blackness spread around them, 'without the Duchesne key I can't translate the clay tablets. But Ian's studying the ceramic pieces. Maybe they will cast some light on what we have found.'

She tasted the coffee, her eyes on the pitch-black plateau that went on forever. 'How's your knee?'

'My knee?'

She looked at him. 'You said you stopped climbing because you blew out your knee. But you did fine at Jebel Mara.'

'So did you. Better than fine.'

He waited, thinking she might want to talk about her panic on the summit. But she said, 'I noticed back in Los Angeles you didn't carry a weapon when you were on duty,' pointing to the gun in his lap.

'I prefer dialogue to bullets.'

'Does it ever bother you being around the violence?'

Every single day of my life. 'It isn't all car chases and shoot-outs.'

She saw his lips lift in a smile. A fond memory? 'Tell me,' she said, and sipped her coffee.

A taste of the brew first, conceding that while Hawthorne might have his faults he knew how to make a good cup of java, and Glenn said, 'Before I made detective, I worked patrol in the Valley. My partner and I get this call about animals running loose. It's rural, out beyond Chatsworth, and we find this billy goat in the street. We manage to get a leash on it and as we're leading it back to our squad car this pedestrian who's standing there staring at us, says, "Don't you guys use German Shepherds anymore?"'

They laughed together. Then they fell silent.

'What now?' Candice asked.

Glenn knew what she meant. 'We have what Philo wants and he knows where we are.' He looked up at the stars, expecting to see helicopters descending from the sky, men in military fatigues jumping down, brandishing weapons, Thibodeau stepping from a cockpit, calmly holding his hand out for the tablets.

Glenn didn't get it. He had been sure Philo, or at least his agents, would be here. Why hadn't they come for the tablets?

'Maybe he's expecting us to take them to Damascus.'

It was a possibility. But that wasn't going to happen. Not now. Turning the tablets over to the authorities was no longer an option in Glenn's mind. Besides, it had not been a viable plan in the first place. As Candice had said, Philo's wealth opened any locked vaults, persuaded an army of guards. Glenn now felt a personal duty to protect the tablets.

And something else.

The small scar on her neck made him understand something he had not understood before. Philo's man hadn't killed her at her mother's house because that was not Philo's intention. He had needed Candice, her archaeological expertise, to find the tablets. But now that they had been found, she had served her purpose.

She was expendable.

Glenn now had two fragile treasures in his safekeeping.

He sipped the hot, rich coffee. His uneasiness grew. Something wasn't right. Reviewing the past forty-eight hours, he saw now that they had gotten out of Palmyra too easily. Had Philo laid a trap?

187

'Glenn, the secret society your parents belonged to, the Alexandrians. Have you figured out yet what do they do?'

Glenn had brought his mother's emerald-silk journal to the lookout to read by moonlight. 'From what I gather here, it is a religious order of some sort. Beyond that, I don't know.'

'You said she wasn't religious.'

'She wasn't. Not in the traditional sense. My parents never went to church. They never taught me to pray.'

He opened the journal and passed it to Candice. Setting her empty cup on the stony ground, she laid the book on her knees and read.

> There is no death. Our bodies pulsate with the same energy that created worlds, and the First Law of Thermodynamics tells us that energy can neither be created nor destroyed. The total amount of energy available in the universe is constant. Einstein's equation, $E = MC^2$, energy is equal to matter times the square of a constant, proves that energy and matter are interchangeable, which suggests that the quantity of energy and matter in the universe is fixed. Where does the energy of the once-living go? It can't die, so it goes somewhere.

As Glenn drained the last of his coffee he noticed that, while Candice read, she touched a fingertip to the cameo. He followed the pink ribbon around to the back of her neck where, with her hair swept up, he saw how the ribbon was tied. It was delicate and old fashioned, feminine. Candice bit her lower lip as she read. *Kissable lips.*

He stood abruptly, thrusting the gun into the waistband of his pants. 'You'd better get some sleep. You must be tired.'

'I am,' she said, surprised. She had thought Ian's strong coffee would keep her awake. 'But you must be, too.'

He was, suddenly. Aware of heavy eyelids as he stifled a yawn. But he had to stay awake, think of what to do next, how to use the tablets as bait to catch Philo.

The hired men had left them with two sleeping bags, to one of which Candice retired, staying close to the fire in the security of the boulders, and when Ian came up to the lookout, insisting it was his turn to sit watch, Glenn acquiesced, taking the gun with him down to the camp, where he unfurled his sleeping bag on the other side of the fire.

He woke abruptly, the cold night upon him, the desert dark and silent. He saw Ian up on the promontory, looking out over the plain. Leaving the warmth of his sleeping bag, Glenn quietly made his way to the Pontiac. Inside, on the front seat, was the metal box that held Esther's legacy. And then he saw the key in the ignition.

Glancing back at Candice asleep by the fire, Glenn realized there was only one way to protect both her and the tablets.

Philo saw trouble coming before he even got up to give his acceptance speech.

At the back of the banquet room, Ygael Pomeranz was making a scene, while Philo's two men tried to calm him down. Philo would have to intervene himself, and so he cut his speech short.

The five hundred in attendance, only a few of whom were Alexandrians, listened attentively to the man who had just been handed the most prestigious humanitarian award in the state of Texas. They had paid a thousand dollars a plate for the privilege of breathing the same air as philanthropist Philo Thibodeau. They adored him. He had just donated a new wing to St. Jude's Hospital. As they rose to their feet to applaud his modest thank you speech, the women in gowns and men in black tie did not see the gentleman at the back of the room being restrained by hotel security.

Excusing himself from the dais, where politicians and members of the hospital board graciously smiled and clapped, Philo slipped away, motioning to the security men to bring the agitated Ygael to a private back room.

'You give money to hospitals but you steal holy books. You are a whitened sepulcher, Philo!'

Rossi took a step toward him.

'It's all right,' Philo said. 'Please leave us alone. My dear Ygael, to what do I owe this honor?'

Ygael Pomeranz wore a yarmulke and a fringed prayer shawl beneath his black coat. At sixty-eight he was a master of the cabbala and Jewish mysticism. A man of deep faith, he might have been a rabbi had he believed in the existence of God.

'I know what you have been doing, Philo. Don't ask me how I know.'

'I wasn't going to,' Philo said calmly.

'You have been making unauthorized acquisitions. And how? Stealing! Dealing with smugglers, grave robbers, thieves. Using extortion, blackmail, and intimidation. For how long? *Years*, I find out.' The scowl deepened. 'It is beneath you, Philo.'

Ygael traced his lineage back to a sixth-century Talmudic scholar, which made him a highly esteemed and powerful member of the Alexandrians.

A man the others would listen to.

Still, Philo was not worried. Whatever Ygael knew, he didn't know about the bombs. Philo was certain of that. 'Are you going to tell the others?'

'Tomorrow, after my daughter's wedding. In the history of our Order, Philo, this has never happened. We have no precedent. We cannot dismiss you from the Society, but we can watch you from now on. And return the stolen treasures to their rightful owners.'

'And expose our existence?'

'There are ways. François Orléans—'

Their man in Interpol. 'Have you told him?'

'Tomorrow. After I bless my daughter and her husband.'

Philo rose calmly and walked around the table. 'I am deeply troubled, old friend. What you have heard is an error, or perhaps an exaggeration. But what troubles me is not what this does to my reputation – I have enemies, I am not ashamed to admit, but what wealthy man does not? What troubles me is that you, old friend, are distressed. This cuts me to my heart.'

He laid hands on the man's shoulders and looked him in the eye. 'Ygael, first and foremost you are my brother. I would rather chop off my right arm than hurt you, and stealing for the Order would do just that, harm you. Whatever you have heard, it can be explained. I wish only for your peace of mind. Do you believe this?'

Ygael was caught in Philo's penetrating gaze, Philo's compelling voice, Philo's magnetism. 'I could not believe my

190

ears,' he began, uncertainty in his tone now, 'when I heard. I said, "No, this is beneath Philo." But I was shown evidence—'

Philo's voice a whisper as he closed his eyes and said, 'Vipers at our bosom, dear brother. For seventeen centuries we have been attacked. Did not our mothers and fathers flee for their lives while the Great Library burned? What lies and deceit did they have to deal with then? And even today we must be vigilant.'

Ygael's eye widened, glistened with tears as he recalled how his ancestor, a Knight of the Flame, had been tortured in Jerusalem. Yes, the Order had had enemies for centuries and must be forever vigilant.

'Let us praise the Name of God,' Philo said softly, pressing his fingers into Ygael's shoulders so that his friend felt Thibodeau's energy flow through fabric and skin and flesh and find its way into his blood to fall under Philo's spell once again.

'The Name of God,' Ygael whispered.

They embraced and Ygael asked for forgiveness.

After the man left, Philo returned to the banquet hall where the gathered guests applauded his return.

The next day Ygael Pomeranz dropped dead dancing at his daughter's wedding. A shock, since the man had been in such good health. The coroner would pronounce it a heart attack and conduct no further investigation. Even so, blood analysis would not have detected the drug that had been slipped into Ygael's 1993 Taittinger Brut Rosé champagne, an excellent vintage at three hundred dollars a bottle.

Twenty-One

The coffee smelled good. It was what woke her. That and the bright sunlight spilling over her.

Candice rubbed her eyes and blinked. The sun seemed high. Why had Ian and Glenn let her sleep so late? And why *had* she slept so long? She felt groggy, not rested. Ian's strong coffee would invigorate her.

But when she crawled out of the sleeping bag, to rise shakily to her feet, she looked at the remains of the camp fire: cold ash. The aroma of coffee had been her imagination.

And then her foggy mind registered that the Pontiac was gone.

She frowned as the biting wind whipped around her and she searched for Ian and Glenn, calling out their names, squinting over the plateau that went on into eternity. When she turned her eyes to the south she saw a cloud of dust.

A military jeep carrying men with rifles was coming straight toward her.

When Jessica Randolph was fifteen years old her preacher father had locked her in a closet until she found God. After four days without food and water, she hallucinated that her father was God. This sufficed. Her name was Ruby Frobisher, a barefoot girl from the wrong side of the tracks who let boys do things to her because she believed their promises. When she ran away from home at sixteen, her back still blistered from her father's belt, she vowed never to let men have power over her again.

It took several years of struggling before she realized that in her own climb to power she needed men of power, to use as stepping stones. And so she modified her vow. This was the reason for her brief fling with Ian Hawthorne, impressed by the 'Sir' and the ancestral home, before she discovered Ian was determined to make a ruin of himself.

Philo Thibodeau, on the other hand, was something else.

It wasn't Philo's obvious power that she was drawn to, the immense wealth, his connections in government and industry, his sway over commerce and finance. It was Philo's *personal* power – something not all men of wealth and authority possessed. Her father, though impoverished, had had such power, stemming from the soul and radiating out like a sun. Charisma. She had run from her father's charisma and had gravitated towards Philo's. Of her own volition, she told herself, because she wanted to be part of his power. And Jessica believed it, having convinced herself that Philo was different from her father, that white-haired Kentuckian Jebediah Frobisher was nothing like the polished and rich white-haired Texan.

In her con-artist days, when Jessica had worked lucrative swindles and scams, she had perfected the art of reading human body language, facial expressions, vocal inflections. She was almost a mind-reader, and what her talents were telling her these days was that Philo was up to something. Fire burned from his eyes, his body was tense, like a corporate czar planning a major takeover. She had seen it in her father, who had expected the Second Coming to occur on his doorstep and was prepared each day to find Jesus standing there.

But what exactly Philo, and his secret society, was planning she had no idea.

Her inquiries among fellow art brokers had been casual, a friendly competitor comparing notes. And what she had learned of Philo's purchases shocked her.

The Hopi Prophecies, written by Thomas Banacyca himself. The earliest version of *Black Elk Speaks*. The hidden sermons of Paramahansa Yogananda. The parables of Yohannes Septimus, scripted in his own hand. A twelfth-century book of visions authored by Hildegard of Bingen. A private collection of writings by Thomas Merton.

All items Jessica had never heard of.

And all religious.

So now she had come to the fortress mentioned in the Raymond of Toulouse letter. Her fall-back plan.

She knew Philo had hired Ian Hawthorne to steal the Star of Babylon, and Jessica had planned to get it from Ian by offering a higher price. Then use the Star, whatever it was, as bait for Philo. But so far she had not heard from Ian. Which meant putting her back-up plan into action. The Raymond of Toulouse letter. She had yet to tell Philo she had it.

First she needed to know about this secret society Raymond spoke of.

They had warned Jessica in the village to stay away from the fortress, high in the Pyrenees; that evil lurked there, the monks worshipped the Devil. But why should that stop her? The whole world worshipped the Devil. Then they said the road up to the fortress was blocked. That didn't stop her either. There were ways around road blocks. Finally, there were guards. She was concerned about those least of all, because of the hidden weapon she carried. The villagers didn't know about that.

As she guided her royal blue Lamborghini Diablo convertible up the narrow winding road, her hair flying in the wind as the car squealed around hairpin turns and through the cool mile-high mountain pass, Jessica glimpsed the peaks and spires of the ancient château nestled among the peaks and spires of mountains. As groves of beech and oak sped by, the road taking her higher into the lofty summits and farther away from civilization, she smiled in satisfaction.

Philo's secret was about to be revealed to her.

When Glenn saw the jeep, he started running. He had left Candice alone at the camp, still asleep.

Closer it came, racing across the sand, a battered military vehicle carrying three ragged men, armed and looking desperate.

He scrambled up the boulders behind the camp, keeping low, watching their speedy progress. The vehicle was going to pass within feet of their camp.

Where was Candice?

The Jeep came to a halt, raising a cloud of dust that briefly blinded him. The men spoke in Arabic, kicking the remnants of the dead campfire, squinting around in the dawn. Excited speech, cries of triumph. Glenn reached the top and looked down. The men had found something.

Candice!

He reached for the gun in his waistband. It was gone.

He saw what they were excited about. They had found the pistol in the sand. It must have slipped out. But where were the sleeping bags?

Then he saw Candice, wedged between boulders. She had dragged her knapsack and the sleeping bags with her. The men were widening their search for more treasures. Coming too close to Candice.

Glenn broke into a sweat. He had to go down there, lure them away from her hiding place. Would his policeman's badge intimidate them or would it be a challenge?

The leader, laying his rifle down as he gripped the pistol, moved closer to where Candice crouched. Glenn saw her hair blow in the wind, chocolate-brown wisps like flags. A blind man could see them.

He inched along the crest of the boulder, pressed flat, keeping an eye on the men. When his hand brushed rubble, which drifted down near where the lead man was standing,

Glenn held his breath. Candice looked up. Her face was white. He motioned her to stay where she was.

The wind dropped abruptly and stillness descended over the scene. The sun was suddenly hot and Glenn's face ran with sweat.

The head man was almost upon Candice, his back to her. If he turned he would see her.

Glenn scrambled to his feet and, before the man below could register the sound, flung himself off the boulder. He landed on the gunman, sending them both sprawling on the sand as Glenn tried to wrestle the pistol out of his hand. The man fought. Glenn's fist shot out and connected with the gunman's jaw. A crack sounded in the air and the man went slack.

The other two came running, laying hands on Glenn, dragging him off their unconscious comrade, throwing him against the rocky wall. Pinning him down, they proceeded to deliver blows to his ribs and abdomen – until another crack was heard and one of them cried out, reeling backwards, his hand clutching his head.

The third spun around, but too late to dodge the rifle butt that Candice swung into his face, hitting him so hard his feet flew out from under him and he landed with a thud.

'Are you all right?' she said, rushing up to Glenn.

He pulled her to him and kissed her hard. Dropping the rifle, she threw her arms around his neck and kissed him back, clutching to him in a breathless, desperate embrace.

'I thought you'd left me!' she cried.

He held her face in his hands, drove his fingers into her hair as if to hold her to him forever. 'My God, why would I do that? Ian took off. I traced the tire tracks. Candice, he has the tablets.'

'Oh no!'

One of the soldiers regained consciousness and, groaning, started to lift himself up, reach for his rifle.

Glenn seized the sleeping bags and threw them into the Jeep. Then he grabbed Candice's arm. 'Come on!'

As he started the engine, the soldier managed to get up on one knee and take aim. Glenn shifted gears and floored the gas as a bullet pinged off the side of the vehicle. They raced away in a zigzag pattern, kicking up dust, flying over rocks and shrub as bullets struck the Jeep, until they were far enough away and out of danger.

But Glenn didn't slow down. The soldiers might have been part of a patrol and have comrades nearby. 'I couldn't understand why Philo hadn't caught up with us and taken the tablets,' he shouted as they raced across the plain. 'It came to me in my sleep that Ian might be working for Philo. So I took the keys out of the Pontiac and put them in the one place Ian couldn't get to them without waking me up – under my pillow.' His jacket, wadded up. 'It didn't work. I went back to sleep and when I woke up the keys were gone.'

'Why didn't it wake you?'

'Because we were drugged.'

'What!' Then she remembered: the coffee last night. The Jeep hit a large rock. Glenn and Candice flew into the air and jolted back down. 'Where are we going?'

'Ian's tire tracks headed north. Let's just hope we catch up with him before someone else catches up with us!'

It would give her power over him. Threaten to expose his secret, and his society. How could he refuse her terms?

Jessica laughed and the wind snatched away her laugh, leaving her open mouthed as she raced up the lofty mountain, her royal blue sport car flashing like a sapphire in the sun. Nothing, the villagers said, would persuade the monks to open the gate. Many had tried, all had failed. Jessica was unfazed. She was simply going to frighten the monks into opening the gates. A foolproof plan because she knew what men feared most.

When she saw the red-tiled domes, tall arched windows, and round towers of the Romanesque château, she was reminded of the fairy tales she had read as a girl, filled with heroes who rescued fair maidens, and how she had dreamed of those men of power coming to her rescue until she grew up and vowed she would be the one in power. Ironically, the childish dream had in fact come true. Although Philo Thibodeau had worn no armor nor ridden a stalwart charger, he had rescued her all the same.

She slowed the car.

Here, according to Raymond of Toulouse, at this ancient crusader fortress, once lived a brotherhood known as the

Knights of the Flame. Lived here nine hundred years ago and, miraculously, lived here still.

She drove up to the gate, the weapon concealed beneath her skirt. 'Hello there! Can you help me please?' she called out in perfect French. 'I have lost my way. I am looking for Boncourt.'

The guard sat in a sentinel box that looked two hundred years old yet was outfitted with a computer screen, electronic equipment. He surprised her when he came out. Dressed in a long white robe with a monk's cowl, he had long hair and a beard, sandals on his feet, and emblazoned on his chest a stunning red and gold symbol that looked like tongues of flame.

Like Philo's ring.

'Sorry, madame. You must turn around.'

She got out of the car. 'I was on the road to Boncourt when I took a wrong turn. May I use your telephone?'

His eyes went down to her skirt, and she saw the change of attitude, the sudden wariness. A fear as old as humankind, which made every man skittish: the pregnant woman.

'I am sorry. You must turn around, go back down the road.'

She walked up and his ill-ease grew. In her con-artist days, Jessica had pulled in big bucks with her pregnant act. She had the walk down perfect, a rolling waddle with her hands resting on her large belly. 'May I use your telephone?'

He held up his hands. 'No, no. Go back. No phone here.'

'Oh!' she said.

'What is it, madame?'

'My pains! It is too soon! Please help me.'

Horror on his face. 'You cannot come in here.'

She pressed her hand to her groin and ruptured a concealed bag of water. Fluid trickled down her leg. 'The baby is coming. Right now!'

A hasty call for help on the phone, and within minutes white-robed monks came running. They laid her on an old-fashioned stretcher and hurried her up the hill, her cries of pain bringing startled faces to the windows.

She was carried through stony corridors, under ancient arches, past wooden doors heavy and silent. A place little used. Not many monks in residence. A secret society that was dying out? Unless the fortress was used for something else.

Strangely, no crucifixes. No rosaries. In fact, no sign of Christianity anywhere within the fortress.

In the infirmary they transferred her to a cot with starchy smelling sheets, a room out of time, with bare stone walls, wooden cupboards, jars and bottles that might belong to a medieval apothecary. She grabbed the infirmarian's hand with wet fingers and saw the revulsion in his eyes. He rushed to the sink, stripped off his gold ring and lathered. Then he stepped out to make a phone call. The woman would need to be helicoptered to the nearest hospital.

When he returned, the cot was vacant except for a small round pillow he had never seen before. The woman was gone.

And so, to his horror, was his ring.

'Why have you stopped?'

Glenn slammed a fist on the steering wheel. 'We're out of gas. From here we walk.'

In the middle of nowhere, with just the wind and sun, sand and snakes, and the ever-present threat of soldiers. They didn't speak as they shouldered the sleeping bags and Candice's backpack. With no food and just one bottle of water between them, they set off northward into the desert.

The blue Lamborghini Diablo raced down the winding mountain road, Jessica's red hair flying like a pennant of war. She was still reeling from what she had found in the château. After slipping out of the infirmary, she had made her way through the warren of rooms and corridors to find the same thing at every turn: books, scrolls, manuscripts, letters, monographs. Knowing that the monks were searching for her, she had not stopped to read everything – but one item was enough.

It had so stunned her that she had nearly gotten caught, riveted before a papyrus preserved between two plates of glass, the Aramaic text translated into English and French on a typed sheet next to it: *The Lost Ending To The Gospel According To St. Mark.*

Then she had run, jumped into her convertible, and shot off down the mountain before the monks could stop her.

She sped past trees and goats and farmhouses, but saw none of them, only words in typed text, as if they had been burned onto her corneas: *carbon-14, infrared and ultraviolet spectrometry, graphology. Verified date: + – 40 CE.*

Jessica had never heard of the document. The oldest known gospel fragment was dated fifty years later. But this was written only ten years after the Crucifixion . . .

She was frightened, exhilarated, giddy all at the same time, and felt like letting out an old-fashioned Texas whoop. She knew now what Philo was up to. Nothing less than global dictatorship. Because the lost ending to the Gospel of Mark, it if was real, would bring the Catholic Church to its knees.

And that was only the beginning.

Twenty-Two

They trudged through a moon-like terrain with towers of rock upthrusting from a plateau of unrelenting beige beneath a sky that looked as if it could never be blue again.

'How could I have not seen it coming?' Candice said as she took a small sip from the water bottle. 'I thought I knew Ian.'

'You had no way of knowing.'

She looked at Glenn. 'The two drivers didn't cause the cave-in, did they? It was Ian.'

'He most likely paid them off, sent them back to Palmyra.'

'So he could sell the tablets to Philo,' she said bitterly, furious at Ian's betrayal.

As the desert wind whistled around them, Candice shivered with apprehension. Lenore Masters, writing in her journal: *Philo frightens me. I sense a growing mania.* And in the Professor's letter: *Do not let Philo get the Star of Babylon. He will use it for evil. He plans a great devastation.* It no longer mattered what was written on the tablets, only that Philo in his delusion perceived them as being vital to his insane plan. To do what? Destroy the world?

Glenn saw how she pressed her lips together, her face taut as she peered into the eternal distance of this barren plain. He knew she was afraid.

199

And then he remembered their kiss, the feel of her body against his.

Shifting the weight of the sleeping bags on his shoulders, Glenn said, 'This reminds me of Sammy Blanco. He was a robbery suspect we picked up. We were sure he was guilty but he insisted he was at the movies during the time of the hold-up. So we put him in a line-up, see if witnesses could identify him, Sammy Blanco and five other guys – two of them cops. Just as I'm instructing the men to step forward one at a time and say, "Give me all your cash or I will shoot you," Sammy blurts, "That's not what I said!"'

Candice laughed and Glenn said, 'Your turn. Tell me a funny Egyptology story.'

'There is no such thing. We are very serious people. Okay,' she said, recalling an embarrassing but fond memory. 'I was an undergrad volunteering on a dig at the Giza Plateau, we were excavating the workmen's village near the Great Pyramid. Among some broken bits of pottery I found a unique object, small, strangely shaped and colored; I couldn't imagine its function. So I kept it and carried it around with me for a few days, hoping a brainstorm would tell me what it was and I could impress the director of the dig. When it wouldn't come to me I finally went to the head man himself and proudly showed him my discovery, confessing that I had no idea what it was. I was secretly hoping it was something so unusual the Metropolitan Museum would beg for it. He inspected the item, handed it back and said, "Petrified dog shit."'

Shadows grew long and the sun dropped behind the horizon. Cold came quickly to the plateau, but the ground was damp and there was no fuel for a fire. They agreed to keep moving, that to stop and rest or sleep would give Ian the edge, so they each took a sleeping bag to wrap around themselves as they walked.

Night crept across the desert. As Candice relived their astonishing, breathless kiss, wondering what to make of the way Glenn had impulsively pulled her to him, pressing his mouth on hers, Glenn was looking at the moon, an orb of a thousand glowing whites and ivories, the starlight pure silver against the deep purple of the desert night, and wishing he had his paints. He looked at Candice, her face in profile, pale and ivory and feminine, like a cameo. What a canvas he would create.

GLOBAL HUNT FOR SACRED TIBETAN TEXTS

The *Los Angeles Times* headline did not please Philo Thibodeau. Having learned of the missing books, he had already been on their trail when a reckless reporter had divulged their existence. Now every Tom, Dick, and Harry was going after them.

Which was why Philo had changed his strategy and was now in a helicopter swooping up the Himalayan slopes, past terraced gardens, stony peaks, blankets of snow, swinging up to the courtyard of an ancient Buddhist monastery set ten thousand feet high with breathtaking views of the snow-capped Everest range to the east. The buildings were painted in the bright primary and earthen colors of Himalayan monasteries, accented by the tall prayer flags on the roof. A retreat as yet unsullied by modern tourism, where maroon-robed boys in an outdoor classroom ogled the descending craft.

When the chopper touched down and the rotors slowed, Philo saw Jessica emerge into the sunlight, red hair flying in the mountain breeze, her body encased in chinchilla.

She shaded her eyes as she watched him step to the flag-stones. This was a first. Philo never interfered with her trans-actions. 'The lama won't part with the books,' she said when he met up with her.

'I'll give it a try. You take my helicopter back down. I'll return in the other one. And Jessica, stay on top of the Raymond of Toulouse letter. *I must have it.*'

At the helicopter she paused to watch him stride across the courtyard, flanked by his ubiquitous companions. Did Philo know she already possessed the letter? Or was she just being paranoid?

As the chopper lifted off, carrying Jessica back to the valley below, Philo signaled to the men at the second helicopter and they began at once to unload crates labeled FOOD and MEDICINES.

The lama was a Rinpoche, Tibetan for 'precious one,' a man who had achieved, through years of study and practice, a high spiritual awareness. This particular Rinpoche was also

201

a Tulku, the incarnation of a highly evolved individual who has been practicing compassion and selflessness through many lifetimes. In addition, he was a repository of truth, Dharma. The traditional way to greet him was to prostrate oneself three times. Philo offered an American handshake.

Attendants stood by to see to the lama's needs, and to make sure the visitor did not impose upon him unduly, for the lama would never himself express dismay or make his wants known; even if a visitor fatigued him beyond endurance, the patient lama would not say a word.

While an attendant served tea, Philo said, 'Is it true Jesus stayed here?'

The lama nodded. His head was shaven and shiny. He was twenty-three years old. 'Yes,' he said in accented English. 'Two thousand years ago, to prepare for his holy mission.'

'And he read your sacred texts?'

'Yes.'

'He read about light in those texts?'

'The Light of God, yes, in the book *Downpour of Brilliant Light*. And then Jesus took the holy message to Jerusalem,' said the Buddhist monk.

While the little boy-monks chanted lessons outside, Rinpoche inspected his mala rosary cupped in his hands. 'But they are not for sale.'

'May I at least see them?'

A shrine room is a place where a person might contact the highest aspect of his or her nature, a place to open the Buddha-nature that resides within, and to hear the word of truth. Philo was there to negotiate a deal.

When Chinese communists invaded Tibet in 1959, monasteries were burned, thousands of monks put to death. Of the sixty-five original volumes of this sacred masterpiece, only seven were known to be in existence. This was the eighth. Collectors were scouring the world for it.

The paper looked like the skimpiest gossamer but was surprisingly strong, and silky to the touch. The unbound pages were covered in black Tibetan script that discoursed on enlightenment. And Philo had to have it. 'I've got to be straightforward with you, Rinpoche. You see, these sacred texts got a write-up in a popular newspaper and now a lot of people are hunting for the rest of the collection. Some of those treasure hunters are less scrupulous than I. They will come here, offer you money, maybe even try to steal the books. Now, I have brought you handsome gifts. When you open those crates, your eyes will widen in disbelief. Food and medicines for all your people. Blankets and lamps, generators to give you electricity. I know you need these things, being so remote as you are.'

Rinpoche did not dispute this. Lamas and their students had needs like anyone else. Nonetheless, he said, 'The book must remain here.'

Philo looked around. The monastery was ancient. 'You don't look very secure here.'

'We are well protected,' the lama said.

'Then may I beg a promise from you? Will you let me know if the book at any time leaves this monastery, either by your own transportation or, God forbid, theft?'

'The book will never leave this place.'

'But do I have your promise?'

'I will let you know.'

Philo offered his hand. 'Then I will take my leave. The gifts remain, as a gesture of my good will.'

As Philo's helicopter swooped up and away, the little boy-monks looked up and waved. Philo waved back and said, 'Now.' Mr. Rossi pushed a button and four enormous balls of hot brilliant fire exploded below, simultaneously, in the courtyard, setting the buildings instantly on fire. The curved smiles of the boy-monks turned to round circles of shock. As Philo watched the blaze, he ignored the startled faces, the screams, the children and monks running in fiery robes, skin blistering and blackening. He didn't take notice of the little boys dropping and writhing in agony, the older monks throwing themselves on top of the children in an effort to suffocate the flames. He was interested only in the bombs his men had planted while he had chatted with the lama.

Within minutes the courtyard was littered with burning bodies, a few still writhing, the buildings going up in flame, roofs caving in, doorways collapsing, tongues of fire lifting cinders and charred remnants of ancient sacred books up to the sky.

'Excellent,' Philo said, satisfied with the demonstration.

As the helicopter turned away to head back to the valley, Philo's satellite phone rang. 'We have the tablets, sir,' the voice on the other end said.

Philo was pleased. But what came next did not please him. 'We have lost track of the man and the woman, sir.'

'Find them,' he said. 'When you do, leave Armstrong in the desert and make sure she doesn't get out.' Doing her a favor. As an Egyptologist it would be her dream to die in the desert. 'But bring me Glenn Masters.'

He needed Glenn. His plan could not succeed without him.

A human sacrifice was demanded.

Sunrise broke over a flat, gray world. Wordlessly, Glenn and Candice continued their northward trek, eyes fixed firmly ahead as if willing a settlement to materialize out of the plain. They were exhausted – bone-weary, thirsty, and hungry. Their feet were sore, their backs ached. But they pushed on.

Noon delivered a thin sort of sunshine, and as Glenn helped Candice across a narrow ravine he saw that she was suddenly looking past him, a puzzled look on her face. 'What's that?' she asked.

He turned. A brown hump on the tawny plain. 'A camel?' The Pontiac!

They ran with their last reserves of strength to find Ian Hawthorne sprawled on the sand, lifeless, his eyes glassy and staring. Glenn didn't need to feel for a pulse.

'Oh my God,' Candice whispered, slumping against the car.

There was another one – a man in a Hawaiian shirt, a few yards away, two bullet wounds in his back. He, too, was dead.

'Hawthorne didn't have a gun,' Glenn said, looking around. 'Looks like a double cross, or maybe Hawaiian Shirt was silenced by his employer.' Was the third party still nearby? 'We have to get out of here.' Glenn looked inside the car. No keys in the ignition. 'Whoever did the shooting might suspect we would wind up here, and come back to finish the job. We need to find the car keys.'

Candice gathered herself together and searched the car while Glenn went through Ian's duffel. 'The tablets are gone,' she said.

'But Hawthorne held onto these.'

'The ceramic shards!' Esther's *second* story.

'And here's his phone.' Glenn punched buttons. 'No luck. The battery's dead.'

'It had to be Philo,' Candice said. 'He was in the corridor outside the ICU and would have overheard Ian telling me to call him if I needed help. Philo then got in touch with him, offered money to report on our movements.'

Glenn found the keys in Ian's pocket. 'Let's go!'

'Glenn—'

He turned.

'We can't just leave . . .'

He looked at the bodies. Then he retrieved a shovel from the trunk of the car.

'Hawthorne didn't have to die,' he said over the fresh graves. 'If only he hadn't been so desperate.'

Candice didn't want to talk about Ian – the staring dead eyes. Part of her grieved for him, part was angry because it was Ian who had put her and Glenn in this perilous situation. And Ian had betrayed her. She knew it would be a long time before she could forgive him, even though she knew that eventually she would.

As they tossed Hawthorne's duffel into the back seat, a small envelope fell out. It contained a microcassette tape labeled INSURANCE.

Glenn examined it. 'It looks like a telephone answering machine tape.'

'Ian had a habit of recording his phone conversations,' Candice said.

'But why did he have this one with him?'

And then they both knew: for when he made the exchange. In case the buyer of the tablets went back on his word, Ian had proof of their agreement. When they played it, would they hear the voice of Philo Thibodeau?

'What now?' Candice asked as she climbed into the passenger side of the car.

'We head to the coast, one of the ports. See if we can find a friendly ship captain. Latakia would be best,' he added, studying the map.

'How far is it?'

'Three hundred miles.' He started the engine.

'Glenn, there might be checkpoints, soldiers, patrols. We could be stopped and questioned, forced to produce papers. They could even arrest us as spies or smugglers.'

'We have money. We'll bribe our way.'

'And after that? Once we have a ship? Where do we go? Glenn, we haven't a clue where Philo has taken the tablets.'

Not a clue, Glenn thought as the Pontiac sped away from the fresh graves. And the world was a very big place to search . . .

Twenty-Three

Southern France, 1534

The young doctor was a keeper of secrets.

Hélène was certain of it. She had watched with lively interest the handsome stranger with the silken auburn beard and beautiful expressive eyes. Like the other citizens of Agen, Hélène knew little about him except that he was a learned man, for he wore the red robe of a scholar and the flat velvet hat of a physician. His patients affectionately called him Dr. Michael because he was not like the stern doctors of their experience, aloof and arrogant men who dosed patients with physics or bled them nearly to death. Dr. Michael was gentle, listened to their woes and administered sweet medicines that not only soothed but cured. His detractors, doctors who failed to heal and who were losing patients, grumbled that he practiced the Devil's arts. More than one had asked local Church men to investigate, suspecting he was a Protestant sympathizer, which, in the eyes of some, was worse than being a Satan worshipper. But nothing was ever found. Dr. Michael was held to be an exemplary Catholic who achieved astonishing cures.

Hélène, eighteen years old, suspected otherwise.

'How is my mother, monsieur?' she asked from the doorway of the bed chamber.

'Your mother is much improved, mademoiselle,' Michael

206

said as he closed his medical bag. 'I have given her something to help her sleep.'

Traditionally, lungwort was used for chest ailments because the leaf was shaped like a lung. But Dr. Michael used an uncommon method – a bowl of steaming water steeped with peppermint leaves, a remedy that filled the whole house with a heady aroma. Where other physicians had failed, this new man had worked a miracle. Hélène's stepmother was breathing more clearly than she had in years.

But there was more to healing than mere medicines. Any university-educated doctor worth his diploma practiced medicine in tandem with astrology. With his charts, zodiac wheels and calculations, Michael studied aspect analysis, transits and cycles, planetary movements, house cusps and moon nodes, as well as the patient's heartbeat, skin color, temperature, and level of pain. His ministrations to the sick always involved the preparation of the patient's natal chart, paying particular attention to the lunar return, one of the predictive tools of astrology, for the placement of the moon and the ascendant – the zodiac sign rising over the horizon at the time of birth – indicated the course of treatment and the patient's prognosis.

As Hélène watched Dr. Michael gather his charts and instruments, she filled her eyes with the sight of this elegant man so recently come into her life. His costume was that of a gentleman of means and good taste. Like all men of fashion, Dr. Michael's attire gave him an exaggerated broad-shouldered look, yet Hélène was of the impression that if he were to remove his garments broad shoulders would still be revealed. He had a high forehead, long straight nose, and eyes that looked as if they could see straight into a person's soul. In the days that he had stayed in this house, as her father's guest, Hélène had observed that Dr. Michael was taciturn by nature, a man who thought much and said little.

But what intrigued her most was his mystery. Where did he come from? Who were his people? She had often espied him in the garden, gazing up at the night sky. What did he see among the stars and comets and phases of the moon? He wore a distinctive gold ring, and when she had once asked about it, to her surprise, he had laid his other hand over it, a blush tinting his cheeks as if he had been caught at a deception.

Sensing her eyes on him now, Michael straightened from the bed and looked at the vision in the doorway.

His heart leaped.

During his short stay in this house, being treated as one of the family instead of a servant, he had grown to know Hélène, and had guessed long before she told him her birth date that she was a Pisces.

She was beautiful and she terrified him.

'We must let your mother rest now,' he said, needing to break the silence and the long awkward moment in which their eyes had locked. Michael wondered if it was time for him to leave this town and move on once more, as he always, inevitably, must.

Hélène led the way along the narrow passage and down the stairs to the ground floor of the house, where a fire roared against the spring chill, and where Michael's host awaited them with warm bread, creamy goat cheese, and wine.

Hélène's father was a wealthy man who could afford to clothe his wife and daughter in gowns made of Florentine silk, a man who enjoyed expensive novelties – dining this evening on a strange new bird recently brought back from the New World by Spaniards, a fowl called a 'turkey', which he declared would never replace the goose. This region of France was famous for its plum trees, which had been brought back from the Middle East during the Crusades, and Hélène's father owned the largest orchard, turning out sweet plum wine and prunes that were shipped all over Europe. Thus was the family able to afford such luxuries as pearl-handled forks at the dinner table, glass panes in their windows, and candles made not of tallow but the more costly (and less pungent) beeswax.

Nonetheless, for all their wealth, Dr. Michael perceived them as a quiet and modest family. The lady upstairs was his patron's third wife, the first two having died in childbirth, and Hélène was the man's only offspring to survive childhood. Still, the plum merchant declared he was content. And should his wife not thrive under Dr. Michael's care, and succumb to her lung troubles, he had confided to Michael that there were eligible young women in the village who would be happy to run his home and warm his bed. Hélène's father firmly believed that, in a world where nearly half of all babies died in their first year, it was a man's duty to sow his seed where he could.

The two enjoyed evening dialogues in which they might debate the value of translating the Bible for the common man to read, or discuss the merits of the comical novel *Gargantua* compared to the previous *Pantagruel* (and the fact that the two books, wildly popular throughout Europe, were banned in France seemed not to faze Monsieur a bit). Tonight it was religion, and Hélène observed that Michael was suddenly ill at ease.

'Religious reform is in the air, my friend,' her father declared as he decanted wine. 'With Luther in the north protesting Church practices, and King Henry in England separating from Rome so he can divorce his wife, and grumblings in the faculty of theology at the University of Paris, Mother Church is threatened, I fear. What is your opinion on this, monsieur?'

Michael could not read the man's eyes. Was he a follower of Luther and inviting a debate, or was he a Catholic hoping to catch a heretic? It was a mere seventeen years since Martin Luther had nailed his grievances to the door of the church in Wittenburg, yet the wave of reform fever had swept across Europe like a fire-storm and continued to burn out of control. The Church, in panic, was starting to fight back, and so every man was wary of every other man, and all men were cautious in their speech. So Michael said, 'I am a scientist, monsieur. My faith is in the stars and my medicines.'

When the man's cryptic gaze stayed on Michael a heartbeat too long, Hélène rose and said, 'Shall we take the air of the garden, monsieur? It is delightful this time of the evening.'

Once they were out of the dimly lit house and under the bright moonlight she saw a patina of perspiration on Michael's brow. Was he ill? And then she thought: it was talk of the Church and the protesting heretics. Was this handsome young doctor sympathetic to the reformers?

Hélène was right in her suspicion that he carried a secret, but what she did *not* know was that Michael's secrets were dangerous to himself and that he must keep them hidden or risk trial for heresy – or, worse, witchcraft. The secrets were the reason he moved from town to town, never staying in one place long. Nor did Hélène know that, in her desire to know more about him, in her determination to uncover those secrets, she imperiled him.

He wished he could confide in this lovely creature, unburden his soul and place his secrets in her gentle care. But he dared not. He was under the scrutiny of the Office of Inquisition, and they followed him wherever he went. But there *was* something he could share with her, a passion held close to his heart, and as he spoke of it now, earnestly, in this moonlit garden filled with the perfume of spring blossoms, Hélène saw his eyes glow, heard the energy in his voice, and felt Michael's own power radiate as if from a brazier.

'We are living in a new age, mademoiselle. The Florentines call it *rinascita*, rebirth, for the world is awakening to a new awareness. There is thirst for knowledge in the land, and a quest for new understandings like there never has been before. It is no accident that men like Luther are questioning the practices of the Church. Mind you, I am no protestor, but God gave us minds and a free will, did He not? To question and debate is a good thing. New worlds have been discovered, whole continents and new races of people.' He stopped suddenly when he saw how she stared at him. He wanted to tell her more, that he felt he had been born to a certain destiny, that he traveled the earth searching for it. But the astonished look on her face, her blue eyes wide . . . He had gone too far.

Michael had misread her. What immobilized young Hélène was a new excitement burning within herself. She had never met a man with such energy and drive. It thrilled her. But also rendered her speechless. So instead she picked up her lute and played it, as she sat on the marble bench, and she sang an accompaniment in an exquisite thin high voice that made Michael think of spun silver. The song went straight to his heart like an arrow, piercing him in sweet pain. If only he were free to fall in love with this enchanting creature. But his personal demons would never allow it. He liked this town and its people and wished he could settle here. But he knew that soon he must move on, before his secret was discovered.

The hour late, the candle burning low, Michael was at his desk with his charts and instruments and calculations, searching for an answer.

The Shadows had come for him again.

So it had been ever since he was a boy. His curse. He never knew when the Shadows would come; he could be at any occupation, alone or in company, and they would find him, and he would not be able to eat or drink or rest until he had deciphered their cryptic message. He had learned long ago that the decryption lay in the stars, where all of life's answers lay, and so he labored now, with his quills and equations, his astrolabe, protractor, and compass, searching the ever-changing celestial map for the answer.

And there it was: Mars, a malefic planet, was in Aquarius. Michael gave a cry.

The terrible event the Shadows forewarned was to take place tomorrow. And it involved Hélène.

He shot to his feet and paced the small space of his room beneath the sloping roof, wringing his hands. What to do, what to do? If he warned Hélène, everyone would say afterwards, 'How did he know?' He could say he read the omen in the stars, but people would say, 'How did he know to look?' They would not understand about the Shadows.

He wrestled with the dilemma until he was sick with worry and he knew there was only one answer. Hastily packing his bags, he slipped out of the house and, under the cover of night, collected his horse and pack donkey from the stable and quietly left the sleeping town of Agen.

It was not the first time he had fled thus, nor, he knew, would it be the last. For the Shadows drove him, cursing him to a life of restless searching and loneliness, a man without friendship, family, or love.

Beyond the town gates, however, he stopped on the road and looked back. *Hélène.* He could not leave without warning her. If it meant his own death, then so be it.

She thought it was a mouse, the scratching was so faint. But when Hélène came fully awake in the darkness, she realized the sound was a tapping at her door.

She looked out and was startled to find Dr. Michael standing in the narrow passage, fully dressed as if for travel.

He spoke in a whisper. 'Do not go to the marketplace in the morning, mademoiselle.'

'Why not?'

'Pray do not ask, for I cannot tell you. Promise me only that you will stay at home until noon.'

'But, monsieur, I always go, every morning. Papa will wonder—'

'Make an excuse. I beg of you.'

Such starlight as filtered through the open bedroom window illuminated Michael's face: it was pale and damp, his eyes burning with an intensity that alarmed her. But they implored as well, and she felt her heart go out to him, this stranger who had wakened her to the rebirth in the world.

'I will think on it,' she said.

Michael retreated to his room where he spent the rest of the night in a vigil of prayer, begging God to make Hélène heed his warning.

Feigning a headache, Hélène sent servants in her stead to fetch the day's bread and meat. And as she busied herself at quiet occupations, reliving Michael's visit to her room, wondering if it had even really taken place, she suddenly heard shouts in the street. She looked out. People were calling for Dr. Michael. A horse-drawn wagon had rampaged through the marketplace, they told her. People dead, others with broken limbs, blood running in the gutters. Dr. Michael was urgently needed.

But he was already there, he had left early that morning with his medical bag. *He had known.*

'I call them the Shadows,' he said wearily, taking his first rest from a day of setting broken bones and treating wounds. Seven dead, in all. But Hélène was not among them.

She sat next to him in the garden, pale faced and tense, still reeling from the shock of what might have been.

'They sweep over me when I least expect them, and fill me with a feeling of almost-knowing. I do not know where they come from, or how to hide from them, for they always find me. It is something I was born with, and I cannot explain it.' He looked at her. 'And I am Jewish, Hélène, and hiding from the Inquisition.' It was a time for confessions, Michael knew, and if she were to get up and walk away he would not blame her.

But she remained at his side, waiting.

'When I was nine years old, my family were forced to convert from Judaism to the Catholic faith. As ex-Jews we

212

were particularly watched by the Church, especially when I went to study medicine at Montpellier. Once I had my license to practice, I went out into the countryside to help plague victims. I was so successful in saving lives that when I returned to Montpellier to complete my doctorate I was commanded to explain the unorthodox remedies and treatments I had used. As there was nothing untoward found in my remedies, and because my learning and ability could not be denied, I was granted the doctorate. But my revolutionary theories in medicine caused trouble and so I had to leave. Wherever I go, men of learning, men of the Church are suspicious of me. But,' he settled piercing eyes on her, 'I have found warmth and friendliness here in Agen. And in you, Mademoiselle Hélène.'

She was breathless.

He boldly took her hand and said with ardor, 'Since the Chaldeans of Abraham's time, men have believed that the pattern of the stars bodes good or ill at certain periods, and indeed even diverts the course of a man's life. If there be any truth to this science, my stars must have found themselves, after centuries of toilsome waiting, in that precise position designed to bring to my soul a love and delight that I had never thought possible.'

He felt her hand tremble in his.

'To you alone shall I now confess my most preciously guarded secret. All my life, Hélène, I have felt destined for something special, outside the experience of ordinary men. Yet I cannot name it and I fear I shall die before I realize it. Do you think it boastful of me to say it was no accident that I was born into this age? I was born for a purpose, but I do not know what that purpose is. And I fear that I will miss my destiny.'

She smiled, her eyes dancing. 'I know what your destiny is, Michael. I sensed it from the moment I met you. Because I, too, carry a secret.'

A secret! Blessed, enchanted creature! 'Pray tell me, mademoiselle, that I might cherish it and keep it in my heart.'

She lowered her head to observe him from beneath long lashes, and said, 'You have to marry me first.'

* * *

213

She took him to the chateau in the Pyrenees built by her ancestor Alaric, the Comte de Valliers, the crusader knight who had united the Alexandrians. And, now that Michael was her husband, he was given the gold ring of the secret society, modified since Alaric's day with a new flame motif, inscribed with the words: *Fiat Lux*. He wore it next to the gold ring his father had given him and which he had once hidden from Hélène: a ring that had belonged to his grandfather, a rabbi, and which bore an inscription in Hebrew.

As they rode side by side on horseback up the narrow mountain road, she told him the story of Alaric and the Knights of the Flame and their stunning victory in Jerusalem in the year 1099, after which they had brought back the Mary Magdalene letters, and much more besides, to be housed in this fortress built by Alaric. From that time to this, the Alexandrians had devoted their lives to gathering illuminated writings from around the world.

'What do they do with this collection?' Michael asked as they rode through dappled sunlight.

'We keep it safe,' she said.

'To what purpose?'

They reached a place on the road to rest and to water the many horses and mules in their train. Here, as they shared a loaf of bread and a wheel of sharp cheese, Hélène revealed the true mission of the Alexandrians.

Michael was initially shocked, then skeptical. But he kept this to himself as he said pragmatically, 'If that is indeed the mission of the Alexandrians, then it is not enough merely to collect and store. You will not reach your goal in that manner. The writings must be read, translated, analyzed, and searched for hidden meaning. Only then will the mission of the Alexandrians be realized.'

Forty-three men and women resided at the Château de Dieuvenir, devoting their lives to the ancient books under their care. Michael was unprepared for this priceless repository of wisdom, for he had imagined a few shelves with a few volumes. Yet he was shown vast halls filled with the arcana and the occult of the ancients, the astrology of the Chaldeans, the secrets of the Hittites, the lost wisdom of Babylon! And, as he looked upon all this accumulated knowledge and illumination,

214

he knew that in this place he would find the answers to the Shadows that plagued him.

It was the nature of the Alexandrians to be democratic, with no leader, each member carrying an equal vote with the others. And so they gave ear to Michael's ideas and, after debate, embraced them.

Michael told the Alexandrians that they must do more than just collect, they must read and translate and analyze and look for hidden messages. 'You are the guardians of the future, but for that you must harvest the past.' Thus with the arrival of the new member came changes, and the château was wakened to industry and purpose, its residents imbued with fresh energy and vision, for they had been shown that they were more than mere curators of ancient words.

As Michael explored the vast archives, finding such treasures as books by German mystics Hildegard of Bingen – 'In my forty-third year I worshipped a heavenly vision, and I saw in it a mighty brilliance.' – and Matilda of Magdeburg – *The Flowing Light of the Godhead* – he realized that much of the library's collection was about light.

'Alaric called his experience the Luminance,' Hélène explained. 'In a vision of light, he saw the greatness of the order of knights that he was to create.'

Michael trembled with hope. Could this light dispel his Shadows? 'How does one experience this Luminance?'

'I do not know. It is said that the Luminance comes to us all, but rarely in our lifetime. Jesus experienced it, in the Transfiguration.'

Michael was anxious to experience the Luminance, for he knew that in the light he would find his salvation.

'Dr. Michael! Dr. Michael!' The boy banged on the front door with both fists. 'Mama is sick! You must come at once!'

Hélène stirred at her husband's side and Michael threw back the covers and put his feet on the floor. 'Must you?' she murmured. The night was cold and Michael felt good next to her. Her question was rhetorical: Michael never refused a patient's call.

Opening the window shutter, he looked down at the boy below. 'Who is there?'

'Jean, the baker's son. Mama is ill.'

'Very well. Stop making that racket now. Go home, I shall be there shortly.' Michael drew back inside, and while he got dressed Hélène left the bed to check on the baby.

They had lived five years together in a loving marriage; Hélène had produced two children, they had their own house, and were prospering. Michael set broken bones, couched cataracts, extracted teeth, administered balms, lotions, and teas. He carried powders and herbs in sheep's horns hanging from his shoulder and belt. He carried also in his medical kit a new invention of great novelty: small sharp scissors that made such tasks as cutting hair and sewing much easier. But mostly he read people's stars.

In his spare time, he pored over books from the château, and twice a year visited the fortress in the Pyrenees, now a center of industry as scholars labored over the collected texts, authenticated and catalogued them, examined and translated them, so that the Alexandrians were the most enlightened men and women on earth. Yet they kept their wisdom a secret, for religious unrest was troubling the land, as more and more voices, in every village and town, spoke up against the Church and the Church fought back.

The baker's wife had a fever and lay moaning. When Michael drew the bed cloths back he received a shock: bright red lumps protruded from her neck. Further examination revealed swellings in her armpits and her groin. He stared in horror.

The Black Death had come to Agen.

The plague swept through with brutal swiftness. Within a week infected families were boarded up in their houses, patients were abandoned in plague hospitals, the dead buried in mass graves. Michael toiled ceaselessly. The standard treatment was to apply red-hot cautery irons to the swellings caused by the plague, searing the flesh and causing agony for the victim. But, as this did nothing to stop the illness, Michael used a special treatment devised by him. He believed the plague was spread in the air and that it was important to keep one's breath and the air around oneself medicinally clean. He made pills of sawdust, irises, cloves, aloe, and pulverized red roses, and distributed these among the townsfolk, telling them to hold the lozenges in their mouths at all times.

Secretly, Michael was sick at heart. He consulted the stars and was shocked to find five planets in Scorpio, clearly heralding this new outbreak of plague. How could he have missed it?

Soon death was everywhere. Fathers abandoned their infected sons. Lawyers refused to come and make out wills for the dying. Monasteries and convents were soon deserted. Bodies were left in empty houses, and there was no one to give them a Christian burial. The disease struck and killed with such swiftness that Michael recorded in his journal: 'Victims of the plague often eat lunch on earth and dinner in the hereafter.'

But there was something else besides the plague for him to be frightened of: when the Black Death first came to Europe in 1348, killing people in the millions, citizens needed an explanation, a cause. And, although Jews also perished of the plague, the terrified survivors turned their anger and grief upon the Jewish population, slaughtering them in the belief that *they* had brought the disease to Christendom. Now the plague was back, and people were going to look again for a scapegoat.

At the first outbreak, Michael had ordered Hélène to stay at home until the pestilence had passed, not even to open the shutters, to burn incense day and night, and most of all to keep the lozenges in her mouth and the mouths of their two children.

Days and then weeks passed, and finally the sickness began to withdraw from Agen. The dead were burned and people tried to pick up the pieces of their broken lives. A third of the population was gone. Half the women were widowed, many children orphaned. Michael returned home after his long absence, weary and haggard. Hélène met him at the door.

He kissed her cheek and she bared her throat. Three angry red buboes marred her white skin.

He could not save them.

First Hélène died, a mere three days after he came home,

217

and then the boy and finally the baby. He was left alone with three silent corpses while in the streets people were celebrating the end of the plague.

His howls of pain kept neighbors away, as they thought he had lost his mind. But then some recalled how he had ministered to them when he himself had gone without sleep, so they pushed their way into his house and pried the body of Hélène from his arms. He fought and cried, and it was only by forcing one of his own potions down his throat, putting him to sleep, that they were able to carry the deceased out to the cemetery on the edge of the town.

In the weeks that followed Michael lived like a ghost in his house, never setting foot outside, brooding, talking to people who were not there. As his perceived madness continued, the townsfolk grew less passionate and more afraid. Their troubles during the pestilence forgotten, they began to resent Michael's refusal to come and set a broken leg or treat a feverish child. And then they began to talk among themselves and wonder what sort of doctor it was who could not save his own family. His patients abandoned him, turning to home remedies and such doctors as passed through the town. Hélène's father, listening to the gossips and wondering the same thing himself, tried to sue Michael for the return of Hélène's dowry. And, finally, he was accused of heresy because of a chance remark made to a workman casting a bronze statue of the Virgin. Michael's plea that he was only describing the lack of aesthetic appeal in the statue was ignored and the Inquisitors sent for him to stand trial in Toulouse.

He planned to flee under the cover of night.

As he packed his bags to leave the home where he had known a short spell of bliss, he stopped in the process of adding another book to his satchel – and he remembered the Alexandrians and their boast that they did not believe there was a God.

That was what had killed Hélène and the little ones! God's punishment of Michael for allying himself with heathens, for reading pagan works. In rage and grief he gathered together all the ancient books and scrolls he had brought from the château, heaped them in the flagstone yard of his house and set them afire. While tears streamed down his cheeks and soaked his auburn beard, he cursed his luck, God, and the stars. He shook a fist heavenward, shouting at the planets and moon and celestial bodies that they were cruel tricksters. And as the bonfire of relics grew hotter and larger, Michael felt the heat recede and a coolness wash over him. Soon the fire encompassed the yard, the walls of his home, the flowers in his garden. But it was not a hot conflagration. He let the flames consume him yet he felt no pain. Instead, a cloud of peace and joy engulfed him. His eyes were filled with the images of incredible things: cities made of towers of glass, strange chariots speeding along wide roads, flying machines, people watching pictures forming from thin air.

He sensed unseen beings all around him, whispering, telling him secrets, and he knew they were showing him the future.

When he regained consciousness, it was to find himself in the flagstone yard, his house and the walls and garden still intact, only a pile of ashes where the books had burned. He knew then that he had been shown a special glimpse into the Luminance. He went to the Alexandrians to bid them farewell and to beg their forgiveness for having cursed them, and for having burned some of their precious books.

The Alexandrians cautioned him whom he told, because not all men would accept that his gift of prophecy was holy, but would think it the work of the Devil.

He left them and continued his questing, searching the lights of heaven for his answers, recording in journals his visions, keeping them secret. He still believed the answers lay in the stars, for what were stars but light? And thus he roamed the land for twenty years, a homeless man with no family, no real friends, a wanderer in search of something he could not even put into words, nor could he speak of it to another soul for it would stamp him a heretic and a witch.

The Alexandrians had given him a book called *De Mysteriis Egyptorum*, which contained the ingredients for magical practices. From this rare volume Michael learned the art of conjury and spell-casting, soothsaying and telepathy, horoscopy and augury, the power of crystals, the magic in certain plants and drugs, and how to summon guides from the astral plane. But mostly he used the book to recreate smaller Luminances, in which he saw visions of the future.

He sensed invisible beings come to him in each luminosity, Aristotle and Plato, the great men of the enlightened past, coming to this man in the era of rebirth to show him things to come. Michael wrote his visions down, but, because he still lived in fear of persecution, he kept his journals a secret. Finally, he no longer dreaded the Shadows, for he illuminated their darkness with light.

In 1554, after fifteen years of adventures and explorations, Michael settled down in the town of Salon, France, where he married his second wife, Anne Ponsart Gemelle, with whom he would raise six children.

On the night they were wed, he confessed his secret and showed her his journals. 'I am caught in a dilemma, my dearest. I must write these prophecies down for others to read, and yet I could be condemned as a sorcerer.'

Anne wisely said, 'You know that astute men, of clear mind and thought, will grasp that what you have to say as divine. Therefore, couch your prophecies in riddles. Such men as you wish to enlighten will have the minds to solve them.'

And so he compiled and published the first of many books that were to make him famous throughout Europe, a compilation of visions of the future, and he included in this first book a preface to his infant son, César:

> These predictions came to me through divine power, for nothing can be accomplished without Him whose goodness is so great that prophetic heat approaches us like the rays of the sun. Occult prophecies are received only by this subtle spirit of fire.
>
> I had at my disposal many books which had been hidden for centuries. I consigned them to flames, and as the fire came to devour them the flame that licked the air shot forth a brightness brighter than fire, like the light of lightning, illuminating my house, as if in sudden conflagration. And I saw that, in the far future, when the

planet Mars finishes its cycle, the world will end in a universal conflagration, brought by the angels of fire of God the Creator.

Now, my son, take this gift of your father, Michel Nostradamus.

Salon, the first of March, 1555

But there was one prophecy that Michael kept out of the version book for public circulation, for it concerned only one small group of people. He gave this prophecy to the Alexandrians in the Pyrenees, assuring them that the day would come when one of their own would decipher the code to reveal the hidden meaning and future foretold in the 83rd quatrain of century 7.

Part Three

Twenty-Four

On a hilltop overlooking Los Angeles, Sybilla Armstrong, sporting her new frizzed hairdo as if to show people what a dynamo she was, surveying her world, the 'new' fifties house she had just acquired for a small fortune, looking out at the city lights and saying to her daughter, 'What's it all about, Candy?'

Candice, in graduate school, her nose buried in a text on the Wisdom Literature of ancient Egyptian sages, looking up from her book, mildly surprised at her mother's philosophical question, so unlike her; Candice wondering if success and wealth had brought out the spiritual in Sybilla, about to reply with something wise from the ancient book, interrupted by Sybilla, who cried, 'Winning! That's what it's all about, Candy. Nothing else.'

No, Mother, Candice thought now as she gazed out at the infinite desert. You're wrong.

Glenn took his eyes off the highway to look at her. She had been silent since leaving Ian's grave. The gas in the Pontiac had lasted until Palmyra, where they had refilled the tank, bought snacks, and then hit the main highway westward. And Candice had said little. He knew the reason for the silence and he thought she should talk about it. But it was up to her to choose the moment.

As if sensing his eyes on her, she turned to him. The window was down. Her hair danced in the breeze. 'I'm sorry about Ian,' she said. 'But he played a dangerous game. He was self-destructive.'

Glenn waited. He knew that was not what preoccupied her.

'Your father once told me I was searching for my soul,' she said after a moment, her eyes fixed on the tawny desert that stretched away to the deep blue sky. Ahead of them, a petroleum truck belched black smoke. 'He was right. All my life I've tried to find something to believe in, but I searched in books, in other cultures, other eras. I never searched within myself. And then, Jebel Mara . . .'

Glenn swung the Pontiac around the truck, got in front of it and sped up. 'Candice, I know the experience on Jebel Mara frightened you. I've seen it before in novice climbers. Many of them, once they get back on the ground, never climb again. It's only natural to—'

She shook her head. 'It wasn't about fear. I wasn't frozen because of panic. I can't explain it. I've been going over it and over it, trying to make sense of it, to put it into words. Glenn, what happened to me on the summit of Jebel Mara was *wonderful*. It was almost . . . a religious experience. Does that make sense?'

He looked at her, framed by the lion-colored desert, palm oases, sky the color of cornflowers, wisps of chocolate-brown hair snapping like pennants. She belonged here, he thought. The desert gave her a surreal beauty. He knew the colors he would use – titanium white for her skin, midnight black for her hair, raw sienna for the shadow on her neck, her soft brown eyes burnt umber, her lips red rose.

'I was filled with such awe,' she continued, 'an exhilaration I've never experienced before. I never went to church, Glenn. I never knew what a spiritual moment could feel like. But that was how I felt on top of Jebel Mara, in the setting sun, and it hit me in that instant that that was what God must be like.'

'You experienced climber's rapture,' he said, startled by her unexpected confession.

There was more, but she hadn't the words, it was too personal, but she had questions now, as if the blazing sunset on Jebel Mara had opened a locked door in her soul and set free questions: Why are we here? What is our purpose? Where are we going? Questions that people must ask in church, and when they pray, which her beloved Egyptians would have asked long ago, Nefertiti in her serenity perhaps knowing the

223

answers, but Candice, having no experience with spiritual matters, not knowing where to begin.

'There was something else.' She looked away, squinted through the windshield toward a collection of small mud dwellings at the side of the highway, clothes strung on lines, children playing in the dust. 'This is going to sound crazy,' she said, 'but when I froze on the side of the cliff, when you told me not to fight the mountain . . .'

He waited. The children waved as the Pontiac sped past.

'I froze, and then I gave myself to the mountain, and then I found the courage to climb up.'

'I remember.'

'Glenn, I thought I sensed a presence with me.'

He nodded. He had sensed the same thing during his fall and his glimpse of the Luminance. A being at his side, telling him everything was going to be all right. He had never told anyone.

She fell silent then, because she needed to think about what she had just said, and Glenn, by reaching for her hand and holding it tight, let her know that he understood.

Desert gave way to verdant countryside, rich with orchards, citrus groves, corn fields, and great hedges of cypress trees. In the mountains they sped through forests and breathed in the invigorating air, and by the time they made their descent to the coastal plain the sun was setting in their eyes.

Latakia was a beautiful, ancient city on the sea, with magnificent public gardens, lush groves of palm trees and oleanders. The Pontiac joined the heavy traffic along the corniche boulevard, and as they drove past the harbor they saw huge cargo ships riding at anchor offshore, boats and other craft weaving about on the water, coming in for the night to tie up or to disembark passengers from ferries and other passenger ships. Among the warehouses and immense grain silos were the buildings that housed the customs and security services and the tourist information bureau – the very places Glenn and Candice wanted to avoid. Signs directed passengers heading to Cyprus, Beirut, Alexandria, and the western Mediterranean to embark at the north quay, so Glenn said he would conduct his search in the southern part of the harbor.

He chose the Meridien Hotel, since it was full of foreign tourists and no one would notice an American woman whiling away the time in the cocktail lounge. She wanted to go with him, but Glenn said he would work best alone. It was going to take money and the right, discreet enquiries. 'I don't know how long this will take. If I'm gone for long, register in a room for the night. I'll find you.'

'Glenn,' she said, taking his arm. The anxiousness in her eyes said everything. 'I'll be careful,' he said, and he was gone.

To Candice's surprise and relief, he returned within the hour. 'Good news. I found a captain who'll take us. His ship is bound for Southampton. The captain said he'll help us to disembark there. He assured me he is a discreet man and has taken passengers before under these conditions.'

'Conditions?' Candice said.

'He understands that, for personal reasons, we wish to avoid immigration and customs. We board the ship tonight, after dark. It's a large cargo vessel but there's only one cabin for people who aren't crew members.' He hesitated.

'What's the problem?'

'I had to invent a story about us. Although Captain Stavros said he understands about being discreet and that people have their reasons for not wishing to trouble themselves with the paperwork and wasted time of visas and so forth, he appears to be a very outgoing and sociable man. He said he's looking forward to our company on the voyage. I paid him a lot of money for not asking questions, but I'm afraid it's in his nature to do just that. So to guarantee our privacy, I had to tell him . . .'

'Tell him what?' Candice said.

'Well,' Glenn actually blushed, 'I told him we're on our honeymoon.'

'Welcome, welcome!' Captain Stavros boomed, pumping their arms in hearty handshakes. A stout man with a captain's cap pulled tight over a head of thick black hair, a prodigious black beard reaching the polished brass buttons of his naval jacket. Though the *Athena* was old and rusty, Stavros himself appeared to be shipshape, as did his two smiling second officers, also Greek, in crisp white uniforms.

The hour was late. A crewman from the *Athena* had met them at a secluded spot on the wharf and brought them back to the ship, which was the length of half a football field and operated by Greek officers and a Burmese crew. The *Athena*'s run, Stavros explained effusively, was from Syria, where he picked up figs, dates, and olives, thence to Greece for more olives, Italy for yet more olives, Spain for wine, and up to Southampton to unload and pick up silk, English biscuits, and umbrellas for the return run.

'What adventurers!' Captain Stavros said loudly, gesturing to a deckhand to collect his guests' knapsacks and duffel bag. The man was Burmese, like the rest of the crew, and wore an ankle-length sarong. 'When your friend told me you were tramp steaming around the world,' Stavros exclaimed, 'I thought at first two young men, for that is my typical passenger. And then when he said a woman,' small dark eyes twinkled at Candice, 'I thought young hitchhikers, for we carry those too sometimes. But a married couple! And newlyweds at that!' He winked and a gold incisor flashed among white teeth. 'We shall make a point to leave you two alone.' He snapped his fingers and a steward in a white uniform appeared. 'He will escort you to your cabin and will be seeing to your needs during the voyage.'

The cabin was modest and cramped, but clean. There was only one narrow bed, but the sofa could be used for sleeping. In between was a small dresser, a desk, and a chair. The port-hole was rusted shut.

'Well, darling,' Glenn said as the steward was closing the cabin door, 'it appears we got the honeymoon suite.'

Candice laughed and then fell silent. With the door closed, the cabin was small. 'I'll need—' she said, intending to finish the sentence with something about the small desk and spreading the ceramic shards on it, since the sea journey was going to take a few days and she would try translating them, as that was why they were here, why they had left the safety of Los Angeles and come this far, to fulfill a promise to his father, to find out why Philo wanted the tablets, to catch a killer. She needed to say these things to remind herself of them, because so much had changed and she was terrified of the new feelings struggling within her, but she had no breath in her throat to finish the sentence because Glenn filled the cabin with his tallness and his masculinity, and she was still feeling the press of his lips upon hers when they had impulsively kissed at Wadi Raisa.

'I'll take the sofa,' he said.

As the bomb broker explained the detonation sequence to Philo Thibodeau, Philo's mind shifted elsewhere.

Jessica had found out about the fortress in the Pyrenees. He was not surprised. He had sensed her growing curiosity about his acquisitions, his private life. Despite their years of association, she knew little about him. But she would read the Raymond of Toulouse letter, compare it to prior acquisitions she had made for him, perhaps discuss his purchasing patterns with others in the field, and put two and two together. Especially as the letter mentioned the ring and Jessica had seen Philo's ring.

He knew she was in love with him. Women could not help fall in love with Philo. He knew that his charismatic nature, his virility were more than they could resist. Like poor Mildred Stillwater. But they could not have him, not even with Sandrine gone. He was saving himself for Lenore.

The question now was what to do about Jessica.

The logical response would be that since he had created her he could destroy her. But was that necessary? She had served him well, and could continue to do so until the end. Not that she, or anyone, knew that the end was coming.

The bomb broker pointed to something on the blueprint, arming devices, he said, while Philo thought back to the day, seventeen years ago, when 'Jessica Randolph' had been born. He didn't need to know the inner workings of the bombs, only how to set them off.

He had not been in the restaurant to eat. It was where he had last seen Lenore, three years earlier, when she had wanted to plan her son's initiation into the Order. A full meal had been set before him, which he left untouched, when he had overheard a conversation at the next table.

By the way they were talking, Philo gathered the man and woman were strangers. Blind date? Call girl and client? She looked pricey. Listening to her, she was knowledgeable on art

– almost. Cultured, almost. Educated, almost. The English accent forced. She needed polish. Not quite the diamond. She confused a Cézanne with a Degas, but her companion didn't seem to notice.

Philo tried to return to his memories but there was something about the woman at the next table. A tilt of the head. A wave of the hand. She was a natural. A pearl buried in an oyster.

The couple finally left and Philo returned to his silent contemplation of the past.

The woman came back ten minutes later, distraught about losing a ring. Manager, waiters, nearby customers, everyone questioned. No one had seen it. She offered a generous reward and told them where she was staying. Then she left.

Philo went into the men's room and was not surprised that another man followed him, very excited, saying he had just found this fabulous ring on the floor outside the ladies room. 'I'm in a big hurry,' the stranger said. 'If you give me, say, five hundred dollars, you can have the ring and claim the whole reward.'

Philo took out his platinum money clip and the man's eyes bugged at the wad of bills. Philo offered him the lot, five times the reward for the ring, if he would take him to the woman.

'I don't know what you're talking about.'

Philo penetrated the other man's eyes with his own dagger gaze, cutting to the shallow core of the petty swindler, and didn't have to say another word.

They went to a seedy motel – not the posh hotel she had told the manager and where their hapless mark would not find her – and she was furious when she saw her partner bring a stranger in.

'Please forgive this intrusion, dear lady,' Philo said in his Southern gentleman way that had a softening effect. 'But I have an offer to make to you. A very generous offer. I wish to hire your services.'

'I'm not a hooker.'

He placed his hand on his chest. 'I assure you, dear lady, I have only the most noble of intentions. It is a *business* transaction. If we may speak privately?'

228

Three seconds to assess the stranger and come to one conclusion: rich. 'Dan, leave us alone.'

'Hey, we work together.'

'I said go.'

The man glowered from the woman to the stranger, then turned, muttering, 'Bitch!'

Philo stayed him with a hand. 'Sir, I ask you to apologize for that remark.'

The man snorted.

'Apologize to the lady.' Calmly.

'She's no lady.'

'To a gentleman all women are ladies.'

'And if I don't?'

'You will wish you had.'

Another snort. 'Who cares? Okay, Ruby, I'm sorry.' He stormed to the door, yanked it open, called back, 'I'm sorry you're a bitch,' and he was gone, door slamming shut.

Philo stared at the closed door, made a mental note, then turned to the woman. 'What is your game?' Philo asked. 'Pigeon drop? Ponzi schemes? Bait and switch?'

She shrugged. 'Whatever works.' She narrowed her eyes. 'How did you guess?'

'I watched you at dinner. You weren't wearing a ring.'

'Very observant. What's the business transaction?'

'I wish to retain your services as an art broker, mainly to make purchases for my private collection. You will be free to take on other clients if you wish, so long as such work does not interfere with your work for me.'

Her name was Ruby Frobisher. Philo said the name was the first thing that had to go. And her hair, she had to change it to red. She needed to work on her carriage, stance, way of speaking, dressing. He would arrange for it all. Her name, too, was Philo's invention, christening her Randolph, the maiden name of the wife of Robert E. Lee, a daughter of the finest family in Virginia and great-granddaughter of Martha Washington. It had added the final touch of class.

And if Jessica ever found out that her former partner in crime, a man disrespectful to women and who needed a lesson in manners, had had his tongue cut out by midnight visitors, she never let on.

But now she knew about the Alexandrians, and Philo's plans.

The bomb broker had shifted to detonation caps, explaining how everything was controlled from one hand-held device, and therefore he now had Philo's full attention. 'These bombs rupture on impact and spread burning fuel gel on surrounding objects,' said the man, who dealt regularly in the illicit sale and distribution of weapons around the world. 'You ordered the Mk 77 Mod 4 fire bomb, which holds seventy-five gallons of fuel gel mixture and weighs five hundred pounds when filled. When the bomb is released from an aircraft these arming wires are pulled from the fuses, thereby arming them. When the bomb impacts the target, everything around it will burn like Hell, literally.'

Philo already knew. He had seen the demonstration at the Buddhist monastery.

He had also decided what to do about Jessica.

Twenty-Five

Captain Stavros was suspicious from the start.

Standing in the wheelhouse, he was able discreetly to observe the actions of his two curious passengers. Their very first night on board, the gentleman had stayed in the ship's salon until the light was out in their cabin, and the next day the steward reported that the two had slept in separate beds – the lady in the bunk, the gentleman on the sofa. A lover's quarrel? Or perhaps they were not really newlyweds, not unless the world had changed since he had courted his own sweet Maria years ago.

Granted, the first day at sea the lady had been queasy, and that could be a deterrent to romance – sometimes. But a packet of ginger powder, pressed upon her by Stavros himself, who had spent forty years at sea and knew every cure for seasickness, had done the trick. Nonetheless, that night and the next her husband had waited in the salon, playing solitaire while the captain and his three officers enjoyed cigars and ouzo, and had only retired when the cabin light was out. Perhaps it was a game they played? Some secret entertainment between two lovers? The lady waiting in the dark, and so forth? Possibly, Stavros conceded, yet he had the feeling that the gentleman was in fact waiting for the lady to get undressed and into bed before he himself undressed in the dark and slipped into the makeshift sofa-bed.

Stavros watched them when they took infrequent walks on the aft-deck – not holding hands, he noticed – talking so quietly that no one else could hear. Sometimes the lady sat by herself in a deck chair, looking at pieces of pottery and consulting a book, pausing now and then to write in a note-book, while her taciturn husband stood at the rail as if searching for his soul out on the waves. He would read from a book with an emerald cover. It looked like a diary. An important one, the Greek captain surmised, to demand so many readings.

Stavros asked himself: what did it matter if they weren't really newlyweds? And his own answer was: it mattered not at all, unless one wondered why they would invent such a story in the first place.

Glenn stood on the deck beneath the clear night sky. With the captain's help he had been able to get Ian's satellite phone recharged, and the first thing he had done was attempt to retrieve the last number Hawthorne dialed. Unfortunately, Ian had deleted all numbers from the phone's memory.

Glenn contacted Maggie Delaney at Hollywood Division; she was in charge of his father's homicide while Glenn was away.

'We've been frantic,' she said now, her voice coming crystal clear from the starry skies. 'Why haven't you called?'

'It's a long story. Any news on my father's case?'

'Nothing. And we can't find Philo Thibodeau either. He's vanished. But he's doing crazy things. Selling everything he owns, all his companies and corporations – he's dumping shares, liquidating his financial empire, unloading everything. Wall Street's nervous. Everyone thinks Thibodeau knows something the rest of the world doesn't. Does he, Glenn?'

231

He didn't respond. Something from his father's letter came back: *Philo has taken Nostradamus to heart.* 'Maggie, see if you can get me information on a Nostradamus quatrain. Century seven, number eighty-three. And find out if there are any unusual astrological aspects being reported at the moment.'

She called back within the hour. 'The quatrain doesn't exist, Glenn. And as for that other stuff – I telephoned the astrological desk at the *Los Angeles Times*. They say Mercury is in retrograde until the twentieth of the month, going from Capricorn to Taurus, with the moon in Aquarius. What's it about, Glenn?'

'A hunch,' he said. 'Just pray I'm wrong.' He snapped the phone shut and looked up at the light glowing in the cabin window. Candice still awake, hard at work. He wanted to go up there, step into that small space, close the door, and pass the night in her arms. Instead, he turned his back on the temptation, went to the rail, and looked at the starsplashed sea.

He would not go up to the cabin until the light was safely out.

As she laid out the ceramic shards, Hebrew letters in faded ink still legible, Candice pictured Esther with her head bent over her work, cleaning a piece of ceramic, mixing her ink, making careful letters and allowing no mistakes, pausing every so often to listen to the hustle and bustle of the city beyond her door. What did she look like? Was she small? Was she pretty? Did she have a husband? Children? Perhaps a lover?

Candice did not work alone but with the assistance of a woman she had met only once, in the corridor outside the Intensive Care Unit, yet who had become a familiar companion over these past few days. Dr. Mildred Stillwater, plump, ageless, smiling in a peculiar way. What had happened to her after the publication of the Hebrew source book? Had she married? Raised a family? Given up ancient studies? For Stillwater's generation, the world of archaeology had been the jealously guarded domain of men. Had it been too much for the mild-tempered woman? Had she acquiesced and retreated to the kitchen of a suburban home, which, for a woman of her generation, was her place?

Candice thought of Paul, asking her to marry him, although it had been more of a casual suggestion than a formal proposal: 'Since your career is on the skids, you might as well come live with me in Phoenix. We could even get married if you wanted.' That was when she had vowed not to get involved, to focus on her career, to make a success of herself as her mother had, without the help of a man. But the vow was made before destiny had brought Glenn Masters to her door and linked him to her in ways she would never have thought possible, which made her think of him even now as she concentrated on the ceramic fragments.

She froze.

The piece in her hand: *My great-grandparents were among the captives taken by Nebuchadnezzar.*

So Esther *was* writing during the Captivity! A Jew in exile after the destruction of Jerusalem, writing something in secret, something in code, something forbidden. Hastily consulting the source book, Candice confirmed the years of the Babylonian Captivity of the Hebrews: 586 to 538 BCE.

Bless you, Mildred Stillwater!

The last pieces were translated now. Candice had only to sort them like a jigsaw puzzle until she completed the picture. The story of Esther of Babylon. And an explanation of the clay tablets Ian had sold his soul for.

A tap at the door, and Glenn looked in. It surprised her. The cabin light was still on. 'Is everything all right?' she asked.

'I finally got a call through to division headquarters. They have nothing new on my father's case.' He looked at the ceramic pieces.

'It's finished,' she said, handing him the translation she had written on a sheet of stationery obtained from Captain Stavros. 'Esther's story.'

He sat on the edge of the sofa and read.

> I write in secret and in haste. Little time is left to me. I fear I have been found. I am the last of my line. After me there is silence.
>
> I am called Esther. It is not my real name. It pleased

233

my Persian master to call me this for he said I was beautiful, like a star. My real name is of no consequence, for I am but the messenger of one who is greater than I, and it is her name that must live on.

My great-grandparents were among those taken captive by Nebuchadnezzar. They saw our king blinded and bound in chains to be brought to Babylon. There I was born and grew up; but I am not Babylonian. I lived with that company of exiled Jews who prayed daily toward the west, where our temple once stood.

Long before Jerusalem fell and we were dispersed and taken into exile, a select group of our people was chosen to carry the sacred words of our faith in our hearts and pass them to our progeny. To my ancestress was given the Song of Miriam, just as the stories of men were given to men. My distant mother memorized the words and carried them in her heart. She vowed to pass the secret to her daughters, that the heroic deeds of our ancestors would never die.

The Persians set us free, but I was not made free, for I caught the eye of a man who made me his slave and gave me a new name. He did not understand that I am the last of a long line of daughters to whom a sacred task was entrusted. He forbade me to fulfill this task, which has been my calling since before my birth, for it was my mother's calling, and her mother's before that, back through time to our first mother, Eve.

But now I am a runaway slave. If I am captured, I will be put to death. I ran from my master not for my own sake, but for the sake of generations who will come after me, and because, at the hour of my birth, my body and my life were dedicated to the guardianship of a sacred book.

I know my Persian master is searching for me. I made my escape during the night, with friends helping me to secure passage on a boat upriver to the city of Mari, where I struck southward on the caravan route that would lead me to Jerusalem.

But Jerusalem is far to the west and I am exhausted. This city provides good shelter from the winter rains and storms that impede my progress. Here, while I wait for the weather to improve, and hide from my master's guards, I will commit to writing the story that was impressed upon my mind as a stylus impresses words upon damp clay. I preserve in this clay the life and words of she who taught us that the Living God created us not to perish but to fulfill our destinies; she who taught us that in our darkest hours the sun always rises, God shining His nourishing light upon us; she who taught us that God watches over all of us, even the humble chick in its egg; and she who taught us that God always takes us to the other side of the sea.

And now a final request: Though I am in darkness, I shall soon be in light. I do not fear death, for I return to the Father, who is light. I ask only one thing in my last moments: that whosoever finds this place and my poor remains, I beg of you to please seek out my sisters in Jerusalem and give them this book which is their legacy. And tell them that my final thoughts were of them.

'The Song of Miriam,' Glenn murmured. 'A lost book of the Bible, left out because of Esther's capture and burial.'

'Then who is the "astronomer's wife"? Miriam?' Candice asked as she noticed Glenn had brought the pungent scent of the sea into the cabin. Would he also *taste* of the sea, she wondered? 'The Books of Moses say Miriam was a singer and dancer, probably a musician as well. Since we know Miriam approached Pharaoh's daughter and told her about the baby's mother, it follows that Miriam could have stayed in the palace, possibly growing up there with Moses.' An image blazed in Candice's mind, bright, sharp, and full of color: a mural from the tomb of Nakht. He had been an astronomer, and his wife a musician. Was it possible that the woman in that painting was in fact Miriam, sister of Moses?

'Glenn, what is written in the Song of Miriam that Philo Thibodeau so badly wants to get his hands on it, enough to kill for it?'

He looked at his ring.

'What?' she said.

'I told you I thought the secret society my parents belonged to was a religious order. I'm starting to remember more. Things I forgot long ago. Candice, the Alexandrians are atheists.'

'Then what possible use could they have for a lost book of the Bible?'

He could tell her now. He was safe. In control. His mother's last words in the journal had empowered him. He was master of his emotions again. *In two months, Glenn and I journey to Morven for his initiation into the Order. But I fear for my son's life. Philo grows increasingly delusional. I sense Glenn is in danger from him. What shall I do?*

'Morven's a place,' he said. 'I don't know where, but Philo is there.' His mother's final words: *Philo is after my son. He must be stopped.* 'Stavros said we dock at Salerno in the morning. We'll find a way to get ashore, fly to England. From there, find Morven and Philo.'

Soon, now, Philo thought in anticipation, Glenn Masters was going to have the supreme honor of sacrificing his life for the sacred cause. He might resist at first, but he was after all Lenore's son, was supposed to have been initiated into the Alexandrian order long ago. Philo was confident that once Glenn understood his destiny he would willingly give up his life.

He paced as Mildred Stillwater toiled over the clay tablets beneath the fluorescent lighting. To decipher the code she used the 'key' – the photocopy of the Duchesne stone, stolen from Candice Armstrong's hotel room in Palmyra.

Mildred had declared how generous it was of Armstrong to share the key, and then to hand the tablets over to Philo. That, of course, Mildred decided, would be the doing of Glenn, who knew by now that he was an Alexandrian, one of them.

'Is it what we thought it was?' Philo asked, curbing his impatience.

'Oh yes,' she said with joy. 'A treasure! One of the finest in our collection.'

Philo agreed. Except that, for him, the tablets meant more: that his twenty years of work were nearly at an end. The Jebel Mara tablets were the final piece of the puzzle.

Poor Mildred, never questioning, always doing what she

was told. Years ago she had been on the verge of marrying and starting a new life. Philo could not have this. As the world's foremost expert in ancient Near Eastern languages and alphabets, dialects and sub-tongues, Mildred was a valuable asset. He needed her here, working for him. He had worked a seduction on her so complete that she had left her groom standing at the altar.

Mildred stopped work to look at him with hungry eyes. Her yearning moved him. She had given up everything to be with him. Had lived a dry, sexless life. Not for her a man's embrace and the fruits of a womb.

Suddenly moved by her devotion and sacrifice, he did something he had never done before: Philo cupped his hand under her chin, lifted her face, bent his white head and kissed her gently on the lips. Lingered there, for it was her first man's kiss in thirty years, and it would be her last.

He drew back. Mildred was transfixed. Her eyes shone like twin suns, glistening with gratitude.

Philo smiled. It had not been an unpleasant task and such a small gesture. He could afford to be generous since the world, as everyone knew it, was about to end.

A bleak sky overhead, a lonesome wind blowing, not a soul, not a bird, not a plant for miles. A desolate landscape. Candice plodding through sand, each footfall sinking deeper until she is up to her knees and cannot move. Farther ahead, between the two sheer walls of the wadi, Glenn half buried, one arm sticking straight up to the sky, fingers curved like claws. His eyes glassy and staring. Dead.

She screamed.

When she opened her eyes she found herself sitting up in the bunk, Glenn immediately at her side, taking her into his arms. She pressed her face to his bare shoulder. 'I dreamed you were dead,' she whispered.

Silver moonlight streamed through the open porthole. He stroked her hair. 'Not yet. I can't die because I have a lot to do still,' he said in a soothing voice, marveling at how small she felt in his arms. She wore a T-shirt for a nightgown, but it felt like nothing at all. 'There's this giant ball of twine, the largest in the world, in Kansas, I think. I haven't seen it yet.'

237

She made a sound and he thought she was crying. But when she made another, he realized she was laughing.

'And there's a house,' he added, 'in Oklahoma, I think, made entirely of Cadillac tail fins.'

She drew back and looked at him with sparkling eyes. 'You made that up. I've heard of the ball of twine. It's in Minnesota. But the house of fins, you made that up.'

'And there's the Shrine of the Holy Tortilla. Don't laugh, I'm serious. There really is such a thing, in Lake Arthur, New Mexico. Jesus' face appeared on this tortilla and it supposedly heals people. I'm going to take a road trip and see all the wonders of America.'

She wiped her eyes. 'Stop trying to cheer me up.'

'I was merely explaining why your nightmare was wrong. I have too many plans to die just yet.'

The silver light through the porthole made Glenn's muscular arms and shoulders look as if they were carved from marble. 'Do you think you might want company on this road trip?' she asked, barely finding breath she was suddenly so achy with desire.

'I don't know. Are you good at folding road maps?'

And then they fell silent because they realized this was the moment. There was Candice's uncontrollable hair, going this way and that over her shoulders, covering one eye in a sleepy-sexy way. And Candice felt tendon and sinew beneath her hands because Glenn slept only in shorts, and she felt the scar on his shoulder blade from when he had fallen and seen the Luminance.

Glenn looked at her neck and said, 'Where is she?'

'Who?'

He laid his forefinger in the hollow of her throat.

'I take her off at night.'

He didn't remove his finger, but stared at the place where the amazing voice came from, the cavern of her vocal cords, filled with heat and honey. He bent his head and pressed his lips to the delicate skin. Candice moaned. She curled her arms around his neck and pressed her lips to his ear.

His embrace tightened, mouth seeking hers, the kiss tentative—

He snapped his head up. 'What's that?'

The ship's engines had stopped.

He pulled slacks up over his shorts and threw open the cabin door. Men were running on the deck.

'What is it?' Candice said, bunching the blankets to her chin.

Stavros appeared, drawing suspenders over meaty shoulders. 'Nothing to worry about, sir. Engine broke down. Happens all the time. We will have it going in no time.' Stavros crossed himself and hurried on.

When Glenn turned back into the cabin and closed the door, he saw that Candice had hastily pulled her jeans and blouse on. 'I thought we were going to have to run for the lifeboats,' she said.

They stared at each other across the small space, remembering what the failure of the engines had interrupted. But how to get it started again? They could hear men shouting below decks, the clang of metal against metal, and knew that, as Stavros promised, the engine would most likely get going again. Humans, however, were not as simple. Restarting an engine was a lot easier than restarting a romantic moment. Neither knew what move to make next. But they hungered now for each other, and ached with desire.

The silence of the sea was almost eerie. Now they could hear what had been drowned out by constant engine noise: creaking, groaning, water lapping the sides of the ship. And the deeper silence beyond their vulnerable vessel, stretching out across the black Mediterranean.

Glenn looked long at Candice, wondering how he had lived without her, unable to imagine that previous, lonely life.

And something else: she had given him a gift.

The climbing that he had gotten away from; but a yearning now filled him, to go back to it, to an endeavor that was more than a physical endurance test, was a spiritual quest. How could he have forgotten the silent realms of Yosemite's big walls, the soft sounds of blowing air accentuated by clips of carabiners and tapping sounds of hammer against piton? She had made him remember this glory that he had forgotten.

'Candice,' he said, filling his mouth with her name.

The engines started up – chugging and throbbing until they relaxed into a steady hum and the boat surged forward once more, resuming its gentle roll on the sea. Candice and Glenn reached for each other across the small space. Starlight glowed in the round glass of the porthole, the only illumination in the cabin, enough light to see each other's faces, to look into each other's eyes. The rest of the darkness heightened the exquisiteness of touch and feel, discovery by hand and mouth. He took a lock of her hair and rubbed it between thumb and forefinger, as if testing fine silk. She placed her hands on his chest, exploring hard muscle.

The first kiss was hard and hungry. Hands moved voraciously, pulling at clothes, peeling them away. Glenn's fingers caressed her bare breast. Candice cried out. They collapsed onto the bed, Glenn driving his fingers into her hair as he tasted her mouth, neck, shoulder, Candice pulling him to her, murmuring, 'Yes . . . yes . . .'

In the silver-mooned twilight Glenn opened his vulnerable heart and gave himself up to passion and desire and yearning, to *feel* for the first time in years. And Candice opened her body to him, holding him inside, clutching him tightly to her, feeling the heat of his breath on her neck, his hard kisses setting her on fire. They whispered each other's names. He tenderly kissed her closed eyes as they moved together in exquisite rhythm. Candice relished the feel of him, his hardness and weight, hot skin against hers.

Tears of ecstasy streamed from her eyes as she shuddered and gave a cry. A moment later, Glenn also, but they continued to hold onto each other, prolonging the embrace, the rapturous moment as, overhead, in the deep night sky, Orion chased Taurus in eternal pursuit.

Glenn woke holding her in his arms, her eyelids fluttering in slumber. He was rocked by a violent protectiveness. Making love with Candice – he had never felt so helpless, nor so powerful. She made him feel like a boy, and a god.

What had he been thinking, allowing her to go to Morven with him? Twenty years ago his mother had thought he was in danger from Philo, when Glenn was only eighteen years old. How much greater was that threat today?

He could not expose Candice to such danger. 'I'm sorry,' he whispered tenderly as she slept, brushing a strand of dark-brown hair from her forehead and kissing her softly on the cheek. 'Please forgive me.'

Tomorrow morning, when they anchored in the Bay of Naples, he would jump ship after paying Captain Stavros to see that Candice was safely delivered to Southampton.

By the time he saw her again, everything would be over.

As the homely *Athena* chugged her way across the moonlit Mediterranean Sea, with her cargo of figs and dates, and embracing lovers and sleeping crew, her captain sat at the communications radio, describing to the listener at the other end the interesting objects the steward had espied while delivering meals to the cabin. 'Very ancient,' Stavros said quietly. 'Writing done in ink, on pieces of pottery. I believe the alphabet is Hebrew, but it could be Aramaic. Yes, yes, we dock in Salerno tomorrow. I can have the man and woman conveniently out of the way.'

He broke the connection and stretched. The Greek captain was extremely pleased with himself, for not only did he ply a lucrative trade in olives and wine to Great Britain, silk and English biscuits to the Middle East, he dabbled in a profitable sideline as well – trafficking in illegal antiquities. And he had been getting rich on it for nearly ten years. After all, who paid much notice to the jolly captains of rusty old boats?

Twenty-Six

'What do you mean, a health inspection?' Glenn shouted. The *Athena* was riding at anchor outside the harbor at Salerno, waiting for permission to dock. The Burmese crew in sarongs were already busy about their work in the cargo holds, while Captain Stavros, squinting in the bright sunshine, had just broken some bad news to his passengers.

He shrugged apologetically. 'It happens. I can do nothing about it. A ship coming from a port where there has been disease must be checked before being allowed to dock. I am sure the official will do nothing more than examine your vaccination certificates.'

Glenn and Candice exchanged a look. They didn't have vaccination certificates.

'And then what?' Glenn asked, glad now he had changed his mind about jumping ship and leaving Candice with Stavros.

'If you are inoculated for the disease they are worried about, you will be allowed to disembark. If not, you will be placed in quarantine.'

'Quarantine!'

'The officials might wish to inspect your bags as well, to see if you have any fruit, meat, or contaminated water. If you are uncomfortable with this, I can perhaps place your bags where the inspector will not see them?'

As tempting as the offer was, they did not like being separated from their possessions – in particular the pottery shards. So they spent a few minutes packing their knapsacks and Ian's duffel, just in case. They would come up with a story if their things were searched.

Beyond that, there was nothing they could do. They stood on the deck and watched helplessly as harbor traffic went to and fro – ferries and hydrofoils, cargo vessels and luxury cruise ships – and seagulls swooped around the *Athena*, hoping for snacks, before moving on to the more promising fishing boats. The shore, with its seawall and busy docks and quays, seemed impossibly far away. The Amalfi coastline was breathtakingly beautiful between blue sky and bluer water, with its arresting bluffs and villages nestled in coastal ravines. Yet Glenn and Candice barely saw it. Their eyes were fixed on each other as they stood speechless in the face of a new development in their lives.

Neither had spoken the word 'love.' It was all too new and stupendous and frightening. They had kissed and embraced and slept in the small intimate cabin of the gently rocking *Athena*, arms and legs intertwined, heartbeats thumping in unison as desire and desperation fueled their passion. But now it was morning and the sun was sharp, the sea breeze cutting, and they both felt naked in their raw emotions.

A small boat bearing official insignia came streaking through the water, weaving its way between the many bobbing craft. It throttled back noisily and tied up alongside the *Athena*. Two men in neatly pressed khaki uniforms made their way up the ladder.

242

After introductions, Stavros directed one of the men to the wheelhouse, where the first mate would make all necessary health documents and papers available to him. The second man stayed on deck, scrutinizing Candice's and Glenn's passports. As he handed them back, he said in excellent English, 'And now, please, your medical papers?' He held out a smooth, olive-skinned hand.

'What's the problem, doctor?' Glenn asked. He noticed that, while the man's badge identified him as a *medico*, he was wearing a sidearm.

'There has been a reported outbreak of cholera in the west of Syria and so we must check all ships that are coming from there. You need proof of inoculation for this disease. But if you do not have this proof, we must take you into quarantine.'

'For how long?'

The man shrugged. 'Days. Weeks. It depends.'

'Weeks!' Candice blurted.

Glenn laid a hand on her arm and thought for a moment. 'Doctor, when my wife and I went to Zaire a few months ago, we were inoculated against cronny bronitis. That's similar to cholera, isn't it? Wouldn't inoculation for cronny bronitis be good enough?'

The man blinked. 'Well, yes. But . . . *mi dispiace*, you still need the paper of inoculation.'

When Candice gave Glenn a puzzled look, he discreetly shook his head.

Saying goodbye to Stavros and his officers, they collected their gear and followed the two doctors onto the small medical boat.

They arrived at a waterfront crowded with pedestrians, cars, and motor scooters, and food vendors pushing carts piled high with everything from eggplant to pizza. The boat's pilot climbed out to tie the lines, with the two officials remaining on board to stand close behind the Americans. Candice was assisted up to the dock, and then Glenn.

The first thing he noticed was a large black car parked at the far end of the wharf, its windows tinted dark so that the occupants could not be seen. The second thing was a boy in shorts and T-shirt pushing a small cart filled with lemons, peaches, and yellow plums. He was calling out his wares in shrill Italian as he moved along the dock, hoping to tempt hungry seamen and dockworkers to make a purchase.

The two uniformed *medicos* flanked the Americans and, holding each tightly by an arm, proceeded toward the car. Glenn said, 'That fruit looks awfully good, and my wife and I missed breakfast.'

Their escorts remained resolutely silent and didn't break their stride.

'Hoy there!' Glenn called to the boy, who immediately redirected his rickety wagon toward the potential customers.

'I have money right here,' Glenn said, digging into his shirt pocket. He didn't bother to count the bills, but he knew it was more than enough to compensate the kid. In a quick move, before their two escorts could react, Glenn pressed the money into the boy's hand and tipped the cart over, sending red, orange, and yellow fruit rolling every which way on the wooden dock. Grabbing Candice's arm, he pulled her around the cart and together they ran, gripping their knapsacks and duffel, while the startled *medicos* slipped and slid on the fruit.

Dodging in and out of traffic, getting themselves out of sight as quickly as they could, Glenn and Candice didn't stop running until they fled down a narrow street with a steep incline, and were so far from the wharf that they decided it was safe enough to stop and catch their wind.

'What was that all about?' Candice said breathlessly as they retreated into the protective recess of a doorway.

'I had a feeling the *medico* wasn't a doctor and they weren't taking us to any quarantine center. So I tested him. I had chronic bronchitis as a child and I called it cronny bronitis. A real doctor would have said he'd never heard of it. This guy couldn't take that chance, in case it was something a doctor should know.'

He squinted toward the end of the street, which opened onto the sunlit harbor. 'Philo almost got us this time.' He took Candice's arm. 'We have to get to London. Fast.'

Twenty-Seven

Philo kept up a steady pace on the Stairmaster, like a warrior preparing for battle.

He relished the feel of sweat dripping from his body, the heat and energy in his muscle and sinew. In this private gym that offered every piece of state-of-the-art exercise equipment, Philo Thibodeau kept himself in shape with all the religious determination of a saint. Seventy years old with the body of a fifty-year-old, he needed to stay vigorous, youthful. Time was racing. The Hour was almost here.

After a bracing shower and re-dressing in white silk pajamas and white silk dressing gown, he stepped out onto the picturesque deck of his chalet, a mountaintop aerie he retreated to periodically to refresh his soul, and he surveyed the world with a 360-degree sweep of his eyes. Philo took in the peaks and the snow, the ravines and valleys, the forest-carpeted slopes, the deer hidden there, the trout swimming the streams, the people in the village below, and then looked to the horizon where he imagined all the villages and towns and cities, and the people teaming in them, six billion souls – all belonging to Philo Thibodeau.

No one else knew this of course. But they would, soon. On the day of trumpets and angels when Philo walked side by side with God. On the day when Philo met the Pope, and the Pope kissed Philo's ring.

'I know what you're up to.'

He turned to see Jessica standing in the open French doors, flaming hair lifting in the breeze, a tall woman in black pleated slacks and cream silk blouse tucked in at a narrow waist. She had arrived an hour earlier by private helicopter.

He lifted an eyebrow. 'And what is that, my dear?'

She retreated indoors, detesting the alpine chill on the deck. She was barefoot because, with the exception of the kitchen, every floor of the chalet – a total of eight thousand square feet – was carpeted wall to wall in polar bear fur, a delicious sensation underfoot. Jessica eyed the buffet that had been laid with a feast and wondered if, for once, Philo was going to share a meal with her.

'At the château,' she said, her eyes devouring the peeled shrimp, wedges of cheese, bunches of plump, dewy grapes, 'I saw a few things.'

They had discussed her visit to the fortress in the Pyrenees when Philo had telephoned to invite her to join him at his chalet. She had freely admitted to duping the gate guard in order to get inside, and to having snooped, once inside. She had thought Philo would be angry, but he wasn't, saying he did not blame her for being curious. She wondered if he would be as calm when she dropped the bombshell and outlined her demands.

'What did you see?' he asked, watching her, a beautiful, artificial woman not to be trusted.

'A papyrus,' Jessica said, shifting her eyes to Philo, to watch his reaction. 'The label said it was the earliest known version of the Gospel of Mark. Is it real?'

'No doubt about it.'

'The earliest manuscripts have Mark ending at the eighth verse of chapter sixteen,' she said, picking up a wedge of cheddar, breaking off a piece, 'when the angel appears to Mary Magdalene at the empty tomb. The subsequent verses, describing Jesus meeting his disciples in Galilee, are an obvious add-on by a later writer. It's always been a mystery why. So the château has the *real* ending.'

Selecting a pipe from a rack of Meerschaums, Philo said, 'Analysis has proven beyond a doubt that it was written a mere decade after the Crucifixion, the only document of its kind in the world. All other New Testament material was written many years after the last of Christ's followers was dead and buried.' Opening a tobacco pouch, scooping the pipe into it. 'As you pointed out, my dear, modern scholars believe the current version of Mark is longer than it originally was, that it originally ended at verse eight: "The women said nothing to anyone, for they were afraid of—" Most translations have it as, "were afraid," because that makes it tidy. But the correct translation is "afraid *of*." Of what were the women afraid? And why did the Gospel end in mid sentence? Some say it's

246

because Mark died before he could finish it. Others say Mark's ending was chopped off to cover something up, like maybe the original ending didn't jibe with the thinking of the day.' He tamped the tobacco. 'Did you read the translation?'

'I had just enough time to jot it down. I memorized it. "For they were afraid of the angel. And so the angel said to them, 'Women, why are you afraid? Do you not know me? Look upon me and say who I am.' And Mary Magdalene looked and she saw that the angel was her Lord, risen from the dead. She beheld the wounds in his hands and the wounds in his feet and the wound in his side. And the Lord said, 'Proclaim to all the world that I am risen.'"' Jessica added with a smile, 'What I wonder is, why not tell the world? Why keep it a secret?' She held up a slender, pampered hand. 'Never mind, I know why.'

'You do?'

She plucked a handful of burgundy grapes from the buffet and cradled them in her palm. 'The papacy of the Catholic Church is based on the fact that Peter was the first person to whom the risen Christ passed on the mandate to preach to the world. But the document at the château, a Gospel fragment predating any other on earth, says that the chosen person was Mary Magdalene. The man at the tomb isn't just a gardener or an angel, as later Gospel versions claim, but Jesus himself. Can you imagine walking into the Vatican and informing the Pope that he has to vacate the throne of St. Peter because it belongs to the sisterhood of Mary Magdalene, and has done so for two thousand years? What's the feminine of "pope," I wonder?'

He studied her, the smug smile, the self-confident manner. Popping grapes into her mouth and chewing juicily. 'You are coming to a point, I suppose?' he asked softly.

'The Mark Gospel, all those ancient books and writings, the religious works you have had me and others purchase for you over the years, I know what you are planning.'

'And that is?'

'Religious blackmail,' Jessica said.

He blinked. He was impressed. 'To what end?'

'Global domination. Control the world's religions and you control the world,' she said.

'You came to that conclusion because of a Gospel fragment?'

247

Another purple grape between her red lips, white teeth biting down, lavender saliva at the corner of her mouth. 'Expose that fragment to the world, and Catholics everywhere realize they've been hoodwinked for two thousand years. And if they start questioning this, then what about the rest of Catholic dogma? I would bet that somewhere in the château, or in your own private collection, Philo, is a document or a letter that could alter the Koran, or prove that the Buddha never lived, or that Krishna was just a myth. Debunk the world's religions and chaos and anarchy ensue. Leaders of organized religions would do anything to keep this information quiet.'

'Very clever, my dear.'

Jessica smiled in satisfaction. This was going more smoothly than she had expected. Philo would have to agree to her terms. Ruling the world. An idea she could get used to.

'You draw an interesting conclusion,' he said. 'But it is incorrect. Yes, we are a secret order, and we call ourselves the Alexandrians. But let me tell you the true purpose of the Alexandrians.' And he did. And after hearing about Alexander and the secret priesthood, the burning of the Great Library, two millennia of obtaining and preserving special writings, Jessica was confused. 'All that just to have the world's largest library?'

'That is only the first part. Have you ever wondered, my dear, *why* I recruited you in the first place? The Alexandrians are collectors. But they weren't collecting quickly enough. I needed to step up the pace, and I needed to do it secretly. It was also necessary to make certain acquisitions that the Alexandrians would not have approved of but which I needed for my purposes.'

She frowned. 'Your purposes?'

He told her the truth then, what no one else knew, not even his late wife Sandrine.

As his soft voice filled the afternoon air, mingling with the roar and crackle coming from the golden flames in the fireplace, as words spoken in a gentlemanly Southern accent told of a plan Jessica could not have imagined, she felt a cold fear creep into her bones. He was serious, dead serious about the destruction he planned. 'Philo,' she said when he was finished and had set his pipe aside unlit. 'Philo, that's insane.'

His manner turned cool. 'No prophet is honored in his own house. Jesus understood this. And it has been my cross to bear. But soon the world will know the truth.'

Jessica was just realizing what a horrendous error she had made, how drastically she had underestimated Philo, wondering how she could not have seen this madness in their years together, and was thinking of her exit, how to get out of here and away from him, when one of his ubiquitous yes-men, the one with the strawberry mark, came in.

'Contact has been made, sir,' Mr. Rossi said.

Philo closed his eyes. *Contact.* The last piece had fallen into place. The beginning had ended and now the ending had begun. 'I leave at once,' he said, starting for the door. He flicked his hand toward Jessica. 'Take care of that.'

Rossi reached into his jacket and brought out a gun. Jessica's eyes widened. 'Philo?'

He turned on her. 'You betrayed me. You were going to expose my glorious cause before the appointed hour. Had I not acted in bringing you here, I might have lost forever my chance to be with Lenore again.'

'Who?'

'*No one,*' he said, white brows lowering over thunderous gray eyes, 'interferes with my destiny.'

Rossi advanced on her. 'No, Philo!' she cried.

'Not here,' Thibodeau said to the man, pointing to the expensive white polar bear fur carpet. 'Out there.'

'No, Philo!' she said again as Rossi took her by the arm and led her, stumbling, out onto the deck. 'No, Philo, I swear,' a third time, like Peter denying Christ. The gunshot echoed off the surrounding mountain peaks like a crack of thunder.

Ian Hawthorne's flat was located in Bloomsbury on a small street midway between the British Museum and University College London. In the recess of a bookshop across the way, Glenn and Candice watched the building to make sure it wasn't under surveillance.

They had caught an immediate flight from Salerno to Rome, and from there a connection to London. Since their passports contained recent Middle Eastern customs stamps, they had been rigorously questioned by security at either end, body-searched and finally allowed to proceed. The delays had heightened their anxiety and the fear that Philo, or his agents, would be lying in wait at Ian's apartment. But nothing seemed to be out of the ordinary. They let themselves in with keys found in Ian's duffel.

Candice felt strange being in Ian's home, and sad, too, remembering his tragic end in the desert. The flat was crammed with books and artifacts, pottery, statuary, ancient coins; walls covered with photographs, framed letters, news articles about Sir Ian Hawthorne; chairs holding personal effects. The summation of a man's life in two and a half rooms.

On board the *Athena* Glenn and Candice had played the tape labeled INSURANCE, found in Ian's duffel. But the recording had been poor, indistinct in places, and so they had come to his residence hoping to find clarification of the tape's message. While they searched, Glenn slipped the tape into the answering machine and hit 'Play'.

This machine produced a cripser, clearer playback than the one on the *Athena*, so that Ian's voice came out loud and clear, from his flat in Amman, Jordan, placing and receiving calls. They listened to Ian making wagers on horses, dogs, soccer games, telling someone the check was in the mail, requesting additional funding for his dig.

And then Candice's voice. 'Ian? It's Candice. You said if I ever needed a favor . . .' Only weeks ago but seeming like years.

They listened keenly now. The next call was incoming. 'Mr. Hawthorne, we wish to hire your services.' A man's voice, not Philo's. 'We understand that Candice Armstrong has requested your help getting into Syria. We would like you to accompany her wherever she goes.'

They listened further. Ian agreeing, negotiating, coming to a mutual price.

'You are to give us periodic reports by phone, Dr. Hawthorne. The number is . . .' Glenn grabbed a pencil and wrote it down.

'Tomorrow evening, in the lobby of the Al-Qasr Hotel on Abd al-Hamid Sharif Street. Our agent will give you three things: the first half of the payment, a satellite telephone, and a gun.'

Ian protested the gun.

'You are to use it if Armstrong gives you trouble.'

They heard Ian's stunned silence, and then the call was disconnected. The tape ended there.

'Ian was supposed to *shoot* me?' Candice looked at Glenn. 'But not you. Why not you?'

Glenn's face was grim. 'Philo wants the showdown. He wants me to find him.' Twenty years ago, an argument between two men. The words 'blood' and 'sacrifice' spoken. Glenn knew now that it had something to do with him.

He picked up the phone and dialed the number Ian's caller had provided as the contact number. The voice at the other end said, 'Thistle Inn.'

'Thistle Inn?' Glenn said. 'Have I reached . . .' And he repeated the number.

'That's correct, sir.'

'Can you tell me where you are located?'

'How's that again?'

'I need directions to your establishment.'

Glenn wrote them down and when he hung up, said, 'It's in Scotland.'

They found an atlas among Hawthorne's books. Glenn located the area where the inn was, in south-west Scotland. In small print: *Morven*. It was an island.

Candice turned anxious eyes to Glenn. 'What do you think we'll find there?'

'I don't know. But one thing is certain – it will be heavily guarded.'

Twenty-Eight

London, England, 1814

'You have to listen to me!' Frederick Keyes shouted. 'Desmond Stone plans to lay hidden traps around Morven! Deadly snares, nets, pitfalls with sharpened spikes.

251

Spring-loaded steel traps, such as Canadian fur hunters use to catch bears. All operated by unseen trigger mechanisms. This is irresponsible, cruel, and inhumane!'

'Come now,' Stone drawled. 'Cruel and inhumane? To protect what is ours? Trespassers and spies deserve to die.'

They were meeting in a London men's club, and, because the hour was late, they had the smoking room to themselves.

'And innocent passers-by?' Keyes said, turning on his rival. He and Stone had been competitive since their days together as architecture students. 'Those who happen upon Morven without knowing they are danger? Are you insane?'

Stone shrugged. 'In war there are always innocent casualties.'

'Casualties!'

'Gentlemen,' said a white-whiskered older man who held up his hands, 'we must be civil about this. Frederick, we agree with *you*, but unfortunately the safety and security of the Library is above all other considerations, including the safety and well-being of tourists and passers-by who unwittingly stumble upon Morven.' The older gentleman had spent the past weeks meeting with Alexandrians in Britain and on the Continent, collecting their votes on the vital and urgent issue of Morven's security. 'Frederick, the virtue of Stone's plan is that it is in place and can be implemented at once. You, Frederick, have not even come up with an idea.'

'I need time.'

'There is no time. You know this. You saw what happened when revolution broke out in France. The château was almost discovered. That is why we came across the Channel. Can you imagine what Bonaparte would do with our collection if he found it? My God, man, he would use it to conquer the world!'

'But innocent people will get killed. Anyone passing near Morven—'

'Then for God's sake, man, come up with an alternative!'

'It takes time—'

'You have precisely one week. After that, we go with Stone's plan.'

As they retrieved their top hats and canes, Desmond Stone said with a smug smile, 'You'll never make it, Frederick. You're out of ideas.'

But Frederick Keyes was made of stern fiber. 'I will stop this barbaric plan of yours, Stone, if it's the last thing I do.'

It was past midnight and Frederick was burning precious oil, laboring over sketches, drafts, designs. But no ideas were coming to him. And he had only three days left.

Bang. Bang. 'Open up!'

Frederick started, knocking over his ink bottle.

The fists pounded again. 'Open up for the law!'

He unlocked the door and peered out. A large man in the uniform of the Night Watch pushed his way in. 'Frederick Keyes?'

'Yes. What is this about, Constable?'

'You are to be taken before the magistrate. Come along quietly.'

Frederick looked at the men behind him, officers of the Watch patrol. 'On what charge?'

'Treason.'

And they clapped iron manacles on his wrists.

The judge's voice rang out in a courtroom rich in wood paneling and history: 'Frederick Keyes, did you aver, in front of the witnesses who have testified here, that there is a higher power than the Crown and God?'

Everyone waited in hushed silence: the barristers in their white wigs and black gowns, the public gallery packed with noisy spectators. The case was treason and therefore held in Court Number One, the most famous and oldest part of the Old Bailey in London.

Frederick Keyes, standing in the defendant's box, said, 'If my lord will permit—'

'Answer the question. Were those your words?'

'Yes, my lord.'

Shouts of shock, outrage, and indignation thundered up from the gallery. The judge banged his gavel. Lowering thick brows, he said, 'And what is that power? Is it the Devil?'

'I cannot say, my lord.'

The judge leaned forward. 'Are you a Christian?'

'No.'

'Are you a Jew?'

Laughter from the gallery.

'I am of no established religious faith.'

'Do you deny all that the witnesses have testified to here today? That you spoke words of treason and blasphemy?'

Frederick Keyes straightened his shoulders and stood tall, his voice strong. 'My words were misconstrued.'

'*Do you deny them?*'

'No.'

'The witnesses said you made use of the word "we." Who are these "we"?'

'I cannot say.'

'You mean you *refuse* to say.'

A pause. 'Yes.'

The judge leaned back, his tone dispassionate as he said, 'A godless man who puts himself above God and king.' Draping a black cloth over his powdered wig, he said, 'Before I pronounce sentence, has the prisoner anything to say?'

A whisper: 'I am innocent.'

'Mr. Keyes, you have been found guilty of treason for which the only sentence is death. You will be taken to Newgate Prison, there to be hanged by the neck until you are dead. I cannot see how you, an avowed atheist, can expect to receive mercy on your immortal soul, nonetheless it is my duty, as I pass sentence, to utter these words: may God have mercy on your soul.'

'It is a sad state of affairs,' Jeremy Lamb declared to his valet as he inspected his freshly shaven jaw in the looking-glass, 'when a man is reduced to wearing the same cravat *two days in a row*.'

'Right you are, sir,' said the valet, who always agreed with his master; even if Lamb were to say white was black, Cummings would agree because he wanted to keep his job.

Lamb stepped back to inspect his appearance in the glass: shined Hessian boots, dark pantaloons, blue coat, and buff-colored waistcoat. Jeremy approved. At thirty-six, Lamb was a fussy and fastidious man, always taking hours to dress and habitually using three hairdressers – one for the sideburns, one for the forelock, and one for the back of the head (although on this morning of a sad state of affairs he had to make do with just Cummings).

'Clothes make the man, Cummings, never forget that,' he said as he turned away to address himself to the day's prospects, which, under these conditions, were sadly paltry. Still, there was the rumor of a new prisoner coming. Always good for a bit of diversion.

No sooner had Jeremy addressed his breakfast of bread and ale than the rumored newcomer was brought to the barred door. It got the attention of all the cell-mates, as any diversion would, so that, for a few minutes at least, Jeremy was able to eat unmolested (the others were always begging for scraps, but if he shared with them all, then what would *he* eat?). Once the new man was looked over, assessed, and deemed worthy of ignoring or stealing from, the usual deafening din of the prison cell would rise again, spoiling Jeremy's breakfast.

He scrutinized the new man.

Not your ordinary criminal. In fact, Jeremy recognized a fellow gentleman, for the man wore a long cut-away tailcoat over a striped waistcoat and traditional white breeches. He looked like any gentleman out for a stroll – not some poor bastard who'd just been thrown in Newgate Prison, the most hellish spot on earth. Jeremy's interest deepened when he recognized the tailoring – a Bond Street man he himself used, gifted in the knowledge of how the grain of the fabric should be used, the direction of the weave and warp. Jeremy wondered what the poor fellow was in for. Embezzlement, most likely. Didn't look like a common thief or debtor. Possibly he was in for transportation to Australia, as many were, most declaring they would rather hang. Now that the American colonies had broken away from Britain, England needed a new dumping ground for her undesirables. Australia was chosen, but the voyage was so long and hazardous, many did not survive it.

The newcomer was frantic, struggling against his jailers, protesting his innocence, as if that would do any good. And when the door clanged shut and locked, the man grabbed the bars and continued to shout his innocence.

After a while he turned away and surveyed the nightmare into which he had been thrown. The look on his face was pure shock. Jeremy himself, two weeks prior, entering the prison for the first time in his life, must have worn such an expression. The hellish noise, the roaring and clamor, the stench and

255

nastiness – it hit one in the face and took some getting used to.

One thing Jeremy noticed about the newcomer was that he didn't have the heavy leg manacles that were attached to most of the other prisoners, keeping them secured to chains anchored to the floor and walls. A prisoner could pay to have lighter manacles fitted – an easement of irons, they called it – or have them removed entirely, *if* enough money changed hands. So the newcomer was not without money, Jeremy noted, like himself, his father having grudgingly paid to have his son's iron manacles withheld.

Jeremy watched the newcomer pace restlessly, slamming fist into palm, murmuring to himself. He tripped over a prisoner sitting with his back to the wall, legs stretched out. 'Sorry,' the new man muttered. But the other didn't stir, and the newcomer noticed the man had a queer pallor. He shook the man's shoulder and the fellow fell over. 'There's a dead man in here!' he shouted, running to the bars.

'You're wasting your breath,' Jeremy said, rising, hand extended. 'They'll come and collect it in a day or two. Jeremy Lamb at your service.'

The newcomer stared at the offered hand as if he had never seen one before. Then he delivered his own into it for a handshake, saying, 'Frederick Keyes,' in a strong voice.

'You can share my space as clearly you are a fellow gentleman.'

Keyes, glancing toward the barred door as if expecting it to spring open and the jailer to announce that he was free, hunkered down on the straw.

'That's Cummings,' the younger man said, pointing to the wretch anchored to the floor by a long chain. 'I pay him to sit watch while I sleep, make sure no one steals from me. He also serves as my valet. If you can afford it, and by the look of it you can, I suggest you work out an arrangement with one of the fellows here. They work cheap and can be trusted.' He pointed to Cummings' heavy chain. 'Can't get away with anything.'

Keyes looked in amazement at Jeremy's corner of the vile cell: a wooden pallet covered in a foul straw mattress, a wooden crate upon which were laid out a gentleman's toilet articles, an overturned bucket that served as a stool, and a plank on two bricks with dishes and a cup set upon it. Nailed to the wall were a looking-glass, and hooks for the man's clothes.

Keyes surveyed the rest of the cell, large and crowded, infested with lice and rats – most prisoners were chained to the floor or walls, but a few had cleared spaces for a mattress and blanket. Those who were free of chains used a communal pail near the door as a latrine, the rest lay in their own waste. Keyes' eyes went to where the dead man lay.

'It's a mercy,' Lamb said, resuming his breakfast while Cummings licked his lips in anticipation of scraps. 'The poor sod was slated for hanging. But as he had no family or friends to bring him food, he starved to death. I am told only a quarter of the prisoners survive until their execution day.'

The newcomer gave him a fierce look. 'Are you to be executed?'

'Dear me, no! I am serving a sentence of three months, after which my father will pay the release fine and I shall be free. Wouldn't do to have the only son and heir perish in jail.'

'Why are you here?' Keyes asked, glancing again at the barred door, leading Jeremy to wonder if he was expecting a visitor.

'I had rotten bad luck. I was dining at my club with the Duke of Beaufort when word reached me that I was to be arrested for debts. A friend lent me his carriage, and I traveled all night with four horses, reaching Dover where I hoped to hire a vessel to carry me over because, as you know, debtors cannot be followed to France.' He sighed. 'I almost got away.'

'Gambling debts?'

'Gambling, sir, is for fools. My folly runs to sartorial matters. I owe every tailor and haberdasher on Bond Street. Mother always covered my debts, but she passed away last year and Father was resolute.'

'He would not pay your debts?' Keyes said, unable to believe a father would abandon his child to such horrendous circumstances.

'My father is the sort of man who wanted heirs but no children. Unfortunately he could not have one without the other and so he tolerated my sisters and me. If we saw him at all when we were growing up it was to administer corporal punishment when our naughtiness became too much for Mother.'

The rest he did not divulge: that he had done what he could to gain his father's pride by attracting the attention of the Prince Regent, gaining a post in the prince's own regiment – the 10th Dragoons – earning rapid promotion and gaining a captaincy. It didn't work. Not a word of commendation from Lamb Elder. So Jeremy started rebelling, notably in his mode of dress, following Mr. Brummel's example. Surely that would have gained the old boy's notice, as Lamb Elder still believed in velvet coats with gold buttons and powdered wigs. When that failed to elicit a response from his father, Jeremy gave up, in the meantime having discovered a lifestyle he quite enjoyed.

'Father requested that I be put in prison among the condemned, instead of in debtors' prison, to teach me a lesson.'

Jeremy waited, but the newcomer was not forthcoming with information about himself. Upon closer inspection, the man appeared healthy, in his late-forties with a touch of gray at his side whiskers. Clean, impeccable dresser. Jeremy cleared his throat. 'Might I ask what you are in here for?'

Frederick assessed his affable companion. How to respond? Keyes had fallen into a trap laid by Desmond Stone, as surely as if he had tumbled into one of Stone's savage pitfalls. In laying his trap, Stone had taken advantage of Britain's current economic troubles, which had spawned agitation for social reform. The government's response was repression, creating laws aimed at squashing dissent. And with Britain fighting so many fronts – the Americans, the Spanish, the French – paranoia was rife, suspicion was in the air, and every man had to watch his tongue. The slightest word could be misconstrued and there were spies everywhere.

In the men's club, two nights after the secret meeting of the Alexandrians, on a busy evening, Desmond Stone claiming to have a 'throat', which necessitated him leaning close to Frederick and speaking in low tones, thus ensuring his own words were not overheard. 'I don't see why we can't do away with all the secrecy about the Order. After all, we are *in the modern age.'*

And Frederick, unaware of the trap he was walking into, saying, 'You know as well as I how dangerous it would be for our secret to be revealed. We are atheists, Desmond, yet the most god-fearing of men. And we owe our allegiance to a power that is higher and mightier than even that of the British Crown. No one would understand.'

The witnesses at the club had not been part of Desmond's scheme, but merely honest men who had reported what they'd overheard. Frederick blamed none of them, just Desmond Stone. And himself.

'I am in for treason,' he said to Jeremy Lamb.

For once in his life, Lamb was at a loss for words. The man was to be hanged! Jeremy fumbled about, then said, 'But at least you can make your stay here as comfortable as possible, as you see that I have done. Tell your visitors to bring money – my father sends a weekly allowance by way of a servant, which I turn over to the jailer for favors.'

'No visitors,' Frederick said, watching now as prisoners began to strip the clothes from the dead man.

'What do you mean?'

'There will be no one coming.'

'Surely you must have *one* friend?'

'No friends . . .' They were having trouble getting the breeches off the corpse because one leg was chained to the floor. They were twisting the foot . . .

'But how will you eat?' Jeremy said, ignoring the mayhem in the corner. He had seen it before. 'The jailer is only required to provide one crust of bread per day, one cup of water.'

Keyes turned almost angry eyes to him. 'I have no one.'

Pity rose so suddenly and sharply in Lamb's heart that he was brought to tears. Bringing out a handkerchief, he declared, 'Then you shall share my space and my bounty. It doesn't do for a fellow not to have friends,' added Jeremy Lamb, who had hundreds of friends.

Keyes was pacing again, like a caged tiger, Jeremy thought. The man hadn't slept, he refused food, and now he went to and fro, his eyes on the barred door. The day before, he had said no one would be coming, so what was he expecting to see at the door?

Poor fellow, Lamb thought as he inspected himself in the looking-glass. Cummings was combing Jeremy's hair, as if they were in a Mayfair townhouse. No one had told Keyes

259

when the hanging was to take place. It could be today. It could be a month from now.

'Terrible punishment for speaking one's mind,' Jeremy said, but not too loudly lest his own words be taken for treason. 'Only the other day I was saying to Her Royal Highness, the Duchess of York . . .' His voice trailed off and his eyes grew large. 'I say!' he blurted, and Keyes turned to see what had caught Jeremy's eye.

'Emma!'

Jeremy glimpsed a vision of apricot and yellow and then it was blocked by the mass of bodies that were chained nearest the bars, pressing against them now, skeletal arms stretched out, begging for food, money, freedom. The jailer's voice boomed over the clamor, and he dashed his club against the bars, driving the creatures back. They slinked back to their places by the foul-smelling wall and watched as the bars swung open and a lady in gown and bonnet was admitted.

'Emma!' Keyes said again, rushing to her. 'I told you not to come.'

'Frederick, I couldn't stay away. I—'

The breath caught in her throat as her eyes widened at the sight of the skeletal wretches moaning in sickness, the outstretched grasping hands of the starving. She looked in horror at the naked ones, filthy and bug-bitten, with beards down their chests; the forgotten, the homeless, in prison for stealing bread or picking a pocket, crying out for food, water, mercy.

Jeremy quickly cleared a clean space for the lady and Keyes helped her to sit. Frederick clasped her hands and scolded her again, gently, for coming. But added that he was glad to see her.

Emma Venable was the second reason Keyes was going to hang.

He hadn't known her prior to a year ago, even though she was born into the Alexandrians. The membership numbered in the thousands now and was scattered all over the globe – some even lived in America – thus it was impossible to be acquainted with them all. He met her at a funeral. Her parents had died at the hands of a highwayman who had stopped their coach on a country road and demanded their money or their lives, ending up taking both. The man was caught and hanged at the crossroads of the nearest town, his body left up for weeks as a deterrent to other brigands.

Frederick saw much of her after that, and out of that friendship a gentle love had blossomed. They were to have been wed – and then he was arrested.

Because another had eyes on her.

Emma Venable descended from Alaric the Knight and was therefore held in great esteem by the Alexandrians, making her a prize bride. Keyes suspected that Desmond Stone, the man who had framed him and sent him to this terrible place, harbored secret ambitions: more than just to be the architect for Morven's security, he wished to dominate the Order, use its growing wealth and power for his own ambitious ends. Although Alexandrians were supposed to be democratic, and all members equal, one could not ignore the fact that Stone claimed an astonishing bloodline, all the way back to High Priest Philos. For this reason, many Alexandrians deferred to him. By marrying Emma, Stone would create a sort of royalty within the Order, since the priests and priestesses who served at the ancient Library had always been members of Egypt's royal house.

Keyes' fear now was that, once he was out of the way, Desmond Stone would charm or pressure orphaned Emma into marriage.

Jeremy watched the two, his eyes fixed on the young lady's pale oval face, dainty curls peeping from under her bonnet, and found himself desperately hoping the beautiful creature was Keyes' sister.

'Oh, Frederick dearest, what a terrible place! I cannot bear to think of you in here.'

Emma knew nothing of Stone's treachery, and neither did the Alexandrians, for if Frederick were to tell them that his arrest and conviction was Desmond's doing, it would rip the Society apart, divide it into factions, with members taking sides, suspicions rising in their minds, brother becoming mistrustful of brother. For the sake of the Order, Frederick Keyes would take his secret to the gallows.

Emma clasped his hands in hers. 'Let us be wed, here, now, right away.'

'I will not make of you a widow, nor will I let you speak sacred vows in this vile place.'

Jeremy suddenly saw Keyes in a different light than the night before. He wasn't the lost, friendless soul Jeremy had supposed. When Keyes had said no one was coming, Jeremy had concluded the man was without friends, not that he had told them to stay away. Unlike Jeremy's friends, who had stayed away of their own volition.

This gave Jeremy pause. He knew himself to be a pleasant fellow, always robustly welcomed wherever he went, invited to the best parties. But, for the first time, he saw the people he thought to be his friends were not his friends at all. Until now he had given it no thought, telling himself he didn't blame them. What a dreary prospect, to visit someone in prison. Yet it didn't seem to matter to this lovely Emma.

It made him feel strangely unsettled.

'My dearest,' Emma was saying, 'Horace Babcock is taking your case directly to the Home Secretary to appeal for clemency.'

'I know. I had hoped it would have come through by now. But I shall be freed soon, fear not. In the meantime, Emma, I must work on my plans for Morven's security.'

'But there isn't time! Already Desmond Stone is at Morven, overseeing his project.'

'Emma, it is never too late. While I draw breath, I shall fight Stone's barbaric plan. I promise you I will come up with a humane way to keep the Library safe.'

'When you were in the courtroom – oh, Frederick, how they misunderstand! And how brave you are not to reveal our secret.' For therein lay Frederick's ticket to freedom: to explain why he had spoken words that sounded like treason but in fact were not. Yet the explanation would necessitate revealing the existence and purpose of their order.

And now this insupportable irony! That to him was commissioned the task of making the collection secure from thieves and spies while the only way to carry out that task meant revealing the existence of the very structure he was meant to protect!

When the bell ran for visitors to leave, Frederick gave Emma a list of things he needed, and the next morning she appeared with drafting paper and his architect's tools, along with food, blankets, and a change of clothes for Frederick. She stayed the whole day, serving baked eggs, fresh bread, and ale. She had brought playing cards, books, and gossip, making herself at home in Jeremy Lamb's small corner of the foul prison cell, keeping bonnet and gloves on as if she were paying a call to people of high social standing, while Frederick cleared space for his work. Both knew that the Home Secretary was going to intervene at any moment and Frederick would be set free, because the Alexandrians were men of wealth and connection. In the meantime, Frederick drafted experimental plans while Emma chattered about the scandalous new dance that had come from Vienna and was sweeping Britain. 'Imagine a man and woman embracing for an entire four minutes in the middle of a crowded dance floor! But I should love to try the waltz myself. Perhaps after you leave here, Frederick.'

All the while, Jeremy watched. And what he saw in Emma's eyes when she looked at Keyes – something more than love: respect and admiration, almost worship, as if Frederick Keyes was her *god* – reminded Jeremy Lamb that he was god to no one, not even to a dog.

When the barred door swung open and the prison chaplain entered, Frederick almost fainted with fright. Each day he woke thinking it would be his last, and each night he lay down thinking tomorrow would be his last. And now here it was – the chaplain had come to pray with him!

But the chaplain had come for another, and, as the man picked his way through the stinking gloom, Frederick felt ashamed at his relief that the gallows was not meant for him.

'They hold services here inside the prison every Sunday,' Jeremy said as he and Frederick watched, and while Cummings boiled water for tea over the small spirit lamp Emma had provided. Her visits were improving the conditions for everyone: Cummings now had bandages beneath his leg irons, and ointment for the sores. 'I went once, for diversion,' Jeremy was saying, 'and the chaos was such during the sermon that the chaplain had to shout to be heard.' He didn't add that they also held services for the condemned. Gathered around their coffins, the prisoners had to listen to a lengthy sermon on the Sunday before they were taken to the gallows. 'The chaplains are supposedly bringing them spiritual peace of mind, but they're usually more interested in getting prisoners' stories so they can sell them to the scandal sheets at huge profit, the reading public being what it is.'

The next morning, shortly after Emma's arrival, the bell in the tower began to ring – the signal that a hanging was to take place – and a man came through the cell block with a hand bell, pausing outside the bars to cry out:

> All you that in the condemned hold do lie,
> Prepare you, for tomorrow you shall die,
> Watch all, and pray, the hour is drawing near,
> That you before th'Almighty must appear;
> Examine well yourselves, in time repent,
> That you may not t'eternal flames be sent:
> And when St Sepulchre's bell tomorrow tolls,
> The Lord have mercy on your souls!

Jeremy and his two companions looked on as the poor man was finally released from his manacles and dragged from the cell. He put up no resistance as he was mere skin and skeleton. But Emma saw the bewilderment in his eyes, as if he had no idea where he was or why.

'What was his crime?' Emma asked, her face tight and pale.

'He was a postal letter-carrier, sentenced to death for stealing a letter containing ten pounds. Been awaiting execution six months, I'm told.'

Emma started to cry, then forced herself to stop. Frederick was not going to suffer that fate. She had faith in the Alexandrians to sway the Home Office to intercede and grant him his freedom.

Keyes did not sleep – nightmares plagued him and rats crawled over him. But more than anything was his obsession with stopping Desmond Stone's brutal plan to protect Morven. Frederick paced the damp stones, trod the rotting straw, ignored the moans and cries of those around him, and blocked out the unending chatter of Jeremy Lamb – *How to make the Library secure?*

264

When Emma arrived, both men saw at once the red, swollen eyes. They jumped up to fetch her from the door and escort her to a seat. She could barely speak. The news had come: there was to be no clemency for Frederick.

Emma wept while Frederick stood over her, his face chiseled in firm resolve. Desmond Stone, with his own wealth and personal connections, had seen to it that the Home Secretary denied Frederick's request.

'Emma,' Frederick said gently, 'I want you to go home.'

'No!'

'Please, my dearest. I need to think. I have to come up with—' His throat closed over his words. He looked down at the useless drafts and drawings he had sketched on the paper. Stone was right: Keyes was out of ideas.

'I hate this place,' Emma said softly. 'The jailers demand money at every step. I even have to pay a shilling to be brought to you, for I could not do it on my own, this place is such a maze. Theseus himself, searching for the Minotaur, could not find his way through such a labyrinth.'

Frederick stared at her. 'What did you say?'

She lifted damp eyes. 'The myth,' she said in puzzlement. 'The labyrinth of Minos. You know it.'

'Tell me again.'

'Why?'

'Just tell me.'

'Aegeus, King of Greece, was forced to pay tribute to King Minos of the Minoans in the form of seven youths and seven maidens. Frederick, why do you want—'

'Go on!'

'The fourteen sacrificial victims were sent underground, into a maze where a monster called the Minotaur lived, a hideous creature that was half man and half bull. The victims became hopelessly lost in the labyrinth and were eaten by the Minotaur.'

'King Aegeus' son, Theseus,' Frederick interrupted, suddenly excited, finishing the story, 'wanting to slay the Minotaur, volunteered to be one of the sacrificial victims. He was successful! Theseus killed the monster and then found his way out of the labyrinth by the trail of twine he had laid upon entering!'

265

'Frederick?'

'That's it!' he cried.

Now he knew what he must do, but he had little time. The hangman's noose awaited him.

Now Frederick had an even bigger problem. The solution to a human-security plan for Morven had been found. But how to get the plans to the Alexandrians? Emma was the only one he could trust, but she was young and naïve. Desmond Stone would be watching. Keyes would in fact be placing her in danger by giving her the plans.

Emma was sitting with her embroidery, wearing bonnet and silk gown, though she had removed her gloves. She refused to stay away despite Frederick's protests. Another Alexandrian had approached the Home Secretary on her fiancé's behalf, and she resolutely believed he would be successful; therefore she would visit Frederick every day, until the order for clemency came through.

Unfortunately, Frederick knew otherwise.

He was puzzling over what to do with the plans when he happened to glance up and catch the expression on young Jeremy's face.

And Frederick saw the solution to his second problem.

Jeremy didn't know what to make of Keyes. All men, once they knew they were headed to the gallows with no hope of reprieve, were soon overcome by hopelessness and gave up. But Frederick Keyes refused to cave in. Working day and night on his great sheets of paper laid out on the filthy floor, on his knees tracing lines, scribbling numbers, fanatically working with drafting tools, compass, T-square, rulers, triangles, protractors, calipers, parallel rule. All in a great race against the clock – he had to finish before the hangman called.

It baffled Jeremy. What man spends the last days of his life *working*?

Jeremy understood Keyes' motivation. A place called Morven. That was everything – and the security of some sort of collection. Nonetheless, it was sobering for Jeremy who, at thirty-six years of age, had absolutely nothing to show for his life except a wardrobe full of expensive clothes. When he looked down the road into his future he saw himself as a laughingstock, a man not aging gracefully but becoming a buffoon. He had seen such men, elderly fops, whom people made fun of behind their backs. But what sort of alternative future was there for him? It would be insufferable drudge to work in his father's accountancy firm. Jeremy was too old to go to university and he couldn't learn a trade. What, at the end of it all, was it going to say on his gravestone? *Here lies Jeremy Lamb. A good dresser.*

Emma arrived with food, clean clothes, and news: the new theater on Drury Lane was finally completed; Beethoven had performed his newest symphony, No. 8; a Swiss explorer had found a magnificent temple in Egypt at a place called Abu Simbel; and everyone was speculating on what Monsieur Champollion was going to discover when he finished translating the Rosetta Stone.

But instead of spending precious moments with her, Frederick said, 'Emma, why don't you play a game of cards with Jeremy while I work on these plans.'

And so she did.

Frederick's next request was: 'Emma, would you bring some of your special ointment? Jeremy is plagued by rat bites.' And then: 'Emma, bring some of your special jam tarts for Jeremy, I'm sure he's never tasted anything so heavenly.'

And finally: 'Emma, why don't you tell young Jeremy about our mission to restore the Bible to its original form.'

So subtle was Frederick's campaign that neither Emma nor Jeremy, who was thrilled with this new attention, had any inkling what Keyes was up to.

'Isn't the Bible in its original form now?' Jeremy asked, delirious with this sudden attention from the lovely Emma, her perfume, her nearness, turning this hellish prison cell into heaven on earth.

'There were hundreds of gospels and epistles,' she said, 'being circulated in the early years of Christianity, splintering the new faith into competing sects and conflicting beliefs. One group decided there could be only one, so they got together and decreed what would be canon, what would not. Those writings left out were declared heretical and became lost, like the Gospel of Thomas. The Alexandrians have spent centuries

267

searching for the omitted writings to put them back into the collection.'

'Astounding,' declared Jeremy, marveling at such knowledge inside that lovely head.

'The Old Testament is likewise incomplete. Books are missing from the collection.'

'If they're missing, how do we know about them?' Jeremy asked, noticing that in the pale-blue iris of one of her eyes, a small black dot floated.

'The Bible itself mentions them. Joshua ten, thirteen: "And the sun stood still, and the moon stayed, until the people had avenged themselves upon their enemies. Is not this written in the book of Jasher?" We believe there are eighteen more books besides the Book of Jasher that for one reason or another were left out of the Old Testament.'

Encouraged by Jeremy's keen interest, for he leaned forward, elbows on his knees, hands earnestly clasped, Emma continued, 'We're getting close to completing the collection. There is a Song of Miriam we are searching for, and perhaps one or two more gospels. And then we shall have a perfect Bible, in its original state.'

Jeremy's attention was upon Emma's bonnet. Decorated with ribbons and flowers, she never removed it, which became his secret obsession. Curls poked out around the edges, auburn curlicues that teased him maddeningly. The more she kept her bonnet on, the more he wanted to tear it away and drive his fingers through her hair. He fantasized about the tresses beneath the hat: thick, shiny locks twisted into elaborate chignons that cried out for a man to set them free.

Emma produced a small book. 'I know this will interest you, Mr. Lamb.' *The Gospel of Thomas.* She read from it.

'"The disciples said to Jesus, 'Tell us how our end will be.' Jesus said, 'Have you discovered, then, the beginning, that you look for the end? For where the beginning is, there will the end be. Blessed is he who will take his place in the beginning; he will know the end and will not experience death.'

'"Jesus said, 'If they say to you, "Where did you come from?" Say to them, "We came from the light, the place where the light came into being on its own accord."'"'

The curls trembled and Jeremy ached to touch them.

"'Jesus said, 'It is I who am the light which is above them all. It is I who am the all. From me did the all come forth, and unto me did the all extend. Split a piece of wood, and I am there. Lift up the stone, and you will find me there.'

"'And Jesus said to his disciples, 'I have come forth from the First Mystery which is the last mystery, the mystery that is the head of all things that exist. It is the Completion of the Completions, it is the Treasury of Light.'"' She closed the book. 'We call it the Luminance.'

Jeremy thought Emma was the luminance. She had brought light into his dark world, she was his beacon. And he was falling desperately in love. 'Tell me,' he said, his voice choked.

'A great, wondrous light awaits us all, Mr. Lamb, as was foretold to Alexander the Great twenty-one centuries ago. The Luminance. God coming to us in light, uniting all of human kind, past and present, in the light. For we are *made* of light, and to light we will return, to be reunited with loved ones.'

'How I wish I could believe it,' he declared, silently adding: my dearest Emma.

'Death is not darkness, Mr. Lamb, it is light. Death is not an ending, it is a beginning.'

And Frederick Keyes, bent over his ruler and diagrams, looked up at the woman he loved and saw, with great pain in his heart, that his scheme was working.

Frederick was laboring over his plans and Emma and Jeremy were at a game of cards when Emma looked up and was star-tled to see a group of people gathering at the barred door. They peered in and pointed, some laughing, some shaking their heads, two ladies sobbing into handkerchiefs. 'Who are they?'

'Tourists. They pay to get a look at the condemned awaiting execution.'

She jumped up, the cards tumbling from her hand. 'What is wrong with you horrible people?'

''Ere, 'ere,' said the jailer. 'No need for that, missy. They's paid their money, thank you.' He turned to the group and said loudly, 'We 'old 'angings every Monday morning. Good seats for everyone. Them that wants a seat at one of the windows overlooking the gallows will be expected to pay ten pounds. Well worth it, in my mind. Right, let's move along then.'

Frederick interrupted his work to console her, drawing her away from the hearing of others. 'There, there,' he said, calming her down.

But when he casually enquired, 'What do you think of young Jeremy?' she drew back and gave him a searching look. 'Why do you ask?'

'Just tell me, dearest.'

'He is not young to me.'

'You know what I mean. Do you like him?'

'I do not dislike him.'

'A woman could do worse.'

Her look turned to shock. 'Frederick, what are you saying?'

'My dear girl, you are without a protector.'

'I have you.'

'I am hardly in a position to take care of you.'

She lifted her chin. 'I am twenty.'

'Precisely my point. I don't trust Desmond Stone. He seeks your hand for all the wrong reasons, not one of them being affection.'

Shock became puzzlement. 'Desmond Stone? I have no intention of marrying him.'

You might not have a choice, he countered silently, not wanting to alarm her. 'What would you say if I were to ask Jeremy to look out for you after I am gone?'

'Frederick, you mustn't give up hope!'

He took her by the shoulders. 'Emma, I need you to be strong, for me and for our brethren in the Order, and for all of humankind. I need you to take these plans, when they are finished, to Morven and see that they are implemented. We cannot wait for a clemency that might never come. Young Jeremy will be released soon. I want you to go with him. If not, I fear the Luminance will be imperiled by the secret ambitions of Desmond Stone.'

The plans were finished.

'I will give these drafts to Emma to take to the Alexandrians,' Keyes said to Jeremy. 'I am worried she will not be safe carrying them. There is a man, Desmond Stone, who will want to destroy them, and possibly hurt her in the process. She needs a protector, someone to take care of her.'

'For the love of God, why me?'

'Because I see how you look at Emma, with such love and tenderness, and I know that Emma looks upon you with favor.'

Jeremy stared at him. 'My dear Mr. Keyes, I am flattered, but I am not the man for the job. People do not count on me. I am an unreliable cad. I am fickle and vain.'

But Keyes smiled. 'There is more to you than that, my friend. You are a good man, Mr. Lamb. Your generosity when I first arrived, for no obvious gain to yourself, because you believed I had no friends. You befriended me out of the goodness of your heart, and in this prison, where it is every man for himself, that counted for a lot. But more than that is the look on your face when your eyes are on Emma. It is with tenderness, not lust or possessiveness, the way Desmond Stone looks at her, as if she were an object. And so I know you will be good to her.'

Jeremy was sick at heart. As much as he loved Emma, it was too big a responsibility. She would never look upon him the way she did Frederick. And could he live with her, knowing the ghost of Frederick Keyes would always be between them? 'I cannot be counted on for anything, sir, I am sad to say. It is a fault that lies deep within my make-up, and, as the old saying goes, an old dog cannot be taught new tricks.'

He wished Keyes hadn't asked him. It was all Jeremy could think about, it plagued him as nothing ever had – the care and keeping of Miss Emma Venable. Except for this brief spell in prison, Jeremy's life had been a smooth sail, and he expected it to be so upon his release, to be reunited with old friends, get back into the social rounds, the parties, the good times. He did not want the responsibility of another person! Especially not one so fragile and precious as Emma. And who was Keyes, anyway, to have such a high opinion of him? No one had a high opinion of Jeremy Lamb, least of all Lamb himself. Did Keyes think him a simpleton, that he would believe such balderdash? 'You are a good man, Mr. Lamb.' Rubbish.

Jeremy restlessly paced his small area, by turns angry, frustrated, disgusted with himself, and hopelessly in love, while the oblivious Keyes polished and perfected his architectural plans spread out on the floor. Jeremy had more important

271

things to worry about: his release from jail would come danger-
ously close to the opening of shooting season at the Duke of
Norfolk's, and Jeremy needed to get to Savile Row and have
his wardrobe put together. He prayed his cutter was available,
for to use another—

'And 'ere we 'ave, ladies and gentlemen, the place where
we keeps the most dastardly and bloodthirsty of our criminals – men waiting to be 'anged or men locked in for life.
Step close and see for yourself.'

Tourists again. Jeremy was thankful Emma wasn't here yet.
He felt like tossing the slop bucket at them.

'When is that fellow due for execution?' came a smooth
voice in an upper-crust accent. The man was pointing at
Frederick on the floor. Jeremy gave the tourist a closer look.
Tall, imposing, the best tailoring on his lean form. But something else – a hardness about the eyes, cruelty around the
mouth. Jeremy was familiar with the type.

But why was he pointing at Keyes?

'Don't know yet, your lordship,' the jailer said. 'The gallows
is busy, I'll tell you. Judges send them in 'ere faster than we
can 'ang them. Now, if we move along, we'll visit the women's
section next, where London's most scandalous women of
pleasure are . . .'

The group moved on but the tall man lingered, staring down
at Keyes, his lips curving up in a cold smile. As if sensing
him, Frederick glanced up, and the look that passed over his
face made Jeremy's blood run to ice.

He knew who the tourist was.

The tall man said, 'You are too late. The traps are being
set.' He laughed softly and sauntered away, while Frederick
remained immobilized on his knees.

Jeremy was quick to help him up. Keyes had broken out
in a sweat, his face a shocking gray. 'Stone . . .' he whispered
as Jeremy held a cup of water to his lips. Stone, the man who
had put him in here.

And who wanted Emma.

Frederick spoke quickly. 'We haven't much time, Jeremy.
Your release is tomorrow. Now I need to tell you a secret.'

It was seeing Desmond Stone that had changed Jeremy's

mind. He could not let that devil get his hands on sweet Emma.

'I stood trial for treason and was sentenced for declaring that there is a higher authority than the Crown and God. Jeremy, I was referring to humankind, but could not tell the Court this for it is the Alexandrians' most preciously kept secret.'

Jeremy didn't understand, but it didn't matter. They both had the feeling that Stone's appearance at the bars was a sign that the day of execution was imminent. Keyes' architectural plans were finished, waiting for Emma to take them away. All that remained was letting Jeremy in on the secret. For Emma's sake, he had to be told.

'We are not madmen, Mr. Lamb. Alexandrians are educated, thinking men who know that humanity stands at the brink of an astounding change. This new era will bring an explosion of new technologies, the likes of which the world has never seen. Steam-powered locomotives, you have heard of them, such as are used in mining operations, will expand and grow and criss-cross the globe in a network of iron roads. Men will build machines that will fly, ships that will go faster, and ways of communicating that we cannot now even dream of. Mother Shipton, of whom you have heard, in 1550 prophesized: "Around the world men's thoughts will fly, Quick as the twinkling of an eye."'

Keyes leaned forward. 'Listen to me, my friend. Whether you believe my words or not is of no consequence. What is of consequence is that we stand at the dawn of a new era, that our days of quietly collecting and guarding are nearly over and that we are about to begin our true work.'

Jeremy gave him a wary look. 'Which is?'

And when Keyes told him, Jeremy said, 'Preposterous!' But it got him thinking. And he agreed that the security of the Library was vital.

He lay awake all night, excited now, feeling strong and important, making plans, fantasizing about Emma. Tomorrow was his freedom! He was going to turn over a new leaf. No more running up debts, no more purchases on credit. He would settle down to a real job of work, perhaps join his father's accountancy firm. Of course, he would keep his friends. One did not discard a lifetime of habits overnight. And it *was* a fellow's duty to look his best, keep up with fashion, let people know his stature by the clothes on his back. He would retain perhaps just one or two of his favorite tailors on Bond Street. And the haberdasher, the bootmaker, the importer of silk cravats, and one must always have a variety of gloves and snuff boxes . . .

He dozed off into the best slumber he had had in weeks.

Jeremy awoke to a shock.

The chaplain had come to counsel Frederick while Jeremy slept, and so he wakened the next morning to learn that today was the day of Frederick Keyes' execution.

Emma arrived. Keyes held her in his arms as she wept inconsolably. He spoke tenderly, to hide the pain and anguish that ravaged his soul. 'Promise you will stay close to Jeremy. Go straight to Morven from here. Do not attend my hanging. Leave with memories of me alive.'

She sobbed onto his chest.

'Promise me, Emma!'

Jeremy watched them and was heartsick. No woman had ever, or ever would, love him as Emma loved Keyes. He saw his future, laid out before him as perfectly as a bland quilt – an endless round of parties, gossip, and tailors, empty year following empty year until his deathbed, lying alone and unloved. His name forgotten because he did nothing with his life.

And then he thought of Desmond Stone, a formidable man, rich and powerful and ruthless. And Jeremy knew he was no match for such a one, that he would not be able to protect Emma from him.

The answer came to him as clear as a summer's day.

Swallowing for courage and balling his hands into fists, he blurted, 'Frederick, you go. Take Emma and your plans to Morven.'

They spun around. 'What?'

'When they call my name, *you* will answer. I shall stay.'

'No!' cried Emma.

He spoke quickly, his body trembling with dread. *The hangman's noose*— 'The release money has been paid, the jailer will call out for Jeremy Lamb. He doesn't care who's who, as long as he has the correct body count at the end of the day. And when the call comes for Frederick Keyes, I will answer.'

'Good God, man, I can't let you do this!

'Do not talk me out of it. I have never done a brave thing in my life. Do not rob me of this.'

Keyes refused to listen. 'I will not send an innocent man to the gallows.'

'Your life means more than mine. You have purpose, where I have none. Others need you, Frederick, no one needs me.'

'I will not do this!' Frederick said with a strangled cry.

'My friend, listen: you once said I was a good man. Let me fill those shoes. Let me prove you were right.'

Keyes desperately searched for another tack. 'Desmond Stone is sure to be among the spectators and will realize that the man on the scaffold is not I.'

'From what you have told me of him and his duplicity, he would not dare to complain to the Alexandrians that you had escaped the noose for it would bring suspicion upon himself.'

'Still I cannot let you do this!'

Jeremy seized Keyes by the shoulders, his eyes blazing with passion, though his face was shockingly white. 'Not a soul visited me while I was in here. All these favors and luxuries – not a single one given to me, but all paid for with my own money! I have lived a worthless life, Frederick. This gives me something I have never had nor hoped to have – meaning and dignity. If what you say is true about the Luminance, then we shall meet again.'

Keyes looked deep into the anguished eyes and saw a soul in turmoil. 'What about your father?' he said in a hoarse whisper, his throat had gone so dry. 'He is expecting you to be released.'

'He will think I did my usual cowardly thing, that I've run off to France to avoid other debts. And when he does not hear from me after a while, he will presume I have met a bad end through misadventure. He will not miss me.'

'*I* will miss you,' Emma said softly, her face wet with tears.

He took her hands and said, 'Promise me, *promise me*, that what you say about the Luminance is true.'

'With all my heart and soul and being, Jeremy Lamb, I promise you it is true.'

Lamb asked one favor of Emma: to remove her bonnet.

She did so, and at the sight of her glorious hair tears came to his eyes. He kissed her hand and thanked her.

'One last request, Frederick. When you can, come back and pay Cummings' release fee. He stole money only to feed his children. He's a decent chap and served me well. Now go quickly. Ride night and day and stop Desmond Stone.'

'Jeremy Lamb!' the jailer called out, keyring jangling at the lock.

Frederick embraced his new friend one last time, then turned and cried, 'I am Lamb!'

As they hurried down the corridor one way, up the other way the bellman for the gallows was coming. He called out, 'Frederick Keyes,' and faintly Frederick and Emma heard Jeremy say, 'I am here.'

Outside in the blessed fresh morning air, the bells in the tower rang out as the paid spectators pushed inside to grab good seats for the hanging. Frederick and Emma hurried past, Frederick knowing that Jeremy Lamb's sacrifice would haunt him for the rest of his life, that he would forever ask the question: If I survive at the expense of another man's life, have I really survived?

And Emma, until the day she died, would remind him that the arrangement had not been one-sided, that Frederick had given Jeremy a precious gift: knowledge of the Luminance.

Part Four

Twenty-Nine

'It looks deserted,' Candice said, peering through binoculars.

The eastern end of the island was flat and covered with
rich green grass and clover; the western end was hidden in
dense forest and mist. No sign of human life.

After a short flight from London they had rented a car and
driven through the lush countryside of south-west Scotland,
with green golf courses and rolling hills, quaint farms and
small seaside resorts. The man on the phone had said, 'From
Ayr you take the A78 going south. Not the main road, mind,
but what they call the scenic route. The inn is on the right
side, on a cliff overlooking the sea. If you reach Culzean
Castle, you've gone too far.'

At the signpost they had pulled off onto a lane and come
into a tiny hamlet with a narrow paved road. The Thistle Inn,
looking hundreds of years old, was the dominant establishment. The pavement ended shortly past the inn, and beyond
it wild pasture stretched to the edge of a cliff that overlooked
the calm waters of the Firth of Clyde.

They stood now on the cliff surveying an island, identified
on the map as Morven.

'Do you think Philo is there?' Candice asked as she squinted
in the late-afternoon sunlight.

Glenn looked back at the village, the Thistle Inn that was
Hawthorne's contact. Then he surveyed the coast along the
mainland – sandy beaches, jagged rocks, hidden coves –
noting the steep footpath that twisted down to the beach below,

and a rocky jetty where a motorboat was moored. 'Let's find out.'

The boat was old, but the outboard motor looked in good condition. A few hefty pulls on the cord got it stuttering to life and Glenn and Candice sped away from the mainland.

They sat side by side, not looking back at the receding cliffs, but with their faces to the wind, toward the mysterious island that even now was growing increasingly shrouded in late-afternoon mist. When they reached the rocky shore, they slung their knapsacks over their shoulders, dragged the boat onto the beach and struck off inland, boots crunching over gravel and coarse sand. But soon they were treading spongy grass and soft peaty moss.

Where the woods began, a sign was stuck in the earth:

QUARANTINE. BY ORDER OF THE SCOTTISH EXECUT-
IVE HEALTH DEPARTMENT, PUBLIC HEALTH DIVISION.
KEEP OUT.

Senses heightened, they plunged into the trees, boots trampling dead leaves and boggy soil, mushrooms and toadstools, breathing air damp and dewy, and thick with the smell of decay and mold. They came to a rusting barbed wire fence with another sign, old and weathered, the lettering faintly seen: MORVEN LABORATORIES.

'Laboratories!' Candice whispered. 'What *is* this place?'

Climbing through the wires they entered a forest rich with loamy scents and the sounds of unseen creatures beginning their nocturnal business. The fog swirled about their legs as if it were a living spirit.

And then suddenly the ground gave way. Candice let out a yelp and vanished.

Glenn fell to his knees. 'Are you all right?' He switched his flashlight on. Candice lay covered in leaves and twigs.

'Yes,' she said. 'What the heck is this?'

'Looks like an old pitfall.' He reached down to lift her out. 'We'd better be careful. This whole area could be booby-trapped.'

They pressed on, and when they broke through the dense trees, they stopped short.

'My God,' Candice whispered. 'That is the biggest house I have ever seen!'

Although swathed in mist, much of the mass of the structure could be made out, and, in the dying dusk, some of the details: massive square tower turrets, medieval battlements, Gothic spires, ornate gables, giant columns and pilasters, and a central clock tower looking for all the world like Big Ben. The house appeared to be part castle, part palace, three stories tall, longer and wider than a city block, immense and gaudy. And, to Candice, spooky and creepy.

Not a single light glowed in the hundred windows.

'It's deserted,' Candice said in a hushed voice.

'Not quite,' Glenn said as he pointed to one of the many chimneys. Smoke spiraled up.

They retreated into the protection of the trees and, crouching low, crept around to the north side of the house, from where they could see an earlier structure to which the rest seemed to have been appended: an ancient stone tower with narrow slits for windows, crenellations at the top. They continued their circumnavigation until they reached the rear of the castle. Here they saw the remnants of an ancient moat, dried up, choked with weeds. Glenn could see, through his binoculars, a small, dark flaw in the brickwork.

'Does that look like an opening to you?' He handed Candice the glasses.

'An old drainage ditch from inside probably.' She shuddered. 'And full of rats I'll bet.'

Glenn started to take a step forward, but stopped suddenly, pulled her to him and kissed her hard on the mouth.

'That was for luck,' he said and took her by the hand before she could catch her breath.

They made a dash across the spongy turf and reached the opening, which, to their relief, was larger than had first appeared. Inside, it smelled dank and had an unearthly feel. They heard skitterings as Glenn's flashlight beam swept the floor and walls. The ceiling was domed and constructed of brick. 'Looks like some sort of storage place,' he murmured. At the far end, the dim circle of light illuminated a heavy wooden door.

The floor was uneven and slippery with moss, the air icy

cold. Despite their jackets, Candice and Glenn shivered, and the breath from their mouths came out in little steam jets. They reached the door at the other end. Glenn ran his flashlight beam over it, and then onto the floor, noticing how the bottom of the door had scraped the flagstones over the years. He crouched to examine the scratches. 'This door hasn't been used in a very long time.'

He seized the giant handle with both hands and pulled on it. The door creaked open.

Before them yawned blackness, and a fetid, musty smell rushed at them, as if a ghost had been waiting to be set free. They imagined men in chain mail clanking about, sharpening their swords, readying for battle. But there were no men, only narrow stone stairs that spiraled upward.

It was steep going. They took the steps slowly, feeling the wall with their free hands. At the top they encountered another wooden door. This one opened more easily.

A dark, empty corridor stretched before them in cold gloom. As they advanced a few yards, they came upon a crossroads: the corridor continued ahead, yet it also branched off to the right and left.

'If my orientation is right,' Glenn said quietly, 'the newer part of the castle, the main house, is that way.' He shone his light to the left.

They paused to listen. But all they heard were the tiny squeaks and rustling of rodents. And, in the distance, the lonely call of a foghorn.

'Glenn,' Candice said, her eyes wide, 'what kind of laboratory would have been here? Why did the government health department close it down and what does Philo have to do with this?'

Following the corridor that branched to the left, they came upon a door unlike the previous two. Made of steel, it was posted with WARNING and AUTHORIZED PERSONNEL ONLY signs. Glenn tested the push-bar. The door swung silently open.

A vast chamber lay before them, stretching away into the darkness so that their flashlight beams didn't reach the end. The air was strangely dry, startlingly so after the dampness of the outer corridor. Neither warm nor cold. And silent.

They entered slowly, allowing the door to whisper shut behind

280

them, closing with the barest audible click. Circles of flashlight beam swept over a bewildering interior: there were no windows, and the polished linoleum floor and modern, soundproofed ceiling with banks of fluorescent lighting did not match the castle's ancient exterior. Instead of the suits of armor and medieval tapestries Candice and Glenn had been expecting, the enormous hall was lined with steel flat-file cabinets, the kind with three-inch-deep drawers used to store blueprints or artwork, and they were stacked up to the ceiling so high that the topmost could only be reached by tall ladders attached to rolling tracks. The cabinets extended several feet into the room so that the path down the center was just wide enough for two people to walk comfortably shoulder to shoulder.

'What *is* this place?' Candice whispered, her eyes stretched wide. None of the cabinets or drawers appeared to be labeled.

There was only one way to find out. Choosing the file cabinet on his left, Glenn hooked his fingers over the small metal handle of a drawer and pulled. To his astonishment, the drawer slid open on quiet ball bearings.

'These cabinets aren't locked. The owner obviously isn't worried about thieves,' Glenn murmured as they swung their flashlights over the contents of the drawer.

Candice gasped when she realized what she was looking at. Beneath a clear Plexiglas cover, sealed against the environment, was a fragment of papyrus with faded writing on it. Next to it, a white sheet of paper with typed information: *Book of Malachi, earliest known copy, verified by F. N., Zurich – carbon-14, chemical analysis. Date: + – 98 BCE.* And then a translation of the script: *Surely the day is coming [text missing] the sun of righteousness will rise upon wings of healing . . .*

'I don't understand,' Candice said in a low voice, glancing toward the door they had just come through, expecting armed guards to burst through at any minute. 'Is this the laboratory mentioned on the sign outside? Morven Labs?'

'Not a medical or biological lab, apparently.'

'What about the notice from the health department?'

'Fake, to keep snoopers out.'

Her perplexity deepened when they opened the next drawer and their flashlights illuminated part of an Aztec book, with a typed sheet containing analytical data verifying date (sixteenth century) and authenticity (by thermoluminescence and gas chromatography), and a translation of the text: *In the month of Toxcatl, the people of Tenoctitlan celebrated the feast of Tezcatlipoca [text missing] and he would live for one year . . .*

Their puzzlement growing, Candice and Glenn opened drawer after drawer and found letters, missives, memoirs, and treatises, from all ages and cultures, written on parchment, vellum, papyrus, and onionskin, in Hebrew, Greek, Latin, Asian calligraphy, Sanskrit, and alphabets they could not identify. Some were paintings on bark, others were scratches in stone. There was correspondence from sixteenth-century Germany, documents from Medieval England, knotted message ropes from pre-Columbian Peru. But in every case the specimen was accompanied by a typed sheet giving a translation, description, and verification of authenticity and age by means of laboratory tests from scanning electron microscopy to pollen analysis.

'This is an archive,' Candice said a little loudly, so filled with awe that she forgot for the moment the danger they were in.

'With a religious theme,' Glenn said as he continued to sweep the endless banks of storage drawers with his flash-light, a golden circle that flew over blackness and illuminated here and there parts of the whole peculiar picture. Every drawer they opened contained words about Heaven and Hell, God, the soul.

'But you said the Alexandrians are atheists. Why do they want these sacred writings?'

Coming to another open space, they found glass cases, hermetically sealed, with gauges giving steady read-outs of temperature and humidity. Inside these cases were larger speci-mens: books, tablets, enormous scrolls. More languages and alphabets, more godly revelations.

Candice's eyes nearly bugged out when she came upon a large, flat display case, several feet long. Inside, carefully preserved between sheets of glass, was an opened-out papyrus scroll covered in Egyptian hieroglyphics. 'It's the Egyptian Book of the Dead,' she whispered in disbelief. 'But a much earlier one than any I'm aware of. The writing dates it centuries before the oldest known copy.' She bent close to read the data, and received a second shock. 'Glenn, this papyrus was translated and authenticated over a hundred years ago! How can I have never heard of it?'

They resumed their forward progress toward the end of the hall, where they could make out a set of double doors.

'Glenn,' Candice whispered, 'you said the Alexandrians are atheists. Why do they have all these religious writings? Are they trying to prove or disprove the existence of God?'

He froze. From the silence and the shadows came a voice chanting in gentle cadence, a lesson being taught to a little boy, words forgotten long ago:

'Who are the Alexandrians?
We are gatherers of god-knowledge.
To what purpose?'

'Glenn? What's wrong?'

'I'm remembering something. A catechism my mother taught me. It's about the Alexandrians gathering knowledge about God.'

'Why?'

'I can't remember.' He took her hand. 'Come on.' Urgency in his voice.

They encountered another steel security door. It opened onto a small vestibule that offered two options: a stairway and an elevator. They chose the elevator and, inside, saw five buttons: there were two more floors above them and, surprisingly, two below, which meant there was a basement beneath the castle.

'Down,' Candice said, thinking she would feel a little more secure closer to the ground, and Glenn pushed the button.

The elevator opened upon a long hallway, paneled in wood, with wall sconces flickering. But no doors. When they came to a dead end, Glenn ran his hands over the paneling. 'The interior of this building has been altered. There is hollow space on the other side of this wall,' he said, thinking of secret passages built in the days when the master of the house paid late-night calls upon lady guests.

283

As they explored, they discovered that the castle was laid out in an unpredictable floor plan, with corridors suddenly appearing, doors opening upon nothing, stairs going up, elevators going down, a honeycomb of passages that went nowhere. Such doors as did work were either locked or opened upon deserted rooms – mostly archives and libraries – but one startled them: a beautifully furnished parlor glowing with light from a chandelier and flames roaring in the fireplace. It struck Candice as being like a gentlemen's club, furnished with deep leather chairs, trophy heads on the walls, hunting rifles in a gun case. Despite the lights and the fire, the room was unoccupied.

They hurried on.

Coming to another blind end, forcing them to retrace their steps and turn down another corridor, Candice said, 'Why is it such a maze?'

'For security. It would have been the best they could do in the nineteenth century. Thieves get in but they can't get out.'

They came across a brass plaque: *Completed AD 1825. Designed by Frederick Keyes. In Memoriam – Jeremy Lamb.*

Candice looked around with a shiver. 'Glenn, do you have the feeling we're being watched?'

'I've felt it since the minute we stepped foot on this island. And I have a good idea who's doing the watching.'

The hidden passageway ran through the heart of the castle and only one man knew its beginning and its terminus. Philo Thibodeau, hurrying down the dark corridor, his way lighted by flashlight, white clothes glowing ghostlike. He had finished the last of his secret work.

He looked at the luminous dial of his watch. The detonation devices had been set. The countdown had begun. Timing was everything. The bombs had to be launched with precise synchronicity.

He shivered in ecstasy. *Soon, Lenore . . .*

Their search through the labyrinthine castle led Candice and Glenn to more locked doors, stairs that went nowhere, deserted rooms. But no people.

Finally, another steel security door, locked, but with a

small window so that they could peer in. The room was vast, brightly illuminated, and cluttered with work tables, electronic equipment, microscopes, test tubes, and a chamber with glass walls and signs that said: WARNING! CLEAN ROOM! COVER-ALLS AND MASKS MUST BE WORN! And the answer to Candice's question: people of different ages and nationalities, wearing jogging outfits or white lab coats, working silently, moving among the benches and equipment, a beehive of industry.

Candice stared at the statues being restored, papyrus undergoing analysis, machines humming, lights blinking, and—

'Dr. Stillwater!' Standing at a large table covered with clay fragments, making notes on a clipboard. 'And those are the Jebel Mara tablets.'

Glenn pulled Candice away from the door and looked around. 'We have to find Philo before others find *us*. Come on!'

They found a library stacked floor to ceiling with shelves of rare and antique books. Scanning the titles, they saw a different theme: 'Doomsday!' Candice said, feeling unseen eyes on her. 'Is that what this society is all about? The end of the world?'

He had a strange look in his eyes when he finally looked at her. 'Yes,' Glenn said. 'But . . . it's also about God.'

She frowned. 'But the Alexandrians are atheists.'

'They believe in God,' he said as the memory coalesced in his mind. 'They just don't believe He exists.'

'What do you mean?'

'God has not yet come into being. That is the purpose of this society – *to create God.*'

Thirty

Philo had touched no food in forty-eight hours, and drunk only mineral water. Yet his vigor was at its peak; he had never felt stronger. In his private suite in the castle, he sat in a steam bath to sweat out impurities, then performed meticulous ablutions with the purest soap made from virgin olive oil and bottled water imported from the Swiss Alps, drying off with thick white Egyptian cotton towels.

Laid out on the bed were brand new London tailored clothes he had ordered for this night. The pure white shirt made from single-fiber, raw-filament silk obtained from the inner cocoon of the mulberry moth, hand-dyed and handwoven, a fabric so fragile it could be worn only once. White pleated slacks of the finest Belgian linen. Instead of shoes, white satin slippers, because he would be walking on holy ground. Clipped beard and moustache, hair trimmed, nails manicured; on his wrist, a custom-designed watch, the steel band locking in place with a tiny key. The countdown timepiece.

Lastly, into the pockets of the slacks, a pair of four-inch, pearl-handled Derringer pistols, each only a single shot, but deadly at close range, enough for his purposes.

He was ready.

Candice stared at Glenn. 'To *create* God?'

'The catechism my mother taught me. It's coming back: "Who are the Alexandrians? We are gatherers of god-knowledge. To what purpose? To bring God to earth. How will we bring it about? When all the knowledge is gathered, and we *know* Him, God will be born." Candice, these people believe they are creating God. That's the purpose of this place.'

'How can they create God? God created us!'

Retracing their steps, Glenn said, 'The Alexandrians believe we were never created, that we simply came into being, evolving from the primal star-stuff of the universe. But we didn't come into being by accident, we evolved for a purpose – to bring God to life. Without us, He could never exist. That is their job here.'

'How?'

'When all the books and writings and wisdom and visions have been collected – when humankind knows everything – then we will know God and He will be born.'

'But God exists in the Old Testament. How can the Alexandrians have overlooked that?'

'I remember my father pointing something out to me once. Moses and the burning bush. "I am what I am" is a mistranslation. The original Hebrew reads, "I will be what I will be." God telling Moses that He was in the *process* of being, referring to Himself in the future tense. Jesus spoke in the future tense, too, when he mentioned the coming of God. When he prayed, he said to his father, "Thy kingdom come." The Alexandrians even named their fortress in the Pyrenees the Chateau-de-Dieuvenir.'

'The Castle of God-Is-Coming,' Candice said.

Another flight of stairs. It only went down.

Their footsteps echoed off the stone walls as Glenn said, 'It has to do with global consciousness. One hundred thousand years ago there was but a handful of humans on earth, and only just becoming aware of themselves, let alone of a higher power. But now we number six billion, conscious, aware. In our cave-dwelling days, we were cut off from one another. The peasant in his field thought his village was the world. But now the world itself is becoming a village. We are connected by telephone and satellites. And at the speed with which this is increasing, it won't be long before everyone in the world is connected to everyone else. We shall form a global mind. At least, that's the theory.'

At the foot of the stairs, another doorway. 'The Jesuit priest, Teilhard de Chardin, said that mankind is evolving, mentally and socially, toward a final spiritual unity called the Omega point.'

This door wasn't locked and swung open under Glenn's hand. They faced an enormous hall, where suits of armor stood among medieval tapestries and antique furniture.

They cautiously entered, noting that lights blazed here, too. But also, on massive sideboards, in handsome armoires and hautboys, votive candles flickered in ruby-glass jars. And Candice was startled to see, in beautiful glazed vases, bouquets of fresh flowers, some still dewy about the petals.

Someone had been in here recently.

There was no one here now, yet it was inhabited all the same, by people trapped in gilded frames, on canvas and wood, carved in small marble busts, frozen in time and costume, staring out into the twenty-first century as if just as baffled as the two visitors who now looked around wide eyed. On walls and shelves and table tops were family crests, coats-of-arms, and linen embroidered with family trees. The Society's history, Glenn and Candice deduced, and the people in the paintings, the busts in the niches, the framed needle-points of name lists, were prior members.

One portrait in particular, dominating the room, caught their attention.

A Crusader, a giant of a man, handsome and stalwart, dressed in chain mail, armor, and a long gray surcoat. It was the symbol on the surcoat that most arrested them, for embla-zoned upon it was not the red cross of the Knights Templar or the Maltese cross of the Knights of St. John, but a circle of golden flames.

The symbol on Glenn's ring.

'Glenn!' Candice said. 'Look at his hand, the one resting on the sword.'

Glenn stared. The crusader had a sixth finger on his right hand.

Candice looked over her shoulder, thinking she heard sounds inside the walls. 'Where *is* everybody?' she whispered, staying close to Glenn as they continued along the gallery of portraits, some magnificently huge, some no bigger than the palm of a hand, men in armor, women in crinolines, Tudor next to Victorian, eras comingled as every inch of wall space was used.

At the end of the hall, on a carved mahogany sideboard, a papyrus document written in Greek was sealed under glass. An accompanying card explained that the papyrus dated nearly three hundred years before Jesus and was the initial charter for the Library, bearing the royal seal of King Ptolemy.

'Look at the first name,' Candice said quietly.

'Philos,' Glenn said, remembering. 'The first High Priest. My mother traced her bloodline to a member of the house of Ptolemy, a woman named Artemisia, a royal princess and a high priestess at the Great Library.' He pointed to the Crusader portrait over the fireplace. 'And that man, the Comte de Valliers, a lineal descendant of High Priestess Artemisia, was my mother's forefather.'

'Which makes him *your* ancestor as well,' Candice said. And then her eyes fell upon a portrait. 'Glenn! Look at this!'

It was the portrait of a bearded man in Renaissance clothes, holding an astrolabe. A brass plate at the bottom of the frame identified him as Michel de Notre Dame.

'Nostradamus!'

'Look at his ring.' Gold flames over a ruby. 'He was an Alexandrian!'

On the table below the painting was a large book. *The Prophecies of Nostradamus*.

It was open to century 4, quatrain 24:

> Ouy soubs terre saincte d'ame voix feinte
> Humaine flamme pour divine voir luire:
> Fera des seulz de leur sang terre tainte,
> Et les s. temples pour les impurs destruire.

Underneath, a translation:

> Beneath the holy earth of a soul the faint voice heard,
> Human flame seen to shine as divine:
> It will cause the earth to be stained with the blood of
>   the monks,
> And to destroy the holy temples for the impure ones.

Glenn turned the brittle pages until he came to the seventh chapter. Here the quatrains did not end at forty-two. And there it was: quatrain 83.

> In the fourth month when Mercury is in retrograde,
> In that shining ornate temple where lamp and candle
>   burn,
> Seven generals command seven suns,
> In great Luminance, the earth reborn.

Glenn stared at the page. The Luminance. The vision he beheld as he was falling off a vertical rock face. The splashes of light on his canvases. He knew now what it was. The Last Days. Armageddon.

The end of the world.

'"The earth reborn,"' Candice murmured, the back of her neck prickling with fear. 'What does that mean?

289

'Nostradamus wrote in riddle and code, invented words and changed proper names by swapping letters. He did it to avoid standing trial as a magician. No one really knows what the quatrains were about.' Glenn looked around at the red votive candles, golden flames in ruby jars, flickering like tiny stars. '*This* could be "the ornate temple where light and candle burn."'

Candice looked at him with eyes like dark pools. 'And "seven generals commanded seven suns?"'

'Candice,' he said quickly, urgently, 'the Alexandrians are a Doomsday cult. The Luminance is the end of the world. I remember that now.'

'The end of the world—' The breath caught in her throat.

'I don't know how all this fits together – the religious writings, Nostradamus, the Alexandrians. But Philo needed the Jebel Mara tablets for a reason; he's planning something. The great devastation my father wrote about in his letter, the reason my mother was afraid of Philo.' He looked at the quatrain again, remembering his phone conversation with Maggie Delaney. 'We're in the fourth month and Mercury is in retrograde. Philo is going to fulfill the prophecy in this quatrain.'

'What are the seven suns—?' She could hardly breathe.

Glenn's look said it all. He didn't have to utter the word: *bombs.*

'But *why*? Why would Philo want to destroy the world?'

Thirty-One

'Listen to me now.' Glenn took Candice's hands in his, looked deep into her eyes. 'This is between Philos and me. I want you to leave. Now. Take the boat back to the mainland—'

'I won't go without you.'

'You know I have to go through with this.'

'Then we face it together.'

*   *   *

290

'The detonator is radio-frequency operated,' the weapons dealer had explained. 'Effective range two miles. Eight megabyte memory, programmable up to twenty functions.' But Philo wasn't going to be two miles away, and he only needed seven functions.

As he stared at the glowing red numbers on the digital read-out, he thought: Alexander the Great conquered the world with fire. Philo Alexander Thibodeau could do no less.

They were under the castle. Fluorescent lights showed on bare concrete walls and floor. 'It looks like an old bomb shelter, probably built back in the fifties.' Up ahead they saw a massive steel door.

Unlocked, it swung open on silent hinges.

Glenn and Candice were unprepared for the sight that dazzled their eyes.

Glass cases displaying treasure beyond imagination: crowns and tiaras, jeweled orbs and dazzling scepters, ermine robes and golden shoes, a gem-encrusted throne.

'Philo!' Glenn called out as the steel door swung shut behind them. No reply.

They moved cautiously among display cases filled with golden goblets and jade goddesses, ivory crucifixes and silver chalices.

'What's that smell?' Candice said, pausing beside a display of rare Byzantine icons.

'I don't smell anything.'

Candice sniffed the air. 'Gasoline.'

Glenn called out Philo's name again. They listened. 'There's no one here.' They hurried back to the door. It was locked.

'Wait,' Candice said. 'I hear something.'

'I hear it, too.' A steady *beep . . . beep . . . beep.*

They followed the sound through the maze of glass cases, where emeralds and sapphires glinted blindingly beneath fluorescent lighting, until they reached the rear of the vault, where they stopped short at a sight that rendered them both momentarily speechless.

The bomb was six feet long, army green and bullet shaped – and wired to a mechanism from which the beeping emanated.

'Is it nuclear?' Candice whispered, as if her voice could detonate it.

291

'No. You were right about smelling gasoline. This bomb is filled with napalm.'

'Napalm!'

'Jellied gasoline. This bomb is designed to spread flaming gel in its blast radius, setting everything in its path on fire. The outer casing is thin aluminum and that explosive device is—' He stopped.

They saw glowing numbers on a digital read-out. Counting backward.

'It's going to go off! Can you disarm it?'

He shook his head.

'Philo brought us here to kill us?'

'He wants us to witness his power.'

'But why is he going to blow up the castle?'

He looked at her. 'To stop the Luminance. He doesn't want the world to end. He doesn't want to share his power with God. The only way to stop the Luminance is to destroy all of this. And now *we* have to stop *him*.'

Glenn eyed the small cassette player perched on the explosive mechanism. Carefully picking it up, he hit 'Play' and Philo's voice came out: '"*The final hour is at last begun, when first we begin to worship the sun.*" That is the way out, Glenn. I shall meet you in the Hunting Room.'

'"Worship the sun." What does it mean?' Candice couldn't keep her eyes off the digital display – the numbers ticking backward.

'It means,' Glenn said, looking around, 'Philo is playing games with us, he has been from the start, making us jump through hoops. He doesn't want us to die down here. He needs us alive so he can gloat to us. He must have rigged a secret device for opening the locked door. And we have exactly,' he added, his eye on the glowing red numbers, starting the timer on his wristwatch when the numbers read 5:00, 'five minutes to find the release mechanism.'

'Play the tape again,' Candice said. They listened. Their eyes met. *Worship the sun.*

They ran to a giant Aztec sunburst made of solid gold and pounded every inch of its surface – glyphs, figures, the serpents' tails, and the face in the center, its eyes, nose, protruding tongue. The security door did not unlock.

'What next?' Candice looked frantically around and saw sun-worship icons all over the room. The countdown stood at four minutes. 'There isn't time for all of them!'

'You take that side, I'll take this.'

They smashed open cases and seized sunbursts made of copper and bronze and silver, Assyrian winged suns, symbols of Apollo and Ra.

Three minutes.

'Sun symbols can sometimes be a wheel, disk, or circle,' Glenn said. 'Sometimes the sun is associated with an eye. Louis XIV called himself the Sun King.'

'We can't get to it all!'

Glenn looked at his watch. *Two minutes.* 'Maybe we're looking for the wrong thing. Maybe it isn't the sun.'

Her mind racing, Candice recited: '"The final hour is at last begun, when first we begin to worship the sun." Wait a minute. I thought I saw—'

She found it behind a display case containing an ancient Roman mosaic of the sun-god Helios: a medieval tapestry hanging on the wall. In vivid colors and rich detail, it depicted men gathered on a mountain, their faces lifted to the sky. In the top right and left corners of the scene, two symbols: alpha and omega.

First and last.

And rising above the heads of the kneeling men, Jesus ascending to heaven.

'Glenn! Over here!'

He came running.

'It isn't the sun in the sky,' she said excitedly, 'it's the *son of God*!' They pulled the tapestry aside and saw . . .

Thirty-Two

An elevator.
One minute.
'What's the Hunting Room?'

293

'Where we saw the animal heads. What floor was it on?'

'Six,' Candice said. 'No, five! Or was it four?'

He pressed four and the small lift shuddered upwards at an agonizingly slow pace. Glenn took Candice's hand and gripped it as they watched the buttons light up and wink off with each passing floor.

But Glenn's watch moved faster. They had only reached the second floor when the sweep hand stood at twelve. *Zero*. Time had run out. He pulled Candice to him; they held tightly to each other.

And waited.

Seconds ticked by. A minute. Silence surrounded them, and the stillness of the massive castle, as the little elevator trembled upward past the third floor.

'Did it go off?' Candice asked.

'We would have heard or felt something.'

'Was it a fake bomb?' Candice said in disbelief. 'A prop to scare us?'

'Or Philo interrupted the sequence from a remote control.' Glenn saw the high color in her face, the rapid throb of pulse at her throat. 'Now listen, Philo's crazy. And we're on his turf. Let me handle this. No rash actions. Promise me.'

'Glenn—'

'Candice, he's counting on us to lose our heads. Stay frosty.'

At the fourth floor the elevator opened upon a vestibule with three doors. The ones on the right and center were locked. The third swung away under Glenn's hand.

They recognized the room glowing with light from a chandelier and flames roaring in the fireplace, furnished like a gentleman's club with deep leather chairs, animal heads on the walls, hunting rifles in a gun case. And Philo Thibodeau, a vision in white, standing beside the mullioned window.

'I see you solved the riddle,' he said. 'I knew I could count on you.' He smiled. 'Did you enjoy the maze, Glenn? It was created by your great-great-grandfather, Frederick Keyes. Did you know that? Seeing to Morven's security was to have been *my* great-great-grandfather's honor, Desmond Stone, but Keyes cheated him out of it.'

As they cautiously entered, Glenn surveyed the room. No

one else was there, nothing out of the ordinary. Philo's hands empty. 'The bomb,' Glenn began.

'Do not worry,' Philo said in a gentle voice. 'It is not yet time.'

Glenn gave him a wary look.

'The countdown you saw was not toward detonation. It was to *arm* the bombs. And now they are armed.'

'They! There's more than one?' Candice said. Glenn felt her tense up at his side.

'There are seven located throughout the castle,' Philo said calmly. 'In the treasury vault you saw the seventh – the largest and most powerful.' He lifted his arm and drew back the sleeve of his white silk shirt. The wristwatch caught the chandelier's light. 'The bombs employ radio fuses which are ignited by this remote device. It's a marvel of technology, my own design actually. This watch is anti-magnetic, fire-proof, and so shock-resistant it cannot be destroyed with a hammer. That is the failsafe feature. Once the sequence is set, there is no way turn it off. And should you think that overpowering me will do anything, the steel band has been locked in place and cannot be removed from my arm without the key.'

'Why?' Candice said.

'Glenn knows why. It's the reason he is here.'

'I am here,' Glenn said evenly, in control, 'to take you in for questioning in the case of my father's murder.'

'No, that is not why you are here. And you do not have to question me. I killed him.' Philo raised an eyebrow. 'I see you are not surprised.'

He went to the fireplace, picked up a poker, and jabbed burning logs. 'Your father didn't approve of us, of our work here,' he said, his face illuminated in the fire's glow. 'John only tolerated us because of your mother. That's why she didn't bring you here when you were young. John forced her to keep silent until you turned eighteen. He had no right to keep you from us. You belong to the Society. You are of the blood.'

It all fell into place. Twenty years ago, someone shouting, 'He is of the blood!' His father saying, 'Stay away from my son or I will kill you.'

'So you carried out your revenge,' Glenn said, his eye on Philo's wrist. *Could* he set off the bombs with that device?

'Revenge? Partly, yes, but also because John had to be gotten out of the way. For your mother's sake.' Philo replaced the poker. 'When John told me he suspected the Star of Babylon involved the lost Book of Miriam, the final missing piece of the Bible, I knew the Luminance was at hand. I couldn't have John around when Lenore returned. It might confuse her. Which man to go to – the one she had been married to or the one she loved?'

Glenn gave him a puzzled look. 'My mother is dead.'

'In the Luminance we will be reunited.'

The two stared at him, Candice with a blank, uncomprehending look, Glenn's puzzlement deepening.

'The glorious Luminance!' Philo cried. 'There have been thousands of prophecies of the event. Our mutual ancestor, Alexander, was not the only one. We have found references to the Luminance in the religious writings of cultures thousands of miles apart and separated by centuries. Around the globe, from the Pygmies of Central Africa to the California Indians, from a twentieth-century Swedish physicist named Lundegaard to a Coptic monk in the tenth century – minds independently conceiving of the same idea: God coming in light when humanity is ready.'

'And the bombs?' Glenn said, surveying the room, searching for ways to distract and overpower Philo.

'Do you know what your mother did when she came here? She studied the works of Hypatia of Alexandria, a fifth-century mathematician. Your mother devoted her life to Hypatia's equations and theorems. Searching in them for evidence of God. After religion and philosophy, science is the next evolutionary step in the process of God's being. With each age, more knowledge is revealed to us. Primitive man living in caves thought the moon was a spirit. Thirty-five years ago, man *walked* on the moon. Galileo was thrown into prison for saying the earth revolved around the sun. Now we know there are other planets revolving around other suns. A century ago physicists said that science had come to the end of its purpose. There was nothing left to study or explore. And then quantum particles were discovered and a whole new science was born. After subatomic reality what's next? What *could* be next, but God? And it will be a day of angels and quantum particles, trumpets and quarks. Religion marrying science. A wedding day at which the Ethereal Creator weds Glorious Substance, with humanity as the guests!'

'You've made your point,' Glenn said. 'Disarm the bombs and we can talk.'

A tap at the door, and Mildred Stillwater entered with a tray of tea. Placing it on the antique mahogany coffee table, she set out four cups, bone China decorated with pink roses. The cups rattled in the saucers.

'It looks lovely, my dear,' Philo said to her. 'Earl Grey. The only civilized tea on the planet. You know what would be extra special? A few sprigs of fresh mint. From our greenhouse.'

'Yes, Philo,' she said. But first she turned to the visitors. Mildred wore a buttercup yellow cardigan over a tweed skirt and white blouse. 'You look surprised,' Mildred said, taking Candice's cold hands in hers. The scientist's eyes smiled behind glasses that gave her an owlish look. Her hair, drawn in a tight bun, made her head appear small and round. 'You didn't know I was a member of the Society? My father was a member. Our bloodline goes back to the seventh century.'

To Glenn she said, 'My condolences over the loss of your father. His accident was a terrible blow to us all. And thank you for so generously giving us the Esther tablets. It's a beautiful poem, the Song of Miriam.'

'Mildred,' Philo said. 'The mint, please?'

'Right away, Philo,' she said, flustered. Her buttercup-yellow cardigan was buttoned wrong. Candice thought: *she is in love with him.*

Did Mildred also know he was a murderer?

'I loved your mother, Glenn,' Philo said after the door closed behind Mildred. 'As no man has loved a woman, past or present. When she died I thought I should perish from grief. My consolation was that I knew I would be reunited with her in the Luminance. The Book of Daniel says: "Multitudes who sleep in the dust of the earth will awake to everlasting life . . . they will shine like the brightness of the heavens . . . and like the stars forever and ever." But I was impatient. I could not wait. I remembered that I had been chosen to bring God to the world. I would simply hasten the process.'

'You're going to *command* God to appear?' Candice said in disbelief.

'My forerunner, Jesus, thought *he* was bringing God. But that glorious task was meant for me. Jesus was simply paving the way for my work.'

'But why the bombs?'

'They are my instrument for sending the message to God.'

She stared at him. 'You're going to burn down the castle in order to create God?'

'Burn *up* the castle,' Philo corrected. 'But it isn't the castle, it is all the sacred words and writings housed here. We weren't meant to just collect books and sit on our backsides waiting for God to be created. We have to send a message to Him. With fire. Words flying heavenward to awaken the nascent Almighty, stir Him from His fetal slumber and call Him to His glory.'

Philo turned his face to the fire, eyes glowing. 'Alexander the Great began his conquest of the world by burning the city of Thebes to the ground. He cut a fiery swath across three continents, burning everything in his path, and at the end set fire to the great palace of Xerxes at Persepolis, burning it to the ground.' He turned blazing eyes to Candice. 'Should I do less?'

'My superiors know where I am,' Glenn said, fighting to stay calm, keeping his eye on Philo's wrist. If Glenn did overpower him, would he be able to cancel the detonation sequence?

'It does not matter who knows you are here. They are helpless. I control everything.'

'And the others? The people in the lab?'

'They don't know about the bombs, Dr. Armstrong.'

'You're bluffing,' Glenn said. 'You won't destroy two thousand years worth of human insight and divine revelation. Not even you.'

Philo went to the window and said, 'Let me show you something. Look there, down below. Do you see the greenhouse?'

Light spilling from windows beneath them illuminated the

flagstone path from the castle to the glass and wood structure filled with tender plants. 'Watch,' Philo said. 'There.' A bright spot of yellow appeared below – Mildred Stillwater in her buttercup cardigan, hurrying along the path. 'Fetching mint for our tea,' Philo said softly.

They watched her enter, the door swinging closed behind her. Philo said, 'Keep your eyes on it,' pressed a button on his wristwatch, and an explosion blinded them.

'Oh my God!' cried Candice as she stared in horror at the flames leaping to the sky. 'You killed her!'

'I did it for her own sake. The poor thing was going to suffer, and now she won't.'

Glenn grabbed Candice's arm. 'Get out of here, go!'

But she held onto him, tears streaming down her shocked face.

'That was the first,' Philo said, admiring his handiwork, pleased that it had gone well, which meant the other bombs would perform perfectly. 'I placed the six other devices in key locations – the Science Archive, the Ancestral Hall, the Jesus Vault, and so forth. You saw the seventh downstairs. I will detonate them in order. And where I placed the bombs the walls are filled with incendiary chemicals. Morven will go up in a blaze of glory.'

Glenn stared at the burning greenhouse, shrubs and bushes also aflame, sparks flying up to the stars. An inferno from which no one could have escaped. But there was something wrong . . .

And then it came to him. No one was running out to investigate.

Reading his thoughts, Philo said, 'I have locked all the doors within the castle. No one can get out.'

Candice was nearly hysterical. 'You're going to kill everyone?'

'Do not worry, they will be martyred, just like their ancestors seventeen centuries ago.'

'Let them out!'

'I cannot have them going for help or starting a bucket brigade.'

Glenn frantically cast about for a strategy. 'Philo, let's talk. Disarm the bombs—'

'I have heard of your powers of persuasion. You talk jumpers down from ledges. Why haven't you asked me why I brought you here to Morven?'

'What do you mean, you *brought* us?' Candice said, shaking so badly her teeth chattered. Mildred in the greenhouse—

'I engineered everything. But not the two of you, just Glenn. He was meant to come alone. I tried everything in my power to keep you out of this, Dr. Armstrong. But you are the wild card your reputation says you are.'

To Glenn he said, 'I followed your progress from the minute you left California. We lost you for a while in the desert, but we picked up your trail when you boarded the *Athena*. I was the one who sent the fake medico at Salerno to pick you up. I learned that Captain Stavros was planning to steal the ceramic shards and sell them on the black market. No doubt getting rid of you two in the bargain.'

Glenn's jaw tensed with fury. 'All that just to bring me here to kill me? Why not kill me along the way? Or back in Los Angeles. Why the dramatics?'

'Kill you! My dear boy, that is not why I brought you here at all.'

'Then why, for God's sake?'

'Why, to rule at my side, of course.'

Thirty-Three

Flames danced and crackled in the fireplace while outside the conflagration roared to the sky, sparking the tops of trees, setting them on fire. And faintly heard on the floors below, people shouting.

'I did not bring you straight to Morven after your father died,' Philo said, savoring the stunned look on Glenn's face, 'because you needed to prove yourself first by undergoing the trial by fire, as every god must. And you *have* proven yourself, in deed and courage and strength. Now you will sacrifice your old life for the new. No longer will you be an

300

ordinary mortal, but one of the Supreme Beings. We are the bloodline of Alexander the Great! Charged with the sacred task of bringing God to the world,' Philo cried. 'Can you deny your birthright?'

'My birthright—' Glenn stuttered.

'Alexander died in Persia, leaving Ptolemy to rule Alexandria in his stead. But it was Alexander's *son* who carried on the holy mission to build the Great Library and fill it with the world's knowledge. That first High Priest of the Library gave birth to sons who gave birth to sons and daughters, creating a lineage which we can trace all the way down to this very night, in this very room, to Philo Alexander Thibodeau and Glenn Alexander Masters.'

Glenn reeled with shock. 'Your middle name is for an uncle,' his mother had once explained. Yet he had never met or heard anything about the uncle.

'Sandrine could not bring a child to term,' Philo continued. 'When she had her fourth miscarriage I took it as a sign that you were the son I was meant to have. Had I married Lenore, you would have been mine. And now here you are to rule beside me.' He laid a hand on Glenn's shoulder and said, 'You were born to create God.'

How many times had Philo himself heard those words in his boyhood? Bathsheba saying, 'You were born to bring God to the world. It is your destiny, my dear son.' The Luminance, she had called it. God's light. Not destructive, not the fires of hell and Armageddon. The fires of the Luminance would be cool and refreshing, brilliant but not blinding, and the flesh would neither seer nor blacken nor fall away from bones.

'We shall rule as a trinity with Lenore – mother, father, and son.'

Glenn licked dry lips, looked around the room, at Candice's white face, the fire at the forest's edge. He had not been prepared for this. 'By killing me and yourself as well?'

'Our death will be but a wink in time. We cross the threshold and are reborn in light.'

In that moment Glenn realized what he was dealing with. A man who not only did not mind dying, but *wanted* to die in order to gain a greater reward. Nothing in Glenn's experience had prepared him for dealing with a suicide bomber.

301

'You can't do this!' Candice said, unable to stop thinking of Mildred's final moments in the inferno.

Philo turned a wrathful face to her. 'And Paul said to the Thessalonians, "Do not put out the Spirit's fire, do not treat prophecies with contempt." It is because of you my son has not embraced his destiny. Look at him! Confused, uncertain. Because of you. Like Delilah, you have weakened him.'

He slipped a hand into the right pocket of his white linen slacks and drew out the Derringer. 'Step into the next room, Dr. Armstrong. What will transpire next is not for outsiders to witness.'

'Okay, Philo,' Glenn said, holding out his hands. 'Put the gun down.'

'Do not provoke me, son, for I *will* shoot.'

As Candice backed toward the other room, Philo said, 'It's your own fault, Dr. Armstrong. I tried to dissuade you from this path. When threats on your life did not work, I tried another tack. The job in San Francisco had already been given to the nephew of one of the museum trustees. You were never considered for the position. In fact, they did not want you. You are a laughingstock in your profession, Dr. Armstrong, with your Pharaoh Nefertiti theory. Mr. O'Brien said you would bring ridicule to his institution.'

She stared at him. When tears threatened, she tipped her chin defiantly.

'A sizeable donation to the museum persuaded Mr. O'Brien to see you in a different light. You were to have taken that job, Dr. Armstrong. But you did not. Stubborn and impulsive, your colleagues call you. And look where it got you.'

'Let her go, Philo,' Glenn said. 'This is between you and me.'

But Philo stepped toward her, gun leveled, and Candice fell back.

'Philo, I'm begging you. Let her go. Release the fire doors. Let everyone out. I'll rule with you. I'll help you bring God. Whatever you want.'

Philo shook his head. 'Empty words, son. You do not mean them. It's because of her.'

When Candice stepped inside the adjacent room, Philo

302

closed the door, shutting it with a decisive click. Glenn grabbed the brass knob. It didn't turn.

'These security doors are very strong,' Philo said. 'I will demonstrate.' He pushed another button on his wristwatch and they heard a muffled explosion within.

And a scream.

Glenn grabbed the knob again but suddenly it was hot. Fire on the other side. 'The chamber is engulfed in flames,' Philo said. 'There is no exit, no way out. But the oxygen will be consumed quickly, she will not suffer long.'

'Get her out of there!' Glenn bellowed, lunging at Philo.

The older man was nimble, sidestepping with ease. 'You will see things differently after the Luminance.' He produced the second Derringer and, before Glenn could react, squeezed the trigger. The bullet sent Glenn flying across the room, where he hit the wall and slumped to the floor.

She couldn't breathe.

As soon as Philo closed the door behind her, Candice had seen the incendiary device. She had run across the room before the bomb blew, sending flames up the walls and over the door.

Now the fire was rapidly approaching her, consuming furniture and drapes, filling the room with smoke and a heat so intense it seared her lungs.

Coughing and choking, she pounded the walls, calling for help. Dizziness overcame her, tears streamed down her cheeks, her lungs felt as if they were on fire.

'Help!' she screamed, fists banging on the walls.

Flames rushed at her, the air so hot she couldn't draw breath, smoke stinging her eyes, blinding her. '*Help!*'

Suddenly a panel in the wall slid open and she fell through. It slid closed as she dropped to her knees and found herself in a lightless passage. Coughing, trying to draw breath, she pulled herself up and plunged into the darkness, away from the heat and smoke.

She was in a dark tunnel, feeling her way like a blind mole, hands scraping stone and brick. She walked into a wall, hit a dead-end, backtracked. The castle shuddered. Philo had set off another bomb.

303

She smelled smoke and gasoline. Heat rushing through the passages. *Like the floodwaters at Jebel Mara.* Except that Glenn wasn't there to guide her out. She heard others screaming, calling for help, pounding on locked doors. She fell through another sliding panel and found herself in a space no bigger than a closet. She tried to backtrack but was trapped.

Buried alive like Esther of Babylon.

Agonizing pain. The stench of smoke and chemicals.

When Glenn's head cleared, he found himself on the floor, a pool of blood beneath his left shoulder.

He sat up, nearly fainting as pain washed over him. He looked down at his bloody shirt. Why hadn't Philo killed him? *Because we are all going to die anyway.*

Staggering to his feet, he looked around. Candice? And then he remembered.

Philo was gone, the mullioned window standing open to admit cold night air and ribbons of smoke.

Snatching a linen runner from the mahogany sideboard – sending vases and candlesticks to the floor – he stuffed it into his shirt over the wound, packing it tightly to stanch the blood flow. Then he ran to the window, where he saw Philo scrambling on the rooftop, around domes and parapets, silhouetted against a backdrop of flames.

Glenn heard screaming closer in and realized it was Candice, trapped within the walls.

'Candice!' he shouted, pounding on the wood paneling. 'Over here!'

He stepped back to frantically survey the wall. How to get her out?

Another loud boom, the castle shook. The sound of glass shattering, balls of flame flying up to the sky.

'*Candice!*' His fists hitting every seam in the paneling, searching for a mechanism. Pain swept over him again, and nausea. *Don't faint. Keep it together.*

He renewed his assault on the wall, following Candice's cries on the other side. When he came to a bookcase, he pulled books off shelves. As he hefted *The Collected Works of Jules Verne,* a panel slid open and Candice collapsed into his arms.

She coughed and gulped air. He swept the hair from her eyes and said, 'Thank God.'

'You've been shot!'

'It's all right—'

'No it isn't. Glenn, let me take care of this.'

'Candice, Philo is out there. He's setting off the bombs.' They ran to the window. The east wing of the mansion was on fire, tongues of flame leaping from windows and through a charred crater in the roof.

And Philo, arms raised, the wind whipping his white hair as he cried, 'God said, "Let there be light," and there was light, and God saw that the light was good!'

They followed him out, picking their way over slate tiles. 'Philo!' Glenn shouted.

'The science archives!' Philo responded, an arm flung outward toward the burning wing, where sparks and cinders floated up to the stars, and fire brighter than day blinded them. 'The laws of Isaac Newton, the letters of Copernicus, the equations of Albert Einstein – flying to God!'

As Glenn drew near, Philo dashed across a chasm that had been laid ahead of time, Glenn saw, with a board. When Philo reached the other side, he kicked the board off so that Glenn had to stop. Morven's roof presented a challenging skyline of varying heights, chimneys, spires, mansards, skylights, hipped gables – a manmade Grand Canyon. There was no way to get to Philo.

'How do you know you haven't overlooked something?' Glenn shouted. 'What if you burn all this down and God doesn't appear? You will have set the work of the Alexandrians back two thousand years.'

A gibbous moon rose over the treetops, casting the scene in a preternatural glow. The starlight sharpened, as if Philo's insane plan was working and nature was preparing for the birth of the Luminance.

'I am not one of your bank robbers, Glenn! You cannot talk me out of this. I know what is going to happen tonight, and if you had an ounce of smarts in your skull you would see it too. But never mind. In a moment you will be a believer.'

Glenn shouted, 'You are destroying everything our ancestors worked hard for and sacrificed for.' There was more being

305

incinerated here than wood and stone and glass: the relics he had seen, robes worn by Alaric and Christofle when they rode to Jerusalem; a lock of Emma Venable's hair; the love letters written by Cunegonde that never reached Christofle; the walls of the humane maze created by Frederick Keyes – twenty-three centuries of passions and dreams and self-sacrifice, going up in flames to be erased from memory forever.

But Philo replied, 'Jesus said, "I have cast fire upon the world, and see, I am guarding it until it blazes. He who is near me is near the fire, and he who is far from me is far from the kingdom. For no one lights a lamp and puts it under a bushel, nor does he put it in a hidden place, but rather he sets it on a lampstand so that everyone who enters and leaves will see its light."'

Glenn wiped perspiration from his forehead. *Think like Philo. Get inside his head. What is he most afraid of?* 'Philip and Alexander will be back, too,' he shouted. 'Have you thought of that? They will claim world rulership!'

'They were weak! Philip got himself assassinated and Alexander drank himself to death. I am stronger than the two together!'

Philo touched his watch. Another explosion. The castle shook. More flames leaped to the night sky. The air filled with the acrid stench of incendiary chemicals. And people screaming.

'Is destroying Morven enough?' Glenn shouted, fighting pain and weakness, his left arm growing numb. 'Shouldn't you be setting fire to the Vatican archives as well?'

'I have everything sacred that I need from the Vatican. They are left with copies, fragments, and forgeries. And I am not destroying Morven! I am sending it up to God, to bring Him to earth, and, with Him, my beloved Lenore.'

Where Glenn stood the roof pitched sixty degrees. He steadied himself against a dormer window and looked down the ventilation shaft that separated him from Philo. His shoulder throbbed and he felt faint.

'What if Nostradamus was wrong?' he pressed, relentless. 'What if you misinterpreted the quatrain? The seven bombs might be the "seven suns," but who are the seven generals? You can't just use part of the prophecy and overlook the rest.

Philo, think about it. If you've made a mistake and it's too soon, and it isn't time yet for the Luminance, you destroy all of this and you destroy forever our chance of bringing the Luminance and being reunited with my mother.'

Philo's head snapped around. Fury blazed from his dark-gray eyes. 'Your mother and I will be together again tonight!'

'Then why did she say she was afraid of you?'

Philo froze.

'In her journal,' Glenn said, fighting for breath, resisting the pain, 'you can read it for yourself. She said she was afraid of you.'

'Lies!'

'She won't come back, Philo. Open the doors. Let everyone out!'

'They have to die! God needs their souls.'

Glenn spun around and ran back to the Hunting Room, where he smashed open the glass gun case and grabbed a hunting rifle. Slid back the bolt – the chamber was empty. He found a box of shells, inserted a five-round clip into the magazine, retracted the bolt and pushed it forward to slide a cartridge into the firing chamber. With the rifle cocked, he returned to the window.

As Philo ran across a lopsided parapet and up three steps of battlements to reach the flagstaff platform, Glenn steadied the rifle's stock hard against his right shoulder and sighted his target. 'Okay, Philo, not another bomb. Stop right there!'

'You won't kill me. You are a man of reason and words.'

Glenn fired. The shot rang out and a roof tile went flying. 'Remove the detonator, Philo!'

Philo ducked nimbly around a massive chimneystack. 'You're a man of peace, remember?'

Glenn fired again. Another slate tile flew off the roof. 'The next one takes your arm off!' Glenn shouted as he slid the bolt and took aim.

Philo raised his hand, reached for his wristwatch, 'Lenore!' he cried to the star-filled sky. Another explosion. The castle shook, flames shot up from the west wing. Philo and Glenn and Candice were now surrounded by a ring of fire.

'Where is he going?' Candice said.

Their eyes stinging with smoke and blinded by the brightness of the flames, they saw Philo disappear around another chimneystack and materialize on a lower roof. 'He's heading for the center of the castle. Directly over the treasury vault. The last bomb.' *The largest and most powerful.*

Through smoke and intense heat, deafened by the roar of the fires, Glenn surveyed the rooftop as he would a cliff he was about to climb.

And suddenly two men appeared with guns, both aimed at Glenn. Philo's ubiquitous companions, the African and the one with the strawberry mark.

'Don't you know he is going to kill us all?' Glenn shouted at them. 'You as well?'

'It's what they are counting on!' Philo shouted. 'They have faith in me.'

Glenn stared at them, saw that they meant to shoot, and slowly lowered his rifle. As he heard the sharp cocking of the guns, another figure suddenly materialized on the roof.

Mildred Stillwater. Her hair standing out, looking like an avenging angel.

Philo's two men turned briefly and in that instant Glenn snatched up his rifle, took aim, and fired. As the African fell, the other turned back, gun raised. Candice seized a loose brick and threw it at him, hitting him squarely on the head.

Glenn clambered over a parapet and offered Candice a hand. They hurried toward Philo, and they heard Mildred cry, 'Philo, I heard you tell them you killed John Masters! I wanted to hear more, so I sent Francesca to the greenhouse. It was cold out, I gave her my sweater. You killed her! But it was meant to be me, wasn't it? You locked all the doors, you monster! I barely had time to let everyone out. You were going to murder everyone. And the others over the years . . . Norbert Williams, Jennie Meade, Ygael Pomeranz. You killed them, too! And *I* have been your accomplice!'

As her words spilled out, they saw pain on her face – the memories flooding back: of the man she had loved long ago and had left standing at the altar because of Philo. The weeks afterward, Andy telephoning, begging to know what he had done wrong, why had she left, pleading with her to come back. A sob escaped her throat. *Andy, can you ever forgive me?*

'God is coming!' Philo cried, ignoring her.

'The only thing that's coming is punishment for your crimes.' She shouted at Glenn and Candice to run away, find safety.

'Dr. Stillwater, get out of the way!' The next bullet was for Philo, right in the chest. Glenn hefted the rifle and chambered another round.

Suddenly Mildred was looking up at the sky.

And Candice said, 'What's that?'

Glenn listened. Rumbling. Coming closer.

Helicopters?

Philo shouted: 'Do you hear? God is coming! The Luminance is at hand!'

And then something hit Candice on the head. She put her hand to her hair and it came away wet.

Another drop hit her, and another.

'My God,' she whispered. From the clear starry sky, rain was beginning to fall.

The wind picked up and the moon vanished. Clouds moved swiftly across the heavens, devouring starlight. And the rain fell harder.

'Where did this come from?' Glenn murmured as fat drops soon soaked his shirt.

Philo looked up in horror. 'No!' he cried. 'Lenore, where are you?'

He didn't see Mildred rush at him. 'Burn in Hell!' she cried, slamming her hands against his chest.

Philo's white satin slippers slid on the wet tiles. Arms flailing, he lost balance and skidded off the roof, tumbling to the edge. He caught the eave as he fell over, to dangle four floors above the cobblestoned courtyard.

The rain fell torrentially now. Flames were being doused, black smoke billowed up.

Philo, hanging from an ancient gutter, with rain pouring down his face. But he was still able to press the buttons on his watch. Holding on with one hand, he swung the other over.

'No!' Glenn shouted.

Philo's finger reached the wristwatch. Through the rain he could see the seventh button, and as he was about to press it, the read-out display went dead.

Philo stared at it. He pressed the button. Again and again.

And then he realized: all the failsafe options he had had included, the fireproofing, shock-resistance, unbreakable wristband, he had overlooked the one feature he had not thought it would need: waterproofing.

Glenn dropped to his knees, laid the rifle aside, and reached down to grab Philo's hand. Their fingers locked. 'Hold on!'

Whipped by wind and rain, Philo threw back his head and howled, 'Lenore, my love, wait for me!'

He looked at Glenn. Their eyes met and held.

And then Philo loosened his grip.

'No!' Glenn cried.

Candice reached the roof's edge as Philo landed on wet, spongy shrubbery below. He lay still for a moment, then rolled to the ground and took off running.

'Where is he going?'

'Into the house. He's going to manually detonate the bomb!'

'How do we get down?' Fire still roared all around them while the roof gutters and eaves ran with rain.

'This way!' Mildred shouted.

The stone steps in the ancient tower were worn and slippery. The three made their way down quickly but cautiously, coughing in the thick smoke, their faces roasting in the heat.

The stairway opened onto the opulent Victorian-Moorish reception hall from which all the wings of the castle radiated. 'That way!' Mildred said. 'The way down to the vault is through the Music Room.'

But the room was an inferno, the Steinway grand piano reduced to mere sticks as hot flame licked up legs and body. Philo stood in the doorway, momentarily stopped. There was no way around. No other way to the vault.

He took a step forward.

'Philo, don't!' Glenn shouted, holding his arm in front of his face, the heat was so intense.

Philo turned, a beatific look on his face. 'The fire can't touch me. I will pass through unscathed.'

He stepped in.

White silk and linen and satin caught flame. And then white hair and white skin. Philo whipped around, his body on fire, blackening as he looked through the wall of flames.

310

A look of surprise. This should not be happening!

But it was, just as it had happened to others long ago – his father on the other side of a locked door, begging to be let out, his mother screaming. The pain was beyond bearing. His very soul was burning up. *Mother, Father, did I really do that?*

His eyes met Glenn's in sudden comprehension – a moment of sanity in the world of his madness – *What have I done?* – and then the scream came out on his final breath. And one word: 'Lenore . . .'

Early dawn shed light on blackened ruins, men and women huddled in blankets, police dogs snuffling through rubble. Before Mildred had unlocked the security doors, those trapped inside had used cell phones to call for help. Boats and helicopters had arrived as the unexpected squall moved on, and now a new day was breaking. People from the mainland were there – the owner of the Thistle Inn, local farmers, a doctor and the constable, all Alexandrians. And François Orléans, Interpol agent, interceding with other local authorities, who were not.

The secret of Morven was safe.

Candice joined Glenn on a low stone wall where he nursed his bandaged shoulder. Her heart did a tumble at the sight of him, and then swelled with love and pride. Glenn Masters, fighter of bad guys. 'How are you doing?' she asked.

After Philo's fiery death, Candice had helped the others to search for victims still trapped inside the castle while Glenn had allowed one of the Alexandrians, a nurse, to tend his injury. Luckily the bullet had gone through, leaving a clean flesh wound. 'It's going to put a crimp in my polo game,' he said, wincing as he adjusted the strap of the arm sling.

He searched Candice's face, sooty and smudged. 'And how are *you*?'

'Invigorated,' she said with a small laugh. 'I haven't slept in two days. I should be exhausted.'

Glenn brushed a fleck of ash from her hair. All these years he had thought that falling in love would weaken him, that allowing himself to feel emotions would leave him open to the darker side. But it was just the opposite, he realized. His love for Candice had given him strength.

Mildred Stillwater joined them. 'I am sure the authorities will be satisfied that Philo Thibodeau died by accident. We blamed the fires on faulty wiring.' She pushed a hank of hair from her face. 'We had no idea. I spoke to some of the others and they said they had noticed Philo's strange behavior lately, but I suppose we were afraid of him'

She looked at the castle, blackened in places, untouched in others. The fires were out, only embers and hot spots remained. The dawn air was thick with acrid smoke. 'Luckily, our most precious treasures escaped harm. The Magdalene Letters, the Gospel of Mark, the Book of Hsu Tsi. We will return the items Philo stole, of course.'

Mildred's hair had come undone and hung in waves over her shoulders. Candice thought she looked strangely young, her plump face unlined and ageless. Without the glasses, one saw almond-shaped eyes, evidence of the beauty she had once been. 'How are the others doing?' Candice asked.

'Everyone is accounted for. A few burns and scrapes, but all are unharmed. Except for poor Francesca, who went into the greenhouse instead of me.'

She shivered in her red cardigan, pulling it tighter as she said, 'Candice, I'm so sorry you went through such an ordeal. After I sent Francesca to the greenhouse, I returned and listened outside the Hunting Room, and when I heard Philo telling you his plans to destroy Morven I went to warn everyone. If I had stayed, I might have saved you being forced into that room.'

'You couldn't have stopped him, Dr. Stillwater. None of us could. The only thing that finally stopped him was the rain.'

Mildred looked up at the clear morning sky. 'Strange . . . Scotland is famous for its unpredictable weather, but the storm last night was unusual, even for Scotland. It made me realize something. We misinterpreted the message in Alexander's vision. We thought God was telling us of His coming at a future date. But He was only speaking of the Luminance, when he would come *again*. God came to us long ago, perhaps at the time of Adam and Eve, and has been with us since, to watch over us and hear our prayers. What awaits us next is the Luminance, when we have earned it.'

'How can you be so sure?' Candice asked.

'Because He brought the rain to Morven to protect His sacred words. How else to explain a storm on a clear night?'

Mildred looked at the half-burned castle, her friends shocked and weary.

'Will you stay, Glenn?' she asked. 'We so need your help.'

'I don't belong here, Dr. Stillwater. I have my work back home.'

Glenn had plans. Captain Boyle was retiring in a year and Glenn was in the running to fill his place. He wanted to keep going after the bad guys, even if it was from a police captain's desk. But he had plans for rock climbing as well, taking his canvas and paints to mountaintops to capture the Luminance for others to see.

He was ready to paint Candice, too. Through the soot and ash on her face, she glowed. By discovering the Luminance around herself, she had uncovered the Luminance within.

'Dr. Stillwater, the society will still continue its mission?' Candice asked hopefully.

'Oh yes. We will keep at it. The Luminance might happen tomorrow, it might happen a thousand years from now. All I know is that God won't be rushed.'

Mildred watched the two, remembering her own youth, and she wanted to give them a gift, to take away from here, something to treasure in their new life together. 'Philo might have been insane,' she said, 'but he was right about one thing: we will be united with our loved ones in the Luminance. Glenn, you *will* see your mother again.'

She excused herself then, saying she had something to see to

Glenn watched her go, mulling over her remarkable words, deciding he would sort through them another day because something more pressing was on his mind. He thoughtfully twisted the gold ring on his right hand – ruby and gold, fashioned to look like fire – and he decided it would be the engagement ring. He wasn't sure yet how he would go about asking Candice to marry him, but he did know he would have to go carefully, design a strategy, because he knew she did not seek matrimony, that she was determined to go through life as her mother had, unmarried. Although, technically, Sybilla was a widow. He wondered if he could use that as a stratagem.

'Candice,' he said, deciding to give the waters a test. 'What would you say if I asked you—'

'Yes,' she said.

'Yes what?'

'I will marry you. That is what you were going to say, isn't it?'

He pulled her into a breathless kiss, oblivious of the looks and smiles from those nearby. Then he drew back and said, 'Promise me you will never stop being impulsive.'

'If you promise *me* something.'

He wanted to kiss her again, take her across the water to the Thistle Inn, where there were rooms above the pub. 'What's that?'

'That you will never stop painting the Luminance.'

As Mildred returned with a scorched carton, passing among colleagues who sipped from Styrofoam cups, she watched Candice and Glenn.

They were embracing. Mildred recalled such embraces in her past, long ago, when she had been about to marry a good man, whom she had left when Philo asked her to come with him to Morven. She thought now of Andrew, wondered where he was, if he had married, deciding she would look him up and see if it wasn't too late for them . . .

'The Jebel Mara tablets,' she said, handing the box to Candice. 'Along with my translation. Please give credit to Professor Masters, for it was his find.'

Candice accepted gratefully. 'What does it say?'

'Here, read for yourself.'

> I am the Living God's handmaiden.
> I carry the sacred lyre,
> I carry the sacred flute,
> I carry the sacred drum.
> I lead my sisters in music,
> I lead my sisters in song,
> I lead my sisters in dance.
>
> Follow me, saith the Living God.
> Across the sea,
> Across the sea,

To the other side,
And sing praise.

For the rays of the Sun are like
The arms of a father, to embrace and comfort,
And we fear no more.
Rejoice and sing praise.

Now Candice realized the terrible truth: Esther's live burial had nothing to do with what she was writing; it had been the vengeful act of her cruel Persian master, from whom she had had the audacity to run away.

'I hope you leave here with a new faith,' Mildred said.

'I have a lot to think about,' Candice said. 'All this talk of the end of the world.'

'The end of the world is not something to be frightened of, my dear. The Book of Revelation, filled with frightful imagery, is but one vision of the end of times. There are many more, from all faiths around the globe, which predict a *beautiful* apocalypse.' Mildred smiled reassuringly. 'Remember your classical Greek. Though the word "apocalypse" has come to mean death and destruction, its definition is simply "an uncovering," a revealing of knowledge. And the apocalypse I speak of is the unveiling of the beauty of God and His luminous universe.'

Mildred pointed to the box. 'There is something else in there. For you, my dear. The Temple of Amon at Heliopolis preserved an ancient chronology of the rulers of Egypt. It was relocated to the Great Library by Princess Artemisia in 310 BCE. I have been aware of your special Nefertiti research for some time, Candice, and I had no right to keep this from you.'

Puzzled, Candice looked in. Her eyes widened.

'It is authentic,' Mildred said. 'The certificates of verification are with it, as well as a chronology of the object's history, as it was passed down through the generations from the Eighteenth Dynasty to the Ptolemies.'

Dawn light illuminated a false beard made of solid gold, a royal emblem worn only by the kings of Egypt. Candice could make out the name clearly in the hieroglyphic cartouche: *Nefertiti.*

315

She was speechless as she embraced Mildred.

Glenn got shakily to his feet, the events of the night catching up with him. 'Are we done here?'

Candice looked at him with shimmering eyes. 'Yes.'

He held out his hand and thought of the strange and wonderful future that lay before them, of the Luminance and of reunions, of a humankind growing together in love, and he thought that although mysteries and questions still lay before them, he knew one thing for certain. He was never going to stop being surprised by that seductive, honey-dipped voice.

'Let's go home,' he said. And as she slipped her hand in his they felt a gentle breeze swirl around them. They thought it came from the sea, but it was a gathering of spirits, singing in golden tones, to thank them and to wish them well – Philos and Artemisia, Alaric the Knight, Christofle the Monk and Cunegonde, Michael of Notre Dame, Frederick Keyes and Emma, Jeremy Lamb, John and Lenore Masters, and David Armstrong, Candice's father.

Whispering: *We shall see you in the Luminance.*